One Man's Music

One Man's Music

Christina Britton Conroy

Black Lyon Publishing, LLC

ONE MAN'S MUSIC
Copyright © 2008 by Christina Britton Conroy

Our books may be ordered through your local bookstore or by visiting the publisher:

www.BlackLyonPublishing.com

Black Lyon Publishing, LLC
PO Box 567
Baker City, OR 97814

This is a work of fiction. All of the characters, names, events, organizations and conversations in this novel are either the products of the author's vivid imagination or are used in a fictitious way for the purposes of this story.

ISBN-10:   1-934912-10-7
ISBN-13:   978-1-934912-10-2
Library of Congress Control Number: 2008906319

Written, published and printed in
the United States of America.

Black Lyon Literary Love Story

For everyone who loves great music.

1.
New York City: December 1961
PRIMO: Leggiero Ritenuto

The composer's name was Eric Ries.

I was ten, it was a few days before Christmas, and my piano teacher gave me a suite of seven short pieces called *A Rainbow For My Daughter.*

The cover page made me giggle. It was a funny drawing of a skinny little girl with long, straight hair, just like mine. She played on a cartoon piano under the bright slashes of a wobbly rainbow. I loved playing the piano. I loved rainbows. And soon I would love Eric Ries.

The composer's name was below the title and an inscription was below that: "To Susannah, on her eighth birthday." I glowered and gave the music back to my teacher. She knew I was ten. I wasn't going to learn pieces written for an eight-year-old. I already swallowed my pride, learning pieces Mozart composed when he was eight.

My wise teacher ignored my pout, and told me the name R-I-E-S was pronounced Reese, like the peanut butter cups.

It's funny how the peanut butter cup image has stuck with me my whole life. Next, she pointed out the inscription.

Susannah Ries made her debut playing a Haydn Piano Concerto with the Cleveland Orchestra when she was seven.

Well, okay! That made all the difference. I had heard child prodigies solo with the New York Philharmonic, envied their talent, but not their lifestyles. They had to get up extra early, practice before and after school, study lots of music theory along with their regular schoolwork, and constantly protect their hands. They never went ice skating, played basketball, did cartwheels, or anything fun. Since I was just a regular ten-year-old kid, it was okay to learn music composed for an eight-year-old prodigy.

My teacher and I sat on the piano bench. She opened to the first page and I felt disappointed there were no words under the black notes. I loved singing more than anything, but there were no words to sing. I wondered if Susannah Ries liked to sing. My teacher played the first piece: *Red*. I had played sweet sounding Mozart and weird sounding Bartók, but never anything sounding like this. It was exciting and bright, and warm, and really, well ... *Red*.

There was a piece for every color in the spectrum and every piece had a different mood. My teacher played all seven while I studied the printed notes. I could almost taste the music. It was like bittersweet chocolate: rich and delicious, but never quite satisfying. I saw that the notes were close together and my small hands could easily reach every piano key. Best of all, there weren't too many black notes.

Years later, I analyzed the harmonic structures and saw the brilliance in Eric's simple scoring. The engaging melodies seamlessly shifted between major, minor, and Dorian modes.

I loved the music and the rainbow colors, but I was absolutely fascinated that a man composed a piece of music as a gift for his daughter. I could not imagine any man loving his child that much. My father didn't even like me. He was away a lot, and when he was home, he never noticed I was there. He walked right past as if I were invisible. I really wanted him to like me. I got good grades in school, worked hard at my after-school lessons, looked neat, smiled, never spoke out of turn, but it was never enough.

Lester Adams, my dad, was sort of like a silent, hostile ghost haunting the apartment. He was tall and slim, and always looked smart in his dark business suits, silk ties, expensive cuff links, and tie clips. His sandy hair was cut short and never seemed to grow. His nails were usually buffed and his gray-green eyes were usually bloodshot. He constantly took off his glasses, rubbed his eyes, and put the glasses back on.

I have the same gray-green eyes, pale brows and lashes. People said I looked like him. He seldom spoke, and when he did, it was usually into the telephone. Whenever he and Mom spoke to each other, they yelled. No matter what I did, I was always in their way, so they both yelled at me. When they were behind closed doors and I couldn't hear their actual words, I assumed they argued about me, accusing me of doing bad things. I suffered in silence, wondered what I had done wrong, and buried my head in a pillow, trying not to listen. I understood nothing about grown-up, married troubles and thought all their quarrels were my fault. I grew up feeling perpetually guilty and believing I was a rotten kid no one could ever love.

School day mornings, Penny, our darling dark-skinned, matronly live-in maid, gave me breakfast at the kitchen table. Mom slept late and never ate breakfast. Some days, Dad sat at the other end of the table, bolting down coffee, stewed prunes, a slice of toast, studying the *Wall Street Journal*, nodding with approval, or cursing under his breath. I longed to know what he was studying, but never dared to ask. I chewed my sugary cereal and sipped my orange juice as quietly as I could. If Daddy happened to look up, I smiled, but never spoke. I felt privileged just to be allowed in the same room. Some weeks, that was the only time I saw him.

Some afternoons, I came home and found him in his big, dark, wood-paneled study, swiveling in his chair, arguing on the telephone. His desk was always buried in papers. Shoulders raised, body tense, he rubbed his eyes and exuded hostility. If he looked up from his papers, he scowled, and I hurried away before he could scold me. Once in a while, he smiled. If he was in a really good mood, I went inside and talked to him. I learned to tell him about important things, like solos I sang in school, because the phone always rang. He picked up the receiver, turned his back, and forgot I was there. If I stayed until he turned back around, he was mad.

Determined to win his approval, I decided on a special surprise for his May birthday. I memorized all seven pieces of *A Rainbow For My Daughter,* and painted a picture to match each color. I planned to present the concert and the artwork together, as a birthday gift. Just after New Year's, Dad packed his bags and left. I sat at my desk, doing homework, when Mom came into my room. It wasn't very cold, but she was wrapped in a warm robe and fluffy slippers.

"Jenna dear, I have something to tell you. It's important."

She sat on the bed and I hurried to sit next to her. Important things were trips or parties, sometimes even visitors. Best news would be that her sister, my Aunt Connie, and her two boys were moving back to New York. I loved Aunt Connie more than anyone in the world. She was the perfect, cuddly mom who knew how to make little kids feel important. I loved sharing her lap with my little boy cousins. She read us stories, played games, baked cookies ... Even when she was busy with grown-up business, she found time to kiss and cuddle us, put Band-Aids on our cuts, and listen to our chatter.

Aunt Connie never seemed to care how she looked and I used to wish she was my mother, instead of her sister Allison: the beautiful, untouchable, ice princess. A few months before, Aunt Connie's husband got a job in San Francisco and the family left town. All at once I lost the only affectionate grown up I had ever known and my two best friends. I cried for a week.

I sat on the bed, eager for Mom to tell me the happy news. She saw my expression, tried to smile back, but couldn't. Her lips trembled and she looked away. I knew something was wrong. My mouth went dry. Her brow creased and she toyed nervously with her long manicured nails. My throat tightened. Every second she waited, my heart beat faster.

Finally, she took a deep breath and said, "Your father and I are getting divorced. He's moving to Los Angeles. That's in California, but nowhere near your Aunt Connie."

A nervous laugh gurgled out of my throat. "But, Daddy's away a lot. He always comes home."

"Not this time. He's gone for good. He's got a house on the beach, and a new ..." She choked. Tears filled her eyes. She reached across me, grabbed a Kleenex from the box on my bedside table, and held it over her mouth. My eyes were like saucers. A new what? A new daughter? He hated me so much he found a new one? Finally, Mom wiped her eyes and swallowed. "He's got a girlfriend."

She forced a laugh. "She really is a girl. Just finished college. He says he's in love." Her face squeezed up, like she was going to start sobbing. I sat paralyzed as she grabbed the whole Kleenex box, pulled out a pink wad, held it to her face, and wailed, "I even redid the bedroom for him. You remember?"

Of course I remembered. For weeks, workmen tore the room apart. When they were done, an oversized color TV and Hi-fi system were built into the walls. Plush pale-blue carpeting surrounded a king-sized bed with a hand-embroidered silk spread and matching headboard. Delicate Wedgwood lamps perched daintily on antique, hand-carved mahogany bedside tables.

She wiped her eyes. "I hoped he'd love the bedroom enough to love me, and we could have another baby." She was crying so hard I could barely make out the words. "I alll-ways wanted to give you a ll-ittle brother or ss-ister. I thought a bedroom fit for a k-king would k-keep him home. It ddd-idn't."

She wailed, then sobbed quietly for a few minutes. I felt sorry for her and sorry for me. I just lost my father. What was going to happen to us? Eventually, Mom stopped crying. The muscles in her face hardened and her mouth twitched. She stared at the floor and her lips moved as if she were having a conversation with someone. She looked like a different person. At first it was just weird, then it was scary. I was suddenly hot and sweaty.

She looked like she was getting ready to hit something and I didn't want it to be me. I inched back against the headboard and pulled my knees up to my chest. Instead of striking out, she lurched off the bed and pulled my ballerina doll off its pedestal. She toyed with the pink tulle on the tutu and spoke to the doll in her fake, charming hostess voice.

"So, you're going to have his baby." Her lips closed into a nasty smile. "Fine, Miss Beach Bimbo. Take the bastard. Have his baby. Let's see how long it'll take before he starts cheating on you." She looked tense, but satisfied, as she tossed the doll back onto the shelf and marched out the door.

I sat paralyzed. This was more information than I could deal with. Babies grew in their mothers' stomachs, but I had no idea how they got there. I didn't know what a "beach bimbo" was, and "cheating" meant copying someone's math test. Confused and very frightened, I chased her down the corridor to her bedroom.

"But, Mom! That's not fair. I've only had time to learn one of the piano pieces."

"What are you talking about?" She kept going.

"I have this great present planned for his birthday."

"He won't be here for his birthday."

"But that isn't fair!" My cheeks burned.

"Life isn't fair!" She stormed into her bedroom, slamming the door in my face. I stared at the closed door, leaned against the wall and started to cry. Tears streamed down my cheeks, but I knew better than to make a sound. Mom hated when I cried. She got really mad.

I slinked back, curled up on the bed, buried my face, and silently sobbed into a pillow. My bony frame convulsed painfully. It hurt worse than a stomachache. Like all the witless children of divorce, I blamed myself. Daddy was going to California to have another daughter, a better one. If I had done better, he would have stayed. I was dying to talk to someone, but without an adult to confide in, I was alone in the world.

If Aunt Connie had stayed in New York she would have explained that it was not my fault, that I was only a little kid, and that I could never control the situation, no matter how hard I tried. She would have told me that I was okay, and not the worthless failure I thought I was. Since no one told me all that good stuff, I was on my own. Eventually, I calmed down and reasoned with myself. I made messes before, lots of times, but I cleaned them up, and everything was forgiven. This was just another mess. I could fix it, change Daddy's mind and make him come home. With the single-mindedness of a dog digging up a bone, I spent the rest of the winter memorizing *A Rainbow For My Daughter.*

One evening in April, I watched Mom dress for an evening out. She wore her matching beige lace bra and panty-girdle, and carefully opened the cellophane on a new package of expensive stockings. She perched precariously on the edge of her bed, held a stocking in two hands, carefully scrunched down the top, and slid her toe into the contoured foot. The stocking gently pulled up her leg, as she attached the front garter, then the back one. She repeated the process with the second stocking, pulling it halfway up her leg, casually remarking, "Oh, next month your father's traveling to New York on business."

Totally thrilled, I screamed, "I can give him his birthday present!"

Pop! Her thumbnail stuck through the expensive nylon. I saw a wide run spread down the front of her leg. Her cheeks burned red under her makeup. Before she could scream at me, I burst into tears and tore into the dark living room. I hid behind a window curtain on the floor, and curled in a ball.

Minutes ticked by. It seemed like forever before I heard her leave the apartment and felt safe enough to sneak out. Everything

I did was wrong, but I could make it right. I just had to. If Daddy liked my present, and saw how good I could be, he'd stay with us and make Mom happy, all of us happy, with me as the heroine.

A week before Daddy's return, I was all ready. I stood at the side of Mom's eight-foot Steinway grand piano, swallowed a nervous giggle, and made myself concentrate. If this project was a success, life would be good. If it failed ... No! It wouldn't fail! Poised, ready to go, I noticed that my school uniform knee-socks had fallen down. They were always falling down. It seemed like I spent half my life bent over, pulling up my socks and winding the tops over thick rubber bands. I was such a skinny stick, I couldn't hold up pants or skirts without suspenders.

Careful not to mess my uniform jumper, I dropped into a squat, pushed back wispy strands of hair falling from my ponytail, and spread my seven abstract watercolor paintings along the floor. Each picture was a splash of colors, emphasizing one color in the spectrum. I had finished the last picture a few minutes before, so the violet paint was still wet and shining.

I left the paintings, raced into the laundry room, and dragged Penny away from her ironing board. She looked around guiltily. The living room was reserved for Mom's guests. I only came in to practice the piano, and Penny only came in to clean, or serve at parties. Penny looked really uncomfortable and I knew she wanted to leave. When she saw my wet painting on the spotless, gold wall-to-wall carpet, she clutched at her heart. I picked up the thick watercolor paper and showed her it wasn't soaking through.

Mom was a harridan when it came to carpet stains, or fingerprints on her pale walls, brass doorknobs, or light-switches. She entertained constantly, so Penny vacuumed, polished, and dusted constantly. Before taking another step, Penny looked around the room, checking off a mental list, making sure nothing was messed up.

Sunshine flooded through the heavy gold-brocade curtains, pulled open with gold tasseled ropes. The matching gold-brocade couch and easy chairs were arranged in comfortable conversation areas. At one end, the shallow fireplace was decorated with a highly polished brass screen, elegant fire shovel, tongs, and poker. I had never seen a fire, but perfectly cut logs were kept ready just in case. The two crystal chandeliers shed cheery light over the large oil paintings, ornate mirrors, and finally, the huge piano fitting perfectly in its far corner.

Suddenly, Penny's eyes went wide. My fingerprints were on the piano's shiny black wood. She pulled a rag from her pocket and wiped the marks clean. "Okay, honey. Now, what do y' want me t' do?"

I led her to the sofa. "You have to sit down and pretend you're my dad."

She lurched with surprise, then perched on the edge of the sofa. "Okay, honey. I'll pretend I'm your daddy."

I knew she was thinking that Daddy would never sit still long enough to hear me do anything. I stepped away, studied the line of artwork, and moved back to straighten the pictures. Sure they were perfect, I walked to the keyboard, took a deep breath, and almost started laughing.

Penny stared back with huge eyes. She loved me so much she would have done anything I asked. Clearly, she had no idea what I was doing, but knew it was important and wanted to help. I closed my eyes, once, then began.

"Daddy, I painted these pictures for your birthday. Each one is for a color of the rainbow: red, orange, yellow, green, blue, indigo, and violet." I held up the piano music. "This is called *A Rainbow For My Daughter*. The composer's name is Eric Ries. It's spelled R-I-E-S, but pronounced Reese, like the peanut butter cups." I pointed out the dedication. "This says, 'To Susannah, on her eighth birthday.' Eric Ries wrote this music for his daughter's birthday, and there's a piece for every color. Of course, I'm the daughter, playing the pieces for my father, on his birthday, so it's sort of reverse."

Penny thought for a moment, then smiled and nodded. "That's good, honey."

I felt like a million dollars. This was really going to work. My face flushed as I put the music back on the piano, and perched on the very edge of the bench. I straightened my back and stretched my right leg so my toes reached the sustaining pedal. I curved my fingers exactly like my teacher had taught me, took a deep breath, counted a brisk, "One - two - three - four, one - two - three - four," played the first two measures and stopped. "Oh! I forgot to say that this first piece is called *Red*." I took another deep breath, counted again, "One - two - three - four," and drove my fingers into the keys.

From the corner of my eye, I could just see Penny listening, tapping her foot to the lively music.

"Penny!" Mom's high-heels clicked over black-and-white tiles in the foyer. "Penny!" She sounded mad.

I stopped playing, guiltily dropped to the floor and collected the paintings. Penny leapt to her feet, frantically fluffing the sofa pillow she had been sitting on. We both froze as Mom, slim, blond, blue-eyed, and fashion model perfect, slithered into the living room, wearing a cream-satin evening sheath. She looked very beautiful and very angry. Hooking the gold wires of opal earrings through her pierced earlobes, she demanded, "Penny! Where's my gold pen?"

"It's by the phone in the kitchen, Ms. Adams. I'll get it." She hurried away.

She saw the watercolors in my hand. "What's that?"

My heart pounded. "It's a surprise ... for Daddy." I nervously bit my lip.

Mom glared. "I told you ..."

"But it's his birthday. I've been practicing *A Rainbow For My Daughter* all winter. If I play the pieces and give him the pictures, maybe he'll like them. Maybe he'll decide to come home and ..."

"Stop this!"

"But ... he might like them." Tears burned my eyes.

"For the last time, your father and I are separated. He lives in California. In a few months we'll be legally divorced and I'll never have to see the bastard again."

"But maybe ..." The tears ran down my cheeks.

"No maybe and no tears!" She was like an ice princess, beauteous and deadly cold. Her jaw clenched. "I'm hosting a UNICEF banquet tonight. You know what UNICEF is." She pointed an accusing finger.

I nodded, frantically wiping my face.

"Millions of little girls are starving to death, so you have nothing to cry about!"

She turned on a sharp high-heel and stormed away. That high-heel slipped on the smooth gallery floor, and she almost fell. Wobbling, then righting herself, she hurried off the linoleum into the hallway and the comfort of wall-to-wall carpeting.

I stood by the piano, forcing back more tears. Afraid of being scolded again, I took the paintings and music, hurried to my bedroom, and curled into a ball on my bed. In a few minutes I heard Mom's voice, the front door open, then close again. She was safely out of the house. I lay back and cried out loud.

Allegro Innocente

Monday through Friday, I rode the Seventy-ninth Street cross-town bus to school and back home, through Central Park. Since I lived in an asphalt jungle, I loved this bit of nature and watching the foliage change with the change of seasons. This May afternoon the park was a gorgeous collage of light greens and bright yellows, but I hardly noticed. Perched rigid on the edge of my seat, I bit my lip and clutched my monogrammed schoolbag with white knuckles.

I looked a mess, but didn't care. One of my navy blue knee socks hung down around my ankle, my school blazer was buttoned wrong, and the collar on my white uniform shirt stuck up at an angle. I totally forgot the polished silver dimes in my new, shiny-black loafers. Penny had helped me polish those dimes. For the first time ever, I was allowed to wear light, slip-on school shoes, instead of heavy-laced oxfords. I felt very proud and very grown up.

A warm breeze blew through the open bus windows, tore at my hair and ripped it from its rubber band, whipping it across my face. I willed the bus to fly across Central Park West to Eighty-first Street, so I could leap off in front of The Beresford, my apartment house, Number One, West Eighty-first Street, and race upstairs.

Today was Daddy's birthday. He was coming home. Even though Mom said he was only coming to empty his files and would leave as soon as he was done, I was determined to make him stay. Early that morning, before I left for school, I tied my seven rainbow paintings with a bright-blue ribbon, attached a Happy Birthday Daddy note, and laid the packet on his desk. I pictured him opening the packet and admiring the paintings, one by one. This afternoon, I planned to play my piano pieces. I whispered to myself, "He'll be really proud of me, and he and Mom will make up. It will be so wonderful." I was only scared that he would have come and gone before I even got home.

As the bus neared the edge of the park, I excused myself, and stepped down onto the exit stairs near the back, ready to be the first one out. The bus rounded the last corner. I stared at the bright-green stoplight, daring it to turn red. We came nearer and nearer, then—no! It turned red. I closed my eyes, clenched my jaw and bounced frantically up and down. My heart beat like a tom-tom.

It felt like two years before the light changed. Finally, the bus pulled across the street and stopped. The automatic doors opened and I lunged inside the building, under the gray canopy. Zooming past Martin, the elderly Irish doorman dressed in his elegant gray uniform, I flew through the marble-walled lobby, into the waiting elevator.

I wanted to scream, "Get me upstairs!" Good manners forced me to say, "Good afternoon, Martin ... Kelly." Kelly was the elevator man.

Slowly, Kelly turned into position, and took his time pulling the brass gate closed. "So, Jenna, how was it at school today?"

Frustrated tears stung my eyes. Those two always teased me and I usually liked it. Just not today! "It was fine, thank you, Kelly. Is my father at home?"

"Sure is. Came in about an hour ago."

I breathed a sigh of relief as Kelly slid the heavy brass door shut and pushed down the round wooden handle, worn smooth from years of constant use. The elevator groaned, then moved upward. It felt like a submarine reaching the water's surface, and I held my breath the entire five floors.

In the past, I had walked in on interesting grown up conversations and the grown ups had stopped talking, spoiling the fun. Now, I soundlessly opened the front door, listened and tiptoed inside. Mom and Daddy were in the study arguing. I missed a few words, then heard Mom say, "Come on, Lester, it won't kill you to smile and say 'thank you.' I can't think why, but your daughter still loves you."

They were arguing about me. This was worse than awful. He was supposed to see my paintings and get happy. I heard papers rustle and Daddy mumble something.

Mom screamed, "You bastard! Why won't you believe me? She even looks like you."

"No, she looks like you." More papers rustled.

Mom yelled, "She has your eyes. And your blood type."

"A quarter of the world has my blood type. What's Fred Miller's blood type?"

"How dare you! You cheated on me our whole married life. I had one short ..."

"One night with Fred and—pop! We were married twelve years. How come we never had a kid?"

"We did! We had Jenna." Mom sounded like she was going to cry.

What in the world were they talking about, and who was Fred Miller?

Daddy sounded really angry. "Listen Al, I supported that kid for ten years, and I've promised to keep supporting her until she finishes college. I think that's plenty generous."

All of a sudden, my book bag slipped off my shoulder, banging onto the floor. I pretended I had just come in and raced into the study. "Daddy, Daddy! I'm so glad you're home."

Mom held my rainbow pictures. Dad glanced at me, then her, sat down in his swivel leather chair, and looked through his files. Mom burst into tears. She slapped the watercolors on his desk, then ran down the hall to her room and slammed the door.

I stared after her. I watched Daddy's back. After a couple of minutes, I half-whispered, "Happy birthday, Daddy."

He turned his head, forcing a smile. "Thanks. Oh, thanks for the drawings. I'll look at them later when I have time."

Since he had actually spoken to me, my courage grew. I stepped toward him. "They're not drawings, they're paintings. Watercolors. One for every color of the rainbow, and I have piano pieces that go with them. They're really short. I can play them for you, any time you'd like. Right now if you ..."

"I won't have time to hear any music, but I'll look at the paintings later." He picked up the phone, and dialed a number. "Mark Katz, please, Lester Adams calling. Yeah, Mark, I can't find the deed to the Florida property. What do we do?" He listened, nodding. When I didn't leave, he looked annoyed and turned his back. "Okay. Have you got his Miami number?"

It was no good. He was not going to look at the paintings or hear me play. I waited another minute, then went to Mom's room. The door was closed, but I heard Mom inside, talking between sobs. Very quietly, I turned the knob and opened the door.

Mom sat on the edge of her bed, balancing the telephone

receiver between her ear and her shoulder. With her free hands, she opened a bottle of pills. "I know, Connie, I am better off alone. I just can't ..." She saw me and glared. "I'm talking long-distance to your Aunt Connie. Go see if Penny's got your dinner."

"Mommy, please don't take those pills. They're too strong. Last time you slept a whole night and day." My stomach cramped and a bitter taste flooded my mouth.

Mom spoke into the phone. "Hold on, Connie." She walked toward me and pushed me out of the room. "I want to sleep until that bastard's back in California. Don't bother me again." She shut me out.

I stood in the hall, panic-stricken. I hurried back to the study. "Daddy! Daddy!" I ran up to his desk.

He didn't look up.

"Mommy's taking some pills. They're really strong. Last time she slept for—"

"Good!" He balled a wad of paper and crammed it into the trash. "Then she won't interrupt me again." He turned back to his files.

"But maybe she won't wake up at all. Maybe she'll die. You're going away and I'll be left all alone." Suddenly, I was screaming, "I know you don't care about me. You're going to have another daughter, but I'll be all alone. Just make Mom stop taking the pills, then you can move away and never come back. Then—"

A flicker of bright red and blue shone through his pile of trash. It was the corner of my rainbow paintings, still tied with their blue ribbon. He kept his back to me, sifting through papers, papers and papers. His agile fingers dug out a strangely marked document. He smiled victoriously and grabbed the telephone. My brave moment of steaming anger melted. He was talking on the phone, again. I did not exist. I could scream the house down and he would never hear me. What had I done wrong? What would his new daughter do that I didn't do? I knew I had done everything right. Everything!

Suddenly, I felt nothing. Emotion drained out of me like water pouring down a rusty gutter. My arms hung heavy at my sides and I was even too tired to cry. Zombie-like, I walked from the room, into the kitchen. Penny stood over the ironing board, pressing one of my white school-uniform blouses. An aroma of roasting meat wafted from the oven and my stomach lurched. The table was set for two and I sat down in front of my empty plate.

"Mommy won't be eating dinner. She felt bad and took a pill."

Penny stopped ironing. She shook her head, sighed sadly, and finished the shirt. "Are you going to play the piano for your daddy?"

"No, he's too busy." I didn't recognize my own voice. "He liked the paintings, though. Really a lot." Tears threatened, then stopped. A lot of little girls were starving to death. I didn't have anything to cry about.

2.
September 1962
Presto Animato

*T*oday was Thursday, the only weekday afternoon without an after-school lesson. Monday was piano, Tuesday ballet, Wednesday ballroom dancing, and Friday art. This was also the third Thursday of the month, the day Mom always hosted the New York Philharmonic Society luncheon meeting. Linda, the Monday through Friday daytime maid, told me that petit fours had been ordered for dessert. I begged her to put some aside, but she said she would get in trouble. If I got home late, all the petit fours might be eaten. My mouth was set for smooth pink-sugar icing, surrounding soft, moist pink cake.

The apartment door was propped open with an ornate brass doorstop, so I hurried on tiptoes out of the elevator to the edge of the living room. Two dozen stylishly dressed women sat in an uneven semicircle on the gold-brocade sofa, matching easy chairs, and dining room chairs that had been brought in just for that day. Each woman held a blue manila folder and looked through the papers inside. I could make out the usual printed pages, concert tickets, and an 8x10 glossy, black and white photo of a dark-haired young man. A pile of long-playing phonograph records sat on the coffee table.

Mom looked really pretty in a brown linen suit with matching high-heeled shoes, a simple pearl necklace, bracelet and earrings. At thirty-five, she was one of the youngest women in the society. Her honey-blond hair was freshly colored and styled into a bouffant flip. It was sprayed good and stiff, so I knew it would stay looking nice for a couple of days. Her pale-blue eye shadow, false eyelashes, and deep-red lipstick were perfect. My natural coloring was so pale, I thought I looked plain and unattractive. I longed for the day I would be old enough to wear makeup and look pretty like Mom.

Betty Newberry, the officious Philharmonic Society chairwoman, addressed the meeting. She was snooty and I didn't like her, so I lurched out of sight. Betty's silk floral-print dress matched her blue-gray hair, rolled up in a French twist. Even though she gestured grandly, swaying back and forth, lecturing women on both sides, her hair never moved. It was solid as a lacquered helmet. In the back of the room, Penny and Linda, the two maids in black-and-white uniforms, set out a silver coffee service for dessert. I was in time. It would be at least another fifteen minutes before the petit fours were served.

Tiptoeing back through the foyer, I passed the wood-paneled study that had been Daddy's office. The rainbow project had failed miserably. Penny had retrieved the rainbow paintings from the trash and stored them carefully in a shirt-box.

Since I never played for my father, my piano teacher suggested we tape my playing and mail him the tape with the paintings. I was dying to do it, but lied and said I was tired of the music. I was too embarrassed to say he would just throw the tape away without listening to it. Besides, he was going to have another daughter. She would be prettier than me and play piano better. I was superfluous.

Mom kept busier than ever with charity work. She always seemed to be in a meeting, on the phone, dressing for a fancy event, or sleeping. Penny kept the house and me in order. That summer I went to music camp, sang solos with the chorus and leads in two operettas. I was dying to take voice lessons, but my conductors both told me to wait until I was fifteen. They said children's voices weren't mature enough for serious lessons. When I got back home, Mom enrolled me in every other after-school class she could find.

This afternoon, my only thoughts were about pink-sugar icing. Speeding past the empty study, I raced toward the back of the apartment, to my bedroom. I tossed my book bag onto the white cotton spread covering my antique Victorian double bed, and raced into my bathroom with its oversized, turn-of-the-century tub.

I hurried to the high porcelain sink, soaked a washcloth, and ran it over my face. The cloth dropped into the sink as I straightened my navy blue flannel uniform jumper, pulled up my knee socks, and rolled the tops over their rubber band garters. I painfully tore the rubber band from my ponytail, raced back to bedroom and my white-marble-topped Victorian dresser. My long, straight ash-blond hair was a tangled mess, but I forced a comb through it. Taste buds aching for creamy sugar icing, I gave myself a quick once-over, decided I looked okay, and headed back toward the living room.

Betty Newberry was still talking. "So, ladies, I'm sure we'll all do our best to make Mr. Ries's Philharmonic debut a great success."

I froze. Had she said, "Ries"?

She bubbled on. "Now, I know that contemporary music isn't everyone's cup of tea. It can be ..."

Mom raised her hand. "Instant Halloween?"

The other women laughed in agreement.

Betty smiled indulgently. "Actually, Allison, Mr. Ries has been criticized because his music is too 'derivative.' I think that means that he writes tunes." The ladies laughed some more and Betty smiled to herself. She gestured to the coffee table in front of her. "If any of you wish to preview his music, feel free to take one of the records."

A woman held up a copy of the photograph. "He's so handsome! My friends will buy tickets just to get a look at him."

The other women smiled and nodded as Betty blushed and fluttered a hand. "Well, yes. I'm looking forward to meeting him myself."

The maids finished setting out dessert and coffee. They sprang to attention as Betty gestured toward them. "If there's no other business ..."

The ladies stood, stretched, chatted among themselves, and moved to the sideboard.

I waited only a moment before grabbing one of the records, and slithering through the women to the dessert plates. I held the record like a tray and Linda smiled, handing me two pink petit fours. Penny made me a cup of sweet, milky tea. I balanced the teacup and cakes on the record jacket, started out of the room, then stopped when I saw one of the 8x10 glossy photographs on the floor. Very carefully, I bent both knees, picked up the photograph between my pinky and fourth finger, and wobbled back to my room.

My eyes were glued to the beautiful flowered icing. I longed to slowly savor the petit fours, and suck each delectable morsel of sugar. I let the photograph drop onto my desk, shuffled to my bed, and laid the record/tray on the spread. I set the saucer on the bedside table, and then, finally picked up a petit fours. I nibbled a corner of pink sugar and exhaled. The taste was heavenly. All the waiting had been worthwhile. I was still savoring the smooth texture and sweet flavor when I noticed the back of the record jacket, lying on the bed. A tiny black and white photograph was at the top. I held the cake in one hand, the 8x10 glossy photograph with the other, and compared the pictures. They were the same.

The back of the record jacket was covered with writing, and underneath the tiny photo was a short biography: "Born in 1933, Eric Ries is the youngest and first American composer ever to win the coveted Neunheim Medal for Composition. The son of a French mother and English father, born in Arizona and raised in Nova Scotia, Ries combines elements of many cultural musical forms. His *Violin Concerto* is among the ..."

I set down the half-eaten cake and tore the cellophane off the record jacket. The new black plastic disk looked like buffed ebony, and the smell made my nose tickle. I carried the thin disk around the bed to my Hi-fi, started back to finish the petit fours, heard the first notes, and stopped in my tracks.

Low string instruments played a series of slow, soothing chords that seemed to wind around my waist. Like soft tentacles, the music hugged me, tugged at my heart, and held me absolutely still. A solo violin took over, sliding through the other instruments, soaring higher and higher in a sweet, poignant theme. Moments later, a mellow French horn countered the violin melody. I couldn't move. I never wanted to move again. I felt nurtured, calm and absolutely safe. I stayed totally still, leaning against the edge of the bed.

Twenty-two minutes later, the needle clicked, then lifted off the record. I still didn't move.

Suddenly, I was hungry for the music again. Like a ravenous dog after a bone, I clicked the arm lever, then raced back around the bed. I shut the door, turned off the lights, and sprawled on the bedspread, stretching my arms and legs. The music started again and I literally bathed in the sounds. The violin soared. The French horn counter-melody crooned again and I found myself humming along. I knew this tune, but how?

Twenty-two minutes later, the concerto ended a second time. I leapt off the bed like a Jack-in-the-box and grabbed my piano music off its shelf. I found *A Rainbow For My Daughter*, reread the dedication, "To Susannah, on her eighth birthday," flipped to the Indigo page and looked at the notes. Yes! It was right there—the same tune he had used for the French horn solo.

Turning the record over, I played his *Four Rivers Suite*, on side two. This was just as wonderful as the *Violin Concerto*, but different. It felt like I was actually riding whitewater rapids, or floating down steamy jungle rivers full of large-toothed, hungry crocodiles. The *Violin Concerto* had soothed me into a near comatose state. The *Four Rivers Suite* energized me into action, driving me to learn about the composer.

I remembered the printed material inside the Philharmonic Society blue folders, and raced back to the living room. Some of the women had left, but most were still sipping coffee and talking. They didn't seem to notice me. A pile of untouched folders lay on the coffee table, so I brought one back to my room. Inside was an article from a London newspaper. I skimmed the beginning and slowed down toward the end.

"... Although he claims to be one-hundred percent American, Mr. Ries is fluent in a number of languages, and divides his time between the music capitals of the world. Recently divorced, he spends a good deal of time with his young daughter, Susannah, who is already an accomplished pianist. Talented father and daughter travel together during their summer holidays. Most recently, they ..."

Below the article was a small photo of Eric with a little dark-haired girl sitting together at a piano smiling at each other. A cold, smothering sadness spread through me. Two Christmases ago, a photographer had taken a picture of Mom, Dad and me. We had smiled for the camera, but the smiles weren't real. I could see that this father and daughter were really smiling. They played music together. They really liked each other. He loved her so much he wrote music for her to play. Her parents were divorced, but she still saw her dad. My imagination soared as I pictured this dad sitting back, listening when his little girl talked, comforting her when she was upset, and the two of them having real conversations. I imagined them eating meals together, and doing neat things like horseback riding and ice skating. She even got to travel with him on trains and airplanes.

She had everything I wanted, didn't have, and would probably never have. I felt awful. The article went back into the folder. I closed the blue cover, and stashed it on the shelf with my piano music. A brand new kind of sadness burned in my stomach. It was sort of like being hungry, but I didn't want any food. With all my heart, I wanted to be Susannah Ries.

The 8x10 photograph smiled up at me from the bed. I took it in both hands and studied the face. Eric's thick dark hair blended into sideburns, then a manicured beard and mustache. He had a high forehead and dark eyes with long, soft lashes. His lips were curved in a nice smile. I looked back at the small photo and held it next to the large one. He seemed very kind. I spoke silently to the picture, introduced myself, told him what a good father I thought he was, and how I wished my own father was like him.

A knock on the door startled me out of my reverie. It opened a crack and Penny waited, still in her dress-uniform. She saw my almost untouched petit fours and now-cold tea. "I was sure you'd spoiled your appetite."

After making such a fuss about getting the cakes, I felt embarrassed and fudged an excuse. "Oh, well, I, I'm saving them for dessert."

Never judgmental, she just took the plate and the teacup. "Okay honey, your dinner's ready."

I slid the photograph inside the record jacket and followed her into the kitchen.

Andante Calma

An hour later, I was back talking to the photograph. I half-closed the door, changed into pajamas, and sat cross-legged on my bed. The photo lay in my lap. The *Violin Concerto* had played once more, then clicked off, but I was so deep into my one-sided conversation, I barely noticed the silence. I had so much to say, my words tumbled out like water overflowing a dam.

I told Eric's picture about the divorce, stuff going on at school, my piano lessons, ballet and art classes, how it was unfair I had to wait for voice lessons till I was fifteen, about my girlfriends,

Penny, Aunt Connie ... Every thought led to another, and the more I talked, the hungrier I was to tell more. Out of nowhere, I found a brilliant best friend. He understood everything, was interested in everything, and had plenty of time to listen.

I was startled when Mom opened the door and walked in. She carried her high-heels and looked ready to drop. Afraid that she'd heard me talking to the photo, guilt struck like a cold wind and I tossed the picture behind me. "Hi, Mommy. Is everyone gone?"

"Finally." She sat next to me and picked up the record jacket. "You played this all afternoon. You must like it a lot."

I smiled and nodded.

She turned her head and looked quizzically behind me, at the now upside-down photograph. "You were having quite a conversation. What were you telling him?"

"Nothing." That was a giant lie and I felt faint. To cover my feelings, I held up *A Rainbow For My Daughter*, pointing out the composer's name.

She smiled with surprise. "My goodness, I didn't know he'd written these." Stifling a yawn, she handed back the record jacket. "I'd better get a move on. Your Aunt Connie's plane arrives in two hours."

"Can't I go with you?"

"Not on a school night. We'll be back too late. You'll see her tomorrow."

"I wish she still lived in New York."

"So do I. Unfortunately, her husband likes San Francisco." I could tell Mom really missed her younger sister and best friend. She yawned. "Did you have dinner?"

I nodded.

"Don't stay up too late." She gave me a squeeze.

"I won't." I smiled as she dragged herself out of the room. As soon as she was gone, I told the picture that that lady was my mom, and that she was in a good mood because she'd just given a party and her sister was coming to visit.

I opened *A Rainbow For My Daughter*, turned to the *Indigo* page, studied the notes, and told to the picture I recognized the French horn tune. I took the picture and the music into the living room, set both the photo and the music on the piano stand, and opened the music to *Indigo*. I slowly settled myself and remembered how the

French horn player had phrased this melody. I could never make a percussive piano sound like mellow brass, but I could still play as musically as he did. I took a deep breath, leaned into the keys and played. The music seemed to wrap itself around my waist, just like the first time I played the record. It felt marvelous. I played it again, then turned the page to *Purple*.

I wished I could play all night, but remembered that I had homework to finish.

Mom was in the doorway, watching me. I couldn't tell what she was thinking, so I assumed she disapproved.

Much to my surprise, she smiled. "That was beautiful. It was so elegant, so mature. You even looked like a concert pianist."

My insides filled with a happy bubble. A smile burst out of me.

Walking away, she muttered, "I wish your father could have heard it."

The bubble burst and I felt like crying. I wished he'd heard it too. Maybe he would have stayed with us.

3.
January 1963
Moderato Giovale Grazioso

Tuesday afternoon, before the Friday premier of Eric's *Violin Concerto*, Mom let me skip ballet class to hear a rehearsal of the New York Philharmonic. I had been going to rehearsals and concerts for years, and knew nearly all the orchestra members. My favorite was Pete, a bassoon player who soaked his double reeds in milky coffee.

Open rehearsals were scheduled one morning a week, and since conductor Leonard Bernstein depended on the Philharmonic Society ladies to sell tickets, he allowed their friends and families to attend a few other rehearsals. Listeners were supposed to sit in the audience, but the sight-lines were lousy, and I couldn't hear the players' conversations. Half the fun was hearing what they said to each other in private. I sneaked into the wings, a couple of feet behind the first violins, and scrunched down against a thick, dusty curtain where no one could see me.

That morning, forty of the musicians had rehearsed a Mozart symphony. This afternoon, eighty-six musicians would be sight-reading Eric Ries's *Violin Concerto*. They took out their instruments and moved into a huge semicircle of folding chairs set on the wide, modern stage of Philharmonic Hall. A row of black metal music stands stood between each row of chairs.

I wasn't surprised to hear them gripe to each other about having to play another American Premier of a modern composition. They usually complained that contemporary composers didn't write tunes, so they couldn't anticipate what note followed another. Sometimes, composers wrote in awkward keys, or interval skips that weren't suited to their instruments. I remembered Mom's joke about contemporary music sounding like "Instant Halloween." I couldn't tell when the notes were right or wrong, and wondered why it was so important to play them right. The musicians got to · play a new program every week and forget the music they hated, so I wondered why they minded it so much. They anticipated the worst from composer of the week, Eric Ries, shook their heads, gritted their teeth, tightened bowstrings, adjusted wooden reeds and brass mouthpieces, warmed up fingers and lips.

I loved watching them prepare. Each one was a great musician with a strong personality, but I knew that in a few minutes all their sounds would meld together, playing Eric's beautiful concerto.

A couple of feet in front of me, in the back of the first violins, Sid and Monica shared a music stand. Sid was an old grouch who scared me. I kept really still, so he wouldn't know I was there. Monica was nice. She was younger than Mom and kind of pretty. She had beautiful long black hair that swung back and forth when she played.

Sid slid his bow across the four strings and played a fabulous three-octave scale. He held a spectacular final note and let it go. The sound vanished instantly. He scowled at Monica. "Nothing! This hall has no sound! Nothing!"

Monica nodded sadly. She pulled her hair into a clip at the back of her neck, tucked her violin under her chin, and played a scale of her own. "I know, Sid. The acoustics are awful."

The concert-master, sitting in the first violin chair, stood up and everyone stopped playing. He nodded to the first oboe player, who pursed her lips and blew a pure-toned A. The concert-master sat down and the entire orchestra tuned to that A. Pete told me that the oboe was the only instrument that played perfectly in tune without being adjusted, so it always gave the pitch for the other instruments to match. In America we tune to an A: 440, and that meant that the sound vibrated 440 times a second. In Europe, they tuned to A: 445, so European oboes were made differently.

Sounds of tuning and practicing musicians washed over the stage. Piping flutes, blaring trombones, and lush cellos all created their own exciting music, which went silent as soon as it was played.

Sid looked up to heaven. "Christ! Why did we leave Carnegie Hall? I don't care if the roof caved in, the sound was so marvelous.

Sure, the paint was peeling, but it still had charm, and we heard every breath, every bow change, everything. We knew we were playing in an orchestra."

Center stage, Pete and his stand partner practiced a bassoon passage. Monica grimaced. "Those guys sound like they're in another room."

Even though the sound was bad, I liked the huge, modern interior of Lincoln Center's Philharmonic Hall. The plain white walls and asymmetrical ceiling disks looked neat.

Monica shrugged. "They're bringing in new engineers to fix the acoustics."

"Better to tear it down and start over. You can never fix—" Sid stopped as conductor Leonard Bernstein walked on stage, talking with a slim young man. "Who the hell is that? Another wunderkind? I've got kids older than him."

I bit my lip. It was Eric Ries. He looked more handsome than his picture, and a lot younger. I had read that he was thirty, but he was dressed in tight leather pants, like a teenager.

Monica chuckled. "Can your kids compose?"

Sid huffed. "Can he?"

"Yeah. I heard his London Symphony recording. He writes like Puccini. You'll like it."

Sid rolled his eyes. "Puccini. Right."

"He won a Fulbright to study with Boulanger."

"Everyone studies with Boulanger."

Sid scowled, but Monica plowed on. "Two years ago, he won the Neunheim Prize for Composition. He was only twenty-eight. The first American and youngest winner ever. Some of the judges thought he was too young, so he grew the beard to try to look older. He lives in Salzburg, but keeps an apartment in Paris. They just picked him up from the airport. He's divorced, with a daughter. He doesn't look old enough, does he?"

"No, he doesn't. He looks like a kid with a beard." Sid's glance shifted from Eric back to Monica. "You know a lot about him."

"Yeah, I … I read about him." She nervously bounced her bow on her thigh.

"You read about him, a lot." She shrugged and he patted her arm. "Listen, kid, your track record with guys isn't too good. How long is he going to be in town?"

"I don't know."

"No? You seem to know everything else about him."

She turned away. I couldn't see her face, but I guessed she was embarrassed.

Sid looked sad. "Monica, sweetheart, do yourself a favor. Watch the conductor, scratch the fiddle, and go home. This guy's too pretty and you're already too hot for him. It spells trouble. I don't want you sittin' here next week cryin'."

I didn't know what they were talking about, but it sounded dangerous.

Monica started to answer, but stopped when music librarians walked through the rows of musicians, distributing parts. I huddled even tighter against the dusty wing curtain, so they wouldn't see me. The librarian placed the large, handwritten manuscript on Sid and Monica's music stand, and they studied their first page together.

Sid huffed. "Okay, Puccini junior, impress me." He glanced over the notes, then nodded begrudgingly. I knew the music sounded beautiful, but had no idea it was technically well written. The four fingers of Sid's left hand would easily find their place on the four strings of his violin. The hand-printed notation was elegant Victorian type copperplate. The music was both readable and playable, he said. Sight-reading would be a breeze. Sid turned the page without further comment and Monica's shoulders shook in a silent laugh.

All over the orchestra, musicians exchanged smiles and nods. I learned later that musicians always loved Eric's orchestrations. He wrote well for every instrument.

Leonard Bernstein stood next to the podium and spoke to the orchestra. At forty-four, this composer/conductor was one of the most famous musicians in the world. I used to watch his Young Peoples' Concerts with the New York Philharmonic on TV. He was short and slim, with thick brown hair. On TV he always smiled. In real life, he yelled a lot. Today, he swaggered proudly. "Ladies and gentlemen, I'm pleased to introduce Eric Ries."

Eric smiled and nodded. He looked relaxed, but I wondered if he was nervous underneath. I would have been. His *Violin Concerto* had been performed and recorded in London, but this was a different orchestra. The players were really critical and Bernstein's tantrums were really scary.

Eric raised his head and put his hands together in a graceful salaam. He looked left and smiled at all eight pairs of first violins, even Sid and Monica in the last stand. I was used to conductors only looking at the first stands, ignoring the rest of the players, and just expecting them to follow his baton. Eric looked directly at Monica and her shoulders tensed. Afraid he would see me behind her, I scrunched down against the dusty curtain.

His smile shifted to the second violins and the string bass players behind them. He looked forward and nodded to the long row of woodwinds. Piccolo and flute players smiled politely. Clarinet, oboe, English horn and bassoon players soaked their reeds in vials of water, or sucked them like licorice sticks, and nodded back. Behind them were the timpani player, two percussionists, and to their right, the trumpets, trombones, French horns, and tubas smiling and nodding. Finally Eric looked right. I couldn't see the cello, viola and harp players, but he looked longest in the direction of Sharon, a beautiful harpist with long blond hair.

Monica sat up straighter, straining to see, and Sid smirked, "Good! Let him mess with Sharon's head and leave you alone."

Monica snapped back, "I don't want to be left alone."

Eric turned back and spoke clearly enough so everyone could hear. "Ladies and gentlemen, I am humbled and honored that you're going to play my music. Thank you very much." He looked like he meant it. Lowering his hands, he made a slight bow. Everyone looked pleased. Some of the string players applauded by tapping their bows on their music stands. Eric broke into a brilliant smile and the whole stage seemed to light up. Wow! He was so handsome! He could have been a movie star.

I nearly screamed when a violin bow bounced off the floor right in front of me. Sure I'd be seen this time, I panicked, pushed back a few feet, and pulled my knees up to my chest. I heard a collective gasp as Monica retrieved her bow, and inspected every delicate inch of polished wood and horsehair. A good bow cost an awful lot of money. Smiling with relief, then noticing that everyone, including Eric Ries, was staring at her, she lowered the bow into her lap. I felt sorry for her. She wanted Eric to notice her, but not because she was a klutz.

Bernstein climbed the two steps onto his conductor's podium. Everyone looked in his direction, so I got brave and slid to the very edge of the curtain. He opened his huge orchestra score and studied the notes. Musicians only read their individual parts, but conductors have to read all the instruments' part at the same time. I could not imagine reading the entire page, horizontally and vertically, in several different clefs, all at the same time.

Eric moved behind the conductor's podium and leaned on the brass railing. His shoulders slumped, his smile disappeared, and he rubbed his eyes. A minute ago, he was full of energy. Now he looked exhausted. Monica said that he came directly from the airport. I guessed that he was jet-lagged.

Bernstein raised his baton. The players lifted their instruments and posed, ready to play. Bernstein set a slow four-four tempo, waving his baton in four directions. On the next downbeat, violins and violas pulled their bows across low strings. Sid and Monica, and the entire first violin section bowed in unison. It was beautiful to watch. Wind players, brass, and low strings all joined, reading Eric's music for the first time. Whenever I listened to his record, I concentrated on the violin solo, not the instruments accompanying it. I knew this was an orchestra rehearsal, without the soloist, but I was still startled not to hear the solo violin play, on cue. It took me a second to adjust, then I got really excited. For the first time, I could clearly hear all the other instruments. It was so great!

Eric looked down and listened hard. His right hand clutched the brass podium rail, his left hand rested on his hip, and he seemed very tense. After a couple of minutes, his shoulders relaxed. He still listened hard, but smiled slightly. When he stifled a yawn, I guessed he liked what he heard. Suddenly, the second violins played something weird. Bernstein glared at them and flipped his baton. The music stopped.

Eric lurched, then forced a smile. "Whoops! What happened there?" Still smiling, he hurried to each of the section leaders and they studied the part together. Bernstein rolled his eyes, impatiently shook his head, and stared at the ceiling. Eric looked at all the players. "I am so sorry. The copyist's notation is beautiful, but some of these eight notes look like sixteenths." He smiled up at Bernstein. "With your permission, Maestro, I'd like everyone to take a minute and check their parts for confusing notation." All the musicians looked hopeful. Bernstein sighed dramatically, shrugged, then told them to go ahead. They all skimmed through their parts.

Monica turned pages and pencil-marked a couple of places in their score. She looked sideways at Sid. "So, how many times have you heard a composer take responsibility for his copyist?"

Sid didn't answer and Monica laughed. I guessed his silent answer was "never."

For the next few minutes, pencils scratched as the players marked their music. Eric went back to his place behind the podium. Bernstein raised his baton again. The read-through started again and continued until the movement was over.

Before starting the second movement, Bernstein leaned over to ask Eric a question. Lithe as a gazelle, Eric loped up the steps onto the conductor's platform. He was only average height, but still taller than Bernstein. They studied the orchestra score together. Monica sat up and stared at Eric.

I stared too. He looked really comfortable talking with Bernstein, and Bernstein seemed to like him. I tried comparing Eric to my father, but there was just no way. Dad was thirty-nine, and Eric was thirty. I was eleven, so nine years seemed like a really big difference. Even so, Eric didn't look old enough to be anyone's father. Every father I knew wore grown-up, conservative clothes and had short-cropped hair. One had a beard. Eric's hair was dark and shaggy, with long sideburns blending into a pencil-thin beard and mustache. He wore a tight-fitting maroon turtleneck, and tight black leather pants that seemed to be sprayed onto his legs and butt. He looked really good, but nothing like I expected. For weeks, I had been talking to the 8x10 black-and-white photo of his face, and imagining that a business suit, like my dad's, was attached to it. Now I would remember this young, teen-age body, and attach it to the face in the picture.

Eric stepped off the podium and Bernstein began again. The rest of the reading was clean and easy. Monica's posture kept shifting and I guessed she kept looking at Eric. Once, her bow slipped. She played some sour notes and Sid glared at her. She sat up straighter, keeping her eyes moving in a straight line from the manuscript to the conductor and back. They read through all three movements and the orchestra manager called a break. I sneaked out, back down into the audience where I left my schoolbag and coat. The few listeners and all the orchestra members seemed really happy. The music was both beautiful and playable. I wanted to stay longer, but had to get home.

I took one long, last look at Eric Ries, still on stage, practically surrounded by musicians congratulating him, chatting and laughing. I wouldn't get to hear the concerto with the soloist until the concert Sunday afternoon. Five whole days away. A lifetime! Mom and some the other Philharmonic Society ladies were having lunch with Eric tomorrow when I'd be at school. It wasn't fair.

•

Friday night, The New York Philharmonic debuted Eric's *Violin Concerto*. I begged to go, but Mom wouldn't let me. Saturday morning I raced downstairs to buy any papers that might review the concert. I found two. One critic praised Eric's technical skill and "fearless sensuality" because he wrote mostly tonal melodies and harmonies. The other critic thought the concerto sounded "derivative." Mom said that meant it sounded like music written by other composers or, worse yet, like movie music. I was upset, but she said I shouldn't worry. Reviews would be published in lots of papers, all over the world, and some were sure to be good. I hoped she was right.

Since all three concerts were nearly sold out, the Philharmonic Society ladies celebrated with dinner at the Russian Tearoom. Since I had helped stuff envelopes for the campaign, I was invited. At seven o'clock Saturday night, Betty Newberry, Mom, myself, and five other Philharmonic Society ladies met at the Russian Tearoom. The food was ridiculously expensive, but I loved the gaudy red and gold decorations, the huge polished samovar by the entrance, the tacky Christmas decorations that were left up all year, and the surly Russian waiters in their folk costumes. Lots of celebrities ate there and we might see some. My mouth was all set for creamy-sweet cheese blintzes smothered with sour cream and blueberry jam. Mom always ordered chicken Kiev. It came in a hard pocket crust that popped hot steam when the top was pierced. We checked our coats and the maitre d' in a tuxedo showed us to a large round table.

The women sat down, and I hurried to the ladies room to comb my wind-blown hair. I washed it that morning, so it was feather-soft, and shining, hanging long down my back. When I left the ladies room, I stopped and stared.

Two men sat in the last booth. One was old and bald. The other was Eric Ries. Their dinner check lay on the table. Their drink glasses were nearly empty and they sat back talking. The way they joked and laughed, I could tell they liked each other. Without thinking, I dodged around to a waiters' station, dropped to the floor and crept on my hands and knees until I was behind their booth. A busboy came by with a tub of dirty dishes, saw me sitting on the floor, and kept walking. It was really funny. I guessed this restaurant had a lot of crazy customers.

I heard the old man sigh, then say, "Leave it alone, Eric. Since when do I care about critics? As long as you get played, forget the bastards. Grit your teeth and compose what you like. I love your music. I always have. I always will. And as long as I'm around, you'll get played."

Eric's voice said, "Thanks Phil. You're a rock." Glasses clinked. "Love y' man." There was silence, then, "I had the oboist last night."

"Judy or Sheila?" The old man chewed a piece of ice. Just hearing it made my teeth hurt.

Eric's voice said, "Umm, the blond."

"Judy. Good. Sheila gave my buddy the clap."

"Ouch. Isn't the second harp Sheila?"

"Sharon. What, you had her, too?" There was silence, then the old man chuckled. "Christ! I thought I used to be a womanizer."

"It was a lot harder in your day. No pill." Eric yawned. "Maybe you should try again."

"No, no, no. Since marrying Ellen … You should try marriage. A really good woman's worth—"

"I've been married." Eric sounded angry.

"That wasn't marriage. That was bondage. What about Colette?"

"Poor Colette … She puts up with a lot from me." He sounded sorry. Who was Colette and what he had done to her?

"Does she know you screw around?"

"We don't talk about it, but she must. I'm gone half the year. Thank God she's busy with her own career. She's lovely, but not worth giving up the rest of the world for."

I thought screwing around meant getting silly and cutting up during ballet class. It didn't seem so terrible.

Eric spoke softer. "There's a woman—back of the first violins.

Dark hair. Pretty in a dour sort of way. Dresses like a nun."

"Monica Jones."

"That's her name? Monica?"

Did Eric like Monica? This was great. She would be so happy.

"You're not interested in her?"

I wanted to shout, "Why not? She's really nice."

Eric said, "She dropped her bow and I got a glimpse of cleavage. Under those size-forty T-shirts, I think she's hiding a beautiful body."

"She's fucked up in the head. Don't get me wrong, she's a great player. For a while she sat principal-second, but couldn't handle being principal anything. She freaked and got demoted. She'll probably stay buried in the back of the section for the rest of her life."

"That's not a bad life."

"For some, I guess." Phil sighed. "Don't fuck Monica. She'll be more trouble than she's worth."

"I know her type is dangerous. That's why I saved her for my last night. Tomorrow's Sunday. After the matinee, I'll be on my way to Salzburg. If she freaks out, I'll be gone."

This was a lot to take in. I knew the "F" word was bad, but didn't know what it meant. Why did Eric think Monica would "freak out"? Sid said he didn't want her crying. Why would she be crying?

Thinking Mom would send a search party for me, I crept back and pretended to come out of the ladies room. I got back to the table as the waiter was leaving. Mom said she had ordered me cheese blintzes and tea. Before I could walk around to my seat at the far side of the table, Eric and the old man left their booth and started toward us.

Betty Newberry saw them and sprang to her feet. "Phil, darling! And Eric. How lovely to see you both."

I nearly broke out laughing when the old man physically shuddered and stopped in his tracks. Eric stifled a smile, looked at the floor, and kept walking until he was all the way around on my side of the table.

Betty gestured grandly. "Ladies, I believe you all know Philip Shapiro, President of Atlas Artists Management ... and some of us know Eric Ries. Let's see, who wasn't at lunch last Wednesday ..."
Betty introduced Eric to the ladies who had missed lunch, and I

stared at Phil Shapiro.

The orchestra players talked about a guy named Phil Shapiro. Could this really be him? He looked like an ordinary old bald guy with a paunch. Phil Shapiro was one of the most powerful artists' managers in the world. He handled the careers of dozens of classical music superstars and every musician wanted to sign with Atlas Artists.

Betty finished introducing the grown-up ladies and saw me standing behind my chair. She pursed her lips and gestured condescendingly. "Eric dear, this pretty child is Allison's daughter, Jenna."

Eric smiled at Mom, stepped over, and offered me his hand. I felt like I was meeting God. Automatically, I took his hand and curtsied. Betty rambled on to Phil Shapiro. He looked really uncomfortable, but couldn't get away.

Eric talked to me. I was thrilled, but guessed that he just wanted to ignore Betty. "So, umm, at lunch ... Your mom told me you like my record."

"I do! I play it all the time."

"Wait a minute." He squinted and pointed a finger. "That first rehearsal ... You were in the wings."

"You saw me?" The blood drained from my face. "Oh, no! I really tried to hide."

He nodded and smiled. "You did pretty well. A couple of times the curtain moved. The first time I thought I was imagining it, then I saw this little rabbit crouched on the floor."

I laughed at his teasing. "I hope Mr. Bernstein didn't see me."

He smiled and shrugged. "He probably did. He probably enjoyed your being there. It's nice when a kid cares that much."

This was fabulous. I was so excited. "It was so great sitting there. I heard the players talking to each other."

"Oh, so you're a spy. I'll bet that's interesting. I'd like to hear what they say about me. Or, maybe I wouldn't."

"They love you!"

He chuckled with surprise. "They do?"

"Yeah! Even Sid. Even some who didn't think they would. Monica really likes you."

He looked surprised. "Monica?"

Afraid he knew I eavesdropped on his conversation with Phil, I stammered, "Uh, yeah. M-monica sits last stand, first violins. She has really long beautiful hair and she's really nice."

He raised an eyebrow. "So you're a spy and a matchmaker."

"No! I—I just heard her talking about you, before the rehearsal. She's read all about you, and heard your London Symphony record."

He nodded slowly. "Okay. That's nice. I guess ... I like Monica too. Thanks for the tip." He gave me a conspiratorial wink. I giggled and he smiled back.

Phil pried himself away from Betty Newberry. He pointed to Eric and inched sideways around the table. "Ladies, forgive me, but I've got to get my boy on stage for his bow. Good to see you all and thanks for all your good work." He rushed out. Eric waved and followed.

I hurried after them. "Mr. Ries!" He turned back. "I have a picture of you. Would you sign it for me? I'll be at the concert tomorrow afternoon." I felt like a puppy begging for table scraps.

He laughed and shook his head. "Yeah, of course. Come back to the greenroom." He reached out his hand, affectionately cupped my chin and cheek, then followed Phil out of the restaurant.

To this day, I remember the smile in his eyes, and the feeling of his hand on my face. To him, it was nothing—a pat on the cheek for a cute kid. For me, it was a miracle. In those few minutes, Eric Ries had given me more attention and affection than my father had given me my entire life.

Allegro Brillante

The next afternoon, I maneuvered Mom into leaving the apartment on time. She was never late, but sometimes on the edge. A full fifteen minutes before the concert started, we were inside Philharmonic Hall, in our subscription seats, center aisle, row J.

I knew every measure of the *Violin Concerto* by heart, but this would be a different conductor, violinist, and orchestra. I was very curious to hear the variations. The concert started with a Mozart Symphony. Next came Eric's *Violin Concerto*. I sat on the edge of my seat, listened hard, watched Leonard Bernstein and his violin soloist, a young man I was hearing for the first time. I was surprised, but not always pleased with Bernstein's interpretation.

In the London recording, the violinist stretched phrases until they brought tears to my eyes. Bernstein pushed his violinist to play stricter tempos, driving the music from one climax to the next. It was exciting and beautiful, but I missed some of the schmaltzy moments.

The concerto ended and Bernstein brought Eric out for a bow. He was dressed in a dark suit and his shaggy hair was combed smooth, away from his face. He looked very handsome this way, and more like he could be someone's father. He bowed, the violinist bowed, Bernstein bowed, the French horn soloist bowed, the whole orchestra bowed, Eric bowed again, the audience cheered and applauded, so there was a lot more bowing. After reading the one bad review, I was relieved that the audience was so kind.

Finally, Bernstein led Eric and the violin soloist off stage. The orchestra followed as the house lights came up for intermission. I had to stay for the second half, but wanted to run to the greenroom and get Eric's autograph right then and there. It seemed like years before the final music ended, Bernstein and the orchestra took their bows, and the house lights came up again.

I knew a shortcut through the backstage area, so I clutched Mom's hand and pulled her against the traffic of audience members, all going the other way. I never carried a purse, so Mom had Eric's photograph in her shoulder bag. As soon as we were backstage, I let her go and sped on alone. The greenroom stairs were straight ahead, but the door to an instrument locker room flung open, blocking my way. Eric raced out. His back was to me as he raced down the corridor, tucking in his shirt. He leapt up the stairs, two at a time, straightened his tie, then disappeared into the greenroom's back door.

I hurried past the open door and saw Sharon, the beautiful blond harpist, inside, straightening her long, full skirt. There was no harp part in the last piece, so I guessed she and Eric had been inside, studying her harp. She combed her long hair away from her face and laughed at nothing that I could see. When she saw me at the open door, her smile vanished and her eyes bulged. She blushed and stammered, "Oh. Hi, Jenna."

I said, "Hi!" back, then hurried up the stairs after Eric.

By the time I got to the greenroom, a long line of fans waited for Eric to sign their programs and record jackets. He sat behind a small table, in front of an oriental folding screen. I stuffed envelopes in this room and knew that the screen hid piles of cardboard boxes filled with fliers for future concerts. Eric signed a man's record jacket, handed it back, smiled and spoke. I couldn't hear what he said, but the man smiled back. Next in line was a middle-aged woman with a program. Eric signed it and spoke to her. She answered back. Eric said something else and the woman left, smiling. Whatever he said to everyone must have been terrific, because they all left looking happy.

Even though he found this process exhausting, he gladly suffered through hundreds of tedious teas, lunches, and autograph signings all over the world. He spoke fluent French, passable Italian and German, and graciously played the role of a charming, grateful musical servant, flattering both men and women. He made them feel like they were the most fascinating individuals on the planet. Smile after smile, handshake after handshake, tryst after tryst, he insured record sales and return engagements.

Monica stood in a corner watching Eric. I zoomed over to her, dying to know if they had gone out on a date.

She smiled kindly. "Hi, Jenna. Great concert, wasn't it?"

"Yeah." I looked from her to Eric and back. "Maybe you'll play the solo sometime."

"No." She looked sad. "I'm an ensemble player, not a soloist."

I didn't know what that meant, but I was too interested in matchmaking to waste time asking. I hedged, "Um, Mr. Ries is really nice."

"The nicest man I know." Her words were happy, but she looked miserable.

"He likes you. He said so last night."

She stared at me.

Not sure what more to say, I blathered, "Last night, at the Russian Tearoom. I was there with the Philharmonic Society ladies, and we met Mr. Ries and Mr. Shapiro. I got talking to Mr. Ries, just for a couple of minutes, but he said he liked everybody, especially you."

"He said that?" Her eyes got watery like she was going to cry.

"Yeah, well, something like that. I don't remember exactly."

She whispered, "We were together last night. It was late, after we'd had drinks with everyone else. He was wonderful." Tears streamed down her cheeks. She wiped them away with her fingers, then dug into her pocket for a Kleenex.

"But, that's great. So ... Why are you crying?"

"He's leaving tonight. I'll never see him again."

"You might. I mean, you could visit or something."

She shook her head, then turned away as Mom came over with my photograph. I felt really confused watching Monica cry. Mom saw a friend across the room and went to talk.

I took the photo and joined the queue. There were two people in front me. Finally, my turn came and I handed Eric the picture.

He took it and smiled. "Ah ha! It's the little spy." He poised his pen, then paused. "To ..."

"... Jenna." My voice was a nervous whisper.

"That's right." He wrote, "To Jenna," signed his name, and handed it back. "I have a daughter who's eleven. How old are you?"

"Eleven. I read about your daughter. Her name's Susannah. I can play *A Rainbow For My Daughter*."

He looked pleased. "Oh, good for you. Do you want to be a pianist?"

"No. I want to be a singer."

"Really! Well, who knows?" He winked and smiled sweetly. "Someday I might write a song for you." He reached past me and took a program from the last person in line: Monica.

I was the best singer at school, and one of the best singers at music camp, but never thought about singing for a living. His light remark about writing me a song cemented the drive into my psyche. From that moment, I was going to be a singer.

I stepped away and Monica moved into my place, leaning her hand on the table. I just had to hear their conversation, and sneaked behind the screen where I could peer through a slot in the panels.

Without changing his expression, Eric covered Monica's right hand with his left, squeezed it gently, and signed her program.

She leaned into him. "Do you have to fly out today?"

He watched her, waiting to answer. When her eyes filled with tears, he smiled sadly and handed back the program. "Yeah. Sorry."

I wondered what he would have answered if she hadn't cried. Last night he told Phil that if she "freaked out" he'd be gone. Was this freaking out?

Monica looked desperate. She whimpered, "It was the best night of my life. I'll never forget you." He nodded sadly. She blinked back tears, took her program and hurried away.

He sat down, watched her go, and shook his head like he didn't believe it. Phil ambled up, wiping sweat from his forehead. He handed Eric a large envelope. "Here's your recording contract. I worked my tail off, and it's good. Bruchman's a thief, so don't play a note until he signs it. Oh, your wife called."

Eric jerked to attention. His whole body tensed. "You mean my *ex*."

"She said to tell you that Susie won a piano competition."

"That was today? Oh, shit! I promised to call and wish her luck." He lurched to his feet. "She actually won? That was a national competition. I expected her to win the regionals, but she beat out, what? Five-hundred kids? A thousand? Those were the best kids in the country. Is there a phone in here?" Suddenly frantic, he scanned the room. Phil looked too. There wasn't a phone, but I couldn't tell them.

Phil gave Eric a sideways look. "Last month, you forgot her Christmas call."

"Yeah. The kid's going to hate me." His eyes opened wide as Betty Newberry fluttered toward him. He whispered, "Not that stupid cow, again. She drooled all over me at lunch."

Phil whispered back, "That 'cow' is chairwoman of the Philharmonic Society. If you want to play New York next season, smile."

"What's her name?"

"Betty Newberry."

Eric smiled and held out his hands. "Betty Newberry, you are an angel!"

Gushing with pleasure, Betty took his hands. "Oh, Eric, your music is so beautiful. I felt like I was watching a romantic movie."

He flinched, then forced a smile.

Phil turned his back, rolling his eyes.

Eric leaned close to Betty, whispering, "As long as you're pleased, That's all I care about."

Betty blushed like a schoolgirl. "You are such a dear man. If there's ever anything I can do for you ..."

"Right now, you can lead me to a telephone. I have to call my daughter."

"There's one in the office, down the hall, second door." She gestured toward the entrance.

"Thanks!" He gave her a peck on the cheek and hurried away.

She looked as if she were going to faint.

I was in pain, holding my stomach to keep from screaming with laughter. Phil shook his head and followed Eric. I waited a second, then followed at a distance, hoping to eavesdrop on Eric's conversation with his daughter.

Before they could reach the door, a young woman blocked the way. Her short blond hair was mussed prettily across her face. She gasped for breath, and I could see her bra outlined under her tight red sweater. In one hand she held a small tape recorder. With the other, she wiped away frustrated tears. "Mr. Ries! I'm so sorry, but I've just driven in from Hartford. My car broke down. I missed the concert and the press conference, but I've got to get something into my editor tonight. It's my first assignment, and ..."

"There, there." Eric stopped and smiled. "Let's get a nice cup of coffee, and you can ask me anything you like."

I was shocked. He needed to call his daughter. Right now. It was really important. Instead of going into the office, he took the reporter's arm and led her toward the elevator. She looked startled, but thrilled when the elevator door opened and he led her inside. Just before the door closed, he shouted, "Phil! Send Susie some flowers with a nice note."

"I already have." Phil grimaced and ambled away.

I tried to digest what I'd just seen. Refusing to believe that Eric Ries wasn't the best father in the world, I consoled myself thinking how happy Susannah would be when his flowers arrived. After all, my father had never sent me flowers.

Appassionato Diminuendo

The next few weeks, my euphoria at meeting Eric Ries put me on a buoyant cloud, bouncing me through everyday activities, making everything seem more fun and more important than it had been before. Years later, I identified this delicious lightness as being in love. At eleven-and-a-half, I just knew it felt good.

One afternoon, I raced home from art class with exciting news.

I threw open the apartment door, sped down the hall to Mom's room, and stopped dead.

Mom stood with her back to me, holding the telephone. Her arms were tight at her sides and her shoulders were tense. She clutched the phone with one hand, and squeezed the other hand into a fist. "No, Lester, I do not! Our lawyers are supposed to negotiate this. I'm not even supposed to talk to you." There were angry tears in her voice. "Talk to my lawyer!" She slammed down the phone and stood over it, breathing hard. I backed away, and stayed out of sight, until I heard her stomp over the plush pale blue carpeting. When I heard squeaking wood, I knew she had planted herself on the delicate antique chair matching the three-mirrored vanity in her dressing room.

I pretended I just came in. "Mommy! Mommy! You'll never guess what happened." I counted to three, raced in, and threw my arms around her neck.

"Watch the hair!" She braced herself and closed her eyes. I backed away from the perfect blond, bouffant hairdo that had just been styled by Mr. Anthony at The House of Revlon. She took some deep breaths, steadied her shaky hands, reached for her under-eye cover stick, and pulled off the cap.

Too excited to wait, I blurted out, "You know the art class exhibit? Well, this time Mr. Irwin—"

"Your hands!" She lurched back.

I looked at my hands and saw fingernails encrusted with green paint. "Oh, sorry." I hurried past her, into the bathroom. Her expensive, pale lavender towels hung in an immaculate row of increasing size: hand towel, small bath towel, and large bath towel. I made sure my hands were perfectly clean before drying them on the hand towel. Hurrying back, I pushed my scrubbed fingers under her nose.

"That's good, dear." She pushed my hands away and reached for her eye shadow. "Now, when's your art exhibit?" She sounded less than enthused.

I dropped to the floor next to her chair. "It's not just going to be an exhibit, this year. Mr. Irwin said—"

"We just got that uniform back from the cleaners." She glared at my reflection, and smoothed pale blue shadow over her eyelids.

"Sorry." I guiltily sprung to my feet and picked carpet threads off my skirt. "Mr. Irwin said we're going to be doing primary color studies, so I told him about *A Rainbow For My Daughter*. After class there was a piano in another room and I played the colors for him. All of them. I made some mistakes, but he really liked them."

Mom's lips twitched into a fast, forced smile. "Good for you." Her lips relaxed back as she dipped a tiny brush into a saucer of water and used it to wet a solid cake of black eyeliner. When the paint liquefied, she filled the brush and drew perfect black lines above and below both eyes. I was still there, so she felt obliged to ask, "Alright, he liked your music. Is there more?"

"Yeah!" I rushed to finish. "One of the other kids, Sarah Beth Samuels, said her school class wrote poems about colors, so Mr. Irwin said we should do a multimedia thing, with pictures and poems, and I should play the piano. Isn't that great? I'm so excited!"

She sniffed, then smiled for real. "Yes, that really is great. I'm proud of you."

I waited for her to say more nice stuff, and felt alarmed when her lips reset in their pursed position. Had she told me the truth? Maybe she really thought the idea was stupid. Maybe she remembered my disappointment, never playing those pieces for my father, or maybe she just wanted me out of the way so she could dress.

"It's nearly six-thirty. You must be starving." She carefully applied adhesive to the back of a false eyelash, concentrated her full attention, and slowly lowered the eyelash onto her eyelid.

I smiled nervously. "I am. I just wanted you to know about the—"

"Thanks for telling me." She secured the eyelash and kissed the air in my direction.

I kissed the air back and hurried to the kitchen to tell Penny. We sat together as I bolted down my dinner. I talked between bites, and explained how hot colors went with major keys, and cold colors went with minor keys. Penny concentrated, listened patiently, and understood almost nothing. When I finished, she gave me a big hug and told me how smart I was. She was a darling and I really appreciated her kindness. I rushed to my room and retold the whole thing to Eric's photo, now in a handsome dark wood frame. He understood everything.

A few minutes later, Mom glided down the hall in a stunning blue satin, ankle-length sheath, with a matching sapphire necklace, earrings and bracelet. She looked fashion model perfect, beautiful, and far too untouchable to be anyone's mother. She paused at my door and I stared with unabashed admiration. "You look fabulous! I wish I could go."

Pleased by the compliment, she opened her arms. I hopped off the bed, but hesitated, afraid of wrinkling the gown. Very gently, I hugged the gleaming satin. She squeezed back, pushed wisps of hair away from my eyes, kissed my forehead, and wiped off the lipstick mark. "It's a hospital fundraiser. It'll probably be a terrible bore. I wish you could go for me. I'll be late, so sleep well."

"I will." I wanted to kiss her back, but was afraid to touch her flawlessly painted face. She started to go, then paused and looked at Eric's photo lying on my bed. She knew I talked to the picture, but never said anything about it. I hoped she didn't think I was crazy. She smiled uncomfortably, and left to get her mink coat from the front closet. I waited until I heard the front door open and close, sighed with relief, picked up the picture and finished telling it about the multimedia art exhibit.

Semplice Mesto Accelerando

That spring, the divorce became final. Dad had moved out more than a year before, so I didn't understand why a paper document made Mom so unhappy. She spent whole evenings shut in her room or on the phone with my Aunt Connie. I heard her crying, felt awful, and blamed myself. Week after week, pill bottles gathered on her bedside table. Sometimes she took a pill right after dinner, fell asleep, and was still asleep the next morning. Those days, I went to school afraid she wouldn't wake up at all. I smiled a lot and pretended nothing had changed, but inside I felt really scared. If the divorce was my fault, her despair was also my fault. I had lost my father. Was I going to lose my mother, too?

Eventually, Mom escaped her depression by burying herself deeper into charity work. Most of her energy went into a fundraising campaign for UNICEF. All fifty states competed to see which one could raise the most money before Halloween, when children collected donations along with trick-or-treat candy. Delegates from each district in the winning state would be honored at a gala dinner in Washington, D.C. Mom joined armies of volunteers who canvassed, called, begged, wrote letters, and knocked on doors. By late summer, New York state was declared the winner. Mom was frantic to attend the award ceremony, but each district was only allowed to send two delegates. They were chosen by their peers, so the vote was a popularity contest. Mom's recent black moods had made her lose several friends. She knew she wouldn't be chosen.

The banquet date was Friday, November thirteenth, the same day as my thirteenth birthday. If a child's birthday fell on a school day, her party was usually held on the nearest Saturday afternoon. Mom told me not to worry. She wouldn't be going to Washington, so my party could be Saturday the fourteenth.

Mom and I sat at the kitchen table planning my birthday party while devouring spaghetti and meatballs. I rolled an overlarge forkful dripping with tomato sauce, shook some off, and slurped up the rest. I giggled at my rude sucking noises, and Mom glared disapprovingly. She looked really funny and I burst into an open-mouthed laugh. Half-chewed noodles fell from my lips back onto my plate and red sauce splattered across my napkin.

Mom looked scandalized, opened her mouth to scold, but I cut her off. "Last year we took everyone to the planetarium." I swiped a napkin over my tomato-smeared mouth. "Could we rent a movie, this year, and show it in the living room?" I smiled angelically. "Some of the girls could sleep over."

Mom glared icily, shrugged off her annoyance, and pretended my face wasn't smeared with spaghetti sauce. "Well, a slumber party might be fun. We could take everyone to the circus. Would the girls like that?"

Sucking in another mouthful, I shook my head and made more rude noises. Another laugh bubbled in my throat, but I knew better than to risk Mom's wrath a second time. I practically gagged, but managed to swallow the noodles.

Then Mom said something really weird. "I wonder how soon you'll start inviting boys to your parties."

Boys? I hardly even knew any boys. I went to a girl's school. The only boys I knew were in my art and ballet classes, and most of them were creepy.

The phone rang and Mom reached behind her. "Hello? Oh, hi,

Liz."

I tensed. Liz was the chairwoman of the UNICEF drive. Mom said she wouldn't be selected to go to Washington, but this was the final word. After listening for a moment, she sadly shook her head. Her eyes lost focus.

I was elated. I wanted to scream, "Hooray! She isn't going. I'll really get my party."

Mom's posture relaxed and she sighed. "I know you did, Liz, thanks. You deserve to go. We did it for the kids, after all, not the glory. Yeah. Thanks, again. 'Bye." She hung up the phone and shrugged sadly. "I guessed it. I'm the third alternate."

"Then ... You still might go?" I forced a smile.

"Not a chance." She picked up her fork and took a bite of salad. I tried not to look too pleased, but my hand was shaking as I wound another spool of noodles onto my fork.

Mom was really disappointed and I appreciated her trying to sound cheerful. She thought for a minute. "You know what? Why don't we have your party on Friday the thirteenth, where it belongs? School's a half day on Fridays. The party could be from three to seven."

I was thrilled, but afraid to show it. I hedged. "But, some people think Friday the thirteenth is bad luck."

"Not for us!" This time Mom smiled for real. "Let's call it a Luck Party."

"I could invite thirteen girls."

"Good idea."

"And rent the movie *Dracula*, and tell everyone to dress like vampires."

"A costume party? Okay. Why not?"

"What if Daddy calls?"

"What?" Mom looked totally surprised. "Oh, sweetheart, he hasn't called in—"

"I know he forgot my last two birthdays, but this one's really important. I'm turning thirteen. It's a milestone." I stabbed a cucumber slice.

Mom sadly raised an eyebrow. "It's important to us, but he's—" I could tell she thought he would forget it, but didn't have the heart to say so. "Well, if he does call, we'll be home and you can talk to him."

•

In preparation for the Birthday Luck Party, Mom designed thirteen wonderfully funny/scary portraits to hang in the foyer as decorations. She spread the sketches over our large dining room table, and we painted them with watercolors.

For the first time ever, Mom and I spent entire evenings alone, having fun together. Three weeks before the party, we sat at the kitchen table. She strung yarn while I addressed thirteen handmade party invitations. The cover of each one had a picture of a pair of dice showing a three and a four, and read:

> *I'm turning LUCKY thirteen.*
> *Please come to my Birthday LUCK Party,*
> *on Friday, November 13th from 3:00 to 7:00.*
> *Please dress like a vampire.*

Inside were my name, address, phone number and RSVP.

Mom strung enough white and silver yarn to make a huge cobweb for the party guests to crawl through on their way into the living room. She suggested leaving it up for her Philharmonic Society luncheon and I nearly fell off my chair laughing. Mom laughed until she had tears in her eyes. "Can't you see Betty Newberry, blue hair and high-heels, climbing through yards of yarn?"

I pictured the comical parade of fussily dressed, middle-aged women bent over, pushing through the web, struggling to keep their balance.

The phone rang and Mom answered, still laughing. "Hello? Oh, hi, Liz." She stopped laughing. She looked thrilled. My blood ran cold. She shouted, "You're kidding! Both of you are busy?"

My hands shook as I slid the last invitation into an envelope, licked the back and sealed it closed.

"Wait a minute, Liz." Mom put her hand over the mouthpiece. "Open those up, sweetie. We have to change the dates." She smiled victoriously. "I'm going to Washington."

"But, Mom ..."

She held up a hand for silence, turned away, and talked into the phone. "The banquet's black tie, isn't it?"

"Mom!" I was frantic.

"Sorry, Liz." Mom turned back, clamped her hand over the mouthpiece, and glared. "What?"

"What about my party?"

"We'll do it the next week."

"But it—"

"This is a great honor, Jen. You should be proud your mother's representing UNICEF."

"I am, but—"

"If you want the party on the thirteenth, you and Penny can do it without me."

"Penny's going to a wedding. She's leaving early Friday morning."

Mom hesitated, and I held my breath, praying she'd recant. Instead, she clenched her jaw. "Jenna, this is much more important than a birthday party. We'll postpone it a week. Alright?"

"No! It's not alright." My stomach was a tight knot.

She glared me into silence and turned back to the phone.

I fled to my room. A few minutes later, she found me sitting on my bed, silently complaining to Eric's picture.

She smiled uncomfortably and walked in. "Jenna, honey. I'm sorry it happened this way."

I was furious. "But Mom. It's all planned. I already told everyone. They're expecting my party to be on Friday the thirteenth."

"Then you'll just have to tell them it's postponed. You've always known the banquet was on the thirteenth."

"But, you said you wouldn't get to go."

"I was wrong."

"But that's not fair."

"That's the way it is."

"But—"

"Just change the date on the invitations." She stormed out.

I followed her. "But, Mom!"

"End of discussion!" She shut her bedroom door.

I stood in the hall, stared at her closed door, then raced back to my room and Eric's photo. He would never do that to his daughter. I was only going to have one thirteenth birthday. This would have been the best party in the world.

It wouldn't be the same, on … I checked my desk calendar. November twenty-second.

Andente Accelerando

Friday, November 13th, was like any other school day, except that my teacher took the customary two minutes to have the class sing *Happy Birthday* to me. That afternoon, I arrived home soaked from a steady shower of wet snow. For the first time in my life, I got off the elevator and had to use a key to unlock the front door. The foyer lights had been left on, but there was no sound. A second later, an ambulance screeched down Eighty-first Street and I was actually comforted to hear the siren. I took my drenched coat and scarf into the laundry room, and tossed the wet clothes over the ironing board.

With just Mom, Penny and me living in the twelve-room apartment, I had often been at home alone, but never overnight. If I needed help with anything, I could use the intercom and buzz the doorman, or push the elevator button and wait for the elevator man to come up. Phone numbers for Mom's Washington Hotel and Penny's family in New Jersey were printed on a pad near Mom's telephone. I was safe, but felt strange being totally alone. To boost my spirits, I played Eric's *Four Rivers Suite,* soaked in a warming bubble bath, and imagined myself floating down the four rivers. Expecting my father to call, I kept my ears tuned for the telephone. Penny left an assortment of dishes in the refrigerator and I sampled everything.

All evening I sat on Mom's bed, watched the oversized TV, did homework, and wished I had thought to ask someone over for the night. I wasn't frightened, just lonely. Twice I started to call girlfriends, then, afraid to tie up the phone, hung up again. Since there was no phone in the living room, I was afraid to practice the piano and risk missing a call. As the minutes crept by, I felt more and more alone. Why didn't Daddy call? I knew California was three hours behind and that he often worked late, so I busied myself with more homework and TV. I pictured Mom at her fancy party and hoped she'd call to say "good night."

By ten-thirty, the phone hadn't rung. I felt tired and angry. Daddy knew what time it was in New York. Why didn't he call? I bet Eric hadn't forgotten his daughter's thirteenth birthday. I wondered when it was. If it was last summer, she might have been with him. If he wasn't with her, he must have called and sent a present. I wondered what he gave her.

When the eleven o'clock news came on, I switched off the TV. I clenched my jaw to keep from crying, and sat on Mom's bed, rocking and thinking hard. I was thirteen-years-old. I wasn't a child anymore. I could make my own decisions.

More nervous than I had ever been in my life, I tiptoed into the wood-paneled study where my father used to work. Mom had taken over the room. Her papers were scattered over the large desk and a bottle of Seconal tablets sat next to the Rolodex. I grimaced, remembering her too often drugged sleep. I sat in the large swivel, leather chair, felt swallowed up, and smiled thinking of myself as Goldilocks in Papa Bear's chair. Carefully turning Rolodex cards, I found one for: Adams, Lester, with a California address and telephone number. My hand shook as I forced the receiver against my ear. I misdialed and had to start over three times before completing the number.

After four rings, a young woman answered. "Hel-lo." Beatles music played in the background.

"Um, hello. Is Lester Adams there please?"

"Not for another hour." The voice sounded cheerful. "Can I give him a message?"

My heart pounded. I clutched the receiver. "Please tell him Jenna called."

"Any last name?" The voice was not as cheerful.

I was shaking. "Adams. I'm his daughter ... In New York. It's my birthday."

"Yeah, right! Who are you really, huh? He doesn't have a daughter." Now the voice was sneering. "He told me he didn't have any kids. Who is this? Is this that ...?"

I froze, then slammed down the receiver. I couldn't move. He told her he didn't have any kids? I felt numb. He told her, he—didn't have—any—kids. The electric clock buzzed for five long minutes before my head cleared and I remembered where I was.

Almost sleepwalking, I left the study, turned off the lights, and made my way to my room. I sat on my bed, staring at the picture of Eric. Now I felt frightened, angry, dejected and totally alone in the world. My insides cramped with emotional misery. I had to talk to somebody, but there wasn't anybody. It was close to midnight, so calling Penny or a girlfriend was out of the question. I pictured my mother, happy and gorgeous at her Washington party, surrounded by friends and admirers, while I was all alone. She made me give up my party so she could go to her own party, and I hated her for it. It was still early in California so I thought about calling Aunt Connie, but that was no good. Aunt Connie and Mom always disagreed about child rearing. If Aunt Connie found out I was alone all night on my birthday, she'd throw a fit. Mom would get upset and yell at me. There was absolutely no one I could turn to.

I fell on my bed, sobbing uncontrollably. The pain was so bad I thought my insides would rupture. I remembered Mom crying like that after the divorce. She took pills and felt better. There was that bottle in the study, and rows of others in the bathroom. I told Eric's picture that I would just take one pill. It would put me to sleep. I would be all right in the morning if I could just sleep tonight.

I took the Seconal bottle from the study, went into Mom's bathroom, and read the labels on all the pill bottles. Not sure which were for nerves and which were for sleep, I brought them all to my room and lined them up next to Eric's picture. I thought about taking them all and never waking up again. No one would care. Father wanted me dead, so I would finally do something that pleased him. Mom would be embarrassed if I killed myself, but she'd get over it, like she got over the divorce.

I looked at Eric's picture. He seemed to be pleading with me not to do it. I played his *Violin Concerto* and lay on the bed. My bony frame shook with silent, wrenching sobs. The sweet, sensual music washed over me as I looked from the pills to Eric's picture and back again. Twenty-two minutes later, I played the record again. Dozing fitfully, I woke up, hearing the needle click and the automatic arm lift off the record. The pillow was wet from crying. The pill bottles waited. Eric smiled. I played the record again, and again, and again. I looked at the picture. I looked at the clock. It was two-thirty.

I was thirteen years, two-and-a-half-hours-old and I hated myself. I hated my parents. Why couldn't I be someone else's daughter? Why couldn't I be Eric's daughter? I made a vow that when I grew up and I could choose the people I lived with, they would all be nice.

I was half-asleep and my eyes were swollen from crying. The pill bottles looked slightly out of focus, and seemed to have magical qualities. I didn't want to die. I just wanted to forget tonight ever happened. More tears rolled down my cheeks and I didn't stop them. My shaky fingers took the Seconal bottle. The label read: *One pill at bedtime, as needed.* I went to the bathroom, filled my water glass, and brought it back. Carefully, I opened the bottle, poured several pills into my hand, and rolled them around like beads. They were nice and smooth. It would be easy to take a bunch, all at once.

One by one, I put them back in the bottle. When only one was left in my hand, I put it in my mouth, took a drink of water, and swallowed. I closed the pill bottle and put it next to the picture. Like a child with my dolls, I arranged the bottles in height order, then smiled at the picture. "Good night, Mr. Ries. Thanks for your music." I switched off the light.

•

"Jenna! Wake up!"

Everything hurt. My mouth felt dry and sandy. My eyelids were too heavy to open.

"Sweetheart, are you sick? What's the matter?" It was Mom's voice.

A glass was at my lips. I opened my mouth and drank thirstily. Some water spilled, but I couldn't move.

Her hand was on my forehead. "You don't have a fever. Jenna, sweetheart. Wake up!" She yelled and slapped my cheeks.

Startled, I opened my eyes. "Hi, Mom." My eyes closed.

"Jenna! Don't go back to sleep. How many pills did you take?"

I forced my eyes open. "Wha—?"

"How many pills did you take?"

"One."

"Which one?"

"Seconal. I almost took more, but I didn't. Just one. I promise." My eyes closed.

"How long ago?"

My eyes opened.

"Darling. When did you take the pill? What time?"

"Two-thirty. I was thirteen years, two-and-a-half-hours-old." My eyes closed.

•

I woke up feeling groggy and sore. My limbs were almost too heavy to move. Bright sunlight poured through cracks in the bedroom curtains and I wondered what time it was. Mom lay asleep beside me. This was very weird. Slowly my mind cleared. I remembered last night, calling Dad, taking the pill. "Mom?"

She woke from her doze, frantically pushed loose hair off my face, kissed and hugged me hard. "Oh, darling. Thank God, you're alright."

"What time is it?" I pushed her away.

She looked at the clock. "Two-fifteen. How do you feel?"

"Okay." I felt awful, but didn't want her scolding me for doing something stupid. "I'm sorry I took the pill. I won't do it again."

"Oh, my angel. I'm sorry I made you so unhappy." She looked horribly guilty and I was glad. I knew she wanted me to say it wasn't her fault, but it was her fault, and I hated her for it.

She tried to hug me again, but I pulled away and slowly sat up. The narcotic made my head ache and my limbs drag, like I was treading water. I struggled up into a sitting position, leaned back against the headboard, reached for a Kleenex and blew my nose.

Mom quickly sat up. "I almost called for an ambulance, but your breathing was regular, so I thought you'd sleep it off. Those pills are strong. I'm thirty pounds heavier than you are and they knock me out cold."

I looked at the pills, still in their neat row. "Daddy didn't call."

"I knew he wouldn't. Oh, darling, I'm so sorry." She really sounded sorry.

"You could have called, just to say 'good night.'"

She hesitated, then blurted out, "I should have. I'm sorry. It was late. I didn't think … You could have called me."

I wanted to hit her, but didn't have the strength. Suddenly, my stomach cramped. I tasted bile and spat out, "I called Daddy instead."

She gasped. "What did he say?"

"He wasn't home. A woman answered. I told her who I was and she said I couldn't be." I started to cry. "He told her he didn't have any kids." I hugged myself and sobbed silently.

"That stinking bastard! Oh, darling …"

She reached for me, but I pushed her away, stumbled into the bathroom and slammed the door.

4.

April 1968

Vivace Appassionato

$\mathcal{B}$y the time I was sixteen and a junior in high school, my life was routine, under control, and headed in a direction that I liked. I was a serious music student, spending every Saturday at Juilliard Preparatory—what they now call their Pre-College division. Eric's casual remark about writing me a song spurred me onto serious vocal training, and Juilliard Prep offered voice and piano, music theory, solfeggio, German, French, and Italian diction, all under one roof, hour after hour, during one very long day. I kept up my ballet class, but dropped my other after-school activities. Regular academic school had become a dreary inconvenience.

After that horrible night of my thirteenth birthday, my mother became another dreary inconvenience. Every few months she tried being a model mother, pretending to be interested in me. Pleased by her attention, I got fired up, explaining my latest project. Before I finished, she inevitably lost interest. I sometimes helped with her charity drives, but since promoting Eric's debut, I never really cared about the causes. Most weekends Mom and I went to concerts or theatre together. Otherwise, we lived separate lives under the same roof.

Every day, I came home and reported to Eric's picture. It was like keeping a diary, but nothing was written down. It was very therapeutic, talking through every intimate detail of my life. It was also very weird. I gave that photo all the love and attention I should have given loving parents, siblings, or friends. Since none of those were around, the picture got it all. A few times I tried breaking my emotional addiction by hiding the picture, and even throwing it in the trash—never hard enough to break the glass. Every time, I realized I had no substitute and the picture returned to its place of honor. I was addicted to the photo, dependant on child support from a father who denied my existence, and governed by a self-absorbed mother.

Some kids smoked pot and loved it, but I wouldn't smoke anything and risk hurting my voice. My one adventure with Seconal swore me off pills forever, and booze was out of the question. I saw too many social drinking grown ups make fools of themselves. Psychotherapy could have been terrific, but Mom saw a shrink once, decided he was a quack, and never went back.

Given the alternatives, being addicted to Eric's picture seemed pretty healthy. My imagination projected a perfect being onto that two-dimensional, black and white photo. I believed that Eric Ries was all-knowing, unconditionally loving, and free from human frailty. Still, some days I heard myself talking to the picture and thought I was going crazy.

One evening, I raced home in a rage and shrieked my woes to Eric's photo. Sarah Smith, the worst dancer in my ballet class, had tormented me again because she had a boyfriend and I didn't. Sarah was only fifteen. She was hideously ugly, had thighs like an elephant, and hair frizzing out of her bun. The boyfriend she was so proud of was a pimply geek, but it still made me furious. Her teasing stung because she hit a sore spot. I was socially retarded.

Except for partners in ballroom dance classes, I had never touched a boy. I had certainly never been kissed, or met a boy I wanted to be kissed by. I was a freak and deserved her teasing. My only recourse was spilling my guts to the photo, damning Sarah Smith to hell.

Mom, a smiling thundercloud, stood in the doorway. "Darling, are you all right?"

Furious at the interruption, I stared at Eric's picture and clammed up. Mom waltzed in uninvited. "Whatever is the matter? You usually move like a silent swan. Tonight you sounded like a Sherman tank."

I clenched my jaw, stifling a scream. "Nothing's the matter. Wow, you look great." At forty-one, my mother was still the most beautiful woman I had ever seen off the silver screen. She posed like a model, showing off her new designer cocktail dress. "This was terribly extravagant, but I'm having dinner with the Newberrys, and you know what a snob Betty is. She's introducing me to the president of the Chopin Foundation and—"

"Yeah. Well … You look great." Tonight, I had no patience for her social climbing. I wasn't finished venting to the picture and wanted her gone.

"Did something happen at school?"

"Yes!" What an imbecilic question. "Something stupid, adolescent, and not worth the time it would take to tell it."

"You won't tell me, but you're telling that picture."

I clenched my fists and stifled my temper. "That picture is an inanimate object. I can waste its time and not bother anyone."

"You're bothering yourself."

I held up a hand in protest, but she wouldn't let it go. Her slim presence seemed to fill the whole room.

"You never seem to talk to anyone real. Teenage girls are supposed to gossip on the phone all night." She looked sincerely concerned, as she sat down and put an arm around me.

Hating it, but knowing she meant well, I gritted my teeth and stayed still.

"You have lovely girlfriends and you haven't entertained for ages. Why don't you invite them over?"

That was the limit. I stood up and pulled away. This was my private space. She was not only intruding, insulting my precious photograph, but deriding my lifestyle. Legs apart, hands on hips, I spat out, "Mom, I was with my friends all day at school. After school, I was in ballet class with my other friends. It's seven-thirty. I'm tired. I'm hungry. I have a history paper due the day after tomorrow, so I will not be wasting time gossiping on the telephone."

"But you're even alone on weekends. When I was your age, I had a date every Saturday night."

I threw up my hands. "I know, I know. You were a social butterfly. You had a dozen boyfriends, but you didn't spend every Saturday taking classes at Juilliard. I come home with even more homework, music to practice, and Sunday is the only day I don't have to talk to anyone."

She shrank back. "Don't be angry, darling, please. I know how hard you work. Your teachers tell me you're very talented."

I wanted to explode. "If I'm doing everything right, what's wrong with venting to a photograph?" The downstairs buzzer sounded like a reprieve from Valhalla. I sighed with relief. "There's your car."

Mom looked totally defeated as I led her into the foyer. "Have a nice evening and stop worrying about me. I'm fine."

"You're more than fine, you're wonderful." She smiled.

Begrudgingly, I smiled back. She took a moment to touch my cheek, then brush back my long, silky hair. It had darkened to an ashy-brown and hung straight, almost to my waist. I was five-foot-seven, ballerina thin, and an inch taller than she was. Her high-heels boosted her to five-foot-eight, and she was pleased she could still look down on me. She smiled sadly and I actually felt sorry for her. She really wanted to be a good mom. She just didn't have the talent. Penny appeared with one of her freshly brushed mink coats.

I escaped back to my room to drown my frustration in Eric's music. He had recorded two more LPs, but my favorite was still the *Violin Concerto*. When the sensual music started, I felt just as warm and nurtured as I had the first time I ever heard it. I settled into my desk chair, and thought back, for the thousandth time, to that evening at the Russian Tea Room when I was eleven. Eric Ries had smiled at me and touched my cheek. I wanted that smile and that touch again, more than anything in the world.

I still thought of Eric as a father figure, but month-by-month my childish fantasies shifted. For years I had lain in bed making up stories about a nurturing father who would rescue me from evil captors. Now, my rescuer was becoming a handsome sweetheart with shaggy dark hair and a finely trimmed beard. Thanks to sex-education classes in school—God forbid Mom would have taught me anything—I finally understood the mechanics of the love act. Drawings of naked men in my biology book made me gag. When a school friend showed me a dirty magazine with real color photographs, I wanted to vomit.

Disgusting as it seemed, I started looking at live men and imagining what they had inside their pants. It was embarrassing, but I couldn't help it. Night after night, week after week, my nocturnal fantasies became more and more daring. Sexual intercourse seemed painful and scary, but my small pink nipples and the tender area between my legs were suddenly alive and demanding. Fantasies of gentle stroking from a handsome and loving male were absolutely delicious.

5.
September 1969
Andante Accelerando

$\mathcal{C}$hoosing a college was a nonstop fight between Mom and me. I loved Juilliard Preparatory and wanted to stay on at the conservatory. Unfortunately, there were no dormitories in New York City and it would have meant living at home, under my mother's thumb, for another four years. That was not an option.

Mom wanted me to stay at Juilliard because she liked having someone at home to boss around. Much more important, the moment I moved out her ex-husband, my ex-father, was going to put her huge apartment, which was legally his apartment, up for sale and move her into a smaller one. Since he agreed to find her a two-bedroom apartment in the Beresford, or an equally lush apartment house and maintain her alimony payments, I didn't feel sorry for her. She would still have plenty of room to entertain, there would still be a maid's room for Penny to sleep in, and I could use the spare bedroom on school holidays. After college I would be living on my own, so the plan seemed good to me.

After weeks of haggling, she agreed that I could go away to school, if my college was close enough to New York that she could drive there and back in one day. I didn't want her that close, but she insisted. There were great music conservatories in Boston and Baltimore, but they were too far away. Philadelphia had The Curtis Institute, but again, no dormitories, so my best alternative was Newell Conservatory, just outside Philadelphia.

The school was only ten years old, but my Juilliard teachers knew some of Newell's faculty, and assured me that the curriculum was great. My theory teacher was absolutely thrilled, and took a half-hour explaining Newell's ground-breaking electronic music studio. Insisting that it was better equipped than anyplace else on the eastern seaboard, he told me about midis and synthesizers, and other sound bending devices I had never heard of. Even though I hated synthesized sounds and didn't care about the studio, I was very flattered he took the time to tell me. That meant he considered me a musician and not just a dumb singer.

Some famous singers are musically illiterate and all singers suffer from that bad reputation. Instrumentalists are reasonably annoyed when they sit down to sight-read a piece with a singer who looks blankly at the music, and waits for someone else to plunk out her part, so she can learn it, note-by-note, by ear. I worked hard to be as good a musician as my violin/piano/oboe playing Juilliard classmates. We were warned about paying too much attention to our solo instruments and too little attention to the scientific arts of counterpoint and harmony. I learned as much theory as the rest of my class and my teacher noticed. It felt really good.

Finally, after nearly eighteen years of maternal torment, my day of freedom arrived. Like Rapunzel escaping her tower, I left home to start my new life as a grown-up college girl. I felt relieved, excited, and secretly terrified.

Mom and I sat in the back of a black limousine, driving down the highway, passing signs to Newell Conservatory Of Music. The trip out of New York and into the country had been an excruciating three hours. I tried to read, pretended to sleep, but nothing turned off Mom's constant, paranoid chatter. I was going to a small college in the country with supervised dormitories, working telephones and indoor plumbing, but she acted as if I were off to Siberia. When the limo slowed to a near stop, then turned into a wooded drive leading onto the campus, I sighed with exhausted relief.

Staring out the window, I watched outside as the sleek black limousine drove past hand-painted signs to dormitories named Beethoven, Liszt, Brahms, Schubert, Bach, and finally my dormitory: Mozart. We pulled up in front of a modern two-story building with a silhouette of the wigged composer on the wall.

Half a dozen normal-looking family cars were parked with their trunks open. Girls my age, their parents and younger siblings, casually dressed in jeans and sweaters, unloaded musical instruments, suitcases, bags, and boxes. I was embarrassed to be in a limo, dressed in an expensive, tailored pantsuit. Stiff and suffocated from the long drive, impatient to get my suitcase, duffle-bag, music, records, and stereo into my room, I sprang out and raced back to the trunk. Totally mortified, I watched the uniformed chauffeur help Mom out. Looking like the First Lady, she stepped out in a pale green silk suit, black patent leather high heels, and gold jewelry. Desperate to fit in, I smiled at the other girls and their families, thought of introducing myself, then decided to wait. Maybe the girls would forget I was the rich kid with the fussy mother and the limousine.

Mom and the chauffeur helped carry my things into the brightly painted cinder block lobby. A friendly, middle-aged woman checked me in, directed me up the stairs and down a long hall. I dragged my suitcase, looking through open doors on both sides of the wide corridor. Other girls and their families moved boxes and bags into identical two-room suites.

I followed numbers on the identical dark-orange doors, found my room, pulled my suitcase past two narrow closets, and lifted it onto one of two adjoining, built-in, blond wood desks. Above the desks, sturdy bookshelves were bolted into the beige cinder block walls. Behind me were bunk beds, made from the same blond wood. I was thrilled to see that the far wall was a large picture window, overlooking bright autumn woods and a lake.

There was barely space to turn around and I started to panic. I had shared quarters at summer camp, but this was going to be close confinement for nine months. A roommate had been assigned to me and I hoped she was nice. Immediately inside the room, across from the closets, a door opened onto a long bathroom connecting my twin bedroom to another. I inspected the shower stall, two sinks with medicine cabinets, four towel racks, and the toilet stall. It was very tight. I would be sharing the most intimate details of my life with three strangers, and prayed the two girls in the other room would also be nice.

The school brochure showed pictures of coed dorms on the other side of the campus, but Mom refused to hear about those. She needn't have worried. The very idea of sex scared me silly and my virginity was locked up tight. I finally had a sort of boyfriend: a shy clarinet player named Tommy. Some Saturday afternoons, we secretly huddled in a dark Juilliard practice room, kissed with our mouths closed, petted above-the-waist through layers of clothes, and said nothing. Tommy was more interested in boys than girls, so our relationship never flowered.

It took two trips to get all my stuff upstairs into my room. After the chauffeur dropped my dufflebag onto the lower bunk, Mom told him to take the car to the main parking lot. She would have lunch with me, then drive back to New York. He nodded politely, wished me good luck and left. I was relieved that he and the limousine would be out of sight. Now I just needed to get rid of Mom.

Frantically, I opened my suitcase, pulled out my precious framed photo of Eric Ries and sighed with relief. Just looking at his kind face helped me relax. Whatever was going to happen to me at college, his picture would be constant and comforting.

Mom pursed her lips. "I was sure you'd bring that with you."

Refusing to take the bait and start a fight, I clenched my jaw and set the picture on a shelf.

Mom crossed her arms. "Most children sleep with stuffed animals."

"I never slept with it."

"Not literally, but it's certainly your transitional object—your blankie. I wish you'd talk to me sometimes."

I wanted to scream. Instead, I hung some clothes in the first closet. "Mom, I've tried talking to you … for years. You never—"

"You started talking to that picture when you were ten years old. It was sort of cute. Now, it's an unhealthy obsession. You're almost eighteen, for heaven's sake." As always, she asked me to talk to her. I tried. And she cut me off. She always cut me off. There was no point trying.

My fingers tightened around a wooden coat hanger. If she didn't leave soon, there would be bloodshed. My gleeful imagination saw the front of her pale-green silk suit dripping crimson from a hanger stabbed through her throat. I came to my senses, remembered that I planned to spend the next four years in college and not on death row, and unpacked at super-speed. I would have to sort the clothes later, but at least the suitcase would be empty and Mom would be gone.

She watched my frenzied activity, then went to work herself, opening my box of records, stacking them on a high shelf. "Bach, Puccini, Ravel, Purcell, Vaughan Williams, Ries, Ries, Ries … The only way I ever know how you're feeling is listening to the records you play. Whenever I hear Eric Ries, I know you're working out a problem."

"Oh, really? And how do you know that? I didn't know you were clairvoyant."

She glared. "I'm your mother. I may not be a gooey, kissy mother, but I know you well enough to know your moods. You can't know how many times I wished there was a tape recorder in that picture frame. At least I could play it back and hear what you were telling him."

Muttering, "It's nothing good about you," I unzipped my duffle bag and heard a dragging sound in the hall. A gorgeous girl with short dark hair, wearing a mini-skirt and shining boots, pulled a heavy suitcase past my door into the adjoining room.

A zaftig, heavily made-up, middle-aged woman followed, carrying two small bags. Jet-black hair was teased high on her head, and she spoke in loud, operatic tones. "Oh, yes! Blame me for everything. I only sacrificed my entire career for you."

Ouch! What was that about? Obviously, I wasn't the only girl with a problem mother. I tried not to be obvious as I glanced through the bathroom doors. I couldn't see the other girl, but I heard her voice.

"What career? You mean the three years you were in New York working as a singing waitress? I still remember the day you came home and Daddy left. I cried for him and you slapped me." Her suitcase crashed onto the wooden desk. "Look Mom, Dad pulled a lot of strings to get you that teaching job. If you hate it, quit. You don't need the money. He pays you enough alimony."

Double ouch! This was awful. Mom and I exchanged glances and surreptitiously watched through the bathroom doors.

A tall, plain girl with long wavy blond hair, wearing loose bell bottom jeans and a fringed jacket, pulled her suitcase into the adjoining room. She spoke calmly. "Hi, Mrs. Ries. Hi, Sue."

The older woman sighed dramatically. "Amy, darling! Thank God you are here. Now I can leave. I know you will take care of Susannah. You always take care of her." She glanced through the bathroom doors. Her eyes moved up and down Mom, and her lips spread into a frozen smile. She looked scary. "Ah! Come in! Let us meet each other."

Mom manufactured her socially perfect smile, and walked

through the bathroom into the other room. "Hello, I'm Allison Adams." She shook hands with the other mother. I slid past her, smiling shyly at the other girls. Mom put her arm around me. "My daughter Jenna's a voice major. She just won an award at Juilliard Preparatory."

"Mom, please!" My cheeks burned. I pulled away and stared at the floor.

"And what voice are you?" The other woman posed grandly.

I swallowed. "Um … Soprano."

The woman shrugged. "I ask because I am Carlotta Ries, mezzo-soprano. Perhaps you have heard of me?" She fluttered a hand.

My memory flashed back through all the singers I had ever heard of. There was no Carlotta Ries. Feeling really embarrassed, I shook my head.

Carlotta's smile disappeared. "Well, you are very young." Not to be outdone, she gestured to her beautiful daughter. "My Susannah's a genius at the piano. We have shelves of her awards—too many to count. And this is her friend, Amy Daniels. She plays flute like an angel."

I stared at the gorgeous dark-haired girl. Her name was Susannah? Her mother was Carlotta Ries? Those dark eyes … Just like in his picture … Hesitating, I took a deep breath. "Susannah, are you related to Eric Ries?"

The girl pulled herself up to a surprisingly forceful five-foot-three. Her figure was slight, but curvy. Beautifully cut, shining hair fell away from her face. Huge dark eyes, framed by heavy lashes, bore into me. "The name is Susie or Sue. I hate Susannah. My father is Eric Ries, and that was the last time we'll talk about him. Understood?"

There was a stunned silence. I felt like she socked me in the stomach, and whispered, "Sure." The room was eerily quiet. Startled by a sound behind me, I turned and saw a compact girl in tight jeans and a denim jacket in my room. "Oh, hi!" Grateful for an excuse to leave, I hurried back through the bathroom.

"Hi." The girl smiled, found an empty piece of floor and dropped a small bag.

I heard Mom say, "Please, excuse us. We'll just go and meet Jenna's roommate. It was nice to meet you all." Happy to leave, she quickly followed me and nearly tripped over a box in the doorway.

I shook hands with my new roommate. "I'm Jenna, a voice major. This is my Mom."

"I'm Kathy, percussion." She had tightly cropped hair, wore no make-up, long earrings, and had an easy, tomboy way about her. I liked her at once.

"Percussion?" Mom smiled uncomfortably. "I don't think of girls playing drums."

"Well, ma'am, there are a lot of us." Kathy looked slightly embarrassed. "I'm just dropping some stuff here. My boyfriend's in another dorm. I'll be sleeping there most of the time. Well ... Nice to meet you." She nodded and left.

Mom looked scandalized but I didn't care. All I could think about were Eric Ries's ex-wife and daughter in the next room. Since Susie refused to even talk about her father, she might freak, seeing his autographed picture on my shelf. I said a silent, "Sorry, Eric," then hid the precious photo in a drawer. Mom watched the photo disappear and smiled triumphantly. I really wanted to slap her. It took all my willpower to shut my mouth and finished unpacking.

•

Late that afternoon, Susie, Amy, and I joined a hundred other freshmen walking across the tree lined campus toward Liszt Hall. Bright green lawns with manicured flowerbeds framed the   buildings. Pristine blacktop walkways gracefully curved, intercepting one another. The flowers were bright and beautiful, but my nose twitched at the pungent scent of organic fertilizer.

A few steps farther and we were assaulted by sickly sweet pot smoke. Two guys shared a joint, right out in the open. I couldn't believe it. Kids in New York smoked pot, but always behind closed doors. One boy offered the joint to pretty Susie. She hesitated, then smiled, shook her head, and kept walking.

Susie and Amy seemed like an odd pair. Loping casually beside me, Amy pushed unruly, long blond hair behind her ears and glanced curiously at the other students. She was a couple of inches taller than me, about five-foot-nine, and broader across the shoulders. Under her oversized T-shirt, sloppy cardigan, and baggy bell-bottom jeans, she seemed to be a thin stick with no shape at all. Despite the cool weather, she wore flat sandals with no socks. She also wore no makeup, so her blond lashes and brows were nearly invisible around her pale blue-gray eyes. Her nose was slightly turned up, her chin was pointy and, when her wide flute-player's lips spread into a smile, she transformed from plain to almost pretty.

By contrast, Susie could have been a cover girl for *Seventeen*. Everything about her was compact, bright, stylish, and stunning. Glossy dark, layered hair fell seductively over her eyes. Symmetrically plucked eyebrows framed huge dark eyes with thick lashes. Her lips were carefully glossed, and her short piano-player's nails were perfectly filed and painted. Strutting coyly in a different pair of shiny new, high-heeled boots, she used the contours of her navy and red designer mini-suit to show off her tiny waist, round little butt and generous cleavage. I used a light blush and mascara, but Susie's bright coloring made me feel drab.

She tossed her head, shook a gorgeous mass of shining hair, and leaned into me. "Sorry about this morning. My mom makes me crazy." She rolled her eyes. "About my dad ... Well, it's like this ..." She took a deep breath. "I practice really hard—four to six hours a day, and I'm damn good because of it. Every now and again I play, and some asshole says my talent's genetic, as if I had nothing to do with it." Her jaw tensed. "Besides that, my dad's a world-class bastard, so we don't talk about him."

I stumbled, caught myself, and nodded as if I understood and agreed. My heart pounded. I didn't understand and I would never agree. For years I had imagined Eric Ries to be the best father in the world—caring, concerned, and everything my own father wasn't. He composed *A Rainbow For My Daughter,* just for Susie. He could not be a bastard.

We walked through the wide wooden doors of Liszt Hall and into a large, square auditorium. At one end, a four-foot-high stage held a grand piano, folding chairs, and half a dozen music stands. It was like the recital hall at Juilliard, but bigger. A short flight of well-worn stairs led up onto stage-right. On stage-left, a sturdy ramp was permanently in place to transport heavy music equipment.

Rows of wooden desk-chairs, with flat surfaces for writing, faced the stage. Metal folding chairs hung in racks against one wall, so I guessed this was a combination lecture hall and concert hall. The light ivory walls and ceiling looked freshly painted and large windows lined both side walls. My hard-soled boots clumped loudly on the unvarnished wood floor, so I knew the acoustics were excellent.

Susie pointed to a narrow, descending staircase near the stage, with a sign: Electronic Music Studio. "Yo!" She grinned, "I can't wait to check that out. That's why I'm here in the boonies. Amy and I almost went to Curtis, then I read about Newell's Electronic Studio. Oo, they're cute! And, they look straight." She made a beeline to another part of the room.

Her quick change of focus threw me until I saw that she was rushing toward three college boys walking in from another entrance. They all had long hair, wore faded jeans, boots, leather jackets, and looked startled. I couldn't tell what she was saying, but the boys glanced at each other, laughed shyly, and blushed. They were obviously flattered that this very pretty, very sexy girl was paying attention to them. She hurried back to us and they followed like dogs in heat. She introduced them: Dave, Richie and Paul.

I was afraid to talk to boys and Susie charmed three at once. She swished her tight little behind at those boys, and I knew I was out of my league. After eight years of ballet, my body was a perfectly trained instrument, without an ounce of fat. I worked hard to get it that way, but for what? I didn't want to dance in a ballet company and I couldn't imagine ever being able to move the way she moved, right now. She even had great tits.

The bumps on my chest looked like they belonged to a twelve-year-old. It was so embarrassing I didn't think I could ever let a man see me naked. Years later, I learned that little-girl breasts can be a big turn-on, but at that moment I glanced around the room, stared at other girls' chests and gasped each time I saw one bouncing. I could actually see nipple shapes under sweaters. Everyone could see them. No one looked embarrassed, or even seemed to notice. This was amazing! Back home, no one dared to go out without a bra, or at least a Band-Aid to flatten the nipple. Since I didn't need a bra, I never owned one that fit comfortably. The idea was scary, but I was determined to try going braless.

The hall filled up and, after twelve years in a girls' school, I was delighted to see almost as many guys as girls. Some guys even had beards. Most students looked my age but a few of the guys looked older. I knew about the GI Bill and guessed that these guys had been in the military, maybe even in Vietnam. They paid no tuition, but started college several years late.

An elderly professor in a worn tweed suit loped up the stairs onto the stage, so we all rushed for seats. Amy and Susie managed to sit together. I sat a row behind them. The professor scratched a bushy gray sideburn, smiled, and adjusted his thick glasses. "Good afternoon, freshmen, and welcome to your first trauma at Newell Conservatory." A few students laughed.

I tensed in my chair. This would be my second trauma. My first had been meeting Susie Ries. She didn't seem quite as threatening as she had at first, but I was still wary.

Most of the students looked scared, so the professor chuckled impishly. "Just kidding, just kidding! I'm Professor Ridout, and this is a placement exam for your music theory and ear training classes, nothing more. No one can fail. Anyone making a hundred percent will be offered a teaching position."

Most of the students laughed. A voice from the back called out, "How much does a teaching position pay?"

There was more laughter as the professor chuckled, shaking his head. "Precious little, I'm afraid. Any more questions?" Looking over the rim of his glasses, he raised a very bushy eyebrow. No one raised a hand.

I took a pencil from my bag and wondered if the test was going to be hard.

The professor gestured to a team of teaching assistants who passed out the exam papers. "You have a half-hour for the first part. Just follow the written instructions. The second part is dictation: rhythmic, melodic, intervals—two and four part harmony. As I said, we do not expect you to do it all. If you don't understand anything, just raise a hand and someone will assist you. All right, you may begin." He smiled and sat down on the piano bench.

The first page of the test was writing scales and two note intervals. I knew how to do that. Great! I finished quickly. Page two was writing or identifying major, minor, augmented, and diminished triads. Again, I felt really cocky. The third page was complex chords and modal scales that I had never learned. The fourth page asked for harmonies and counterpart figures I had never even heard of. I guessed at some, but left most of them blank. My confidence shrank.

The first dictation exercise was rhythm with no pitches. The professor beat a series of rhythms on a small drum. The first time through, I listened for a time signature and approximate number of measures. The second time he beat the rhythms, I listened for the exact number of measures: multiples of four-times-four, and marked a vertical line at the end of each bar. The third time I listened for the length of each note and wrote in as many as I could. The fourth time I completed the exercise. The fifth and sixth times, I checked my work and smiled. It was perfect.

Next was melodic dictation. Child's play! I was home free.

The third exercise was two voices at once. I wrote the top voice, but had trouble hearing the lower one and had to guess at some of the notes. Shit!

The last exercise was harmonic dictation in four parts, like a hymn tune, and harder than anything I learned at Juilliard Preparatory. This was awful. I wrote the soprano voice and a few bass notes, but left the rest blank. I wondered how Susie and Amy had done, and leaned forward, looking over their shoulders. They calmly checked their exercises. They had written every note. Double-shit!

The professor called, "Time out, my friends. Please leave your papers in the bins at the back."

I thought of hiding mine, then dutifully tossed it into a bin with all the others, and followed the traffic outside. Amy and Susie looked bright and cheery. Of course they felt great; they aced the test. I bombed and felt awful.

We joined the slow parade of students milling across the grass, or along the paved path toward the cafeteria. I felt lousy.

We lined up for plastic dinner trays and were suddenly surrounded by Susie's three galumphing boys, Dave, Richie and Paul. After a polite "hi," they zeroed in on Susie, pushing each other, trying to get close to her.

Amy and I let Susie and the boys go ahead of us, down the cafeteria line. Still upset about the test, I barely noticed the awful looking food slopped onto my tray. Susie led the way through rows of rectangular tables with three chairs on each side. Some tables were already full, but she found an empty one and sat in a middle chair. The boys elbowed each other, trying to sit next to her. Richie and Dave won out, sandwiched Susie between, and nearly spilled their trays of institutional ravioli, white bread rolls, soggy green beans, yellow Jell-O salad, and paper cups of milk, or fizzy soft drinks. Paul looked lost, then scurried around the table and sat in the center chair across from her. It was so disgusting, I almost took my tray elsewhere. The other tables filled up with strangers, so I decided to stay with people I knew. Amy sat in one empty chair and I took the other.

Everyone else ate hungrily and talked about the test. I silently toyed with my perfectly symmetrical, dark-orange ravioli squares. When two of the boys admitted that they had "screwed-up," I felt better and ate some watery string beans. Susie and Amy pretended the test wasn't important. I knew it was very important, that they had done well, and were being nice so the rest of us wouldn't feel stupid. Test scores would be posted tomorrow and I would be crying. Susie talked a mile a minute, only stopping to let the boys laugh and blush at her off-color jokes. Amy looked very content, eating and enjoying Susie's clowning. I watched, fascinated, as Amy's long yellow hair swung dangerously close to, but never actually in, her yellow Jell-O.

It was dusk when we finished dinner. Susie looked at her watch. "It's only seven. I've got two hours till I start practicing."

My mouth fell open. "You don't start practicing until 9:00 at night?"

She shrugged. "Sometimes I practice all night. Amy and I don't schedule early classes, and you'll never see us at breakfast. So ..." She turned to the boys. "Who wants to take a walk?" Her closed-mouth smile, raised eyebrow, and sexy hand-on-hips pose were obvious invitations for more than just a walk. I couldn't believe it. She'd just met these guys.

Dave broke into a grin, stepped forward, then stopped and checked his watch. "Shit! I got to call home. Sorry, Susie. See y' guys later." He sent Susie a regretful shrug, nodded to the rest of us and hurried off.

"I need to practice." Amy petted Susie's short silky hair, gave her a squeeze, and started walking away. I followed Amy until she stopped, whispering, "Jenna, there are two boys. Don't you want one?"

I was stunned. Not even sure what she meant, I stared at Susie, then Amy, then back at Susie, now shamelessly flirting with both boys. Suddenly, Susie raced toward the double glass doors, and sailed outside. Both boys ran after her, but Richie ran fastest and caught her. Paul stopped at the door, watched them go, then turned back and looked at me.

Amy gave me a wink and a gentle push. "Have fun." Smiling, she turned and walked away. I wanted to follow her, but thought it would be rude.

Paul shuffled back, looking very uncomfortable. "Your name is Jenny?"

Feeling like an idiot, but determined to look grown-up, I hunched my shoulders and forced a smile. "Sometimes people call me Jenny, it's really Jennifer, but most people call me Jenna."

Paul took a minute to digest all that. "Okay ... Jenna."

I nodded too emphatically. "And you're ... Richie?"

"No, Paul." The poor boy looked embarrassed. He forced a smile, shifted his weight from foot to foot, and bit his lip. Just my height, he seemed to be a gangly mass of arms and legs. A mop of uncombed brown hair hung almost to his shoulders, and a small assortment of pimples dotted his face and neck. His shy smile reminded me of a sweetly pathetic character from the Beverly Hillbillies. "So, um ... Jenna ... Y' want t' take a walk or something?"

I shrugged and forced a smile. "Um ... Sure." If nothing else, he was an actual living, breathing, male person who wanted to be with me. That was enough of a novelty that I couldn't refuse. He led me outside, along a woodsy path, then down a shallow incline toward the lake. The humid atmosphere was thick with the sweet scent of pine and wet leaves. My hungry lungs inhaled great gulps of pristine air. It was like a drug and I felt light headed.

Paul plowed ahead and I followed his heavy footprints. The polish on my dress boots dulled in the fine sandy soil. They would easily clean up, but I felt annoyed, and made a mental note to wear my rubber-soled desert boots the next day. The path got steeper and wetter, the shadows faded, and it would soon be totally dark. My relief at finally reaching the water's edge evaporated when my boots slipped on the moist grass, sending me crashing down onto my bottom, into a thick clump of dry marsh grass. I bounced up before Paul noticed. Afraid to move and slip again, I stood still, staring at the water.

The air was cool and fresh, but our conversation was dreary. We spent an agonizing five minutes exchanging views on the campus and the weather. Paul looked up at the evening sky, becoming bright with stars. "You know, this reminds me of *The Planets*. Do y' know it? Gustav Holst?"

"Sure. *Neptune's* my favorite."

"Oh, yeah? Mine's *Jupiter*. My high school marching band made state finals with that. I'm from Indiana. I play trombone. It was so great!" He paused, savoring the memory. "We should have made nationals, but there was a judge who knew our conductor from I. U. They hated each other, so we didn't have a chance. Did your band play it?"

"My band?" Dear God! A marching band arrangement of that glorious orchestral work? The very idea of majestic strings being replaced by squawky student wind and brass players marching around in gold-braided uniforms was absolutely gross. Still, I didn't want to sound rude. "Um, no. My school didn't have a band. I'm a singer. I play piano, but I've never played a band instrument."

"Don't know what you've missed." Paul beamed like a proud kid. "So, how come you know the piece?"

My eyes bulged. He couldn't be serious. I suggested, "I've heard it played? Lots of orchestras play it. I must have heard it half a dozen times, and I have the Stokowski recording."

Paul's eyes widened. "You've heard orchestras play it? How? Where? I've only heard four live orchestra concerts my whole life."

"Oh, well, I live in New York. My mom's a member of the New York Philharmonic Society, so we go to everything. Lots of times she gets free tickets to ..."

"You're from New York?" Even in the pale light, I saw the color drain from his pimply face.

"Yeah."

"Did you go to one of those music high schools?"

"No, I went to regular school. On Saturdays I took classes at Juilliard."

"You went to Juilliard?" He seemed to shrivel before my eyes.

"Well, yeah. They have kids' classes. It's nothing special."

"I'll bet it is special! I'll bet you had great teachers."

"Well, yeah, I guess ... But we're both here, so you must have had great teachers, too."

"I'm here for Music Ed. I bet you're a performance major."

I shrugged and nodded. Dying to escape, I faked a yawn. "Wow, guess it's getting late. I'm in Mozart. What dorm are you in?"

"Uh, Brahms. Come on, I'll walk you back." He held out his sweaty hand.

I needed help maneuvering up the slippery bank, and clutched his clammy fingers. Holding tight, digging my heels into the sandy incline, I climbed up to the paved walkway. The moment I felt solid ground, I retrieved my hand. A torturous three-minute walk took us to Mozart dormitory and I think we both felt relieved saying, "Good night," and "See ya."

On my way upstairs, I walked through the lobby, past a wall covered with mailboxes. Every girl in the dorm had her name taped above one of these small, open cubbyholes. Since the names were in alphabetical order, I was grateful my name was Adams. I wasn't expecting any mail this soon, so I was surprised to see a paper inside. It was a printed form with my name and audition times.

Jennifer Adams, Freshman Voice Auditions:
Tuesday, September 8
Voice teacher audition 10:30 AM, Liszt Hall
Vocal ensemble audition 12:15 PM, Strauss Building, Room 202

There were five voice teachers, and my Juilliard teacher gave me the names of the two best. Unlike regular faculty members who teach full-time and seldom perform, these two were Artists In Residence: professional singers, often away from campus, traveling all over the world, singing concerts and operas. They took very few students and I longed to be one of those few. There was also an elite twenty-four voice concert choir that toured all over the country.

With more than fifty voice majors, a third of them sopranos, I guessed it was nearly impossible for a freshman soprano to win a place. My biggest worry was the sight-singing audition. After messing up today's theory test, I felt like a musical ignoramus. If I failed that audition, I would have to settle for singing with the large Collegiate Chorus, and the even larger All School Chorale.

Since my first audition was at 10:30, I counted the hours backward, figuring out how early I had to wake up. Lots of singers hated mornings, but I could sing well after only being awake for a couple of hours. If I got up at 7:00, vocalized, ate a light breakfast, with no milk to clog my throat, rested, digested, then vocalized again, I could sing well by 10:30.

I went upstairs, hesitated outside my door, double-checked the room number, and went inside. It was dark and the suite was empty. I switched on the light and saw my pile of voice music. All that talk about practicing gave me a twinge of guilt. It was only seven-thirty, but the day had been stressful and I was exhausted. Back home when I felt like this, I soaked in a warm bubble bath. Since there was no tub, my next best fantasy was curling up in a warm bed. I hung up my blazer and looked back at my music.

Guilt won out over sloth, and I trudged down two flights of stairs to the L-shaped basement. Two long cinder block corridors contained small, soundproof practice rooms on both sides of their narrow halls. Every room had an iron door with a see-through glass panel, and windows that opened. Juilliard practice rooms seldom had windows, so this was great.

The first rooms on both sides were large, and held grand pianos with girls practicing on them. They were wonderful players. Agile fingers flew over the keys as intense faces studied the printed music in front of them. The next rooms were smaller, held spinet pianos and girls practicing on a variety of instruments. I passed a violinist, clarinet player, and a mezzo-soprano practicing one of Cherubino's arias. She had a rich, creamy voice. If all the singers were that good, I had heavy competition. A flute sounded from another room, so I turned and looked through the windowed door. Amy's long yellow hair fell around her shoulders as her body moved with the silver flute in her hands. Her tone was like brilliant crystal as she zoomed up and down scales at super speed. Susie's mother was right. Amy played "like an angel."

The next room was empty, so I went inside and closed the door. All sound stopped. Aware that anyone in the hall could hear me sing, I was almost too nervous to start. I told myself I was stupid, that everyone was practicing and I should, too. I opened the piano keyboard cover, played a C major triad, and sang a series of slow, disciplined exercises. Usually, I could float up to a high C with no problem. Tonight the A# was a struggle. This was bad. I tried again and felt the same strain. I tried a third time and failed again. My eyes filled with tears and my throat automatically closed. Shit! I stretched out my tight muscles by yawning, and stroking my throat. I told myself that it was okay. I'd had a really tough day and I was tired. I'd go to bed, get a good night's sleep, and be fine tomorrow. I just needed sleep. My hands shook as I closed the keyboard cover, and went back upstairs.

I wanted solitude, but opened my bedroom door and saw Susie in her pajamas, leaning over one of the two sinks, brushing her teeth. She rinsed her mouth. "Richie was fun. Green, but fun. I prefer guys who know what they're doing."

I wasn't sure what she meant, but had an idea, and was in no mood to talk about it.

"How was Paul?" Before I could answer, she took a small round plastic disk from the medicine cabinet, and popped a pill into her mouth.

I stared at the pills. "Paul was nice. We took a walk."

"Never seen these?" She smirked, and tossed me the disk.

I caught it awkwardly, shook my head, and studied the birth-control pill container with its tiny sections. It looked fascinating and scary. "Thanks." I felt guilty by association, and handed it back.

Smirking again, enjoying my embarrassment, she put the disk back in the medicine cabinet. "There's a health clinic on campus. I'm sure you can get them there ... when you need them."

My cheeks burned. "Oh, yeah. Amy's practicing... I was, too."

She nodded and walked into her room. I stayed safely in my bedroom, watching her pull on fuzzy slippers and a warm robe.

Her door opened and Amy appeared with her flute. She looked surprised to see Susie. "Back already?" Susie shrugged triumphantly and Amy laughed. "You are such a slut!" She gave Susie a hug and sorted through a pile of music. "I'll go back down with you. I just need ... this!" She proudly held up a piece of music.

Susie squealed, "You got it! Oh, my God! I thought it was out of print." She grabbed a pile of her own music, followed Amy out, and slammed the door behind her.

I leaned against the cold cinder block wall, exhausted and scared. The sudden silence was chilling. My chest tightened. Tears burned my tired eyes. I switched off the bathroom lights and stood in the dark. My eyes adjusted as I gazed out the window at a dazzling, nearly full moon. Carefully opening a drawer, I took Eric's photo from its hiding place and sat on the lower bunk. Moonlight reflected off his kind, familiar face.

I whispered, "Oh, Eric, I don't belong here. Everyone's so much more grown up than I am. I thought I knew a lot about music, but I did terribly on that placement test. I've never had a real boyfriend. I've never smoked a joint. I'd never even seen birth-control pills, and tonight, I couldn't even sing well. Maybe I should just go home." Looking at his friendly eyes, I remembered Susie calling him "a world-class bastard." I'd never believe that. Never!

•

At 10:00 the next morning, I hurried into a practice room, sang my exercises, and was thrilled. I was in outstanding voice. At 10:15, I strutted toward Liszt Hall feeling pumped up and raring to go. Last night's trauma had been for nothing. I just needed sleep. My voice teacher audition was scheduled for 10:30 and I was startled to reach the wide wooden doors and find them locked. I checked my watch, reread my audition schedule for the twentieth time, and tried not to panic. I looked around, saw no one, then started back to my dorm.

Quick, heavy footsteps clomped up from another direction, and a cute, chubby young man huffed up the path, breathing hard. His hair was mussed and his jacket was buttoned wrong. "Sorry I'm late. I overslept. I'm Jeff—graduate voice assistant."

"Oh, hi! I'm Jenna."

We quickly shook hands, and Jeff pulled out a wad of jangly keys. "The faculty will be here any minute. Shit! I am so late." He pulled open one of the doors and rushed into the foyer.

I followed him inside, saw my reflection in a mirror and stopped. My hair was falling into my face, so I brushed it back, and secured it with a heavy barrette. One long piece lay perfectly smooth over the shoulder of my navy-blue blazer. The rest silky-straight down my back. Not sure what to wear for a morning audition, I opted for the blazer over a high-collared, white-linen blouse, a knee-length, navy tweed skirt and high heeled shoes. I looked elegant, but boringly conservative. Yesterday, most of the other freshman had been wearing jeans and baggy sweaters. I guessed they would dress better for their auditions, but I wasn't sure.

Dragging noises drew me into the auditorium where Jeff, now red in the face, pulled two long tables and five folding chairs into the center of the room. He paused to pant, then hurried to a table near the door, and spread out an alphabetized list. I was number one. If my name started with a W, I could have slept late.

A pile of audition forms asked for the singer's name and the titles of five songs. Jeff said I was allowed to pick the first song, and the voice teachers would pick one or two more. I filled out a form as three men and two women, middle-aged and older, arrived and took seats behind the long tables. I hoped that two of them were the Artists In Residence. They all looked very conservative, so I was glad that my clothes were boring.

A young woman with skinny legs and buck teeth bounced up the stairs to the stage, and sat at the piano, ready to accompany the auditions.

The voice teacher at the end of the table called my name. Just as if she flipped a switch, my heart suddenly pounded. I handed her my song list, smiled nervously at all the teachers, and carefully walked onto the stage. I knew that I looked pretty, but I didn't learn until later that most of the other voice majors were plain and overweight. By comparison, I looked gorgeous. I gave the accompanist my Bach aria, counted out the tempo, then moved into the crook of the piano.

Now, my heart banged out of my chest. I had sung in lots of Juilliard recitals and school shows, loved performing, but hated singing auditions and juries. I always got nervous. It was horrible. I had to slow my heart and breathe properly, or I'd sing like a pig. Determined to do well, I stared at the floorboards, and silently counted my breaths: in-2-3-4, out-2-3-4, in-2-3-4, out-2-3-4. As I concentrated on the desperate sadness of the song lyric, my body finally relaxed. I nodded to the accompanist and she played the introduction.

The teachers shuffled papers and chatted quietly. I sang the first phrase, *Seufzer, Traenen, Kummer, Not* (Sighing, Crying, Sorrow, Need), and they all looked up. The aria was slow, high, and technically difficult, but the live acoustics of Liszt Hall made it feel almost effortless. My voice rang out clear and strong. I knew that my intonation was perfect, my phrasing was elegant, and I deeply felt the heartbreaking sadness. Singing like that felt totally erotic. I had never had an orgasm, but that was pretty close. I sang my last phrase, the pianist played her last chords, and there was a moment of silence. I tried not to grin, but knew that I had sung beautifully. I felt really cocky.

The teacher on the end said, "Thank you. That was very nice." She conferred with her colleagues. "Can we hear the Verdi, please?"

The pageboy's aria, *Saper Vorreste* (If You are Asking), from the Masked Ball, is funny and sassy. It's as much an acting piece as it is vocal gymnastics, so I tossed off the high notes, finished with a flourish, and waited, hoping they'd ask for a third selection. I was thrilled when they wanted to hear *Sweet Polly Oliver*, a folk song arrangement by Benjamin Britten. This story of a tomboy who joins her sweetheart's regiment is set to a delightfully bouncy tune, and the clipped English lyrics were really fun to sing. When I finished, the teacher thanked me and said that faculty assignments would be listed on the cafeteria bulletin board that evening. I walked off stage feeling like a star.

Jeff gave me a big thumbs-up. I smiled back a "thank you" as another freshman voice major took my place. He was a good-looking kid, tall and skinny, with short dark hair, so I stayed and listened outside the door. He started singing and I prayed that he was straight. He had the sweetest tenor voice I had ever heard. A few phrases into the song, he hit a high note and cracked. He sang on and cracked on the next high note. It was horrible. I expected them to throw him out, and was appalled when they had him sing another song, and another after that. He cracked on every high note. I couldn't stand it and left. Over the years, I learned that tenors are such rare and wondrous creatures they are nurtured to the extreme. He was straight, but I could never date a guy who cracked. Four years later, at his senior recital, he actually sang some good high notes.

My Concert Choir audition wasn't until 12:30. By 11:30 I was starving, had an hour to kill, and considered eating lunch. I could sing on a full stomach, but not my best, so I made myself stay hungry. This time, Dr. Bradshaw, the conductor, accompanied me himself. I sang my Bach aria again.

People had often complimented the clarity of my voice, saying that I sounded like a boy soprano. Dr. Bradshaw asked me to start the aria a second time, and sing with a perfectly straight tone. I did, and he was thrilled. Next, he had me sight-read a contemporary piece. It wasn't very hard, so I did it well, and left that audition feeling really good. I didn't know if the choir even needed any sopranos, but I knew he liked me.

Feeling great, knowing I aced two out of two, I went to the

cafeteria to devour a huge lunch. It was after 1:00 when I filled my tray, walked into the seating area and looked over the mostly empty tables.

A really handsome guy sat alone, facing the bulletin boards, studying a textbook. I beelined to his table and asked if I could sit down. He smiled, said, "Sure," and kept studying. I sat at the other end of the table, ate in silence, and felt kind of stupid. The more I looked at this guy, the more I liked him. He was tall and thin, with blue eyes and soft blond hair brushed back and hanging to his collar.

An elderly woman came in with a pile of papers, and he watched her pin them to various bulletin boards. Suddenly, a rush of students crowded around one of the boards. It hit me like a brick. These were the results from yesterday's music theory placement exams. My euphoria over singing two good auditions evaporated. The cute guy at my table waited until the woman posted something on the farthest board and went to check it out. I guessed he wasn't a freshman. Paralyzed, I stayed frozen in my chair, watching swarms of students find their names on the freshmen papers, shout with joy, or groan and walk away.

Requirements for graduation included two years of theory and ear training, with a third, optional year, of orchestration and composition. The three years were divided into two semesters each, making a total of six semesters or levels. Level One was the most basic and Level Six the most advanced. I took a deep breath, and gingerly oozed my way over to the bulletin board. My worst fear was that I would be lumped with the dummies in Level One, and my brilliant suite-mates would have passed out of undergraduate classes altogether. I clenched my teeth and braced myself. Level One: nothing. Level Two: There it was—Jennifer Adams, the first name in alphabetical order. Slightly relieved, I read down the rest of the lists. Susie made Level Five, and Amy, Level Six.

The crowd thinned and I was startled to hear Susie's laugh. It was a nasty, mocking kind of laugh I wanted to swat at, like a mosquito.

The laugh got closer and I shuddered. I did not want her reading my name, but it was printed in black-and-white for all the world to see and laugh at. I couldn't believe that she was wearing yet another great outfit. She had more clothes than Saks Fifth Avenue.

Her tight-fitting red mini-dress was complete with military style epaulets and brass buttons, and she looked like a million dollars. She flirted with an older-looking guy holding a trumpet case, then strutted up to me, and rudely pushed the top of her head under my chin. I backed away, looked down at her vibrant beauty, and felt like a long, drab drip of water.

The trumpet guy moved in behind her, tossed his head, and swung shaggy auburn hair away from his eyes. "You're a freshman in Level Five? You must be really smart. I'm pretty dumb. Want to tutor me?"

She smiled seductively and swung her hip against his thigh. "Not if you're dumb. I only teach quick learners. Oh, look! Jennifer Adams - Level Two? Oh, yeah, I forgot. You're a singer." She smirked silently and my knees felt like water. My lunch lurched into my throat and I wanted to fall through the floor. She laughed softly, while rubbing salt into the wound. "I guess singers need empty heads for all that resonance."

That was an old and overused joke, but it stabbed me like a knife. Afraid of bursting into tears, I looked away and blinked hard.

The trumpet player pushed against her. "I'm a really fast learner."

Susie grinned at him. "Oh, yeah? How fast?"

"Fast as you want." Clutching his trumpet case in one hand, he reached his other hand around her waist. Sleek as a cat, she slinked out of his reach, and sped, laughing, toward the door. He followed in hot pursuit.

Determined her nastiness would not get to me, I swallowed hard and took deep breaths.

A few feet away, Amy read her name on the Level Six list. I thought she would feel really proud, but she registered no expression at all. She smiled at me, pushed messy blond hair behind her ears, and read the other lists. "You made Level Two. Good."

"Is it?" I pulled a Kleenex from my pocket and blew my nose.

She shrugged and smiled. "Sure. You'll catch up. Don't worry. Susie and I went to Interlochen. We got all that stuff early."

"But it'll take me two years to catch up." I sounded like a pouty kid. "I'll still be suffering through boring counterpoint exercises, when you two are choosing electives."

Susie's laugh clanged, and we turned to see the trumpet player pull her out of the building. Amy beamed like a proud mother. "Susie is so great. If there's a straight guy anywhere, she'll find him."

I felt jealous and revolted at the same time.

Amy seemed to read my mind. "Do you have a boyfriend?"

"No. I'm a lousy musician and I've never had a boyfriend." Boy, I was good at self-abuse. "I'll bet you have one."

She shook her head and smiled a funny little smile.

Allegro Gioviale

Finally settled into the day-to-day college routine, I was happier than I'd ever been in my life. Dormitory rules were lax, but it was still a safe, sheltered environment. Everyday I made my own decisions about what to wear, what to eat, when to sleep, and I was responsible to no one but me. Most amazing was that all day, every day, I was allowed to study music—just music. I promised to call Mom every Sunday night and that was hell. Whether I told her about friends, classes, or clothes, she always found fault, criticized, and made me feel like a failure. It took me half-a-day to get back my self-confidence. I hated calling her, but it postponed her coming to visit.

I still reported to Eric's picture, but more out of habit than need. When Susie wasn't around, I sneaked the photo from its hiding place, in a drawer between two sweaters. Susie and Amy were always asleep when I left in the morning. We had no classes together, but usually met up for dinner. Susie talked about traveling with her father, about his compositions, his piano and conducting techniques, but never about him personally. I ached to ask questions, but didn't dare.

I was the only freshman soprano to win a place in the Concert Choir. Our first performance was selections from Haydn's Creation, and four soprano solos were awarded by competitive audition. I sang better than most of the others, but didn't get a solo and didn't understand why. Some of the other sopranos were five years older than I was, and jealous snots who treated me like an ignorant kid. Most of the singers were nice.

Most of the guys were gay. The few straight ones already had girlfriends or were real creeps. I went out with a handsome baritone named Nathan. He was twenty-three, home from Vietnam and studying on the GI Bill, so I thought he must be special. When he tried to pull off my clothes practically before saying "hello," I let him buy me dinner, then made a quick getaway. I was tempted to introduce him to Susie, but she didn't need my help.

Three times a day, a well-worn bus shuttled back and forth between Newell Conservatory and The City Of Brotherly Love. Weekends, I joined other students trying for cheap, rush Philadelphia Orchestra seats. The Spring Concert Schedule featured the American premier of *Rosamund Variations* by Eric Ries. Students and faculty eagerly asked Susie if her father was going to be at the premier. Every time, Susie's body tensed and her jaw clenched. "No! He's conducting in Vienna that weekend and can't get away." I kept hoping her answer would change. Every time she said he wasn't coming, my heart broke a little.

One Friday night, I let a pimply freshman bassoon player take me to see the movie Love Story and buy me a milkshake. Sucking up the cold creamy chocolate, I thought about the dialogue line, "Love means never having to say you're sorry." On first hearing, it sounded profound. Later, it seemed idiotic. The film was musically idiotic. Ali McGraw's character was supposed to be a musical genius. They had her playing a harpsichord concerto, sitting with her back to the conductor. Bad as the movie was, the saccharine love story filled me with longing for someone like Ryan O'Neal. I wanted a gorgeous guy of my own.

When we got back on the bus, the pimply bassoon player reached an arm around my shoulder and pushed his sticky lips against my cheek. "Great movie, huh?" He hugged tighter, tried to kiss my lips, and I wanted to vomit. I sat with my arms crossed, and wished I was with anyone but him. The familiar, sickly smell of marijuana smoke drifted toward the front of the bus. By now I was used to pot, hated it, lived with it, and felt like a prude for not indulging in it. A joint got passed up to my row. My date took a hit and offered it to me. I shook my head and stroked my throat. He got that I was protecting my voice, and passed the stinky thing down the row.

•

Every couple of days my roommate Kathy appeared. Typical of girl percussionists, she was gutsy, sweet and funny. I was always glad to see her. She would shower, change into a clean sweatshirt and blue jeans, study, or sack out in the top bunk.

Her major was music education, demanding even tougher music theory and literature requirements than mine. Unlike performance majors who were married to their solo instruments, music education students had to learn every instrument. When I saw her class schedule, I almost fainted. Along with percussion lessons, band, and orchestra rehearsals, Kathy took music theory, lit, keyboard harmony, choral arranging, piano accompanying, beginning violin and beginning flute. Next semester she would switch to beginning cello and clarinet. By graduation, she would be expected to perform on every instrument in the orchestra.

Performance majors like Susie and Amy practiced their solo instruments several hours a day. Singers couldn't practice for more than a couple of hours a day, but we spent time learning Italian, French and German. Kathy practiced on four solo instruments. It seemed preposterous. I would have been ready to slit my wrists, but she took it all in stride.

One evening we studied together at the adjoining desks. I was achingly curious to learn about her tuba playing lover, but too shy to ask. Finally, I couldn't stand it. "Kathy, how come you chose an all-girls dorm, when you knew you'd be spending so much time in Bill's?"

She rolled her eyes and laughed. "My folks chose a girls dorm, not me. My mom didn't even want me at the same college with Bill, let alone in the same dorm. Newell offered me the best scholarship, so they had to let me come."

"But I thought you guys were getting married."

"We are. And that's when my dad thinks we should start having sex."

My eyes bulged. "He doesn't know?"

"Of course he knows." She yawned and leaned back in her chair. "He pretends I'm still a virgin, but he knows better. And he loves Bill. We've been dating since junior high. Last spring, Bill even came home from college to take me to my senior prom. I went to his the year before. He'll graduate a year before me, find a teaching job: public school, probably. The next year I'll join him. We'll get married. I'll find a teaching job, and after a couple of years we'll have a kid. I want three. Maybe four. If we had five, they could be a brass quintet. I don't know." She smiled at the happy vision.

My blood ran cold. Five kids! The very idea was hideous. Guilty for feeling that way, I assured myself that I wanted to get married and have kids. Every normal girl wanted that and I was normal. Wasn't I? Of course, I didn't want a marriage like my mother's, or kids as miserable as I was. I definitely wanted a singing career and the company of a fabulous, brilliant man who worshipped me. I wanted to have sex, too. It was supposed to be great. It also seemed really scary. I watched Kathy, feeling slightly jealous. Her chosen lifestyle was so simple. She had no grand ambitions, nothing to prove and no ego to protect.

Susie was downstairs, pounding the piano. Even as a little kid she had been a piano star, winning every possible competition. She had a reputation to protect, fantastic ambitions, a huge and delicate ego she constantly defended. Sometimes I came back to my room and heard her sobbing. The first time, I rushed through the bathroom expecting some tragedy. Instead, I found her curled on the bottom bunk with her head in Amy's lap. Amy petted her like a lap dog, crooning, "You're right, Susie. You're absolutely right," over and over again. I backed away, pretending I hadn't seen them. Later Amy told me that Susie had gotten a B+ on an orchestration assignment. She thought she deserved an A, and was ready to hang herself. I liked getting good grades, but that was nuts. Susie was in a Level Five class. She was four years younger than some of her classmates, and Professor Ridout was famous for never giving an A during the first semester.

•

Kathy invited me across the campus to visit Bach, Bill's coed dormitory. I didn't know what to expect, thought it would be some sort of whorehouse, and made excuses not to go. Finally, one sunny November afternoon, I agreed and followed her to the den of iniquity.

We approached the square building, older and larger than Mozart, and there were no red lights in the windows. There was nothing to distinguish it from the other dorms, and I was actually disappointed. Mozart always had a woman behind the reception desk, greeting those of us who belonged, and keeping out anyone who didn't. I followed Kathy into Bach, and there wasn't even a desk.

I followed Kathy upstairs, then down a wide hall, trying not to stare as two boys and a girl ambled out of a communal shower room, wearing robes, or less. Forcing myself to smile at the half-naked strangers, I felt embarrassed, then doubly embarrassed that I was such a prude. I thanked my mother for insisting I live in an all girls dorm. We passed opened bedroom doors and I saw walls lined with music festival posters, psychedelic prints, and blowups of celebrities. Some rooms were divided down the middle with makeshift drapes providing an illusion of privacy. The rooms were large, holding two or three single beds. Two of the four floors were supposed to be for boys, and the other two for girls, but the live-in supervisors were graduate students on work-scholarships and barely older than the undergraduate students they were supposed to supervise. After a month, the four floors began to co-mingle. Unofficial coed room lists replaced the official lists kept in the office.

This sex thing was still a mystery to me. At eighteen I was a frigid little virgin, and the exception, not the rule. My generation almost missed the 60s sexual revolution: that amazing time of innocent playfulness. Flower-draped hippies hugged trees and told us to "Make Love, Not War." Masters and Johnson told us that sex was a nice, natural thing we should enjoy. Birth-control pills and legalized abortion made sex nearly guilt-proof. A few months after the Love Story craze, health-care facilities hung posters of an idealized man and woman making love. The caption read, "Love means never having to say you're sorry, until you get VD." But even VD could be cured with a shot in the butt. Twenty years later, AIDS put an end to it all.

For now, sex was safe and our plague was a war in a faraway jungle. Young men were killed and crippled, and most of us didn't know why. Some of our best and brightest ran away to Canada. When the military lottery replaced the draft months later, rich boys hanging out in college, accruing degree after degree, were called up. At Newell Conservatory there was a constant worry: which gifted musician would be forced to put away his two-hundred-year-old violin and pick up a brand new M16 assault rifle?

My head was full of mixed images when Kathy stopped in front of a closed door. She knocked, then casually opened it and walked inside. Twin beds stood against the far walls. A tuba case sat in the middle of the floor, and a chubby young man with long dark hair sat on one of the beds, working out a guitar riff. He looked up and smiled. "Hey, babe. How's it goin'?"

"Good!" Kathy held the door for me. "This is Jenna. Jenna this is Bill."

I had to smile. Everything about Bill was oversized and cuddly. Even his hair was longer than Kathy's. He waved "hello" as Kathy tossed her leather jacket onto the bed, moved his guitar aside, and playfully grabbed the long hair on both sides of his face.

"This gorgeous hunk is my lover." They laughed as she kissed him, snuggling onto his huge lap. They looked so sweet, I wanted to cry. Bill wasn't my idea of a great catch, but I longed for a man to hold me like that—to love me like that. After a minute, Bill groaned, maneuvered Kathy into another position, and tried to straighten his leg. It bent oddly at the knee. Kathy shifted comfortably and kissed him again.

I glanced at his crooked leg, felt embarrassed, and looked away. Kathy told me he broke it as a kid and it never healed properly. They hoped it would make him 4-F. It was awful to be happy about a disability just because it might keep him out of a senseless war and save his life.

I took off my coat and waited for them to unclinch.

Kathy stretched. "Tea, everyone?"

Bill and I shrugged, "Okay."

Kathy took three of four Beatles mugs: Paul, John, and Ringo—from a shelf above Bill's desk and went to get water from the bathroom across the hall. Bill used a rusty immersion coil to heat the water, one mug at a time. Kathy found tea bags and Oreo cookies. We dunked our cookies and made small talk.

The door opened and the gorgeous blond guy I saw in the cafeteria came in, carrying a book bag and a cello case. He saw me and smiled. "Oh, hi! I'm Nick, Bill's roommate." He shook my hand and nodded "hello" to Kathy and Bill.

I smiled back. "I'm Jenna, Kathy's roommate." He seemed really nice, and I prayed he didn't have a girlfriend. Since Kathy spent half her nights in this room, I figured that Nick had to have a girlfriend, and another place to sleep. Bummer.

Nick moved his cello into a corner, hung up his coat and smiled at me. "You're in Concert Choir. I was downstairs in the Electronic

Music Studio and came up during the Creation auditions. You should have had one of the solos."

"Really?" I was pleased and very surprised.

He slipped off his loafers, sat on his bed and tucked his feet under him. "Yeah. You were the best one, but you're a freshman. Dr. Bradshaw always gives solos to seniors, even if they don't deserve it. He figures it may be their last chance."

"Their last chance at what? After graduation, don't they get singing jobs?"

Nick shrugged. "Some do, I guess. Most don't. They may sing in church, or weddings. Very few have careers. Most end up teaching."

Kathy laughed and pointed at Bill. "That's why we're starting out teaching. We'll never be unemployed."

I smiled at her joke, but felt cold. I didn't want to teach. I wanted to perform. I looked back at Nick. "What about you? Are you a performance major?"

"Oh, yeah." He nodded with satisfaction. "And I'm practicing my tail off, but there's lots of competition out there. Lots more cellists than there are orchestra jobs. That's why I'm studying electronic music. It's the way of the future. It could mean a steady job in the music industry."

"My suite-mate says the same thing. Do you know Susie Ries?"

"Susie? Sure. Everyone knows Susie. She's in my orchestration class." He smiled a funny smile that I couldn't read.

Dying to know what he thought about her, I hedged, "She's a great pianist."

"Oh, yeah. She's a great all-around musician. She can also be a little ... Let's just say her personality can be hard to take. How's she to live with?"

I laughed. "Okay. Sometimes ... pretty hard to take." We laughed, then stared at each other for a few uncomfortable moments. I hoped he liked me.

His smile turned shy and he looked away. "Oh, Bill. The library doesn't have the Walton, so I ordered it."

"How much?" Bill scowled.

The guys talked and I got lost in my own thoughts. It never occurred to me that the wonderful singers in Concert Choir might never have careers. I was determined to have a career, no matter how hard I had to work for it.

•

Every Sunday afternoon, a student recital was held in Liszt Hall. Students needed signed permission from their teachers, so the first weeks only upperclassmen performed. The first time freshmen were allowed, Amy, Susie and I were all approved.

I waited nervously, clutched my same Bach aria, and studied the printed program. Susie and Amy were listed first, playing Amy's own transcription of Mandoline, by Fauré. I was second, and six upperclassmen followed. Nick was listed second-to-last, playing part of a Bach unaccompanied suite. Liszt Hall had felt strange the first day when I took the theory placement test. Now it felt like home. Rows of folding chairs quickly filled up with familiar faces. There were only four-hundred students and two-dozen teachers at the conservatory, so I knew everyone by sight, if not by name.

I spotted Nick's golden hair through the crowd. He left his cello case against the wall, and took a seat across the aisle. As he read the program, his head bowed and long wavy hair fell over his adorable eyes. He sat up, his hair fell back, and he saw me watching him. He smiled, and sent me a thumbs-up for good luck. Flattered and grateful, I smiled back, sent him a thumbs-up, and shyly looked away. A minute later, I looked back. He was still watching me. Thrilled and blushing wildly, I crossed my arms and legs, letting my pleated skirt fold gracefully over my thighs. When his eyes ran down my leg and rested on my ankle, my blood pressure surged.

Professor Ridout walked up to the front of the room, welcomed everyone, then asked Susie and Amy to begin. I had heard them rehearse in the dorm basement and they'd been wonderful. In front of an audience, they exploded with energy. Their phrasing was bold, sensuous, and the audience was riveted. I'd never heard a better performance of anything in my entire life. Their last chord was hailed with cheers and applause. Very pleased with themselves, the girls smiled at each other, bowed, and walked downstairs off the stage.

Professor Ridout stood up. "Thank you, Miss Daniels and Miss Ries. A wonderful rendition." The girls moved back toward their chairs. As an afterthought, the professor said, "Miss Ries, you certainly are a chip off the old block." Susie stopped in her tracks and Amy pulled her down, into a chair. Bent over, seething, I could see Susie's chest heave. Amy held her hands, hard.

Unaware of her reaction, the Professor read from the program. "Next we have Jennifer Adams." He smiled and sat down.

Nervous, but excited, I climbed the steps onto the stage. My grad student accompanist waited for my signal. I took a moment to concentrate on the sadness of the lyric, then nodded. He started to play. I started to sing and felt a glorious adrenalin rush. Each time I sang a piece, it got easier, and my muscles were so comfortable with this aria, I don't think I could have sung badly. My voice soared and my spirit with it. It was perfect. There was a moment of silence after the last chord, then enthusiastic applause. I bowed, acknowledged my accompanist, bowed again, and left the stage.

Professor Ridout seemed impressed. He looked back at Susie and Amy. "Well, if you three ladies are typical of this year's freshmen, we have a bumper crop."

I stifled a happy giggle and sat down. Nick sent me another thumbs-up, this time with admiration. I was thrilled.

Susie scurried over and whispered, "That was fabulous. We need to talk," and scrambled back to her seat.

Later in the program, Nick effortlessly carried his cello onto the stage. I knew it was hollow wood, but wondered how much it actually weighed. Facing a chair toward the audience, he sat down, positioned the cello between his knees, and secured the thin metal end-pin into a crack between the floorboards. He held the bow lightly in his right hand, took a deep breath, closed his eyes, and pulled the bow across the strings. Thrilling, deep, resonant tones made me shiver. Nick's phrasing was bold and almost too romantic to be baroque. I loved it. Susie and Amy smiled at each other, seeming to share the same thought.

The next afternoon, Susie checked out the key to one of three harpsichord rooms, then corralled Nick, Amy, and me to read through a dozen baroque ensemble pieces she had borrowed from the music library. She conducted from the keyboard, like a martinet. Amy made great suggestions, and I was pleased when Susie accepted them. Nick offered suggestions, but Susie returned silly, suggestive remarks that made him laugh. I was so delighted to be part of the ensemble, and so terrified of sight-reading wrong notes, I concentrated all my attention on my music.

After two hours, we were tired and excited. A few days before,

Nick had said that Susie was "hard to take." Now he seemed to like her a lot. The way they smiled and joked made me jealous. She set up a strict rehearsal schedule, three times a week, and we were soon performing all over the place. At school there were informal noonday recitals, chapel services, and master classes. Area churches hired us for weddings and funerals, and local Kiwanis and Rotary clubs had us play at lunches. By the beginning of the spring term, we were invited to play on campus in formal early music concerts, and were considered one of the school's best chamber groups.

The more time I spent with Nick, the more I liked him. He smiled at me, and I smiled back, but we seldom spoke. I knew he liked my voice. I loved his playing, but figured that was as far as our relationship could go. We were never alone together. If we had been, I'm not sure I'd have said anything intelligent. I certainly could never make him laugh like Susie. Also, he was a junior and almost twenty-one. I was sure he slept with lots of girls, and liked girls who knew what they were doing. I was clueless.

Spring approached, days got long and warm, and romances bloomed. The campus was so cluttered with clenched bodies, the administration posted fliers forbidding, "The Outward Show Of Affection." Kathy and Bill were happily in love. Susie bragged about every new conquest. Amy spent nights away, but never said where. I had a few more dates with pimply boys and horny ex-GIs. Most Saturday nights I sat alone, wondering who Nick was with, and asking Eric's picture why none of the nice guys liked me.

Appassionate Pesante

A few days before the Philadelphia Orchestra was scheduled to play Eric Ries's *Rosamund Variations*, I walked to my dorm and expected to find an empty suite. Susie sat at her desk with her face buried in her hands. I'd seen enough of her tantrums to know they were self-indulgent and stupid. I had seen her sob and scream, but I had never seen her sit absolutely still. I washed my hands and made enough noise so she was sure to hear me. If she wanted attention, she would yell for it. I dried my hands and waited. She didn't move. I opened and closed my medicine cabinet door. She still didn't move. I waited another minute, then I got scared. "Sue? Are you okay?"

"Yeah, fine." She sat back. Tears streamed down her cheeks.

"What's wrong?" I went in and leaned on the desk.

She grabbed a Kleenex and blew her nose. "I just got a call from my dad's manager. His Vienna concert was postponed and he's on his way to Philly. He'll be here Friday morning."

My heart leapt but I had to stay calm. I pulled out Amy's chair and sat down. "That's not a bad thing, is it? I mean—" I searched for the right words. "You don't really hate him? Do you?"

"No. I love the bastard. Even after …" She stifled a sob, blew her nose again, and shook her head.

Afraid she was going to say that Eric had committed some heinous crime, I held my breath.

She leaned back, swallowed, and closed her eyes. "Let's just say he breaks promises, a lot. He divorced Carlotta when I was six. I don't blame him for that, but he divorced me, too."

"But you spend summers with him. He even wrote you *A Rainbow For My Daughter*."

Susie grimaced. "That was a bribe, the summer I turned eight. The Christmas before, he promised to visit. He didn't. Instead, he called from Paris and promised to visit in June, for my birthday." She shook her head. "Can you remember how long six months were when you were seven? It was a lifetime. He didn't come. He didn't even call. He finally called two days after my birthday. A month later, I got a manuscript copy of *Rainbow*."

My spine stiffened. "Well, my dad's never called since the divorce. Not even once—in eight years."

"You're lucky. If he didn't make any promises, he didn't break any." Nervously thrusting her hands together, she angrily dug at a cuticle.

"But you travel with your father."

"Oh, yes! Carlotta is always glad to ship me overseas, and he takes me to great places. Paris, Vienna, Florence." She smirked. "Each city we land in, he gets busy making music, and all the local broads. Soon as he can, he enrolls me in a really hard music program with sadistic teachers who torture me, sometimes in languages I can't even understand. Even as a little kid, I spent my days buried in practice rooms, so he could have privacy for his affairs. I can't tell you how many of my recitals he missed because some cock-teasing bitch decided, just at that moment, to finally spread her legs …

Christ!"

I tried to match that description with the nice man who had touched my cheek and signed my photo. Buried memories of Monica, the weeping violinist, and the giggling harpist in the instrument locker sprang to mind. I remembered my dismay when he was on his way to telephone Susie, then sped off with a pretty reporter instead. I shrugged nervously. "Well, he's very handsome."

"He's fucking gorgeous! And smooth." She grabbed another Kleenex and blew her nose. "Women fall all over him. In Italy, they chase him like a fucking rock star. Wait till you meet him. You'll fall in love with him, too."

"I have met him." My voice was a nervous whisper. She turned suspiciously and my heart raced. "Just for a couple of minutes when I was eleven. The New York Phil premiered his *Violin Concerto*." Silently debating with myself, I bit the bullet, raced to my room, and came back with the framed photo.

Susie smirked as she took the picture. "That's an old one. Have you had this here the whole time?" I nodded guiltily and she shook her head. "How come you hid it?"

"Well ... That first day ... Do you remember? I asked if you were related to him, and you got really mad."

"Oh, yeah, I remember. Sorry. You never play his records. You've got them all on the shelf."

"I do play them, when you're not here."

She handed back the picture. "So you're already in love with him." She bit her lip, thinking. "I'll tell you one thing. This trip, he's going to hear me play. He'll hear us all play, even if I have to hog-tie him."

•

Friday, at two-in-the-afternoon, the frazzled Philadelphia Orchestra manager ushered Susie, Amy, and me into box seats at the Academy Of Music. The poor guy looked like he had a fever and hadn't slept in a week. "Ladies, please be very quiet. Mr. Ormandy's in a terrible mood. His arm's bothering him, he's being threatened with a copyright suit, and he doesn't like visitors at rehearsals. Mr. Ries's piece is next. I'll tell him you're here." He hurried away.

Afraid to move, we glanced at each other and sat like statues. My eyes roamed the magnificent old concert hall. The classical design of conventional balconies and boxes was very different from the ultramodern New York Philharmonic Hall. I had been told the Academy Of Music's perfect acoustics came from a huge bowl under the floor. Sound resonated from the instruments, into the bowl, then back to the audience and the players.

One by one, orchestra members returned from their break. They looked tense and unhappy, shuffling back to their seats. They picked up their instruments, adjusted brass valves, tightened horsehair bowstrings, sucked reeds, stretched stiff muscles, and muttered to each other. When they were all ready, the concertmaster cued the oboe for an A. Everyone tuned.

A hoarse laugh sounded from off stage, making them snap to attention. Conductor Eugene Ormandy, short, stout and bald, walked on stage, accompanied by strikingly handsome, bad-boy composer Eric Ries. Smiling impishly, Eric whispered to Ormandy, making him laugh. The players relaxed.

I knew Eric was thirty-eight, but looking at his skintight black leather pants, loose green turtleneck, lustrous dark curly hair hanging to his shoulder and blending with his manicured beard and mustache, I would have mistaken him for a grad student.

Susie whispered, "That bastard's smooth as heavy cream. He'll go to hell and charm Lucifer into providing sprinklers."

I almost laughed out loud.

Eric stayed on the floor as Mr. Ormandy climbed the two steps to his conductor's podium. "Ladies and gentlemen, most of you know Maestro Ries."

The string players acknowledged him by tapping their bows on their music stands. Eric smiled and nodded. Ormandy opened the huge hand-printed orchestra score in front of him, raised his baton, and set a tempo. A solo clarinet, accompanied by violas and cellos, played a slow, four bar theme.

I was immediately pulled into the emotionality of a bittersweet goodbye. I felt like I was ten years old again, listening to Eric's *Violin Concerto* for the first time. Lush, bright tones of violins in close harmony snapped me back to the present. Other woodwinds joined, then basses, and finally the brass and timpani. The result was orgasmic and I blinked back tears. Amy listened with an approving academic ear. Susie whispered through gritted teeth. "That's fucking beautiful."

A trumpet *blat* spoiled everything. Ormandy flicked his baton and the music stopped. He scowled at the trumpets. "Again! Same as yesterday. Same bad notes every time. What is wrong with ...?"

Eric raised a hand. "My fault! I'll fix it!" Before Ormandy could say more, Eric slithered gracefully through rows of string players to the trumpets. Totally at ease, in a calm friendly manner, he took his time discussing the difficult passage, asking questions, then marking slight changes on their music. I couldn't hear his words, but his manner was totally self-assured. He had a lot at stake, but seemed sure everything would be perfect. I had never seen anyone with that kind of self-confidence. The trumpet players looked grateful and relieved. Other players watched appreciatively. Eric went back to Ormandy, and marked the changes in his full score. Ormandy nodded. Eric stepped down, looked over the orchestra and smiled disarmingly. "Thanks for your patience, everyone."

Sixty musicians smiled back.

Susie clutched the arms of her chair. "That bastard just seduced the whole fucking Philadelphia Orchestra."

Ormandy tapped his baton. "From the top, if you please."

This time the musicians played with a passion that went beyond good musicianship. The string players leaned into their bowing. The woodwind players bent with the rhythms, and tears streamed down my cheeks. I was lifted out of myself into a place serenely light, nurturing, yet filled with excruciating longing. The piece ended and Ormandy looked pleased. He turned to Eric. "Anything, Maestro?"

Eric smiled back. "Measure 164, in the violas, but that's all."

Ormandy gestured that Eric should speak to the section leader, then checked his watch. "Thanks to Maestro Ries's efficiency, we may finish early this afternoon." Sixty musicians smiled hopefully. "Strauss, if you please." Ormandy massaged his aching upper arm. An assistant went up to the podium, took away Eric's huge score, and replaced it with music of Richard Strauss. Librarians rushed up and down the rows, changing music on the stands.

We three hurried backstage in time to see Eric speaking to the viola section, and smiling at a pretty woman sitting third chair. He glanced into the wings, saw Susie, and left the stage.

Susie flew into his arms. "Oh, Daddy! I missed you so much!"

She clung to him as if she were drowning.

"I missed you too, baby girl." He held her tight, and covered her face with gentle kisses. She kissed him back, then buried her face in his shoulder. He looked over the top of her head, smiled at Amy, then locked eyes with me.

I stared back, then looked away. This was too strange. Susie talked about her father with venom, yet she called him "Daddy" and embraced him like a lover. She was nearly nineteen, but her father called her "baby girl." Jealousy stabbed my heart. No man had ever hugged me like that. Jarring orchestral harmonies of Richard Strauss flooded backstage, coloring the already bizarre scene.

Just as Eric had taken time with the trumpet players, he took time letting Susie settle in his arms. When she finally relaxed, he kissed her brow and let her go. She moved away, keeping her back to Amy and me, pretending she wasn't crying.

Eric smiled at Amy, held out his arms and gave her a fatherly hug. "Good to see you, sweetheart."

She hugged him back. "Gorgeous piece, Eric. Why didn't you write that solo for flute?" She playfully socked his arm.

He laughed. "Actually, the first draft was for flute." He talked to Amy, but looked at me. "When the piano reduction's done, you can transcribe it."

"I will. It'll be beautiful."

Susie turned, saw him watching me, and smiled sardonically. She found his lechery annoying, but wanted him to hear her quartet and wasn't above using me as bait. "Dad, this is Jenna Adams. I wrote you about her. She's a soprano, but she's also a musician. Her voice is gorgeous. You're going to hear her sing with our quartet tomorrow."

"Am I? That's great." He smiled warmly, and offered his hand. "Hi, Jenna. Pleasure to meet you."

I looked him in the eye, smiled shyly, held out my hand, then pulled it back as my brown wool shawl slipped off my shoulder. Twisting to pull it back on, I unwittingly gave him a chance to look me up and down. I wasn't wearing a bra, and my clinging cashmere turtleneck revealed everything I had above the waist. The matching wool skirt hugged my hips and fell gracefully over dress boots. My hair was parted down the middle, framing my face, then draping over my shoulders. Smiling nervously, I rearranged the cloak and took his hand. "Meeting you is the pleasure, Mr. Ries. I love your music. I have all your records."

His expression was open and friendly, his handshake warm and firm, but I was so in awe I had to keep myself from curtsying like I had as a little girl. He held my hand longer than necessary. "I'm very flattered. And the name's Eric."

When he released my hand, I blushed, lowered my eyes, and closed the cloak around me. Susie, hands on hips, looked very sexy in a fringed leather mini-dress and matching jacket. Amy wore a dress-up version of her usual oversized sweater and dungarees. We were a strange trio.

Eric yawned and rubbed his tired eyes. "I'm starving and jet-lagged. Let's get out of here."

Susie led the way. "I made a reservation at Bookbinders."

We were out the door when Susie's introduction finally registered. She told her father that I was a singer, but also a musician. Wow! Did I ever feel proud.

An hour later, we messily feasted on lobster, tossed salad, and baked potatoes. Large paper bibs covered us, necks to knees, as our nutcrackers broke open hard red lobster shells. We sat around a square table, shared stories, laughed a lot, and tried not to squirt each other with lemon juice and melted butter.

It was still early and the old, elegant restaurant was half empty. The tables were covered with bright red cloths, and starched white linen napkins were rolled at each place setting. One entire wall was fronted by a hundred-year-old, carved mahogany bar, with huge mirrors at the back.

Eric sat between Susie and Amy, and across from me. Susie dominated the conversation, but Eric engineered his remarks to include all of us. He started ordering wine, then remembered he was in Philadelphia and not Vienna. Here, we girls were underage. Susie dove into an impromptu monologue about Newell Conservatory, and her comically cruel impressions of our professors had Amy and me in stitches. Eric enjoyed Susie's cutting humor, but seemed concerned at the same time. Amy smiled fatuously, and hung on Susie's every word. Eric glanced back and fourth, and I wished I could read his mind.

I sat across from him, digging every morsel of flesh from my reluctant lobster shell. Determined to get every gorgeous tidbit, I tore off each thin red tentacle, put it between my lips, and sucked out the salty juice. I was on the last one before I glanced up and saw him watching, with a twinkle in his eye. I thought he was laughing at my gluttony and never guessed that sucking can look sexy.

Even as he watched me, his eyelids drooped. He had flown overnight, then gone almost immediately to rehearsal. Suddenly, he jerked to attention. "What, Sue? What's thirty minutes?"

"The drive to campus. We'll wait for you at the stage door, and—"

"Sweetheart, I can't leave the city. I have meetings tomorrow. You'll have to play for me here somewhere." He stifled a yawn.

"You have one meeting, at Curtis, at five o'clock. I'll make sure you're back in plenty of time."

He looked too tired to argue. "Susie, I'm exhausted. I've got to get some sleep. Tomorrow morning, I'll hire a car and drive to—"

"No Dad! I want you to come back with us, tonight!"

"I can't get a car."

"Then come with us on the stinky school bus. You'll have two dozen adoring music students panting at your feet. You'll love it, and I'll be able to keep an eye on you."

Amy stifled a laugh, but I was shocked.

Eric rubbed his burning eyes. "Where do you think I'm going to go? I'll be at my hotel."

Susie glared. "Yeah, shacked up with some broad."

"What broad? I just got here a couple of hours ago. I don't know anyone."

"Bullshit! I know how fast you operate."

I couldn't believe Susie's insolence. Whatever their relationship, she was still the daughter and he was still the father. When Eric shrugged the insult off, I was even more amazed.

"Okay Sue, say I go with you tonight. I'm on Vienna time. I'll wake up at dawn. Shall I get you up for breakfast? I know how much you like mornings."

Susie threw up her hands. "You're jet-lagged your whole life. You'll wake up, eat, and go back to sleep, like you always do. I want you to hear our quartet. We're really good, and I don't trust you to find the campus on your own. You'll get sidetracked and I won't see you for another year. I'll come to the lodge at twelve-forty-five and we can have lunch."

He raised an eyebrow. "Exactly twelve-forty-five?"

Susie glared back at him, and Amy put a calming hand on her arm. "Our first class is eleven to twelve-thirty. Jenna's the only early-bird."

Eric turned to me. "How early?"

"What?" I couldn't believe the question. "Well, I go to breakfast about 7:30."

He nodded wearily and Susie looked delighted. "Great! We'll play for you around two-thirty. I'll hire a car to take you back at four, and you'll be in plenty of time for your meeting."

He shrugged, noticed my shocked expression, and quietly laughed. "I'll bet you don't talk to your father like that."

I felt myself go white.

"I'm sorry. I hope I didn't …"

"No. It's okay. It—it's just that I don't talk to my father. Not since my parents divorced eight years ago." His eyes were full of questions, so I hurried to explain. "I'd like to talk to him. He moved to California. I live in New York. He doesn't call."

"Do you call him?"

The memory of my one phone call, the night of my thirteenth birthday, flooded back fresh and painful. "No … Not for a long time."

"Your father hasn't seen you in eight years?"

I shook my head and felt terribly guilty, like it was my fault. "I sent him a copy of my high school graduation picture. I guess he got it. He never wrote back." I wanted to sink through the floor.

"Does he have other children?" He looked concerned.

"No … At least, I don't think so." Everyone stared at me. I felt like an idiot. "I don't know. He never calls or writes. He sends money every month, but Mom doesn't talk about him. I guess she would have mentioned if he'd remarried. Honestly, I don't know anything about him. It's like he was dead."

Eric looked down at the table, then shook his head like he was angry. I was relieved when he turned to Susie and ran a hand over her shiny hair. "The man's an ass. He's missed watching his beautiful daughter grow up. What a horrible loss."

Pleased and proud, Susie smiled at her father.

I watched jealously. For years, Eric's photograph had taken the place of a father. The real Eric was a father—Susie's father—not mine.

Amy jovially pulled off her paper bib. "And I grew up thinking my parents were boring, because they were always at home. Eric, do you have to fly back tomorrow?"

"Yeah, sorry." He smiled apologetically, stretched and yawned. "This trip is a gift, as it is."

A waiter arrived with finger bowls and offered a dessert tray. Relieved by the mundane activity, we cleaned our fingers, but declined dessert. Eric asked for the bill.

I was dying to tell him how his music had saved my life. "Mr. Ries?"

He smiled. "It's Eric."

I smiled back. "Um, Eric … When I was eleven, you autographed a picture for me. I've …"

Susie ripped off her bib. "Oh, no! Not this story again."

Eric glared at her. "My, but you're rude!" He smiled, encouraging me. "Tell me your story."

I took a deep breath. "Well … Um… Like I said. When I was eleven, the New York Philharmonic premiered your *Violin Concerto*."

Susie charged in. "You autographed a picture for her and she's been in love with you ever since."

I felt mortified. My cheeks burned. Angry tears sting my eyes.

Eric smiled kindly. "I'm more flattered than I can say."

"Bullshit!" Susie rolled her eyes.

"On occasion, jaded child of mine, I actually utter a sincere word." He turned back to me. "I truly am flattered. Please, finish your story."

"Not while I'm around." Susie pushed her chair away from the table and stood up. "Come on, Dad. I'll walk you back to your hotel."

Too tired to fight, he wearily shook his head and followed Susie outside. Amy hurried after them, but I stayed for a minute, thinking hard. He really was flattered. I determined, somehow, to tell him my story.

Dolce Semplice

Late that night, I sat at my desk composing a letter.

Dear Eric,
You can never know how much today has meant to me. I was
ten years old when I first heard your Violin Concerto...

I stopped, remembering the orchestra rehearsal a few hours before. Eric walked on stage. Handsome, confident, friendly ... everything I imagined him to be. The lobster dinner was fun, until Susie got nasty. The concert was perfect. I watched Maestro Ormandy's face, then the players. They loved Eric's music. I loved Eric.

His daughter was asleep in the next room and he was probably asleep in the campus lodge, a quarter-mile up the road. It all seemed surreal. In sixteen hours, I would sing for him. I was nervous about that, but absolutely desperate to tell him how he had saved me from suicide. Susie would never let me talk to him alone, so I had to finish this letter, and somehow sneak it into his bag.

I pulled his photograph from its hiding place, propped it up on the desk, and talked to it the way I had a thousand times before. As soon as my thoughts were organized, I poised my pen over the paper and wrote:

Your music has been my refuge, my haven, a magic place
of escape when real life was just too painful. I've told your
picture all my deepest fears, my wildest fantasies ...

My clock-radio went off at six-forty-five. A cold breeze blew in my window as I leapt from my warm bed. Sleepy but excited, I pulled off my flannel nightgown and dove, shivering, into the shower. The sun was bright and I hoped it would warm up during the afternoon. I had two classes, choir rehearsal, and lunch before joining the quartet to sing for Eric. I sneaked a look at Susie and Amy. They were still asleep.

I pulled on my best boots, tossed a pale-blue knit dress over my head, and wrapped a bulky sweater around me. I double-checked that Eric's letter was safely inside my manuscript book, and joined a parade of students heading toward the cafeteria. Some looked like they had studied or drugged all night and hadn't had time to shower. Most were full of energy, racing across the lawns, past the newly planted flower beds. Some carried musical instruments. We all carried text books and music manuscript books for our various classes.

Three boys yelled and wrestled for a book bag. One boy grabbed the bag and tossed it to a second boy. A third boy lunged for it, got it away from the others, and ran screaming toward the cafeteria. They looked like stupid children. I congratulated myself on acting like an adult, and continued down the path feeling very superior. Suddenly, I did a double-take and totally lost my composure.

Eric stood in the shadow of a large tree. He held a finger to his lips in a silent, "Shh!" He waved me over and moved back into the shadow. Smiling, heart pounding, pretending I hadn't just made a fool of myself, I crossed the lawn. Last night frenzied students had treated him like a rock star. This morning, he was dressed in black and well camouflaged, but I couldn't believe no one had spotted him.

The three boys hooted in a final wrestle before going inside.

Eric laughed. "Those kids are marvelous. Everything's ahead of them. They've no regrets. They've had no major failures." His expression sobered. "And with all the girls on the pill, they won't be nineteen-year-old fathers like I was."

I froze. If he thought all the girls were on the pill, he'd think I was socially retarded. Mom told me men wanted to marry virgins, but she was wrong. College men wanted girls with experience. Obviously, Eric wasn't any different. He took his time looking around the sunny campus. His eyes shone. "This place is fabulous. Just look at all that unobstructed sky— all this green, these trees, the lawn, the lake—the clean air."

Afraid of wasting time on the scenery, I pulled out my letter. "I hope you don't mind, but you said you wanted to hear my story. I didn't think I'd get to tell you, so I wrote it."

He took the envelope, started to open it, then paused and slipped it into his breast pocket. "I'll read this on the plane, but I want to hear you tell it. I'm starving. Why don't we get some breakfast?"

"Do you want to eat at the cafeteria?"

He flinched comically. "No! I had quite enough adoration last night. I'd like to eat in peace. Let's go back to the lodge." He turned to go, then noticed my book bag. "I forgot you have classes."

I hesitated, thinking out loud. "I have theory and Italian diction.

I've never missed, so it won't hurt, this once. I have Concert Choir at eleven. I can't miss that, but—"

Before I finished, he took my arm and led me down a tree-lined path. I went very willingly, but felt like a criminal. I had never skipped a class in my entire life. If Susie saw me with her father, she'd kill me. He held me close and I concentrated on walking in step. The feel of his leather pants against my thigh and the smell his musky cologne were very sexy. He was just tall enough so his soft beard could brush my temple. If I lifted my chin, I could kiss his lips. I smiled up at him. He smiled back. An inch more and we would kiss. Suddenly, my knees buckled. I stumbled, but he held me up. I felt totally mortified, and stared straight ahead the rest of the way.

The Campus Lodge coffee shop was nearly empty. Eric chose a back corner booth, and sat with his back to the door. My knees felt weak and I was grateful to sit down. I slid onto the padded bench across from him, and pulled off my bulky sweater. My hair fell over my face, so I pushed it back, behind my ear and off my shoulder, at the same time pulling the front of my knit dress and showing the shape of my nipples.

He watched, smiled slightly, then opened a menu and glanced down the page. "How's the French toast?"

"It's really good." I smiled nervously. "My favorite."

A uniformed waiter came out of the kitchen and was almost at the table before I saw that it was Nick, looking very cute in a tan smock and cap. Order pad in hand, he smiled at me, then looked startled to see Eric. "Hi, Jenna. Mr. Ries! Wow! This is a real pleasure. I'm Nick McClelland. I play cello with Susie, Jenna, and Amy."

Eric smiled and shook his hand. "Good to meet you, Nick. I'm looking forward to hearing you this afternoon."

Nick beamed. "Thanks. That's really nice of you. I had to work last night, but I'll be at your concert tonight ... Um, what can I get you both?"

Eric looked down at his menu, then at me. "Two number threes?" I nodded.

Nick scribbled on his pad. "Coffee on both?" We nodded. Nick smiled at me and hurried away.

I watched him go and Eric watched me. "Nick's very nice. Is he your boyfriend?"

I forced a laugh. "Don't I wish! I think he's in love with Susie. She has a lot of boyfriends." As soon as the words were out of my mouth, I wished I could take them back. No father wants to hear that his daughter's a slut. I was surprised when Eric calmly nodded.

"She always does. She started sleeping around when she was sixteen." My eyes widened, but he shrugged. "I didn't like it, but she was spending the school holiday with me, and ... Well ... like father, like daughter." He paused, watching me. "You must have a boyfriend."

I laughed nervously, trying to make a joke. "No. Amy and I are both wallflowers."

He didn't smile. "Actually, Amy's not into boys. And you're probably too pretty. A lot of guys are afraid of beautiful women."

This was a lot to take in. I stared at him. For the first time Amy's relationship with Susie made sense, but I couldn't believe what he said about me.

He looked amused. "Don't you know you're beautiful?"

Totally thrown off guard, I stammered, "I—I thought it was because..." I bit my lip, whispering, "We're not all on the pill." Instantly humiliated and sure he thought I was retarded, I was relieved when he smiled, sat back and tried not to laugh.

Nick charged up with plates of food. He seemed to be in a terrible rush, but after the dishes were sorted, he dawdled, like he had something to say. When other customers called, he smiled awkwardly and finally left.

Eric ate hungrily and told me funny stories. He was so charming and so gorgeous, I could hardly stand it. Even his hands were beautiful, with long, slim fingers deftly slicing thin sausages and thick French toast. Occasionally, he started a sentence, then paused in the middle, waiting to finish until I looked at him. Every time I gazed into his smiling dark eyes, my stomach cramped. I was afraid of saying something stupid and making a fool of myself. My French toast tasted sweet and creamy, but I just picked at it.

I also worried about singing for him later that afternoon. Susie had been a harridan, drilling the quartet to perfection. Desperate to sing well for Eric, and dreading Susie's wrath if I screwed up, I suddenly craved nourishment, drove my fork into a sausage and ate everything. We finished and pushed our plates aside.

Eric patted his breast pocket. "Your turn. Tell me your story."

I began tentatively. "Oh … Well, when I was ten, my piano teacher gave me *A Rainbow For My Daughter.* I memorized all the pieces, and painted a watercolor to match each one. I was planning a special present for my father, for his birthday."

Eric sat back, enjoying my story. He laughed at my description of the stuffy Philharmonic Society ladies, and seemed fascinated that a young child could fall totally in love with his *Violin Concerto.* He was amazed that I started talking to his picture. Encouraged by his approval, I continued into difficult memories about my parent's divorcing, Mom's emotional withdrawal, and my ever-increasing dependence on his music. His eyes were glued to mine, and he seemed totally sympathetic.

In the middle of my story, Nick charged up to clear the empty plates. I sat back and stopped talking. Obviously stalling for time, he removed the dirty dishes as slowly as possible. When I stayed quiet and crossed my arms, he reluctantly lifted the full tray of dirty dishes and left. As soon as he was out of earshot, I started again. Nick was suddenly back, with a pot of coffee. I stayed quiet as he gave us refills. Eric asked for the bill. Quick as he could, Nick added up the tab. Eric paid well over the total and told Nick to keep the change. After muttering a nervous, "Gee! Thanks very much, Mr. Ries," he had no choice but to take the money and leave us alone.

Now, desperate to finish, I leaned across the table, plunging through the rest of my story. Eric was riveted when I told him about staying alone the night of my thirteenth birthday, phoning Dad and being told that he didn't have any kids. "I found Mom's sleeping pills, several kinds, stood them next to your picture, and played your *Violin Concerto* over and over. I stared at the pills, then your picture, then back. It was like I was choosing between you. Finally, I took one pill, cried into my pillow, and fell asleep." The emotional memory hurt. I sat back, flushed and tearful. "Talking about it, it sounds pretty crazy."

He shook his head. "It sounds very sane, very sad, and incredibly courageous." He reached out his hand and laid it on the table, palm up. Frightened, but excited, I put my hand into his. He gently closed his fingers and a shiver ran through me. His hand felt wonderfully warm and comforting, just like his music. His voice was soft and clear. "You can't know how your story makes me feel. I've spent twenty years in the selfish pursuit of fame and fortune." Still holding my hand, he sat back, sighing. "Sure, people like listening to my music. They buy records, they applaud, they pay me, but I never know if I'm doing anyone any good. I was a rotten husband, I'm a lousy father, I've—"

I squeezed his hand. "You're a lot better than mine. If he didn't send Mom money every month, I wouldn't know he was still alive." I braved a question. "Why did you marry so young?"

His eyes widened and his eyebrows rose. "I didn't want to. I was an eighteen-year-old piano major, playing for opera school rehearsals. Carlotta was a twenty-two-year-old opera student. Sexy, gorgeous, and suddenly pregnant."

I flinched, so he released my hand.

"One day I was a carefree kid, and the next a father, taking classes during the day, playing in a bar at night, composing and taking care of a baby at the same time. Carlotta was in New York, trying to be an opera star and getting nowhere. I graduated, won a Fulbright. Carlotta came home to Susie, and I left for Paris." As if worn out by the memories, he shook his head. "That's ancient history." He sighed, stifling a yawn. "Oh, sorry. Jet-lag setting in. It's a gorgeous day. I'll walk you back, then I need a nap."

He watched as I slid off the bench and pulled on my bulky sweater. I hung my book bag strap over my shoulder and followed him out. Four music students were in a front booth, finishing their meal and staring at Eric with their mouths open. He nodded cordially, but walked past them without speaking.

I was pleased that the morning chill had gone. Sunshine flooded the path and the air was sweet with spring blossoms. We started back the way we came, until there was a bend in the path. Eric veered sideways, through a clump of trees. I followed him into a small clearing, wondering if this was a shortcut. He looked around, saw no one, and whispered, "Don't worry. They won't have anything to report back to Susie. All I've done is buy you breakfast and kiss you behind a pine tree."

What? I stood like a stone. Very gently, he took my book bag from my shoulder, laid it on the ground, slid his hands inside my bulky sweater, pulled me close, and kissed me. My arms slid tentatively around his neck. He kissed me again. This time I responded, nervous, but happy. He nuzzled my neck and ear. "You are so lovely. Why don't you come back and take a nap with me?"

My heart pounded. I gasped, "I couldn't."

"Of course you could." His lips moved back over mine. "I'm sure there's a back entrance. We wouldn't be seen." His tongue explored my mouth. "We can just cuddle, if that's what you'd like ... If you'd like to explore other things, that would be fun." One hand slid over my breast, gently squeezing my nipple.

Writhing with pleasure, I tried to pull away.

His other hand reached behind, gently squeezing my butt. "I promise to be gentle and slow, and do whatever you'd like." His erection was hard against me. "And stop the moment you ask me to."

I was excited but scared to death. "I couldn't. Susie would—" Torn between desire and guilt, I pushed him away, staggered and lost my balance.

He caught me. "She'll never know."

"She will. This campus is too small. Someone's bound to see."

"I'll risk it."

I pulled free. "I've got Concert Choir! I've never missed rehearsal. Not even once. I'm sorry." I grabbed my book bag.

He looked slightly annoyed, then smiled and shook his head. "There's nothing to be sorry about. Have a good rehearsal. I'll see you later." He started toward the path, then turned back. "I hope Nick realizes what a treasure you are."

Not sure what he meant, I hesitated, then hurried in the opposite direction. Suddenly realizing what I'd done, I stopped and spun back. That was Eric Ries! The flesh-and-blood man whose picture I loved my whole life. He wanted to have sex with me and I turned him down. His boots clipped on the asphalt path beyond the trees. I started after him, and stopped. No! I wasn't that kind of girl. I didn't sleep around. I started back toward my rehearsal then remembered he was leaving that afternoon. I might never see him again. Now, I ran after him, down the path, around the bend, until I could see the entrance to the lodge. He stood in the sunshine, talking to the four music students who'd been in the coffee shop. I stopped dead, heart pounding, breathing hard. I was too late. If I went back now, they'd tell Susie. As it was, all they could say was that Eric and I had breakfast together. That was okay. I checked my watch. It was early. Silently cursing myself, I turned, kicked the ground, and slowly walked to my rehearsal.

At three o'clock that afternoon, Eric Ries, an audience of one, sat in the back of a large classroom. Bright sunshine and a warm breeze flooded through the modern, third story windows, over the pristine white walls and shiny linoleum floor. The space felt bright and safe.

Susie carefully picked her forty-five-minute program so Eric could hear her play in as many styles, with as many combinations of instruments as possible. Amy, Nick, and I sat to the side, waiting our turns. Determined to keep prying eyes away from her celebrity father, Susie taped newspaper over the glass window in the fireproof door, and locked the door from the inside. She started with solo pieces: Mozart, Brahms, and finally a Chopin *Polonaise*. The piece was long, technically demanding, emotionally draining, and she was marvelous. The old, resonant baby grand piano responded with rich, mellow tones. Eric watched his deceptively dainty little daughter draw strength from her whole body, to push her tremendously strong, slender fingers into the keys.

She took a few minutes' break, then accompanied three solos: Nick played part of the Elgar *Cello Concerto*, Amy played the Fauré *Mandoline*, and I sang Ned Rorem's *Ask Me No More*. I knew I would sing well, but hoped my personal best was good enough to please Eric.

For the quartet offering, Händel's *Süsse Stille, Sanfte Quelle* (Sweet Stillness, Gentle Spring), Susie left the piano and conducted from the harpsichord. Eric seemed amused, but not surprised at her easy domination over the rest of us.

He had never heard her play harpsichord and she was eager to prove she had mastered the older style instrument. Resembling a half-sized piano, the tone and touch were completely different. Smaller keys and fewer octaves changed some finger positions. The wires were plucked by hooks, rather than struck by hammers, so the volume never varied. Before she started, Eric looked slightly concerned. A moment into her playing, he relaxed.

Down-stage right and slightly in front of her, Nick sat with his polished cello between his knees, athletically bowing his continuo part. Farthest left, Amy stood behind her music stand, seamlessly weaving her silvery flute counterpoint through the other musical lines. I stood in the crook of the piano, singing my absolute best. Everything I had ever been taught: breathing, resonance, diction, emotionality, and musicality all came together for this most important performance of my life.

We finished and Eric beamed. "That was stunning. Really!" Automatically slipping into teaching mode, he walked toward the harpsichord.

Susie looked up without hostility, but he still stopped to ask permission. "May I?"

"Sure." She smiled and slid over, so he could join her on the hard wooden bench.

He sat down and looked through the music until he found the passage he wanted. "Jenna, do you have a pianissimo high B flat?"

"Yes."

He nodded. "Then, Amy and Jenna, on bar 27, where you have the parallel thirds. On the repeat, I want you both to go up the octave. Everyone see where I am?" We all turned back pages and nodded. Eric looked back another half few bars. "Okay, let's start from measure 24. A little slower, this time. One - two - three, one - two - three."

We played the passage again. I sang my last lyrics, "... *ruhiger Gelassenheit!*" (quiet peacefulness), lightly floating up to the higher octave. It felt wonderful and I knew it sounded great. We finished in perfect ensemble.

Eric was silent for a moment. "Wow." He smiled and the four of us burst into excited laughter. Checking the wall clock, he sadly shook his head. "Damn, this is fun. I wish I could stay." He reached his arms around Susie, hugging her tight. "Beautiful, really. I'm proud of you."

Relieved and very happy, she hugged him back.

He turned and shook Nick's hand. "Wonderful playing."

Nick's smile was radiant. "Thank you, sir. This was a real pleasure."

Eric walked to Amy and gave her a hug. "Beautiful, as always." He let her go, turned slowly, and shook his head. "But ... Jenna." Afraid he was going to say I was no good, I braced myself for the worst. "You have an extraordinarily pure sound. I love it." I sighed with relief, until he raised a warning finger. "In a few years, when you're out in the commercial music world trying to make a living, people will want you to pollute your sound. Personally, I hope that you don't."

"I won't." The words were out of my mouth so fast, everyone laughed.

He held up a hand. "I'm not asking for any promises."

"I'd never change anything you like." There were tears in my voice. My cheeks burned, and I hoped the others hadn't noticed. Eric noticed and seemed to enjoy it. He held my shoulders and kissed my forehead. I gave him a shy hug.

Susie watched, gritting her teeth. "Dad! You ordered a car for four o'clock. Come on, I'll walk you to the parking lot." She opened the door.

He picked up his leather jacket and overnight bag. "Thanks, all of you. This was great." He smiled and followed Susie out.

I sighed happily, then noticed a gold pen on the floor. Sure it was Eric's, I grabbed it and raced to the stairwell.

Susie's voice echoed up. "I hear you had Jenna for breakfast."

I froze.

Eric continued down the stairs, laughing casually. "Actually, we both had French toast." Susie huffed and he laughed again. "Don't worry. Your girlfriend's still a virgin."

"No thanks to you, I'm sure."

"I love you, baby girl."

She scowled, then hugged him. "Love you too, Daddy."

I backed out of the stairwell. To hell with the pen. If it was Eric's, Susie could send it to him. A minute ago I felt wonderful. Now, I felt humiliated and lonely. I shuffled back into the classroom as Amy smiled and hurried away.

Nick loosened his cello's end-pin, and gently pushed it up, inside the hollow wooden body. He lifted the cello into its fiberglass case, closed the cover, and snapped the latches.

I stood at the window, twirling the pen, looking down on Susie and Eric walking across campus to his limousine. He was leaving. I'd never see him again. Why had I turned him down? My vision blurred and I wiped away frustrated tears.

Behind me, Nick chuckled. "That was amazing. I'll have to call home and tell my folks. They—"

I felt so miserable, a sob bubbled from my throat.

"Jen! What's the matter?" He raced to my side. "It went really well. You were great."

Silent tears streamed down my cheeks as I watched Eric and Susie hug and kiss goodbye. Eric got into the limousine and drove away. Susie marched off, out of sight, and I put a hand over my mouth to keep from sobbing.

Nick stammered, "He ... He loved your voice."

I felt like I was going to explode, and desperately needed to blow my nose. I went through my sweater pockets, didn't find any Kleenexes, dredged some from the bottom of my book bag, and blew hard.

Nick followed me around the room. "Really. He thought your voice was beautiful. It is beautiful. You're beautiful."

Taken by surprise, I turned and wiped my eyes.

He looked very uncomfortable, as he reached awkwardly, took my face in his hands, and kissed me hard. Sweat beads popped out on his forehead. "You're the most beautiful girl I've ever seen. And the sweetest. And the most talented."

I was stunned. Was this the same distant guy I lusted after all year?

He pointed an angry finger out the window. "This morning, in the coffee shop, I wanted to kill that guy. The whole year I'd been trying to get close to you, and you always shied away. I couldn't even get you to talk to me. Ries came to town, and in one day you're eating out of his hand. This morning I thought I'd go crazy. God, I wanted to hear what you were telling him. You were spilling your guts to a guy you didn't even know. When you two left, I almost went after you. If he hadn't come back alone, I would have—I don't know what." Suddenly out of steam, red faced and breathing hard, he paced the room.

Not sure what to say, I stammered, "I wanted to talk to you, too, but you were always with Susie. I thought you two were ..." I shrugged. "You know."

"Me and Susie?" He looked shocked. "We study together. Sure, electronic music, composition class, but you didn't think we were ... Oh, jeez! No, no ... She's brilliant, but she's a ..." He made a face. "I wouldn't touch that girl with a ten-foot pole."

I was suddenly glad I was still a virgin. "Do you mean we wasted the whole year not talking to each other?" Tears threatened again, but I sniffed them back.

He looked angry. "We wasted the whole year not doing a lot of things." He kissed me again, roughly ran his hands all over me, and pulled away, panting. "Let's get out of here." He grabbed his cello case.

I hesitated. "Where can we go?"

He laughed. "My room. Bill and Kathy owe me big time. It's their turn to crash somewhere else."

Relieved and excited, I grabbed my stuff and followed him out.

6.
New York City: December 1977
SECONDO: Allegretto Comodo

*E*ver since I was a kid taking voice lessons at Juilliard Preparatory, I imagined myself singing on the international stages of magnificent concert halls and opera houses. I saw myself dressed in gorgeous gowns and heard my voice soar up to the highest balconies. I pictured acres of adoring, screaming fans, and smelled the sweet roses they tossed onto the stage. I even heard the pop of champagne corks and tasted the tart bubbly served afterward at my receptions.

The June I graduated from college, I was twenty-one, broke, and had no choice but to go home. Mom still lived at The Beresford, but Dad had moved her into a two-bedroom apartment. It was lovely, but stifling, and I wanted out.

New York had a lot of paid chorus jobs and, after four years in the Newell Conservatory Concert Choir, I was a great professional chorister. Oratorio societies and the New York Philharmonic Chorus produced high quality performances, but choristers were treated like second-class citizens, and occasionally herded like sheep. My worst job was in the multitudinous Metropolitan Opera extra chorus. I made friends with older singers who had given up dreams of solo careers in exchange for steady work to pay rent and put kids through college. It was sad and scary, but I determined all the more to have a solo career.

I took every job offered, made some good contacts and was hired to sing a few chamber concerts sponsored by music schools and churches. These concerts were similar to the ones I sang with Susie, Amy, and Nick, but at college we were able to rehearse together, long and hard, for free. Professional musicians had to be paid. Since the sponsors were always poor, there was never enough money for adequate rehearsals.

I was amazed to learn that some of the world's best chamber ensembles, like the Bach Aria Group and the New York Pro Musica, rehearsed very little. All the performers were world class soloists and expected to perform brilliantly at their first, and sometimes only, rehearsal. Whether I performed with other solo singers or instrumentalists, I often walked on stage feeling unprepared. Still, these infrequent, low-paying chamber music jobs were thrilling and very prestigious.

I collected a pile of flattering reviews and sent them to every possible artists' manager. One young agent signed me, booked me on a five-month tour with a small vocal ensemble, and took fifteen percent. Once I was on tour, I learned that most of the other singers had booked themselves and paid no commission. Even though I was underpaid, it was a great experience. Touring for five months and singing in different halls every night, I learned to maneuver around odd-sized stages with varying acoustics.

When I got back to New York, I had saved enough to rent my own two-room in a shabby apartment hotel. The walls were nearly soundproof, so the management rented to starving musicians. I landed a steady job, singing solos at First Presbyterian Church. When I was a kid, Mom sometimes dragged me to fashionable churches. Now I never missed a Sunday, but wasn't sure I believed in anything.

At least my love-life boomed. New York was full of attractive, horny men. I had a few casual affairs and minor heartbreaks. During the tour, I fell in love with a tenor, had a wild ten-week fling, then found out he had a wife and son in Cincinnati.

After all these years, my mind still replayed the morning Eric Ries kissed me behind a pine tree. Each time I imagined myself saying "yes," going to his room and being ravished like a goddess. Each time I beat myself up for having turned him down. That same night, Nick McClelland took my virginity. He was sweet, but young and clumsy. It should have been Eric. Nick and I still exchanged Christmas cards. He was married, living in Nashville, playing cello when he could, and working as a recording engineer. He was a pleasant part of my growing up, and I had no regrets about that college affair.

My little apartment was an easy ten-minute walk from Mom's. Every week or so, I went over for dinner. Penny still worked for Mom part-time, and I went to see her as much as Mom. After dinner, Mom always had a new piece of expensive clothing or some edible delicacy for me to take home. I usually said that I didn't need it, then took it anyway. She knew I couldn't afford to refuse her charity.

The years flew by and suddenly I was twenty-six, living in New York, earning my living by singing, but just making ends meet. Everyday life was a far cry from my lush childhood fantasy, but I knew that dreams could still come true.

•

A few days before Christmas, I was dressed in Victorian garb, caroling with a quartet at the South Street Seaport. The alto, tenor, and baritone were wonderful singers and our elaborate musical arrangements were terrific fun. I loved this part of lower Manhattan. It was a long but easy subway ride from my apartment, and within walking distance of Wall Street and the World Trade Center.

The South Street Seaport was New York's newest tourist attraction, and still unfinished. New shops opened every couple of days. It felt like entering a time warp when my boot heels clicked over picturesque cobbled streets leading to Victorian storefronts, museums, expensive boutiques, nautical junk shops, seafood bars, expensive restaurants, and best of all, the ancient sailing ship, Peking. Permanently tethered to the pier, its rickety hull rocked with the tides. Costumed guides led visitors through the ship, then past the canopied stands selling great wines, cheeses, fish, bakery goods, boutique items and handmade jewelry. Beautiful fake gaslights were decorated with hanging baskets of winter greens, Christmas trees, and holly garlands. Our quartet strolled the cobbled walkways, entertained shoppers and posed for pictures with tourists.

The pay and the hours were reasonable. The only problem was that it was freezing. Under my thin, ankle-length Victorian costume coat, I wore layers of sweaters and long underwear. My head was covered with a wide-brimmed, lace-lined bonnet, tied under my chin with a huge satin bow. Under the bow, around my throat, I wrapped two thin silk scarves. My hair was artificially highlighted back to the shining ash-blond I had been as a child. It draped out of the bonnet like a shawl, looked beautiful, and provided an extra layer of warmth. Singers are often neurotic about their throats, but I knew that sickness was just mind over matter. I needed the job, so I was not going to get sick.

Our last set was over at 7:00. At 6:40 I started listening for the tolling of a nearby church bell. Deep in my pocket was a ticket for an 8:00 concert at Carnegie Hall. It was a direct trip uptown on the express subway, but I needed to allow a half-hour's travel time. We were in the middle of a carol when the clock struck seven.

We finished with a rousing, "… Troll the ancient Yuletide carol, fa la la la la … la la la la," acknowledged the applause of passing shoppers, and hurried through a brightly decorated Victorian archway disguising a modern office building. The security guard nodded as we raced by, shivering, then climbed a flight of stairs into an office that doubled as our dressing room.

First in, Don the middle-aged baritone hung up his top hat and thin Victorian greatcoat. Underneath, he wore a down vest. "Payday folks!" He reached inside the vest and pulled out three white envelopes. The tenor and alto quickly hung up their costumes, put on their own coats, took their checks and left.

Too cold to undress, I waited a few moments, breathing in the comfort of warm air. I opened my envelope and folded the check into my bag. "Thanks, Don. I really need this gig."

He scratched his graying hair. "Did I hear the guy at the Oyster Bar ask you to sing with the combo?"

"Yeah. For a hundred a night. I wish I could. I need the money." I sighed and shook my head. "Unfortunately, I can't sing jazz, and I'd choke on the cigarette smoke." I hung my costume coat on a rack with the others.

Don flopped back into a padded, swivel desk chair. "I'm glad you're not going to try. I've seen a lot of really good, young singers come to town, start singing crap and ruin their voices. You've got a beautiful sound. You won't be singing on the street forever. Once you get a good manager you'll—"

"I've heard that a hundred times. When's that going to be?" I knew he meant well, but I was too tired to be polite. "I had a lousy manager who did nothing but take commission. I've been trying to get decent management for three years. Right after college I sang a few competitions. I don't know what else to do."

Don shook his head. "No, your sound's too elegant for that. Showy singers win competitions. You've got to sing really loud or really high for anyone to notice."

"But what else can I do?" Totally defeated, I eased myself into another swivel chair. "Atlas Artists is the only one who really handles my kind of voice. Three times a year I send my reviews. They send back a printed card saying their roster is full." I shivered and the sudden motion helped me warm up. "I have a lot of engagements, but I barely earn enough to live on. Maybe I should try the Oyster Bar." I smirked as my mind flashed-back. "Seven years ago I made a rash promise to Eric Ries that I wouldn't mess with my sound. I kept my promise, but I haven't even seen him since. He probably doesn't remember me, so I wonder why I'm bothering. Maybe I should make some money singing jazz."

I hadn't seen Eric, but every few months I sent him a letter care of Atlas Artists Management. He never answered, so I never knew if he got them. It didn't matter. My feelings were just as strong as when I was eleven, the day he touched my cheek.

Don's eyes widened. "Well, a guy like Ries knows what he's talking about. How do you come to know him?"

"I went to Newell Conservatory with his daughter."

"Really! Did you see this?" He reached for his briefcase and pulled out the latest issue of *Musical America* magazine. The cover was a picture of Susie and two young men in an electronic music studio. She looked beautiful and very happy. The caption read, "Harvard's New Music: Harmony or Humbug?"

Don leaned back, stifled a yawn, and waved at the magazine. "I've finished it. Take it."

"Thanks! Wow, that studio looks like the cockpit of a jet plane. Susie always loved that stuff."

After graduating from college, we girls had kept in close touch. Amy backpacked through Europe, playing everywhere she could. She fell in love with an Austrian girl who played harp, and they settled in Salzburg. Since Amy had no solo aspirations, she was totally happy leading a quiet life and making an adequate living playing duets with her partner.

Determined to have a solo career, Susie drove herself on the grueling competition circuit. Like all young musicians, she spent years developing her emotional sensitivity. Finally mature enough to really express it, she locked it away in order to compete. Just like Olympic athletes, musicians play for a row of judges. The highest scorer wins money, performing opportunities, and sometimes management.

The stress of competition is even worse than auditions or performances, and a lot of people can't take it. Even as a child, Susie competed well. She loved winning, but felt sad for the losers and never fully enjoyed her triumphs. The fierce battle for professional and financial survival began stealing the most precious thing in her whole life: the joy of making music. I was stunned when she wrote that she was entering Harvard's graduate program and staying until she had a doctorate. Choosing to stay out of the public eye meant she had given up any chance of a solo career.

I studied the picture on the magazine cover. "This is great. Thanks, Don." I slipped the magazine into my bag and checked my watch. It was 7:15.

Don stretched and yawned again. "Isn't Ries doing something in New York soon?"

"Tonight. He's conducting the Albany Philharmonia. It's music from 1935-1965. They're playing his *Violin Concerto.*"

"Sixties music." He nodded slowly. "Well, I don't blame him for not trying something new. If the critics had done to me what they did to his cantata a couple of years ago, I'd have slit my wrists."

"I was out of town, but I read the reviews. Two of them were awful. One was good. My mother heard it. She said the audience liked it." Eager to be on my way, I went to the coat rack and started layering for the cold outside.

Don lazed in his chair. "Audiences loved it and we loved it. I sang one of the solos. This is a guy who can really write music. He knows voices and instruments, so the players love him. He puts harmonies together that are actually pleasant to listen to, so the critics say he's 'derivative.' They say he writes movie music, like Puccini or Sibelius —like there's something wrong with that. Christ! It gets me mad."

He dozed off and I slipped out the door, chuckling to myself. Eric's compositions did sound like movie music, the very best kind. They were lush and driven by emotion. That's why audiences loved it so much.

Thirty minutes later, I was sitting in the top balcony at Carnegie

Hall. When I bought my ticket, the box office attendant was surprised I insisted on the second row. I knew from experience that the balcony guard rail was directly at eye level, so people in the front row had to bend down to see the stage. Sight lines from the second row were perfect. The orchestra took their seats and tuned as I opened the printed program. First was William Walton's *Variations On A Theme By Hindemith.* Next were shorter pieces by Samuel Barber, John Cage, George Ligeti, and Pierre Boulez. Last was Eric's *Violin Concerto.*

Applause started slowly. I looked up, but didn't see Eric. A second later, he walked to center stage in pristine white tie and immaculate black tails, looking comfortable as a gracious host in his living room. He radiated self-confidence and was ferociously attractive.

He bowed to the audience, shook hands with his concert master, and mounted the podium. His hair was cut shorter. Otherwise, he looked exactly like he had seven years before. I adjusted my opera glasses and focused on his face. Glimmers of silver highlighted his hair and beard. Slight smile lines gave him even more personality. He was forty-five and still the most handsome man I had ever seen. He picked up his baton, glanced at his score, smiled at the orchestra, and the music began.

I had never heard him conduct, and I studied his technique. His right hand stayed low, and swung in clean short strokes. Every beat was clear and easy to follow. His left hand defined subtle nuances with equal clarity. He concentrated on the first chairs, but glanced back at all the players, even those in the last chairs.

This was a community orchestra supported by rich patrons who booked Carnegie Hall one night a year. The players were a mix of professionals, amateurs, and students, but the sound was totally professional. I was impressed. I hoped the critics would be too. Eric was thoroughly enjoying himself and the players looked happy. I wanted to be on stage, not tucked up in the crows nest with all the nobodies. If I left now, he would never know it, or care. I sat back, feeling sorry for myself. Punishing myself even more, I remembered Susie's smirk, "I hear you had Jenna for breakfast."

House lights came up for intermission and I scrunched down for a doze. I woke when the orchestra returned to play his *Violin Concerto.* I hadn't heard it in a long time, knew it would bring back tons of memories and was almost afraid to relive them. Eric raised his baton in a slow up beat. On his down beat, low strings played the same wonderful harmonies I expected. A young violinist named Richard Reynolds stood to Eric's left, poised to play. On Eric's cue, Richard drew his bow across the strings.

Every measure was familiar, sweet and painful, resonating deep inside me. This music was part of my DNA, as much as my hair, or skin, or the blood pulsing through my veins. The piece finished to polite applause. Eric let Richard bow first, then gestured for the orchestra to rise. When everyone on stage was standing, he turned to the audience, bowed, and followed the violinist off the stage.

I lost no time getting down several flights of stairs, reaching the main level, and ducking into a ladies room. I checked my makeup, brushed and fluffed my hair. My stomach cramped in a hungry growl. Promising myself food as soon as I was away from expensive midtown and back home, I stood back, checking myself.

My loose-fitting cashmere turtleneck hung flatteringly over my matching ivory slacks, and I silently thanked Mom for buying me the expensive outfit. When I pulled the sweater smooth, the shape of my breasts and ribs showed clearly. I let go and the thin wool relaxed back, revealing nothing. The last time Eric saw me, I was eighteen and ballerina thin. At twenty-six, I had gained enough weight to have a few womanly curves.

Carefully preparing, I hung my shoulder-bag over my left shoulder and folded my coat over my left arm. My right hand was free to hold the program and get Eric's autograph. I walked backstage, upstairs to the greenroom, and joined the line of fans waiting to see the artists. I thought I heard Eric's voice among several animated conversations. The slow-moving queue turned a corner, and I saw him talking with a group of attractive, beautifully dressed, middle-aged people. I didn't know who they were, but they had to be important.

My heart pounded. What was I doing here? He wouldn't remember me. He never answered my letters. Maybe he never got them, or worse: he got them and thought they were stupid. When had I written last? October? Did I send him that review? Shit! I was next in line. My cheeks burned as I silently practiced telling him who I was and that I liked the concert. My stomach growled. Please don't do that! Not now! The person in front of me moved away.

Eric smiled, but didn't recognize me. I handed him my program and he signed it. I took a deep breath. "That was a wonderful concert, Mr. Ries. My name is Jenna Adams. I went to Newell Conservatory with—"

"Jenna!" Pen in one hand and program in the other, he stared at my face, looked me up and down, and gave me a hug. "My God! How beautiful you are!" Looking slightly embarrassed, he smiled sheepishly. "Thank you for all those delightful letters. Did I ever answer you?"

Surprised and pleased, I mumbled, "No."

"I am so sorry."

"It's okay. I wasn't sure you were getting them, so I never—"

"I got them. All of them." He glanced behind me. "Are you alone?"

I nodded.

"Listen, I'm staying with a friend. She's giving me a party tonight. Can you come?"

"I'd love to." My stomach growled again, but he didn't hear it.

He looked around and located a stylish middle-aged woman chatting with friends. "Myra!"

She scurried happily to Eric's side, saw me, and clenched her teeth in a forced smile. "Myra, this is Jenna Adams. She went to school with Susie. She's coming to the house."

I followed Eric's entourage into Myra's opulent Fifth Avenue apartment then handed a maid my coat and scarf. Eric turned to tell me something, but Myra clinched a proprietary arm around his waist and swept him out of the foyer. He looked amused, winked, and disappeared into the adjoining living room. Luscious aromas of cooked foods and fresh baked bread pulled me toward the dining room. Caterers laid out a generous buffet of cheeses, pâtés, Seafood Newburg, Beef Stroganoff, noodles, fluffy rice, tossed salad, sautéed vegetables, hot rolls and butter. I took a plate and gave myself small samplings of everything. Other people crowded the table, chatting and laughing, so I retreated to a set of chairs in the corner, and ate like a starving dog.

Between bites, I noticed a young man in an expensive looking business suit standing at the edge of the buffet, watching me. He was an average looking academic type, medium height, slender, with a slightly large nose, short mouse-brown hair, and glasses. He spoke

to a woman standing near him, and nodded in my direction. She
looked at me and shook her head. Without a moment's shyness, he
carried his plate over, and offered his hand. "Hi! I'm Josh Kendal."

My mouth was so full, I tried not to laugh while swallowing
and shaking his hand. "Jenna Adams. Sorry, but this Newburg is so
good! I was singing Christmas carols at the South Street Seaport. It
was freezing and I didn't get dinner. Great way to make a living."

He broke into a lovely, sympathetic chuckle, and ate a fork-full
of Stroganoff.

I laughed back. "Are you a musician?"

"Yeah, but not for a living, fortunately."

The violin soloist, Richard Reynolds, rushed up, looking
miserable. "Sorry to bother you again, Josh. I'm just afraid that—"

Josh looked very annoyed. "It's your own fault. I told you not to
talk to that chiseler."

Richard swallowed hard. Sweat beads covered his forehead.
"But he said my fee was too high, that he'd have to get someone
else."

"And I'm telling you he's lying. Damn it, Richard! You're a great
talent, but talent is only worth as much as it's paid. I'm the agent.
I negotiate, not you. If you're not happy with the way I'm handling
you, I'll tear up your contract tomorrow."

Richard wrung his hands. "No. Please. I ... I'm sorry, Josh. I'm
really pleased with what you're doing for me."

My heart stopped. Josh Kendal was an agent. Dear God, let him
need a soprano.

He still looked furious, but took a deep breath and raised a
warning eyebrow. "Then will you trust me on this?"

"Yeah, of course I trust you. I'm really sorry." Richard hung his
head like a bad kid.

Josh rolled his eyes, then blew in the air. He shook his head,
looked at me, then back at Richard. "Okay Rich, enough. I'm trying
to make time with the most beautiful woman I've ever seen, so get
out of here."

Wow! My cheeks burned. I hadn't had a compliment like that ...
ever.

Josh gave Richard a playful sock in the arm. Richard comically
lurched, pretending it had hurt, then flashed me a smile and raced
out of sight.

Josh looked slightly embarrassed as he took a bite from his now cold plate of food. "Sorry about that. I guess you figured out I'm Rich's manager."

I needed him to find me charming as well as beautiful, so I flattered, "But you're so young. You must be a Wunderkind."

"No," he laughed, "just lucky. And no Kind. I'm thirty-one. Ten years ago I was a composition major at Juilliard and took a part-time job at a talent agency. I love composing, but wasn't masochistic enough to pursue a career. After graduation I stayed on. Last year the director retired and I took over his roster. It's been amazing."

Food forgotten, I stared at this plain-looking young man. Composition majors were the best possible musicians, and this guy was a Juilliard grad: the best of the best. Richard Reynolds was a world-class violinist, so Josh's agency had to be a decent one. Managing classical musicians took a whole catalogue of talents. I tried to imagine dealing all at once with greedy contractors, oversensitive clients, lawyers, contracts, residuals, recording rights, international travel arrangements, housing, rehearsal schedules, stage settings, dressing rooms ... Gulping my last bites, I set the plate on the sideboard. "I went to Juilliard Prep, then graduated from Newell Conservatory with Eric Ries's daughter."

He swallowed a mouthful of salad. "Did you see *Musical America?*"

"Yeah. What a great article."

"You must know Amy Daniels."

"Sure. We write all the time. Susie and Amy and I were a trio for four years. Baroque music mostly. Nick McClelland was our cellist, the first two years."

"I don't know him, but I'd love to sign Susie and Amy." My heart raced, praying he'd sign me. He tasted the Newburg. "You're right. This is good. It's a shame Susie's given up performing. She says it's tendonitis, but I thinks it's nerves. Too often, really talented kids push too hard too early, and burn out. She'll do great things in electronic music, though."

"Do you like electronic music?" I didn't want to admit that I hated it.

"Some of it. What I like is that it wakes people up, makes them uncomfortable, makes them think." He took another bite. "Amy loves living in Salzburg and doesn't want to tour. I can't blame her.

Have you been to Salzburg?"

I shook my head. "She also has a ..." Not knowing how to say that Amy was happily living in a lesbian relationship, I hedged, "I think she's in love with someone."

"Well, lucky Amy." His smile was subtle, but obvious enough. I just needed to glance at some men for their eyes to glaze over, and I had seen his look a hundred times. Right now, I needed a manager who loved my voice, not my looks. I wasn't sure if his crush was a good thing.

I was delighted when Eric joined us, holding a glass of wine. "I see you two have met." He sat next to me. "Your last letter was glowing. You're a busy little singer." He looked at Josh. "She might be a good one for Atlas."

"Atlas Artists?" I stared at Josh.

"Yeah. I'm Eric's agent, too."

I felt faint.

Eric sipped his wine. "Tell Josh what you've been doing."

I grabbed the opportunity. "Last weekend I sang three concerts with the Galliard Consort. I also sing with the Collegium at the Cloisters. I'm the soprano soloist at the First Presbyterian Church, and we're doing a Bach Cantata series. You know I sing at the Seaport, but that's just for the money. When I can, I sing with the New Music Group at Columbia, but they don't pay. I toured with the Larry Reynolds Singers ..."

Josh looked past me. "Maybe she could sing your Sonnets."

Eric looked surprised. "I thought we had Lilly Gottlinger."

Josh wearily shook his head. "She couldn't afford the time. No one with a reputation wants to touch this competition. It'll take a lot of preparation and you can't even afford union rehearsal rates. Even if you win, the prize money stinks. There's minimal press coverage."

Eric scowled. "It's great press coverage for new talent. International reviews like these can launch careers." His dark eyes bore into me. "How does that sound to you?"

"An international competition? With international press coverage? It sounds like a dream come true." My heart raced.

He chuckled. "Maybe a nightmare, but I need to hear you. I'm leaving for Paris tomorrow at eleven. Can you sing for us at ten, at Atlas?"

"What do you want to hear?"

Allegro Gioioso

At 10:10 the next morning, I sang my long awaited audition for Atlas Artists Management. One end of the long conference room held an oval table, covered with papers. At the other end, composer/pianist Eric Ries sat at a Steinway concert grand. Behind him, talent agent Joshua Kendal watched me and the music, and turned pages.

Allowed to choose my first selection, I picked the *Letter Aria* from *The Ballad Of Baby Doe*. In this heartbreaking piece, Baby Doe writes her mother, saying that she's giving up the married man she loves. The aria is musically and technically difficult. I reached the final lyric. "I know he needs me and that I love him, but I have to give him up and we must part forever, forever, *forever* ..."

My last, long note was soft, controlled, and crystal clear. I knew that my pitch was exact, my diction was perfect, and my phrasing was elegant. I was also an actress with the special talent of crying real tears without tightening my throat and distorting the sound. I finished, blurry-eyed. Josh stared with admiration. He stayed silent as I wiped my eyes, and Eric looked through the rest of my music. I brought a big selection including operatic arias, classical and contemporary art songs, and Broadway show tunes. Eric asked for short excerpts from Rorem and Schönberg.

Halfway through the last piece, an office worker appeared at the door and Eric stopped playing. "Mr. Ries, your car's downstairs."

"Thanks." Deep in his own thoughts, Eric stood up from the piano, and sorted papers into his briefcase. Josh and I waited. I knew he liked my audition, so why wouldn't he say anything? I looked at Josh.

He shrugged. "Eric, do you want Jenna to sing your Sonnets?"

I braced myself.

Eric studied his papers. "She has the voice, the musicianship, the temperament, and ..." He hesitated. "She won't mind bunking in the cabin with Susie and Amy. I'm re-scoring the violin for flute. If I use the girls, I won't have to break in a new trio."

I smiled with relief, relaxed for a moment, then started having second thoughts. It would be great working with Susie and Amy again, but where was this cabin, and why us? Were we his last resort? Whatever this was, it was under the auspices of one of the world's best talent managements. How bad could it be?

Eric looked up. "Jenna, I'll need you the last two weeks in March."

"Okay. I have a couple of little gigs, but nothing as important as an international competition."

"Good girl." He looked pleased. "It'll be hard work and no money. I can pay expenses, but that's all. I'll get you the manuscript and you'll need to learn it on your own."

"Okay."

Josh's eyes widened. "But Amy's got engagements and Susie's not performing any more. How can you be sure they'll do this? And don't try rehearsing at the cabin. You'll be like rats in a cage."

"They'll do it, damn it! They'll do it for me." Eric flashed back with a fury I didn't expect. It was scary and sexy at the same time. "Look, Josh, you keep telling me how hard these pieces are. We'll need concentrated rehearsals. I want four days at the cabin … Five, if you can schedule me. Then two days in Paris, before the competition."

"This is crazy."

Bellowing, "Just do it!" Eric slammed his briefcase shut.

Josh threw up his hands. "What about Seattle? Last year, you promised that this year—"

"If they want me so much, they'll change the date." Grabbing his briefcase, he stormed out of the room.

I glanced at Josh, then chased Eric down the hall. "Eric!"

He stopped and turned.

"I'll do a good job. Whatever it is. You won't be sorry you chose me."

His expression softened. "I know. Josh will give you the details. I'll see you in a few weeks." I threw my arms around his neck. He hugged me tight, kissed my forehead, and I hoped he'd kiss my lips. Instead, he touched my cheek and said, "What a beauty," and hurried away.

I watched him go, feeling excited and nervous. When I turned back, Josh was standing at the door. "You've proved you can sing music without tunes, but I'd like to hear more. Could you sing the *Rejoice*?"

"Oh, sure." Startled and thrilled, I found my photocopy of the Handel aria, carefully taped together so that the pianist only had to turn one page. Josh opened it, sat down and played. He set a brisk tempo and wasn't prepared to be pushed into lightning speed as I trilled through the coloratura. In contrast, my middle section was unusually slow, with extra ornaments and high notes I arranged myself. The final section went back to a breakneck tempo. We finished together, triumphantly. He looked pleased and I stifled a jubilant laugh.

Folding up the pages, he nodded approvingly. "Come back tomorrow morning and I'll have a contract for you to sign. Welcome to Atlas Artists."

My mouth fell open, but he didn't notice.

"I never promise to make a client a star, but always promise to do my best."

"Yessss!" I clenched my fists and jumped in the air. All my years of struggling and starvation were finally over. The adrenaline rush sent me gasping for air. Excited tears filled my eyes.

Josh stayed at the piano, chuckling, "I hope those are happy tears."

"Oh, yes!" Laughing, I nodded and blew my nose.

He sat forward, smiling. "I know how hard it is to be a performer. I admire all my clients. I couldn't go out there, facing audition after audition, rejection after rejection. Sit down, relax."

I happily complied, sinking into a padded chair at the conference table.

He thought for a moment, moved to a phone in the corner, and pushed a button. "Sheila, I have a new soprano, Jenna ..." He looked at me. "Jennifer? Adams."

I nodded.

"I want Nicky to hear her." He pointed to me, smiling. "Friday at 12:45. Great, thanks. Who? That's tonight? Yeah, thanks." He hung up. "You're auditioning for Nicholas Braithwaite, Friday at 12:45. He's doing King Arthur, so bring any Purcell, or other English Renaissance pieces you've got. You may as well bring the Rejoice. You know the Wellington Hotel, 56th and 7th?"

I laughed. Every classical singer in New York knew the large, carpeted room at the back of the aged hotel. Auditions and competitions were held there daily.

He leaned back and crossed his arms. "My secretary just reminded me I'm going to hear a new violist tonight at Goodman. Obviously, I go to a lot of concerts, scouting or hearing clients. Would you like to go?"

I heard myself say, "I'd love to," then took a minute to reconsider. Last night, I thought he was going to hit on me. Today he seemed totally different. He was open and friendly, a really bright, nice guy I'd like to spend time with. I didn't find him a bit sexy and hoped that wouldn't be a problem down the road. I smiled and collected my music.

He smiled back. "Great. We can grab a bite before, if you like."

I made a silly frown. "I'd love to, but I'll be singing at the Seaport till seven."

He laughed. "Sorry, I forgot about your survival gig. I'll feed you after the concert, or after the intermission, if the guy's no good."

We ate after the intermission. The violist looked like Adonis, played with adequate skill, but not the stellar talent Josh required for his roster. We sat in a small bistro, sipping red wine, eating great pasta and salad. Josh was quiet, and I guessed disappointed. I tried to cheer him. "Too bad the guy doesn't play better. He's really handsome. I'm sure there are a dozen great violists praying for management. You'll find one soon enough."

"Oh, yes." He smiled sadly. "That's not a problem. The problem is the artist I'm trying to replace. He doesn't know I'm terminating his contract and I'm too chicken to tell him."

"You're terminating a client?" My stomach cramped. "Why? What did he do?"

"He didn't do anything." He sat back, looking very unhappy. "He just got old. His fingers are swollen with arthritis. He can't play anymore. Critics are crucifying him. It looks very bad for Atlas Artists, and I'm too big a coward to deal with it." He rubbed his eyes. "His name is Miguel Salerno. Ever hear him?"

"Yes, of course. He taught a master-class at Newell. It was great. At least, his instruction was great. He didn't demonstrate very well."

Josh nodded. "And that was what, five years ago?"

"Yeah. About."

"Well, for thirty years, Miguel was one of the best chamber players in the world. There isn't a lot of solo work for viola, but what there was, he got. He's also one of the sweetest guys I know. He was kind to me, even when I was just an office boy. Six, seven years ago, his hands started going. Last year, Phil Shapiro wanted to terminate his contract, but Phil's style was so damn brutal, I begged him not to. Phil was retiring the next month, I was taking over the roster and thought I could do it more kindly. What I really hoped was that Miguel would come to his senses and quit on his own.

"He didn't. I have several geriatric clients. None of them play as well as they did in their prime, but the others are such great showmen, audiences love the entertainment and excuse the sour notes. Miguel was never a flashy player. He's embarrassing himself and the agency, and he has to be stopped. He thinks he's got a concert in Brussels next spring. I've replaced him and haven't even told him. The longer I delay, the worse it will be." He looked terribly sad.

I felt like a dark cloak had fallen over us. Why did life have to be so hard?

He saw my expression. "No point in your feeling bad. It's just the cycle of life." He smiled. "Today I had the pleasure of signing a great new talent—you—and tomorrow I have the pain of putting an old one out to pasture. Miguel's still a great teacher. He has a great family. He's financially solvent ... Oh, shit!" He looked down and shook his head.

I read his mind. Teachers and composers can go on forever. Performers have nothing else. If they can't play music, their lives are over.

He rubbed his eyes and sat up. "I'm sorry. Do you want dessert, or coffee, or anything?"

"No, thanks. This was delicious."

"Good. It's one of my favorite places. Come on, I'll take you home. Where do you live?"

"Just up the street, 86th and Broadway."

"Not the Bretton Hall?"

"Yeah. Why?"

He laughed. "I know it well. Some of my Juilliard friends lived there. It's a dump, but it's rent stabilized and you can practice all night. You're actually lucky to be there ... for now. Once you're making some bucks, it'll be different."

At noon the next day, I was back at Atlas Artists, trying to sign my contract. I was ready to sign anything, but Sheila, Josh's elderly secretary, made me sit on a sofa next to her desk and read through every word. She was small, bent-over, wrinkled and sharp as a tack. If central casting booked the perfect Jewish grandmother, it would be Sheila.

She peered over her half-glasses. "Listen dear, this piece of paper can influence your entire life. I've been at this agency thirty-two years, and I've heard a lot of artists complain, after the fact. Make sure you know what you're signing."

I grit my teeth. "I'm trying, Sheila, but it's written in legalese."

"Try harder, dear."

I plowed through a few more lines of gibberish.

She looked up from her filing as Josh's office door opened. Two men came out and Josh followed. The men nodded and left.

I held up the contract. "Josh, isn't this the standard contract every Atlas client signs, even Eric Ries?"

He nodded. "Eric's basic contract is exactly like that. He's had so many recordings issued and reissued, the codicils go on for pages, but that's the basic document."

"Great!" I turned to the last page, signed my name and the date, did the same on a second copy, handed one to Sheila, and folded the other into my bag.

Sheila huffed and turned her back.

Josh waved me inside. "Come here, look where I've got your picture."

I followed him into his office. His large desk had two phones, two large Rolodexes, and three piles of papers. One large, dirty window was framed by filing cabinets. The two remaining walls were covered by 8x10, black-and-white photographs of clients. My photo was in the middle of the wall, right next to Eric's, and facing Josh's desk.

"Wow! I haven't even made you any money yet, and I'm in a place of honor."

"You'll make us both money. I'm sure of it."

Sheila peered inside. "I see you've removed Miguel. How did he take it?"

Josh turned gray. "Actually ..." He leaned on his desk. "I still haven't talked to him, and I left his new phone number at home, so

I'll have to wait until—"

"Go and get it." Sheila's command was soft but stern. Josh stared at the floor like a guilty schoolboy and Sheila sadly shook her head. "Sweetheart, you live around the corner. Go home, get the phone number, and call him." When Josh stayed silent, she continued, "If you won't call him, bring the number back here, so I can call him and set up an appointment for you to meet with him."

"No, I'll do it." He didn't move.

Sheila watched him fondly. "You're just starting to understand what Phil went through, all those years." He looked up, surprised, and Sheila shook her head. "Don't think I didn't see you watching him, judging him, thinking he was some kind of ogre. His meanness was just to cover up. He didn't like making clients feel bad any more than you do."

Josh stayed, nervously drumming his fingers.

Suddenly, Sheila threw an arm around my waist. She only stood as high as my shoulder, but her presence was huge. "Look at this girl, how skinny she is. Take her with you. Go home. You make the call, then you take her to lunch."

"Lunch?" Josh made a face.

Sheila threw her arms in the air. "Yes, lunch." She looked at me. "You've heard of lunch?"

I laughed and nodded.

She pointed to Josh. "This boy doesn't know from lunch. Josh, take the girl, make the call, and eat lunch. Your next appointment isn't till 1:30 with those crazy Italians. They're never on time anyway, so go."

Josh closed his eyes and chuckled silently. "My mother's in New Jersey, but sometimes I think …"

Sheila nodded proudly. "Boys need looking after. Go!"

He shrugged, left the office and went to get his coat.

Before I could follow him, Sheila grabbed my arm. She looked deadly serious. "This is very hard for him, but he's got to do it. He's such a good man, so smart, so kind, but he needs to do this, and he likes you. You're smart, and you like him, too. I can tell. Help him do this." She gave me a squeeze, let me go, and went back to her desk.

My knees felt weak. Suddenly I was emotionally involved with a whole bunch of people I didn't even know. Thinking I should make an excuse and run away, I went back out to the sofa. Sheila winked at me as Josh came back in his coat and gloves.

He smiled, clicked his heels, bowed and offered his arm. It was very sweet. I felt like a coward and thought I was making a mistake, but took his arm anyway. A second later, I had to let it go so we could walk single file down the narrow hall, past offices of subagents, into the main lobby. He waved to the pretty receptionist, "Back in an hour, Ellen."

We walked outside onto 7th Avenue, across 57th Street, and down the block to a beautiful old granite building, across the street from Carnegie Hall. A uniformed doorman opened a heavy glass door, framed with polished brass. The lobby was old, paneled with polished marble, and I felt overwhelmed. Josh obviously made a lot of money. A brass-and-wood-paneled elevator took us to the fifth floor and his one-bedroom apartment. The front door opened into a large living room. An old baby-grand piano stood in the corner, next to a wall of family photos. In front of the sofa, a stereo sound system was connected to speakers hanging in all four corners, and an entire wall was shelves of records and cassette tapes. The entrance to a small kitchen was off to one side and I avoided looking into the bedroom. We dropped our coats onto a soft leather sofa.

"This is an amazing location. How did you get the apartment?"

"I inherited it from a client." He laughed at my stunned expression. "Not exactly inherited. I bought it from her before she retired and moved to Berlin."

I forgot why I was there until he hesitated, then hurried toward the kitchen. "Let me get you a drink. Tea, or juice, or ..." He did not want to make that phone call.

I smiled and planted myself firmly on the sofa. "Thanks, that's sweet, but I'd rather wait until you finish your call."

"Oh, yeah. Right. Guess I'd better call from the bedroom." He looked so nervous, I felt sorry for him. He stalled some more, gesturing to the kitchen. "Make yourself at home. If there's anything you want, just—"

"I'm fine, really. Go make your call."

Finally out of excuses, he went into his bedroom and closed the door.

I wished I could help him, knew that I couldn't, and entertained myself looking over his family photos. There were school pictures of kids, informal family gatherings, and posed pictures from bar mitzvahs and weddings. Josh was in a lot of his family photos and everyone looked genuinely happy. They really liked each other. I looked for pictures of a possible girlfriend, was pleased I couldn't find any, and wondered why I cared.

His record and tape collections were huge, alphabetized, and categorized by type: Opera, Symphony, Choral Music, Chamber Music and Solo Artists. I didn't know when his birthday was, but anyone that organized was probably a Virgo.

He stayed in the bedroom for nearly twenty minutes. I started feeling worried. When he finally emerged, he looked tired but calm. I didn't know if he'd want to talk about it, so I sat in a corner of the sofa, watched and waited. He sat at the other end and sighed, "I'm sorry that took so long. Are you okay?"

"Sure. Are you?"

"Yeah." He smiled, then shook his head. "Fortunately, so is Miguel." He slumped down and leaned his head back against the soft leather. "I didn't know what I was going to say, but I didn't have to say much of anything. Miguel did most of the talking, and venting. I just listened. He was more prepared for this than I was." He closed his eyes. I wondered if he'd gone to sleep, when he said, "Thank you for being here. I don't think I would have done it if I'd been alone."

I rolled my eyes. "Sheila made me come." He laughed and I laughed back. "She really loves you."

"I know. She's great. Pray God she never retires. Atlas Artists would fall apart at the seams."

Dolce Cantabile

Josh and I saw a lot of each other. I sang auditions and he was always pleased. We might not hear the results for weeks, and I might not book anything, but he trusted me to sing well. We went to more concerts and dinners. He was easy company, always calm, considerate, and full of amusing conversation. He still didn't turn me on sexually, but I loved the gentlemanly way he held doors, and touched my back as I went through. His fingers felt nice, gently brushing my hair away from my face, or smoothing it over my shoulders. At concerts, our legs sometimes brushed against each other. We said "goodnight" with a hug and a peck on the cheek. It was sweet and I liked it. The last time we went out, I kissed him on the lips. It was a closed-mouth, high-school kiss, but spontaneous and nice. I didn't know where the relationship would go, but as long as he got me auditions, I didn't care.

One evening, I waited for Josh at the Rumanian embassy. A basso was singing and Josh was scouting. I made small talk with other concert-goers, while gorging myself on refreshments. Josh saw me eating and laughed. He said he could never understand how I could eat so much and stay so slim. I smiled and waved while sipping a cup of luscious hot borscht. "Hi!" I wiped a napkin across my lips and gave him a casual kiss. A bell rang, announcing the concert's start, so I gulped the last of the soup.

Josh stayed close, letting everyone else go ahead of us. The second we were alone, he whispered, "You booked the Monteverdi."

I stifled a scream, grabbed him, and kissed him hard. It was a real-life, grown-up, opened-mouth kiss. It felt natural and really good. Suddenly remembering where I was, I pulled away and hurried into the hall, after the others.

The ornate ballroom/auditorium was small, and the only empty chairs were at the back. We quickly took programs and sat down. Excited by my success and wanting to jump for joy, I made myself sit still and stare at the program. The tallest, ugliest man I ever saw walked onto the small stage, followed by his accompanist and page turner. The music was all in Slavic languages and seemed to be written in a single dreary minor mode. Low tones like brass organ pipes rolled from the basso's bearded face. He looked like Blue Beard, stared straight ahead, and seemed to have marbles in his mouth. He was the most boring singer I had ever heard.

Avoiding Josh's eyes and touch, I sat with my arms and legs tightly folded. *I have a booking—a real booking with a real opera company for real money, and I just kissed Josh—hard, really hard and I liked it. Now what?*

The recital lasted an hour. It seemed like forever. Half way through, I wanted to run out, screaming. Josh loved the guy and stayed long after, talking with him and his people. Fortunately, the refreshments were delicious and plentiful, so I gorged myself on spiced meats, great breads, cheeses, and pastries. I watched Josh open his briefcase, write in his appointment book, and hand out business cards. Finally, he finished talking and we got our coats.

We walked outside and frigid air slapped us in the face. It was ten o'clock. There were no cabs in sight, so we wasted no time diving into the warmth of the nearest subway station. We rode uptown, squeezed between other passengers, and heard an incredibly loud snore. The snoring kept up, and people all around us turned their heads, laughing and straining to find the noisy sleeper. I looked over Josh's shoulder and saw an old man asleep at the end of the car. I felt sorry for him, but couldn't help laughing. I whispered, "Sounds just like your basso."

"He does not." Josh glared at me, trying not to laugh.

"Does so."

Josh shook his head. "I need a basso, Jen, and the man can sing."

I pretended to retch. "But, he's so ugly and boring."

The doors opened at 86th Street and Broadway. Still laughing, we dodged other passengers and climbed up the subway steps.

"There's money in that kind of voice." Josh was determined to win the argument.

I knew he was right, but the patter was too much fun to stop. "Look, Josh, you keep saying seventy-percent of your audiences are women. They won't pay money to hear someone ugly. Now that violist—maybe he didn't play so well, but—"

"You think I should sign a mediocre violist, just because he's cute?"

"He's gorgeous. Besides, all your clients can't be both brilliant and gorgeous."

"Like you, you mean?" I grinned as he laughed and shook his head. "Okay, some of you are brilliant and gorgeous, and I am so pleased you booked the Monteverdi."

"Thanks for getting me that audition—and for being there. Thank you. Thank you."

"I don't often get to hear auditions, but I try to hear new clients. I need to know they can perform under pressure. You certainly can. God, you sang well."

I scurried toward the warmth of my building. "I just wish the production wasn't a whole year from now. I could starve before that."

"Don't worry. I won't let you starve. But you do eat an awful lot."

I stifled a laugh and tried to look insulted.

"Bookings are at least a year ahead. You'll get used to it. I have clients booked six years ahead. It'll take a couple of years, then you should be busy for the next ten."

"Really? That seems like a dream."

We reached the wide steps leading up to my apartment hotel. This was the moment of truth. Whatever happened in the next couple of hours could affect the rest of my life. I really liked Josh, and after this evening's lingering kiss, I was ready to do more than just like him. He had made enough gentle advances that I knew he wanted to sleep with me. I guessed he would be a sweet lover, but my career was more important than my love life.

I had had love affairs that felt perfect, then soured horribly. Josh was a top notch agent. He knew everybody in the music business. If he decided he didn't like me, he could make sure I never worked again. I wished it had never come to this. I wished I didn't like him so much. It was my choice. I could say, "Thanks for the evening," send him home, and keep the relationship purely professional. He might get mad and never ask me out again, but I would still have a great agent, and that was the most important thing in my life. Wasn't it?

He stood on the sidewalk, shivering, exhaling white mist. My insides tightened. He was adorable. I wanted to hold him tight, not send him away. I wanted him to be my agent, but I also wanted to touch him. He had to be more than just a voice at the other end of the telephone.

He must have guessed why I was stalling, because he made a silly frown, posed one hand like a paw and whimpered pitifully. I broke out laughing. "Would you like to come up?"

"Oh, yes. Please." He shivered violently, and sighed with relief. I smiled as we started up the outside stairs. *Crash, bam!* An explosion of sounds erupted from a drum machine and overblown speakers. Josh blinked hard, listened for a moment, and shouted, "Is that supposed to be music?"

I looked over the metal banister and waved to my stoned neighbor, standing on the sidewalk below me, playing an original pop/rock song on his battered synthesizer. A box in front of him held a few coins and dollar bills. His rented room without a bath cost next to nothing, but I was amazed his street music earned enough to pay even that.

I yelled back at Josh. "You said you knew this building." He smiled and nodded as I pushed open the cracked glass doors, led the way over the threadbare carpet and through the huge, shabby apartment hotel lobby. Harsh light glared from naked bulbs in broken chandeliers. I sped across the patchy floor, and made a beeline for the hotel desk with its World War II vintage switchboard.

Bobby, the sweet old guy behind the counter, had greasy hair and dirty fingernails. He smiled and pulled mail from my letter slot. A huge woman in a worn house dress and an antique headset sat next to him, answering a buzz from the switchboard. She pulled a thick black wire from the bottom of the board and plugged it into a hole at eye level. A large yellow dog slept at her feet.

I took my mail and smiled. "Thanks. Good night, Bobby. 'Night, Colleen." They nodded back.

Josh and I joined a dozen other people waiting in front of two freight-sized elevators. One came to a bumpy landing and I yanked Josh out of the way. Like a breaking dam, the wide doors opened and a rock band cascaded out. Josh tried not to laugh as half a dozen half-stoned kids in aesthetically torn jeans and black leather dragged out a truckload of electronic instruments and sound equipment. Everyone waiting to go up fit comfortably inside, with room to spare. The elevator made three stops before reaching the ninth floor.

Everyone had gotten out except Nan, a violinist about my age. I waved "good night" and she grabbed my arm.

"Jenna? Isn't that Joshua Kendal?" I nodded and she looked impressed. "Way to go, girl!"

Josh raised an eyebrow. "Everything okay?"

I didn't know how to react. "Yeah, I guess. Just neighborhood gossip." I suddenly felt cold. There would be gossip, lots of it. Nan was a blabbermouth, but Josh and I had already been seen together all over town. No matter what our relationship actually was, some people would think I was screwing him for his connections. I tried to do everything right and it could turn out all wrong. Shit!

Not sure what to else to do, I led him down two wide corridors, past a row of apartment doors. We heard Bach from a piano,

Ravel from a bassoon, and a tuneless screech from a saxophone serenading us to the end of my hall. I took out my keys, unlocked my double door bolts, pushed open the door, and switched on a light. Josh followed. I doubled back, closing and bolting the door. All sound stopped. No matter how much noise there was in the halls, the thick apartment walls and double-paneled wooden doors made the interiors virtually soundproof.

Josh dropped his briefcase, grabbed me and kissed me. Pleased but surprised, and wishing he had let me get my coat off, I kissed him back, then passively hung my arms over his shoulders, waiting for him to finish. He let me go, smiled sheepishly and unbuttoned his coat. "Sorry, but tonight's the first time you let me kiss you. I wanted to make sure I hadn't dreamt it." He folded his coat onto the daybed. "Ever since I first saw you at Myra's party, I've wanted to."

Turning around, he faced an entire wall of Eric Ries memorabilia. Framed photographs, magazine articles, and record jackets were everywhere. A shelf between the living room and bedroom held the fifteen-year-old, black-and-white autographed picture. "Is this a shrine?"

I forced a laugh. "My mother calls it an unhealthy obsession."

"Is it?"

"What?"

"An unhealthy obsession?"

"No!" That was almost a shout. Laughing nervously, I made myself speak slowly and quietly. "No, of course it's not. I've just always loved his music. You know that. He's the only famous composer I ever met up close, that's all."

He looked me in the eye. "Is that all?"

"Well, of course." My heart pounded. What was happening? All of a sudden I felt like I was in the witness box. Josh hadn't asked anything terrible. I hadn't done anything wrong, but I felt guilty as sin. Not sure how much I should say about Eric, I stalled by taking our coats through the bedroom and hanging them in the closet. I walked back, past the loft bed with a spinet piano tucked underneath, then stopped by the old black-and-white photo.

"Eric signed this for me when I was eleven. It sort of took the place of my father. I told you my parents divorced. It was traumatic, to say the least. My father never liked me, so I was sure the divorce was my fault. I probably had nothing to do with it, but kids don't understand grown-up problems." The emotional memory felt painfully fresh. I must have looked upset, because Josh stayed quiet, waiting for me to continue.

"A few months later, Eric's *Violin Concerto* debuted. Mom's Philharmonic Society had copies of this picture, records and press kits. I fell in love with his record, read about him and Susie traveling together. I could already play *A Rainbow For My Daughter*. He seemed like a really nice father, so I pretended he was my father, too. I talked to this picture, sometimes. I knew it was make-believe, but it made me feel better. You know, it was a kid thing." I forced a smile and sat on the daybed.

He sat next to me. "Go on." His smile seemed sincere, so I felt encouraged.

"Oh, well, Eric came to New York for the concert. I met him a couple of times, just for a couple of minutes. Once he was with Phil Shapiro at the Russian Tea Room. I was just an eleven-year-old kid, but Eric talked to me like a grownup. He signed that picture, and after that I really did wish he was my father. That's all. I didn't see him again till I was eighteen, at Newell Conservatory, when he came to visit Susie." I sat back, smiling nervously. Had that been enough explanation? Too much? My heart thumped. I hoped my face wasn't red. Josh stayed silent. I tried to guess what he was thinking. If he decided I was loony, he'd put on his coat, and never date me again. Deciding that might be best after all, that we could simply stay client and agent, I silently prayed that he wouldn't go.

He studied the wall. "I see you haven't framed any of his bad reviews. When I first went to Juilliard, we made fun of composers like Eric." He laughed sadly. "Britten, Walton, even Copeland ... anyone who still wrote tunes was considered secondhand. At best we called those guys old-fashioned. At worse we said they wrote pop songs or movie music. God, we were arrogant. I went along with the peer pressure, until I started analyzing those guys and finding out that they were good. Again and again, I'd come back to Eric Ries. Something about his construction, his voicings, I don't know exactly. Then, when I started working at Atlas and actually met him ..."

He sat forward with his elbows on his knees. "One day, I was delivering mail. Phil was on the phone, yelling at someone." He rolled his eyes. "Phil was always yelling at someone. The office door was open and I saw Eric sitting inside. I knew who he was, from his pictures. He wasn't exactly hard to recognize. How many composers look like movie stars?"

I smiled in agreement. Josh quietly laughed. "I was only an office boy. I knew it and expected to be treated like one. Well, I dropped the mail on Phil's desk, smiled at Eric and started to leave. He said, 'You're new. What's your name?' He said he was Eric Ries and shook my hand. I said that I was at Juilliard, working here part-time, so he asked what I played. I said piano, but that I was a composition major, and he asked what I was working on.

"Phil stayed on the phone, so I sat down and told Eric I was writing a piano sonata, and how I was having trouble with the middle register voicings. He said young composers needed to work their weaknesses, and that I should expand the middle register, arranging the sonata for piano and viola. At that time I knew nothing about viola, and he started talking about bowing and finger positions."

He shook his head in disbelief. "Well, I tried memorizing everything he said, even though I didn't understand it. But, the wild part was that he was interested. Really interested. He wasn't just being polite. Phil got off the phone. I jumped up, thanked Eric, and made a quick getaway. The next class, I told my teacher what Eric suggested and he thought it was great. So I had to learn to play viola." He sat quietly, enjoying the memory. I waited, hoping for more.

His smile broadened. "It was Eric who convinced me to become a full-time agent. I almost forgot this. One night, just before graduation, I was in the conference room at Atlas, the one you auditioned in. I was practicing a composition for my senior recital. It was the best thing I'd ever written and I was really proud of it. I finished and Eric was standing in the doorway. He said he liked it, and of course that made me feel great. We talked for a minute, then he came over and said, 'Sharp the last A.' I thought he was full of it, but couldn't insult a major client. He must have known I was mad, but he just eased himself onto the piano bench, pushed me off, and turned back to the first page. I stood behind him, wanting to strangle him. Then he started to play.

"It was as if I'd never heard the piece. He played all the notes I'd written, didn't add any or leave any out, but he stretched some and softened others, so I could hear where changes would be good. Then, in the second to the last measure, he sharped the A." He shrugged with disbelief. "That made the piece. That one tiny change made it perfect. That was genius. Real genius. From that moment, I knew I had to spend the rest of my life promoting talent like his."

That story was amazing. I was practically in tears.

Josh looked at the floor and laughed. "I sound like I'm obsessed, don't I?" We laughed together. "You gave him quite an ardent goodbye the other day. Obviously, you don't still think of him as a father figure."

I stiffened. He was right, of course. I wanted Eric to kiss me. He hadn't. I was disappointed, and Josh saw it. "I don't know how I feel. I don't even know him. I hadn't seen him in seven years, and even then, he just spent the one night at Newell."

He smiled at the floor. "That's time enough."

"He propositioned me, if that's what you're wondering. I turned him down."

"You turned him down?" His eyes were huge. He laughed, and relaxed back against the cushions. "That's great. You must be one of the few women on the planet who ever turned down Eric Ries." He kissed my hand. "I've seen him with so many women, all over the world. They throw themselves at him, and why not? He's a hell of a nice guy, handsome, single, so he can do what he likes." Suddenly he paled. "Oh, shit. I almost forgot." He took a deep breath, looked like he was about to do something painful, and opened his briefcase. "I guess I wanted to forget." He handed me a manuscript. "Here are the Sonnets."

Thrilled, I grabbed the spiral bound folder, opened it on my lap, and read the title page. "*Sonnets From The Portuguese.* Music by Eric Ries. Words by Elizabeth Barrett Browning."

The first page contained the printed poems. I read the first lines. *The face of all the world has changed, I think, since first I heard the footsteps of thy soul ...*

"That is so beautiful." Smiling excitedly, I looked up. He didn't smile back. I quickly turned the page to the first musical setting, studied the vocal line and the harmonic structure of the flute, voice, and piano parts. My stomach tightened. I turned to the next page, and the next. "What is this?" I wanted to cry. "He can't have written this."

Josh sighed and shook his head. "This is his response to every critic who's ever said he writes movie music."

"Has he deliberately gone out of his way to make every phrase ugly?"

"That's exactly what he did." He pointed out some complex harmonies. "It's brilliantly crafted: a mathematician's dream. The judges will sit there with open scores, nodding in approval, but the public won't want to hear it."

"Can I learn to sing it?" I turned more pages and started to panic. "I'd better start tonight."

"Not tonight!" he grabbed the manuscript away from me, tucked it safely under the daybed, put his hands on my shoulders, and looked deep into my eyes. "You have three months to learn it and we have much better things to do tonight." Before I could say another word, he pulled me into a long, lovely, deep-mouthed kiss. His hand slid over my breast, my body pulsed, and I was ready to pull my clothes off.

I kept my head long enough to push him back. "Josh, you sweet, darling man, we need to talk." He shut me up with another kiss and I pushed him back again, laughing. "Josh, stop a minute, please."

He sat back, panting. "What?"

"I absolutely adore you, but I'm lousy at relationships. I can never keep a boyfriend, and I need to keep you as my agent. If we start having an affair, and I do something horrible—"

"How horrible could it be?"

"I don't know, but if you get mad at me—"

"I'll still be your agent. I promise."

I sat back, relieved, but not quite believing him.

He pulled me close and kissed the top of my head. "Listen, Jenna, this is also scary for me. My track record with women isn't great. I've been engaged twice. Both times to sopranos." I sat up, surprised and he pulled me back down. "After the last one, I swore off sopranos forever. Then you showed up at that party. I was still at Juilliard when the first one got her claws into me. She was older than I was, beautiful, a great lyrico-spinto, and a Met Opera Finalist. We had rings picked out and everything. I got her an audition at Atlas, she was signed, and suddenly she wasn't ready for marriage."

My mouth dropped open. "That's awful."

"Yes, it was. However, she's still a great talent, and she's still signed with Atlas. She prefers working with one of my subagents, which is fine with me. We get her work, she makes us all money, and the professional relationship continues."

I swallowed. "Okay. How about the second one?"

"Well, that one was different. She really broke my heart." He rubbed his eyes. "About five years ago, I sat next to her at a Domingo master class. She'd studied music at some liberal arts college and had a pretty little voice. She might have gotten work in musical comedy, but never in opera or oratorio. She sang for me, I told her the truth and she took it beautifully. She talked about keeping her music store job until Mr. Right swept her off her feet. She said she wanted a family more than anything. By that time, I was twenty-six, ready to marry, buy a house and have kids. She was pretty, sweet, Jewish, a music lover ... It seemed perfect. We set a date and started picking names for our children. She kept up her vocal coaching, and asked me to hear her again. Of course I agreed. She was better, but not much. I told her so, and she went crazy. All this time, she'd played me along, told me what I wanted to hear, thinking that in the end, I'd turn her into some kind of diva." He sighed loud and long. "And that, my lovely Jenna, is my history with sopranos."

"How do you know I won't be as bad as they were?"

"First off, you're already a client. You'll be my lover later, not the other way around. And second, you're not pretending to be in love with me, even though I'd like you to lie, a little, just to make me feel good." I started laughing and he took both my hands. "You, beautiful girl, are the last thing I think about before I fall asleep, and the first ..."

My laugh bubbled out. "You call me, last thing before you fall asleep, so of course you think about me."

"... and the first thing I think about when I wake up in the morning. At the office, I count the hours until I'm going to see you, and if I'm not going to see you, I count it as a wasted day." He made a grand gesture, looking at the wall-to-wall memorabilia. "I may not be the last guy you think about at night, but ..." He braced himself. "If I can't make love to you, right now, I'm going to explode."

He kissed me again, and suddenly we were pulling off our clothes, kissing, clutching, and barely managing to climb the ladder to my loft bed. We didn't need any foreplay. I spread my legs and he pushed himself in, at the same time asking, "Are you on the pill?" and my groaning,

"Yes!"

We finished in seconds and lay next to each other, gasping. He turned his head and kissed me. Very gently, he nuzzled my neck and shoulders, moved down my front and lingered, running his tongue over my nipples. His fingers explored my very wet vagina, slowly rubbing my clitoris until I gasped and clamped my legs together. I moved down on him, teasing with my fingers and tongue. I lightly stroked his balls, sucked his penis, then lurched back, so he would come in my hand. He lay back exhausted and I giggled, pleased with my skill. I slid down the ladder, returned with a warm washcloth, and gently wiped his gooey genitals.

He sighed with pleasure. "My God, you know how to treat a guy."

I laughed, "We aim to please." He pulled up the covers. I slid underneath, rubbed next to his smooth skin, spooned into a cozy position, and fell asleep.

•

Beep, beep, beep. I was awake. Something was beeping. It was dark.

Josh sat up, and just missed crashing his head into the ceiling. "That's my beeper. Damn! I left it down there, somewhere."

I switched on the bedside, high-intensity light. He started down the ladder as I reached over the railing and switched on the bright piano light.

He rummaged through his clothes, found the beeper and turned it off. "I need to use the phone. Sorry. What time is it?"

I checked the clock and handed the phone down from the loft. "Four-thirty."

He shivered, punched a number and waited. "This is Josh Kendal. You just beeped me. Yeah, hi Melissa. Carol Gilligan? Yeah, Milan, that's right. Yeah, please." He sat at the telephone table, took the pen and note pad, listened and wrote numbers. "You're right. We know those numbers too well. Thanks, a million. Good night."

Half asleep, I leaned over the railing. "What's wrong?"

"A client, flute player in Milan. The bastard contractor promised her a really nice hotel, then put her in a house full of bugs. He's also saying she has to do extra concerts for no extra money. She called my service, hysterical." He sighed and rubbed his eyes. "I'm sorry, but I've got to deal with this now. I'll pay for the calls, of course." He was really shivering.

"No problem. You're freezing. My robe's on the bathroom door."

"Thanks." He wrapped himself in pale green velour. It was too small and looked funny, but at least it was warm. "Go back to sleep. This may take a while."

"No problem." I buried my head under the covers.

Dozing intermittently, I heard his terrible Italian, as he tried to deal with oversees telephone operators. Next he spoke English, commiserating with the client. Next he spoke Italian.

I fell asleep. When I woke again, pale light streamed through the blinds. Josh was still on the phone. He sounded really angry and I guessed he finally got through to the contractor. At first he made polite requests. When that didn't work, he made demands and threatened legal action. When that didn't work, he threatened to withdraw his star clients. Now I was awake. This sounded like a really big deal. I sat up, listening hard. His threat seemed to work. He said, "Okay. If everything isn't fixed in four hours, you'll hear from me again." There was silence, then, "Goodbye, Salvatore. I don't ever want a client treated like this." He hung up and sat back exhausted. I leaned over the loft railing and he sighed, "What a horrible night."

"Does this happen often?"

"No. But, it does happen. Usually I can handle problems during business hours. I ruined your night. I'm so sorry."

"Don't worry about me. The sex was great and I slept through most of the rest of it."

He started chuckling and his laugh grew into an exhausted guffaw. I was relieved to see him relax. "Did you mean what you told him, about pulling your clients?"

He shuddered. "Pray God he never calls my bluff on that one. The clients could sue me. Salvatore's a greedy bastard, but he's also a star worshipper. He lives to be seen with celebrities and won't risk losing that."

I checked the clock. "It just turned seven. Can you come back up for a cuddle?"

He smiled. "A quick one. Then I've got to go home and clean up. I have an important meeting at 10:00."

That morning, I started learning Eric's three sonnets. More than a year ago, they were among three-hundred chamber pieces anonymously submitted to an international screening committee. Three months after that, fifty semifinalists were selected, and three months after that, fifteen finalists were invited to perform their composition live, in Paris.

Eric didn't need this competition. He was already the darling of mainstream classical music audiences. New commissions, royalties, and music sales insured him a very comfortable income. He had enough conducting and teaching engagements to keep him busy for years. The competition could generate international press coverage, and possibly embarrass him. It could also, finally, win him approval from that hard-core, snotty, nose-in-the-air, academic music world he so desperately wanted to please, and join.

This was not a premier where the audience just listens to the music. This was a competition. The judges would read the music, note for note, while I sang it. Any slight mistake would be heard and seen, points taken off, and Eric faulted for writing something unsingable. The music was difficult, but well written. I determined to sing well, boost my fledgling career, win Eric the respect he deserved, and earn his undying affection, all at the same time.

A mug of strong coffee by my side, I sat at my spinet piano and read the words of all three sonnets, over and over. Elizabeth Barrett Browning's poems were passionately romantic and otherworldly. My bizarre addiction to Eric was otherworldly. I understood her completely.

I played the rhythms Eric had written for the first words: *The face of all the world has changed, I think, since first I heard the footsteps of thy soul ...*

The rhythm was four-four time, not in a natural speech pattern, but singable. So far, so good. I played the pitches assigned to the words and was stunned to see a twelve-tone row. This first line was unaccompanied, and since no tone was repeated until all twelve notes in the scale were sung, I had no clue where the melody would go next. I played the phrase over several times, teaching it to my ears, before trying it with my voice. My ears rejected the ugly, disjointed leaps, but I knew that enough repetitions, over enough days, would let it settle in. At least it was in a comfortable range, not too high or too low. Eric knew the mechanics of the soprano voice.

On the next downbeat, the piano and flute entered together, playing two five-four measures. I joined them with the next lyric.

"Move still, oh, still beside me ..."

My entrance was in three-four, against their five-four. That was tricky, but I could learn it. I moved down the page, saw my pencil marks darken the paper, and stopped. I needed a clean copy to mark during rehearsals with Eric, so I took the manuscript around the corner to a photocopy shop and had the entire thing duplicated.

Over the next couple of days, I marked the photocopy with shorthand for every single two note interval on the entire twenty-eight pages. Wishing God had given me perfect pitch so I could find those tones without so much trouble, I worked every day for the next month, just learning the notes. Once I found a starting pitch, I was able to sing the rest of the phrase. My worry was long stretches where the piano and flute played without me. I would have to come back in on a specific pitch, and it was easy when my exact note was played before my entrance. I circled that note on the piano or flute part, drew an arrow to my note, and prayed Susie or Amy would play it accurately. Often, my note was not played. Then I had to use a related note from Susie or Amy and write myself a cue, like: m2↑ (minor second up), or P4↓ (perfect fourth down).

By the middle of February, I knew Eric's sonnets by heart and looked forward to the Paris competition. I had only been to Europe once, when I was eight, on a whirlwind trip with my mother. Eric considered Paris home.

Susie spent a lot of summers there and spoke French fluently. We wrote often and she was even more excited than I was. After four years at Harvard playing synthesizers or pianos accompanied by prerecorded audio tapes, she missed Amy and me and performing acoustic music.

I was amused when she took over, stage managing from her Boston home. She telephoned me in New York, Amy in Salzburg, Eric wherever he was in the world, and reported it all back to Josh at Atlas Artists. It must have cost her a fortune. Josh made our travel plans, and a rehearsal schedule for four days in Eric's cabin. Susie mailed detailed lists of what we needed to pack. Rehearsing

Eric's music on a secluded island in the Canadian woods sounded like paradise.

The night before I left, Josh and I sat in a small Chinese restaurant, sipping steaming bowls of curried noodle soup. He chewed a spoonful of overlong noodles. "Maybe I'm just being an alarmist. I hope so. But with the entire world to practice in, I can't justify Eric locking you girls away like that. Of course, Halifax is an international airport. He won't have to put you up in hotels, which he will in Paris. He can cook in the cabin, so feeding you will be cheap. God knows there won't be any distractions. He doesn't even have a telephone. You have to meet somewhere, but it's hardly a central location. Flying Amy all the way to Nova Scotia, when she's only a couple of hours from Paris, seems nuts."

He made sense, but nothing sounded really bad. I sipped my spicy soup and waited for him to come up with more negatives.

"Eric can be the best guy in the world, but he can also be a controlling bastard. Once you girls are on that island, you're stuck. You won't be able to leave. There's just the one dinky little boat, with an outboard motor. He has a short-wave radio. Susie can probably operate it, but you and Amy can't. Even so, you can't be sure anyone will be tuned in if you need them." He shook his head and finished his soup in silence.

I wound some noodles around my fork. "Thanks for caring so much."

He looked up, surprised. "Of course I care. You're the most important thing in my life. I want to keep you safe."

My throat tightened. No one had ever been that nice to me, especially a man.

"Don't you believe me?"

"I want to. You're so sweet. It's just ... Well, I'm not used to being treated this well."

He reached across the table, and squeezed my hand. "Get used to it. You deserve to be treated well." He sat back and shook his head. "I don't want to scare you with this cabin thing. Maybe it's just me. Did I ever tell you Phil Shapiro sent me up there to get a manuscript?"

"You told me it happened, but no details."

When he sat back and crossed his arms, I knew it would be a good story. "Well, there was this overdue ballet commission. It was about three years ago. Colette, Eric's longtime girlfriend, was still lead dancer at the Paris Opera. This ballet was composed for her. Eric spent weeks in his cabin composing and mailing sections to the ballet conductor for approval. All the usual stuff. When it was finally finished and ready to go to the copyist for the orchestra parts, Colette told him she'd had a fight with the ballet master and he was giving the ballet to another dancer. Eric flew into a rage and refused to send the manuscript, but Phil had already accepted partial payment and was liable if the commission was late. Eric stayed buried in the cabin on that island without a telephone. We called the general store on the mainland and left messages. The store owner swore he passed the messages on, but Eric never called back. It was the middle of winter.

"We were really busy at work, and Phil ordered me to go and get that manuscript. I was used to doing what I was told, but that was crazy. So, a couple of days later I was on a flight to Halifax. From there, I took an ancient bus to this dinky town, Lower Wood Harbour, and met the general store owner. Right on cue, Eric's outboard putted up to the shore. He'd gotten all the messages, knew when I was coming, smiled and waved like I was a long-lost relative.

"I needed to get back to New York and expected him to put the manuscript in my hand. When he said he'd left it back at the cabin, I wanted to kill him. I got in the boat, we sailed to the cabin, and he got settled in for the night. I couldn't get off the stupid island. I felt trapped like a rat in a cage. The cabin is great, roomy but rustic, and there isn't a lot of hot water. I hope none of you girls are planning on washing your hair. I spent the night, and once I calmed down, we had a really nice visit. The next day I took that damn manuscript and flew back to New York."

I sipped my soup, shrugged and smiled. "Well, since I'm not going there mad, it should be all right. Susie, Amy, and I lived in close quarters for four years. We'll manage for another four days." I thought it was a cute line, but he didn't smile.

"That'll be just the beginning. From there you'll fly to Paris. You'll have one day to get over jet-lag, then you'll perform. It'll be tough, physically and emotionally."

I appreciated his concern, but thought he was going way overboard. "Look Josh, I know the music. I trust Susie and Amy.

I'm really not worried."

"Well I am. I trust the girls, but I don't trust Eric. He's up to something. I wish I knew what. Jen, listen to me." He waited for me to stop eating and look at him. "Whatever happens, please remember: this whole thing will be over in a week and a half. If you have fun, great! I'll be delighted. If it's not fun, it won't last forever. In a few days you'll be back here with me, and I'll take care of you." He was so sweet, I wanted to cry.

I leaned across the table, grabbed him by the lapels, and kissed him.

7.
Halifax, Nova Scotia: March 1978
Allegro Vivace

I followed Susie's instructions, and waited by a set of well worn, metal lockers to the left of the Air Canada check-in counter at Halifax airport. I liked to dress up when I traveled, but today, again per Susie's orders, I wore old jeans, a warm sweater, snow boots, and carried my warmest down coat. It was pleasantly cool in New York, but Susie warned me that the Canadian woods would be freezing. Her flight from Boston had supposedly arrived an hour before mine, and Amy's flight from Salzburg a half-hour before hers, so I wondered why they weren't waiting to meet me. Ready to disobey her orders, abandon my post, and check out the coffee shop, I saw two young women walking toward me, carrying large suitcases. We had exchanged performance tapes and photos, but I was amazed to see how much they had changed.

I expected Susie to still be the neurotic, teenage cover-girl who out-played and out-screwed everyone on campus. When a poised young woman walked toward me, wearing no makeup, with flowing dark hair combed over her shoulders, I couldn't believe it. Here was Dr. Susannah Ries, the recipient of prestigious grants and awards. Still slim and beautiful, she was dressed in worn, loose-fitting jeans, boots, and an oversized sweater. When she saw me and smiled, I finally recognized something of my college buddy.

Amy looked half asleep, but prettier than I could have imagined. The once sloppy hippy now wore stylish jeans and a denim jacket that actually fit. Her blond hair was cropped into an adorable cap of short golden curls framing her face. Worn out after sixteen hours of travel, she forced a weary smile and fell into my arms for a long hug.

I gave Susie a hug, and we congratulated each other on looking gorgeous.

Susie warned us to pack small overnight bags to take to the cabin, and leave our dress-up Paris clothes in separate suitcases to be left at the airport. Susie opened her mouth and I felt like we were back at school. "Let's see these dresses. If they clash, I'll kill myself!" Amy and I shared a smile while obeying Susie's command. We opened our suitcases, pulled out our concert gowns, and compared the varying shades of blue. Susie held her cobalt blue gown against Amy's sapphire blue gown, and the two of those against my pale blue gown. Susie sighed with relief. "Yes! This is great. We'll be gorgeous. Paris, here we come." We re-packed our suitcases, lifted them into yellow metal lockers, and pocketed the keys.

We found the bus to Lower Wood Harbour. Cloying smells of metal and exhaust fumes made me gag. I sat next to one of the few cracked windows, breathing the freezing air, trying not to throw up. I never did well on buses and this one was ancient. Most of the windows were taped shut and the torn seats had no shock absorbers. The bus half-filled with other travelers, and we started on our bumpy way. Six stops and an hour later, we three girls were alone with the driver. Amy stretched across the long back seat, dozing fitfully. My motion sickness subsided as miles of thick, snowy woods flew by. Susie reminisced about visiting here as a child. I half listened.

My thoughts bounced between Eric and Josh. I knew the sonnets by heart, sang them well, and looked forward to showing off for Eric. The rehearsals would be great, but would anything else happen? Did I really want anything to happen? If anything did happen, what might it do to Josh? He was the best person I had ever known and the first boyfriend who really cared about me. He was brilliant and sweet, and I adored his company. But I did not love him. Not the way I loved Eric.

The scenery changed from dense woods to rocky coastline, and I felt the powerful beauty of white foam waves crashing against the rocky shore. Eric loved it here. I wanted him to love me. After so many years, it seemed that something real must finally happen between us. A wind gust hurled white powdery snow past the window. Susie sat quietly and Amy slept. I laughed at my fantasy.

I would never be alone with Eric. Nothing was going to happen. Nothing but music, and that was why we were here.

The bus turned a sharp corner, drove down a steep hill, and stopped just before the water line. A faded wooden sign was nailed onto a telephone pole: *Welcome To Lower Wood Harbour.*

"Lower Wood Harbour. Last stop!" The bus driver opened the door and jumped out.

Quickly as I could, I took my bag and coat and climbed down the bus steps. Susie and Amy followed. Crisp, fresh air startled me awake as I shivered, inhaled deeply, and struggled to pull on my coat. I fumbled, then found the zipper and pulled it closed.

On our left was the ocean, sparkling brightly in the late afternoon sun. Farther out to sea was a dotting of small islands. To the right were storefronts that could have been part of a Western movie set. There was a pizza parlor, a general store, a diner, and finally, a movie house showing *Casablanca.* That movie always made me cry. The door to the general store opened and a bearded man dressed like a lumberjack ambled toward us. He looked slightly threatening and I backed away.

Susie ran to him, lunging into his arms. "Uncle Hal. I can't believe it."

He laughed and effortlessly swung her around. "Look at little Susie. Good gracious. You're a grown woman. It's not fair, your stayin' away all these years."

"Well, you could come out of the woods once in a while." She laughed, held on tight, and enjoyed the ride.

He put her down, and looked over his shoulder as another lumberjack came out of the store. "What for?" He pointed to the other man. "Eric here's already had all the city girls. Oh, thanks for sending that magazine. You're going to be a bigger star than he is."

"Damn right, I will!" They laughed again.

I stared at Eric. Windblown, red-cheeked and smiling, he looked more relaxed than I had ever seen him. He also looked thirty-years-old. "Thank God you all made it." He hurried over.

Amy dragged herself over and collapsed in his arms. "Are we finally here? It feels like I left Salzburg a month ago."

He held her tight. "We're almost here. We just have to get over … there." He pointed across a short span water, to a small island. It looked like a perfect Christmas card photo. Snowy trees surrounded a log cabin and a thin stream of smoke rose from the chimney. "If there's anything you girls need, get it now. And remember, there's no telephone in the cabin, so this is your last chance for four days."

Amy and Susie went into the general store. I stayed, looking at a dinky outboard motorboat tossing all too gaily in the gentle waves. I gave him a shy hug. "What happens if there's an emergency?"

Hal's good-natured voice boomed, "He radios me. I'm Hal Ries, this bum's older brother."

Eric laughed as I shook Hal's hand. "I'm Jenna Adams. It's good to meet you."

Hal gave Eric a playful sock in the arm. "I shouldn't call this guy a bum." He socked Eric again. Eric socked back, and the two roughhoused like a couple of bad kids. Hal bent Eric over, squeezing his head in a hammer-lock. "He ran away and got himself an education. Now he thinks he's better than the rest of us." Eric thrashed back and forth, trying to break free. I laughed in sympathy. Finally, Eric twisted his shoulders, pulled loose and sent Hal staggering. Both brothers stumbled, breathless, laughing and panting. Hal pointed an accusing finger. "We all play music. Ever heard Eric play country fiddle?"

My mouth dropped open. "No, but I love his *Violin Concerto.*" It never occurred to me that Eric even had siblings, let alone grew up playing country music.

Eric caught his breath and looked up. The sun was sinking. "We've got to get across the water. Jenna, call Josh. He's at the office. I just spoke to him."

"It's okay. He saw me off this morning. He knows there's no phone at the—"

"Call him. The guy's nuts about you, and he's worried. You won't have another chance."

I shrugged, then followed the other girls into the general store. I picked up the pay phone, reversed the charges, and I found Josh in his office on a conference call. He was pleased I phoned, and interrupted his other call just long enough to wish me luck. I promised to phone from Paris and hung up.

A half-hour later, I sat in the narrow front seat of the tiny motorboat, shivering and holding on for dear life. In the wider, middle seat, Amy wearily leaned against Eric's shoulder. Susie steered from the back. Like a pro, she navigated the delicate craft through icy water. After a few minutes of open sea, she pulled up to a small wooden dock, floating on large metal barrels. The boat bounced lightly against broken car tires nailed to the sides as bumpers. I held on tight as Eric climbed out, took a rope from the front, and tied the boat to a sturdy metal mooring.

Afraid to stand up, I held tight to my overnight bag, grabbed Eric's hand, stepped onto the wobbly dock, and shuffled gratefully toward solid land. Susie leapt onto the dock and sloshed past me to the picture-perfect log cabin.

The porch was covered with groceries and I wondered how many trips it had taken Eric to get them all across the water. We cleaned the snow from our boots and went inside. Susie hung her coat and purse on one of several hooks by the door and chose a pair of soft slippers from a box on the floor. Amy and I followed suit. Eric hung up his coat, kicked off his boots, and made a beeline to the wide fireplace. Within seconds, the logs burst into crackling flames and warmth flooded the single large room.

Josh was right. The cabin was great. To my left, in front of the fireplace, was a well-worn, overstuffed sofa, piles of comfortable-looking floor cushions, and sheepskin rugs. To my right, tucked into the corner, were a small cooking stove, long cutting-board work area, and dining table. The ceiling was slanted and very high. Twilight shone through a skylight in the roof, and large windows opened on all four sides. A baby-grand piano stood at the foot of a wooden staircase, leading to sleeping lofts. A copy of Eric's sonnets sat on the piano's music stand. Under the stairs was the bathroom. Susie and Josh both warned that hot water was rationed, and I was amused to see a sign-up sheet posted, for two morning and two evening showers. Eric's name was written in one of the morning slots. I wrote my name next to his.

Susie and Amy climbed upstairs. I took my bag and followed. There were two attic bedrooms. The smaller one, on the right, had a double-bed mattress on the floor. Eric's clothes hung on wall hooks. The larger guest room loft was on the left. Four narrow mattresses lay on the floorboards. I took one step inside, then ducked under the sloping roof. Susie sorted through piles of sheets, pillows, and blankets. Amy scooped up a pile of bed linen, dropped it onto a mattress, and fell asleep. Susie covered her with a blanket.

A light metal clang sounded from downstairs and I remembered that Eric was alone. Seizing the opportunity, I left my bag, hurried out, and stopped half-way down the stairs.

Eric looked perfectly content, standing over the stove, whistling to himself. He lifted a large wok over the high flame, sautéed garlic and onions, then dropped in large chunks of raw fish. He stirred the fish, lowered the heat, and turned to piles of vegetables spread across the work table. I was useless in the kitchen, but assumed that Eric was expert at everything. When he swiftly and precisely chopped the pile of crisp vegetables, I watched his musician's hands and wasn't surprised at their skill.

I sighed happily. "That smells wonderful."

He smiled as I slid downstairs and stood close to him. His hair smelled of wood smoke and his skin of musky cologne. Even chopping vegetables, he was the sexiest man I had ever known.

"Local fish. I've tried making this in other places, but the fish just aren't the same. Was Josh in?"

I nodded.

"I didn't know I'd become a matchmaker."

My eyes popped open. I did not want to talk about Josh. "I like Josh a lot, but it's kind of early to call us a match."

He looked surprised. "Really? He thinks you're a hot item."

The sensual food aromas and Eric's standing unbearably close were just too much. I heard myself say, "Sometimes, we make love and I think of you."

The knife slipped, and dropped to the table. He showed no emotion as he checked his finger. There was no blood. "Well, he wouldn't be too pleased to hear that." He finished chopping the vegetables.

Not sure if he found me disgusting or alluring, I took a chance. "I think of you a lot. I can't help it."

He watched me for a moment, then added the vegetables to the wok.

I stood close enough to whisper. "Eight years ago, at Newell Conservatory, you propositioned me."

A slight smile spread his lips. "Did I really? Well, well, naughty me."

My heart raced. "I turned you down. I've regretted it ever since."

He bit back a laugh, added seasoning to the wok, and sampled a piece of fish. "In that case, we'll have to make up for lost time." He watched the upstairs landing while nuzzling my ear. I turned my face and we kissed. His beard and mustache brushed softly against my lips. His tongue tasted sweet, and my whole body cramped deliciously. He seemed to enjoy me as much. "Hm. I wish we could go somewhere right now. But, there's nowhere to go. Of course, 'We'll always have Paris.'"

I laughed at his reference to *Casablanca* when a noise from upstairs made us spring apart.

Susie stood at the top of the stairs. I don't know if she saw us kissing, but she was scowling. "Dad, where are those small duvets?"

"In the cellar. Sorry, I meant to bring them up. We'll get them after dinner. Come eat, before these vegetables turn to mush."

"Amy's asleep. She can eat mush later." She started down the stairs, glanced inside the open piano lid and stopped. "What the fuck?" She looked like she'd seen a murder. "You prepared the piano? You didn't say anything about a prepared piano."

I raced to look under the lid. Thin strips of fiberglass were strung through some of the lower wires. I tried a few keys. Some notes sounded normal, others were toneless thuds. Frightened tears stung my eyes. "I need that D, Eric." I pounded the toneless low key, praying it would change to a recognizable D. "On four different entrances, that's the only D to get my pitch."

Susie's body was rigid. "Your harmonies are weird enough without changing the basic sound of the instrument. No one's preparing pianos anymore. It was a stupid fad. It lasted a few years and went out of style."

Eric calmly turned off the stove. "The fiberglass makes a good effect. You'll see."

Susie sat on the piano bench and played. The already atonal harmonies were disrupted by metallic thuds. "You tuned it high."

He nodded. "A: 445. Better get used to French tuning now."

"You're right." Susie played hard, then jerked her hands off the keys, screaming, "Shit! You ruined the fucking action! Do you want me to rip a tendon? This is why I quit performing. I only came back as a favor to you, and now you pull this?" She violently massaged her fingers.

"What's going on?" Amy's sleepy voice made us all turn around. She stood, yawning at the top of the stairs.

Susie held up her cramped hand. "He prepared the fucking piano!"

Eric shrugged disarmingly. "It was a last minute idea."

"Bullshit! You planned it all along, but knew I'd turn you down if you told me. I've been practicing your stinking pieces for two months."

"Then, for God's sake, relax. Let's eat. After dinner, you can try the piano, slowly and sanely. You'll get used to the action in a couple of minutes. I've only altered four notes."

I blinked back tears. "But Eric, you and Susie have perfect pitch. I don't. I need that D!"

Calmly setting out dinner plates, he manufactured his most consoling smile. "We'll find your pitches another way. It'll be fine."

I stared at the piano. It had suddenly become a monster. Josh was right. Eric had definitely been up to something.

Grave Pesante Mesto Sforzando

The next morning, rehearsal was horrible. We expected a difficult read-through, but nothing like this. Susie hated the prepared piano, cursed under her breath, but persevered. Amy's eyes and ears were glued to her music. Her whole body moved in rhythm with her supple fingers. I felt lost. Working with a conventional piano, I found tricky but adequate tonal cues for my entrances. Now, many of those cues were gone. Drowning in a sea of murky sounds, I listened for a pitch, heard a toneless thud, guessed at my pitch, and bravely sang. Since I usually guessed wrong, we had to stop and start over.

After a welcome lunch break, Susie and Amy wrapped up and took a walk. Eric disappeared upstairs. I stayed at the piano, struggling to find my cues. Snow fell, first gently, then hard, driving Amy and Susie back into the cabin. The thick white flakes looked beautiful, but soon collected on the window sills, giving me the impression that we were trapped inside. When Eric called us back to rehearsal, I remembered Josh's warning that we would be like "rats in a cage."

By mid-afternoon, things should have gotten easier. We

managed to plow through all three sonnets once, so the second time through should have been better. It wasn't.

Instrumentalists can play full-out for hours, but singers tire quickly. I tried to save my voice, sing softly, breathe carefully, and pace myself. Frustrated and guilty that I slowed the others down, my neck muscles tensed. My voice felt tired, my throat felt sore, and I wished I could take a break.

All day, Amy listened to Eric's corrections without speaking a word. At 4:00 in the afternoon, her patience wore out. "Eric, if these duplets were triplets—"

"They are duplets!" Eyes straight ahead, fingers clenching the back of the piano, Eric locked his jaw.

Tired and cross, Amy forced her voice to stay low. "I know. And, they're very interesting on paper. But if we can't play them—"

"You have three more days. You'll play them. Jenna!"

I looked up, guiltily.

"You were a half-tone sharp, again."

"I can't find the pitch." My voice was a pitiful wail. "When I learned the pieces, I had a D right before that entrance. Now ..."

Furious, Eric pushed me away from my music stand, found the place in my score, and read backward, a page and a half. "Here!" Pointing triumphantly, he took a pencil and circled a note. "Amy's got this long E flat. Just keep it in your mind and go down a half-step."

"I've been doing that, but there's too much music in between."

"Just concentrate. Damn it!" He walked away, rubbing his aching head.

I frantically studied my music. My throat was seriously constricted and I was sure everyone heard the strain in my voice.

By 5:30, we were all exhausted and annoyed. Eric called it a day. Susie and Amy took turns showering, and we all helped with supper. After a meal in veritable silence, Amy and Susie found solitary corners and books to read. I headed back to the piano, but Eric ordered me to "give it a rest" and "sleep on it." He had a new recording of Schönberg's *Gurrelieder*, and soon the small wooden cabin resonated with lush, sensual orchestral tones. I loved singing Schönberg's soaring atonal melody lines. After an entire day of Eric's music, Schönberg sounded as romantic as Puccini.

By 3:00 the next afternoon, the picturesque living room had

become a torture chamber. Brilliant sunlight flooded through the cabin windows, cruelly mocking the collective misery inside. Susie perched on the edge of her piano bench like a sprinter waiting for the starting pistol. Shoulders raised, eyes glued to the page, she was tight as a rubber band.

Amy gracefully raised her flute to and from her lips. Calm but unhappy, she concentrated on her music. I stood in the crook of the piano, leaned on a metal music stand, frantically beat time, forced my ears to search for nonexistent piano cues, and sang as accurately as I could. I prided myself on being a good actress, always presenting the story in the lyrics. Now I sang like a machine, with no thought to the meaning of the words.

Little by little, we began finding sense within the multitude of notes. It was hard. It was measure by measure, but it was finally happening. Eric stood to the side, focused, scowling, but letting small mistakes go by.

I sang, "Say over again, and yet once over again, that thou dost love ..."

"Shit! Fucking hell!" Susie leapt from the piano, holding her cramped left hand. "The damn tendon snapped! Shit!"

Amy put down her flute. "Is there any ice?"

"I'll get some snow." Eric grabbed a plastic bowl and raced out the door.

Amy put her arm around Susie and gently moved her onto the sofa. "You're okay, Sue. It's just cramped. This has happened before—lots of times. You're more scared than hurt. Just breathe."

Eric returned with a bowl of snow, eased Susie's fingers into the bowl, and piled snow over her entire hand. He watched her for a moment then stood up. "Jenna, Amy, let's work on your cadenza."

Concerned for Susie, we hesitated, then obeyed, and moved back to our music stands. We found the page and Amy gave me a pitch.

Eric beat time. "One - two - three - four - five. One - two - three. One - two - three - four - five."

Amy started and I followed, singing, "Speak once more ... Thou ..."

We lost the rhythm and stopped.

Eric's jaw tensed. "Again! One - two - three - four - five. One - two - three. One - two - three - four - five."

We started again, got lost again, and stopped, shaking our heads.

Eric slammed his hand on the piano. "Christ Almighty, Jenna. What the hell is the matter with you?"

The plastic bowl flew across the room. Melting snow splattered over the walls and furniture. Susie screamed, "It's not her fault! It's yours. You used to write movie music, but at least people could sing it. Now, you're trying to be John Cage and you've fucked up. We're going to lose this competition, big time, if we even get there. Shit! I don't care if—"

"Shut up, everyone." Amy put down her flute, grabbed her coat, crammed her feet into her boots, and fled the cabin, slamming the door behind her. Eric stomped up to his room and slammed his door. I grabbed a box of Kleenex, sat by the fire, and silently sobbed. Susie gently stretched and massaged her cramped fingers. It was deathly quiet.

I heard Eric's door open. He stood on the landing, watching me. Totally humiliated, I blew my nose and swallowed my tears. Susie looked from Eric to me, and back to Eric. Strangely calm, she sauntered to the door. "I'm taking Amy for pizza and a movie. I don't care what's playing. We won't be back till late — very late."

Eric rolled his eyes. "Don't be an ass. If you want to..."

Susie was out the door in a flash. I stared after her, then at Eric, on the stairs shaking his head. He started back up, changed his mind, and plodded down to a kitchen cupboard. He found a bottle of red wine and two glasses, and set them on the table. "I think this calls for a drink."

The outboard motor sounded and we both looked up. The metallic rattle softened as the boat sailed away.

I felt totally ashamed, wanted to hide, and started toward the stairs. "I'm sorry, Eric. So terribly sorry. I'm ruining your music. I'm just not good enough. I thought I was, but I'm—"

"No, Jenna. No, no, no." He hurried over, took me in his arms, and held me as I cried against his shoulder. "I'm the one who's sorry for pushing so hard. You're good enough to sing anything. You have a marvelous ear. All three of you are wonderful musicians—as good as any, anywhere. I've just been pushing the envelope, testing, learning how complex music can be and still be playable. If you three can't play this, no one can."

"But, if I had perfect pitch—"

He laughed sadly. "If I write a piece that can only be sung by sopranos with perfect pitch, it'll have very few performances." He was being kind, but I still felt miserably inadequate.

"What can I do? I'm already doing my best, and—"

"I know you are. Now it's time for me to do mine." He went to the piano and carefully pulled out the fiberglass strips. He played the four notes and they sounded off-key. A tuning kit sat under the piano. He found the tuning hammer, and tightened the wires while playing the keys. Once they were in tune, he sat on the piano bench, opened Susie's music, and changed some notes. "Amy wants triplets, Amy gets triplets. Give me the other scores." Afraid he would change his mind, I held my breath and raced to bring him the other manuscript so he could mark the same corrections on all of them.

For the next hour, Eric edited his precious music. Afraid to make a sound, I picked up the plastic bowl of melted snow, and wiped wet patches off the floor and walls. Eric concentrated, swallowed his pride, and exchanged mathematical brilliance for playable notes. After marking the last change, he piled the scores beside the music stand, and sat back, staring at the piano keys. He looked calm and resolved.

I nearly cried with relief. "Oh, thank you. Thank you." I threw my arms around his neck. He responded with a weak smile and I felt like a fool. I turned away and saw the unopened bottle. "Shall I open the wine?"

"Not yet." He stretched his weary fingers, leaned into the keys, and played a slow, sensual Chopin *Nocturne*. His playing was technically perfect, and terribly sad. I stood mesmerized, afraid of breathing too loud. He ended the piece with heartbreaking simplicity, sat perfectly still, then stood, walked to the fireplace, and removed the screen. Carefully stirring the dying embers, he positioned a large log on top of them, and watched as bright-yellow flames licked the wood. Delicious heat radiated as he moved silently around the room, turning off the lights.

He took his time, piling sheepskin rugs and pillows on the floor in front of the sofa. I smiled, thinking it looked like a nest. Suddenly, I prayed the nest was for me. As if reading my mind, he took my hand, led me to the fire, stroked my hair, pulled me close and kissed me. His soft beard tickled my lips and our tongues explored, hungry for each other. His fingers slid under my sweater, circling my breasts, squeezing my nipples. As they hardened, my whole body tensed. My legs pulled together, but he forced his knee between, unzipped my jeans, pulled down my panties, and slid his fingers up inside me. Already wet and eager, totally losing control, I gasped with pleasure.

Moments later, we lay naked on the soft wool. Gently moving over me, he kissed my mouth, my throat, then my nipples, pulling and caressing with his lips and tongue. His fingers slid between my legs, exploring and rubbing, until my whole body was stiff, and fantastically alive. I writhed deep into the wool, aching to climax. He stretched it, longer and longer. His tongue explored every inch of me, finally lingering on my clitoris, pulsing and swollen.

He whispered, "Are you on the pill?" I nodded and he drove into me, hard. It hurt and I gasped. He looked surprised, gently eased himself out, and back in again. We found our rhythm. Slow and smooth, we moaned, clutching each other, devouring each other's mouths. My head pounded and I thought my insides would burst. He struggled to stay inside, thrusting again and again. I was like a tight glove clutching him, crushing him. He pushed deeper and deeper. In a single move, we gripped each other, stifled screams, then collapsed, still tight in each other's arms.

Released tension sent tears streaming down my cheeks.

He kissed them away. "My God, you're wonderful. Absolutely luscious." After resting a few minutes, catching his breath, he ran one finger around my breasts, down my stomach, and between my legs. His simple touch was painful and I jerked away.

"No more. Sorry. Not just now ... Later."

He smiled triumphantly, rolled onto his back, stretched his arms, then casually folded them, resting his head in the palms of his hands. His eyes closed.

Something in that smile made me uneasy. He looked too comfortable, too detached. Was this just a routine event? Something he had done before, many, many times before? I banished the thought and told myself that I was indeed "wonderful" and "luscious." He was special to me, so I had to be special to him. Didn't I? After all these years, we finally made love. It was thrilling—the final consummation of my one true love. I snuggled close, giggling,

"Wouldn't the girls be surprised if they came back, now?"

He laughed and shook his head. "No, they wouldn't be surprised. Susie wanted rewrites, and Amy wanted peace. They got what they wanted. We got this. Everyone's happy." He leaned up on one elbow, laughed at my shocked expression, and kissed my forehead. "Dear, little Jenna. Do you still talk to my picture?"

I caught my breath. "You remembered that?"

He chuckled softly, running his finger down my nose. "All those letters you wrote me, for all those years? How could I possibly forget?"

Banishing unpleasant thoughts, I rolled over and let myself sink back against his smooth warm skin. I inhaled his deliciously musky scent, and tried to forget everything else. We were finally together. It had actually happened and nothing else mattered ... at least for tonight.

Ritenuto: Poco a Poco Accelerando

Susie was good to her word. She kept Amy in town until midnight. When they got back to the cabin, I was tucked into my narrow mattress, showered and smelling of nothing but soap. I pretended to be asleep, but listened as they crept around downstairs, studied the edited manuscripts and stifled elated giggles.

The next morning, we were all cautiously friendly. No one mentioned the switch in shower schedules, but Susie and Amy took the morning slots. Eric scrambled deliciously fluffy eggs while I made toast and coffee. Susie and Amy laughed about spending the evening in lumpy theatre seats, watching three hours of *Dr. Zhivago* on a small screen. They didn't ask how Eric and I spent the evening.

When the dishes were done, Susie, Amy, and I warmed up and took our places around the piano. The first read-through was overly careful, but amazingly accurate. We played all three sonnets, straight through, without stopping. Amy calmly flew through passages she had struggled with the day before. Susie's supple fingers were still stretched, but finally able to control the multitude of keys. Elated with Eric's rewrites and the return of her conventional piano, she sent me a crooked smile. I wasn't sure what she was thinking, but assumed her smile was friendly.

My entrance cues were clear and consistent. Finally able to find my notes and sing the correct pitches, my concentration shifted to Elizabeth Barrett Browning's words. She was a repressed, middle-aged Victorian spinster, discovering romantic love for the first time. A bedridden invalid, seemingly doomed to live and die in her father's house, she was still able to write poetry and attract famous poet Robert Browning. After a courtship of letters, they married and moved to Italy. Finally, I was able to personalize her sweet, sensual love poems. I pictured Eric in my mind, and sang her words to him.

Eric barely breathed through the entire read-through. He sat perfectly still, listened with an ultra-critical ear, looked gloomy, but resolved. He sacrificed bizarre, jarring effects he had been proud of, but gained a lush bittersweetness that I loved. Still very different from anything he had written before, the sonnets now echoed older, popular compositions by Eric Ries.

We girls finished, glanced nervously at each other, and waited for Eric's critique. After a moment's unsmiling silence, he nodded. "Again, please." We quickly turned back our pages. Eric held up his stopwatch. He had timed the pieces on his own, but never with a live ensemble, and needed to be sure they were within competition boundaries of ten to seventeen minutes. He conducted the musical entrance, and clicked the starter on the downbeat.

Susie, Amy, and I soared through all three sonnets with ease and joy, reaching the final lyric, "Say thou dost love me, love me, love me—toll the silver iterance! Only minding, Dear, to love me also in silence, with thy soul." We ended perfectly in tune. Going from dissonant seconds into consonant triads, then parallel fourths, fifths, and finally octaves, we held our last pure tone. I watched for Susie's cue, sang the "l" of "soul" and we all faded into silence.

Eric clicked the stopwatch. "Fourteen minutes. Perfect. Performance adrenaline will push you, so you'll probably be down to thirteen. You may stretch some places. Either way ..." He looked very pleased. "That was beautiful."

I squealed with happy relief. Amy sighed loudly, smiled, and put down her flute. Susie applauded. "Great rewrites. Way to go, Jenna." I looked startled, as Eric sent his daughter a warning look. Reading each other's sexual innuendoes, they broke out laughing. Amy rolled her eyes, moved to the kitchen, and poured herself a cup of coffee. She always found their humor funny, but tasteless. Eric grinned like a naughty schoolboy needing to make nice, and chased Amy to the coffee pot.

I leaned into Susie. "You know I didn't do those rewrites, he did."

Susie whispered back, "With some heavy prompting from you. I knew he'd never do them for me, but he was dying to get into your pants. I figured if I let him fuck you, his cock would get hard and his head would get soft. It worked."

My stomach knotted. Last night had been beautiful, the fulfillment of a lifetime. I took a deep breath, and pretended she hadn't spoken. At school, she enjoyed humiliating me. Earning a doctorate hadn't changed her that much.

I started going for my own cup of coffee, when she grabbed my arm, whispering, "You know, I've watched that fucker screw around my whole life. Is he really that good?"

I either had to slap her or get out of the cabin. I hurried outside, stomped through the deep snow and slipped, falling into a freezing heap. I was shivering, wet, furious, would probably catch pneumonia, and it was Susie's fault.

A second later, Eric picked me up and dragged me back to the cabin. "Christ, Jenna! Whatever that little bitch said to you, it's not worth—" I grabbed his face and stopped his mouth with a kiss. His tongue darted in and out of my mouth as he pulled me onto the porch. Susie and Amy watched through the windows.

"Eric!" I pulled him to a halt. He looked at me like I was crazy, and I guess I was. "Was last night— What the hell was last night?"

Now, he shivered and looked angry enough to slap me. He held me so tight it hurt. "I love you, Jenna, you idiot, but we won't be able to do anything about it until we get to Paris. Okay?" He kissed me hard and fast, opened the door and hurled me toward the warmth of the fireplace.

Two nights later, composer and trio were at Halifax airport, ready to fly to Paris. Eric studied the seat numbers on the four boarding passes. "We're sitting two and two." He gave one pair to Susie and kept the other. "I want Jenna next to me." I was pleased, until he continued, "I'll be asleep most of the way, so you won't be talking. We only have two days before the competition and I don't want any of you jet-lagged." He focused back on me. "You, especially, need to rest your voice. This is a long flight and you'll get dehydrated. Drink a lot of water and sleep as much as you can." He pulled three sets of earplugs and three eyeshades from his jacket pocket. "I don't care how good the movie is, I don't want any of you staying up watching it."

Susie held up her eyeshade like a hair ribbon and curtsied like a little girl. "Yes, Daddy."

I toyed with the elastic on my eyeshade. "But it's only eight o'clock. I'm way too excited to sleep."

Eric scowled, like I was a demented child. "It's eight o'clock, our time. You only have two rehearsals in the concert hall, and the first one is nine hours from now. Our time, that's the crack of dawn, so sleep while you can."

•

Nine hours later, still in our traveling clothes, dragging our suitcases, jet-lagged and exhausted, we followed Eric into the dusty backstage of a small Paris concert hall. We heard live music and hurried through the small backstage area, into the stage-left wing. A piano quintet was on-stage, practicing a contemporary piece. They played with so much energy and bravado, I wanted to cry.

Amy whispered, "They're really good."

Susie clenched her teeth, snapping into competition/battle mode. "So. Are. We."

I tried to sleep on the plane. It hadn't worked. Now I was almost too tired to stand up. In a couple of minutes we had an hour of stage time. I would have to sing with the other competitors listening, just like I was listening now. I felt weak and sick.

Eric quietly called us, and we scurried backstage. I looked like a bedraggled rat, but Eric looked great. He had slept in his clothes, needed a shave, but still looked fresh. Full of energy, chatting in effortless French, he made conversation with a short, prissy looking, middle-aged-little-man in a morning coat. I guessed he was the Competition Chairman.

Eric gestured toward us. "*Monsieur Ribeaux, je voudrais vous présenter ma fille*, Susannah." Susie shook his hand. Eric continued, "*Et ses amies*, Amy Daniels *et* Jennifer Adams." Amy and I shook his hand.

Monsieur Ribeaux smiled, bowed, and silently clicked his heels. "*Enchanté, mesdamoiselles.*" A telephone rang and he bowed again.

"*Excusez-moi.*" He turned on his heel and left.

The quartet members packed up, but lingered to hear their competition—us. Eric led us onto the empty stage. "Our serious rehearsal is tomorrow from 12:00 to 2:00. The piano's being tuned tomorrow night."

Susie moved onto the bench. "Good. It sounds awful."

Eric nodded in agreement. "You have less than an hour, so just mark through sections. Jenna, you're wrecked. Don't even try to sing full-out." He pulled an envelope from his breast pocket and handed it to Susie. "That's your pension. It's around the corner. You all looked wrecked. Get some sleep."

I shook my head. "I tried to sleep on the plane, Eric. I couldn't."

He patted my shoulder. "I know. It's an acquired skill. Go to bed and stay there till tomorrow. Susie, tie her to the headboard if you have to."

Susie smirked, "I'm not really into that."

Eric laughed and gently pushed me toward her. "Do it anyway. I'll see you all here, tomorrow at 11:45." He walked off-stage.

Afraid of losing him, I raced after him, whispering, "When will we get together? You said ..."

He looked annoyed, faked a smile, and whispered back, "After the competition. Right now, you need rest. I need you singing better than you've ever sung in your life." He looked guilty and quickly added, "It's not just for me—not at all. I mean, this is for you. It's a great chance to launch your—"

"Career. I know, I know. Josh said this could be a stepping stone."

He looked relieved. "Right. He's right. Call him." He stepped away, but I stayed, looking unhappy. He stepped back and kissed my cheek.

I looked up with pleading eyes. "Where are you staying?"

"I have an apartment. Susie has the number. Call Josh."

"I'd rather talk to you."

Ready to yell at me, he stifled his impatience, and spoke to me like I was a spoiled child. "Look, Josh may not be the sexiest guy in the world, but he's a straight arrow, loyal, hard working, and smart as a whip. I've known him a lot longer than you have. He's crazy about you, and you don't want to lose him. Call him!" He took his suitcase from the stage doorman, and hurried outside. I heard the opening bars of the first sonnet, swallowed my disappointment and hurried onto the stage.

Rehearsal was horrible. Eric had told me to mark and not sing full-out, but I tried anyway and failed. Singing is physically demanding and I was just too tired. I ran out of breath and ruined my phrasing. My high notes cracked, and my low notes disappeared altogether. Susie and Amy were also tired and played badly. The next ensemble appeared in the wings and we willingly surrendered the stage.

After checking into our pension, we went to a bistro across the street. I wolfed down a big meal, felt better for it, but was still dead-tired and frightened that I would never be able to sing again. It was morning US time, but afternoon Paris time. I would do what Eric said, go to bed and stay there until tomorrow. I prayed that would be enough rest to get my voice working again. We had tomorrow's rehearsal, another night to rest and then the competition. I had to do well. I just had to.

We walked upstairs to our third floor rooms and passed a telephone booth. I stopped, letting Amy and Susie go on ahead of me. I felt scared and lonely, and needed to talk to someone who cared about me. My two choices were Mom or Josh. Since Mom could never understand the situation, it had to be Josh. I opened the phone booth door and stale air assaulted me. I gave the overseas operator instructions for a collect call to Atlas Artists, hung up, and waited for the call to go through.

Half asleep, I sat back, closed my eyes, and wondered what Eric was doing. I wished he had taken me to his apartment, but guessed he wanted us all here, close to the concert hall. I hoped Josh was in the office and rehearsed cheery lies like, "Rehearsals were great." And, "We're getting along really well." I would never tell him that I couldn't sing. I'd seen him blow up at clients who screwed up, and I was screwing up big time.

Ring! I woke with a start and grabbed the receiver.

"Jenna? Sweetheart? Are you there?" Josh sounded worried.

"Yeah. Hi, it's me." I tried to sound cheerful.

"Thank God! I've been worried sick. Eric called from Halifax. I wish you had."

"I'm sorry, it's just been ..." I forgot my rehearsed lines and started to cry.

Josh nearly yelled, "Jenna? What's going on?"

My throat was so clogged I couldn't speak. I swallowed frantically, and tried to control my voice.

Josh sounded angry. "I knew it was a mistake, rehearsing at that cabin. Jen, tell me, what's going on?"

I finally caught my breath. "Nothing. Really, nothing unusual. Just normal rehearsal stuff. It was hard, but nothing terrible. I'm jet-lagged, that's all. I need some sleep. I'll be fine."

"You'll be more than 'fine,' you'll be terrific, and this will all be over in forty-eight hours. Go to sleep. When you wake up, call me. I don't care what time it is. Okay?"

"Okay."

"Promise? Even if it's in the middle of the night here?"

"I promise."

"Jen, listen to me. I love you. I love your voice, but I love you more."

His sweetness was almost more than I could bear. I swallowed a sob. "Thanks Josh. You're the best." I wanted to say that I loved him back. He deserved to hear it, but my mouth wouldn't form the words. Instead I said, "I'll call you later. I promise. I'm fine, really."

"I know you are. Get some rest."

I hung up and lingered in the phone booth, nearly falling asleep. After a few minutes, I dragged my suitcase up the stairs. Susie, Amy, and I had our own tiny rooms, but shared a communal bathroom. As ordered, Susie tucked me into bed, and left me in comforting darkness. I lay still, thinking about the two men in my life. Josh just said he loved me more than he loved my voice. Eric wouldn't know I was alive if I couldn't sing. What if I couldn't sing on competition day? My career would be over before it even started. I turned my face into the pillow and I fell into a dreamless sleep.

8.
Competition Day
Appassionato Allegro Accelerando

$\mathscr{T}$he small, gilded concert hall had only two dressing rooms, one for men, and one for women. Susie, Amy, and I shared chairs and mirrors with the other female competitors. Fortunately, the musicians were mostly male. The guys' dressing room was really packed, but most of them weren't worrying about mascara and hairspray.

Most of the female players were attractive, but a couple looked so dowdy I was tempted to offer them makeovers. Only twelve of the fifteen finalists had actually made it to the competition. I didn't know why three composers had dropped out, but I was glad. Not only did it lessen the competition, but it lessened the waiting time before we performed, and afterward, when the judges went into seclusion and made their decisions.

I checked my makeup and watched Susie and Amy reflected in the mirror. We were islands of blue in a sea of solid black gowns. Susie had been right, deciding we should wear a color. At least we were going to stand out visually. Hair coiffed, makeup perfect, we all looked beautiful. I looked frightened.

Susie disliked competing against other solo pianists, but she loved this. Eric's music was on trial, not her, so she was having a great time. I listened as she chatted in fluent French, broken Italian and German, and drafted one of the other pianists to turn pages for her. Dark hair sleeked back, dark eyes shining, Susie looked very much like her handsome father. Amy treated auditions and competitions like regular performances. She found a quiet corner, twirled a curl of her short golden hair, and studied her score.

Like a mantra, I kept telling myself, "Eric's music is on trial, not me, not me—not me." It didn't work. I retouched my eyeliner for the fifth time, smoothed my lip gloss, and wished it was all over. We had arrived early enough to do a good warm-up, but that had been an hour and a half ago. I tried to control my breathing, but my heart pounded, and I was wearing out from the extended adrenaline rush. I sipped lukewarm water, hummed quietly, and vibrated my lips, keeping my vocal cords lubricated.

My manuscript was tight in my sweaty hand when I left the crowded dressing room and stepped across a narrow hall into the stage-right wing. Three stagehands waited to move the piano, harp, or harpsichord, as needed, for the next ensembles. Taped to the wall behind them was a large-print list of the twelve compositions, the length of each, their instrumentation, the number of chairs and music stands each one required.

The first ensemble had been the piano quartet we heard the day we arrived. Now a woodwind quintet played an excruciatingly strident composition. The musicians looked very concentrated, playing their wildly difficult parts. I felt strained and uncomfortable, just listening. Mom had called this kind of music "instant Halloween." I smiled at the old joke and my heart slowed.

A side curtain hung slightly open, allowing me to see past the stage into the partially darkened, gilded hall. Ten stern-faced judges sat behind study desks, reading scores, turning pages, and jotting notes onto score sheets. In front and behind the judges' desks, members of the public, music critics, and agents sat listening intently. Unlike usual concert audiences who yawn and fidget, no one budged. There wasn't the slightest sound or movement. I felt their tension. My heart pounded as I moved back against the wall. The woodwind quintet finished and a string quartet took its place. We were next.

Susie and Amy, manuscripts in hand, stepped out of the dressing room as Eric appeared from the other direction. I was amused to see he had dressed to match the colors of our gowns. His slim fitting navy-blue suit was set off with a pale-blue silk shirt and an electric-blue silk tie. Susie reached him first. Careful not to muss her, he squeezed her hand and kissed her cheek. "Love you, baby girl."

"Love you too, Daddy." Careful of her lipstick, she kissed back into the air.

Amy was next. He kissed her cheek. "Give 'em hell."

Smiling confidently, she shook her golden curls. "You know I will."

I tried to appear calm, but felt tight as a rubber band. Eric gently pulled me out of sight, behind a dusty wing curtain. He moved his mouth over my ear, whispering, "You look like an angel." One hand slid around my waist and the other up to my breast. Under the smooth satin, my nipple hardened and my breathing deepened. The quartet music was only ten minutes long. He shifted his wrist to catch the light, looked at his watch, and whispered sensually, "The face of all the world has changed, I think—"

I whispered back, "—Since first I heard the footsteps of thy soul."

He nuzzled my neck. "Do you think Mrs. Browning would be pleased?"

"She is pleased. I know it. I've dreamed about her. She—"

"Good. Now dream about us."

Surprised and thrilled, I followed him back to the other girls.

The quartet finished to enthusiastic applause. The four players stood, holding their instruments, waiting for their gawky, professorial-looking composer to join them on the stage. The five bowed together, then walked into the wings. Stagehands quickly removed two music stands and three chairs. After pushing the grand-piano into place, they positioned a small padded bench in front of the keyboard and a chair next to it for the page turner. The two remaining music stands were moved to the crook and at the end of the piano.

The house lights brightened enough for a set of choreographed assistants to walk into the orchestra, up an aisle and across the judges' desks, removing the string quartet music. A second set of assistants followed, delivering copies of Eric's Sonnets. The elegantly dressed judges opened the music, adjusted their score sheets, raised their pencils, and waited. The house lights dimmed.

The Competition Chairman walked on stage, holding a program. In a loud voice, he anounced, "Elizabeth Barrett Browning: *Sonnets From The Portuguese*. Eric Ries: *États-Unis*."

Bowing slightly, the Chairman stepped back, ushering the next ensemble onto the stage.

Amy took a deep breath, stood tall, and walked past him, into the light. Susie followed. I started after, but Eric grabbed my arm, whispering, "Do you love me?"

Horribly startled, I stammered, "You—you know I do!"

"No, I don't. Prove it! Go out there and sing better than you've ever sung in your life." He let me go.

Shaken, I heard the audience applaud and followed Susie into the harsh lights. I automatically snapped into performance mode. My posture straightened and I smiled. The audience smiled back, as three beautiful young women, swathed in soft shades of blue, moved into our places.

Susie sat on the piano bench and turned the side knobs, raising the seat until she was comfortable. She opened her score and smiled at her page turner, a pleasantly dowdy young woman dressed in black, sitting behind her left shoulder.

Amy's music stand was at the far end of the piano. She moved it slightly forward until she had a clear view of Susie and me. Susie played an A. Amy tuned and waited for me to get settled.

I walked into the crook of the piano, put my music on the stand, and stared at the first a-cappella line: *The face of all the world has changed, I think ...* Yes, the world had changed. Eric's words echoed in my ears. *Prove it! Prove it!* But, how could I prove it? *The face of all the world ... The face of ...* Susie played my first note the way she had dozens of times. I couldn't hear it. I gazed at the music, hearing Eric's voice. *The face of all the world ... Prove it! Sing better than you've ever sung in your life.*

Susie and Amy waited, staring at me, wondering what was wrong. I stared at the words as if I had never seen them before. Susie played the pitch again.

I closed my eyes and pictured Eric, naked and beautiful, on the sheepskin rugs. I inhaled, remembering the scent of his cologne and the feel of his body against mine. Finally, I exhaled and smiled. Slowly, taking my time, I raised my head and opened my eyes. I felt amazingly powerful. An expectant silence filled the hall. All eyes were on me and I was in control. I took a slow breath, and sang the twelve-tone-row with easy assurance, "The face of all the world has changed, I think, since first I heard the footsteps of thy soul ..."

Susie and Amy waited for me to finish the line, watched each other, breathed together, and played their entrances.

The three of us continued as one. "Move still, oh, still, beside me ..." Confident and sure.

Two hours later, bursting with pride, I stood with Eric, Susie and Amy on stage-right, wearing a medal hung on a wide red ribbon. For years afterward, we teased each other that we won second prize on purpose because the blue first prize ribbons clashed with our dresses. Center-stage, wearing blue ribbons, stood the string quartet players and their gawky, professorial-looking composer. Stage-left, wearing third place, gold ribbons, was a piano trio with their elderly lady composer.

Photographs were taken of each group separately, then all of us together. After the composers took their bows, house lights came up and the judges received their applause. There were cheers, hugs, tears of joy, and tears of disappointment. The winners were elated. Some of the losers wept. Everyone was exhausted.

I felt elated. Eric had challenged me to prove that I loved him, and I had. I had sung better than I'd ever sung in my life—better than I ever thought I could sing. He had told me to "dream about us." Now, watching him share congratulations with the other winning composers, I let my imagination soar. We were all supposed to fly home the next day, but he would take me away somewhere, some romantic country inn maybe. We would cuddle under a thick duvet, make sweet love together, then, in the morning, the innkeeper would bring us hot chocolate and croissants. We'd linger in bed ... My fantasy continued, even as I followed the crowd of musicians and audience members upstairs to a rehearsal hall for the champagne reception.

Like rehearsal halls all over the world, this large rectangular room had a wooden floor worn smooth by a thousand pairs of soft ballet shoes. Well lit, with a high ceiling, three walls were lined with mirrors and ballet bars. The only decorations were fantastically colorful, fragrant flower arrangements. Long tables at each end of the room were spread with glasses of champagne, platters of fruit and cheese. I followed the others, taking a champagne flute and sipping the tart bubbles. My arm was bumped, spilling some of the precious liquid onto the floor. I moved away from the crowded entrance, leaned on a ballet bar, stopped and sipped some more.

A short, plump, middle-aged man in a striped suit with a boutonniere, threw up his hands in delight and raced toward me, babbling in French. While not understanding every word,

I clearly understood that he thought I was wonderful. I enjoyed the adoration, looked over his shoulder and saw Eric come in surrounded by fans. The little Frenchman kept up his monologue, unaware that he had lost my full attention,

Like a flame drawing moths, Eric's smile seemed to light the room. He oozed charm, looked impossibly handsome, and appeared to know everyone who showered him with hugs, kisses, and congratulations. Soon they would be gone and he would be mine, alone. His focus shifted and a warmer look came into his eyes. A few nights ago, he had looked at me that way. Who was he looking at now? He excused himself and hurried past his fans. I half watched the little Frenchman, smiled and nodded when it seemed appropriate, looked over the few hairs on the top of his head, and scanned the crowded entrance. A parade of stylishly dressed people poured in.

Standing out from the crowd was a beautiful, slender, dark-haired woman, poised like a ballet dancer. She looked down at her side, smiled and spoke, and I guessed there was a child beside her. Eric spoke to her, reached down and lifted the child. Once they were eye to eye, I saw an adorable, vibrant little boy who looked exactly like Eric. My mouth went dry. I felt cold. Who was this kid? They hugged and teased like father and son, but I told myself that they couldn't be.

The woman moved close enough for Eric to turn his head and kiss her. They were covered by the moving crowd, so I smiled back at the Frenchman. When the crowd parted again, I saw the lady stroke Eric's beard. She looked very proud and his eyes shone with love. The little boy fussed and his parents laughed. The crowd covered them and they disappeared again. I felt empty inside, needed to focus on something real, and stared at the little Frenchman. Whatever I wanted to believe, Eric and his lady looked exactly like a long married couple, still in love, sharing a child they adored. My perfect fantasy weekend in a French country inn melted like dirty ice.

One of the female judges pushed through the crowd toward us. The Frenchman looked so thrilled and flustered, he practically genuflected. She shouted over the noise in heavily German accented English, that she had read about Eric's trio, and wondered how musicians living in different cities managed to rehearse.

Before I could explain, a new, rowdy group poured into the hall. Among the black-clad throng were flashes of blue, which I guessed were Susie and Amy. Most of the group went straight to the champagne tables. I tried answering the judge's question, but she couldn't hear me. I put my empty champagne glass on the floor against the wall, stood up and caught a glimpse of Susie hugging Eric's lady friend, then laughing as she ruffled the little boy's hair. Confused, angry, but determined to hide it, I concentrated on telling the judge how Eric had flown us all to Canada and sequestered us for four days. The judge smiled with approval, put her hands over her ears, shook her head, let the little Frenchman kiss her hand, waved a silent "goodbye" and hurried out of the noisy hall.

Another flash of blue drew my attention. This time I leaned on a ballet bar, stood on tiptoes and had a clear view of Amy, Susie, and Eric's lady talking casually. It took me a moment to locate Eric. He stood in the doorway, holding a large envelope, a plane ticket, and talking with another man. The man turned toward me and I saw that it was Josh ... Josh Kendal? What was he doing here? Eric's lady joined them and Josh kissed her cheek. I felt faint and dropped back onto my flat feet, gripping the ballet bar behind me. The room spun in sickening slow motion. These people were my best friends. I thought I knew them intimately. Now, they seemed to be part of a whole other world I knew nothing about. My heart pounded. Sweat beads plastered my satin gown against my skin.

The little Frenchman squealed happily, and I turned to see Josh approaching us through the crowd. The Frenchman rushed to him, and Josh smiled, greeting him warmly.

Relieved that I had a moment to myself, I escaped into the farthest corner of the rehearsal hall, leaned against the ballet bar with my back to the room, and saw Eric's reflection hurrying toward me. I wished we had some private place to talk. Since we didn't, I turned around and stared at the floor.

"Jenna, I've got to run, but had to say thank you. You were so wonderful. I'm ..."

"Who are they?"

Staying perfectly calm, he stood close and spoke softly. "The boy is my son, Pierre. His mother is Colette Sardon, Ballet Mistress at the Paris Opera."

His calm was infuriating, but I determined not to make a scene in the crowded room. I forced my voice to stay low. "Susie seems to know them well."

"She's known Colette most of her life. We met when I was twenty-two, over here on a Fulbright. Colette was a sixteen-year-old baby ballerina. I was her first. We've been lovers ever since."

"You were almost my first." I clenched my jaw.

"You turned me down." He comically raised an eyebrow and I wanted to slap him.

"Damn it, Eric! You had no intention of spending any more time with me."

"That's not true. I knew I'd be flying to London tonight, but if you hadn't been so jet-lagged, we might have …"

"Bullshit!" I turned away.

He moved close enough to pin me to the wall. "I know you hate me now, but you won't forever. I saw the critic, Gaspard, talking to you. He'll probably have Josh's ear for the rest of the night. A good word from that little frog and you'll be singing all over Europe. That's what you want, isn't it?" Wriggling free, I moved a few feet away. He checked to see that he wasn't being watched and turned back to me. "All right, I lied to you. If I hadn't, you never could have sung the way you did. It was a means to an end, and the end was glorious."

"Really? I don't feel glorious." My heart was breaking.

"You should. You made music today, like few ever do." His dark eyes shone, radiant with passion. "I was backstage. You sang my music and I got a hard-on. My God, I wanted to fuck you. All that sexual energy, that power! You made my music—"

"Music! Is that all life is to you? Music?"

"Yes. Music is dependable. People aren't. Keep music as your lover and people won't be able to hurt you." He shrugged. "At least, not as much."

"Colette seems dependable, sticking with you all these years, bearing your son."

"She won't marry me."

"Really. I can't imagine why." I wanted to scream, but Josh raced over, and I clenched the ballet bar behind me.

"Eric." Josh looked alarmed. "The car's outside. You'll miss your plane."

"I'm out of here." He patted Josh on the shoulder, and smiled at me. "Thanks again. You were wonderful." He kissed my cheek and disappeared through the crowd.

Not sure how I felt, but unable to look Josh in the eye, I stayed leaning on the bar. "You know Colette?"

"Sure, for years. I told you about her. Remember, he wrote her that ballet, then wouldn't give up the manuscript? I had to go—"

"I remember your story. It never occurred to me that they were still together, that Eric could actually maintain a relationship." I made myself take a deep breath, and look at him. His eyes were red and sore. His hair needed washing and his suit was a mess of wrinkles. "What are you doing here?"

"I couldn't stay in New York when you needed me."

His words were so simple and sincere, I couldn't believe it. This was a man with major responsibilities. Peoples' lives were in his hands. I gasped, "But you've got fifty other clients. You can't just close down your office."

He smiled wearily. "The office isn't closed. I took care of what was urgent and left the rest to my staff. Whenever I'm out of town, I call in four times a day. Everything's under control." He rested one hand on the ballet bar, and leaned into me. "Besides, I'm not in love with all fifty—just you." A telltale tear rolled down my cheek. He pulled a handkerchief from his pocket and gave it to me. "I've got a little more networking to do. You should, too, if you're up to it. Then we can get out of here. Okay?"

I nodded, swallowing back tears. Somehow, he sensed that I didn't want to be touched.

His eyes were full of love. "If you'll rest better alone, you can stay at your pension. If you want to come to my hotel …"

"I want to be with you."

"Great." He smiled. "You're a star today, so blow your nose, then let's schmooze."

For the next hour, Josh worked the room. I stayed close to one of the refreshment tables, smearing creamy Brie onto crackers and stuffing my face with grapes. Physically exhausted, emotionally drained, and afraid to practice my schoolgirl French, I watched Josh with admiration. His French was abysmal, but he didn't care. Most of the musicians, critics, and agents heard his terrible accent and switched to English. Those who didn't know him personally knew who he was and were eager to chat. He looked pleased to network with new contacts.

People talked to me, but I was afraid to answer. I listened, smiled, posed for photographs, acknowledged compliments, and congratulated the other competitors. I overheard one comment and laughed out loud. Some guy was amazed that I could be so forceful on stage, and I was so timid in person. He couldn't know that an hour before I almost slugged Eric in public. I hadn't done it, so maybe he was right. I was timid. Around seven, the crowd dispersed. Josh noshed on what was left of the fruit and cheese, then walked me the two blocks to the pension to collect my bags.

Amy and Susie were in their rooms packing. Eager to get back to Salzburg, Amy bid us all a tearful farewell, promised to keep writing, and to contact Josh if she ever decided to tour. He carried her suitcase downstairs and helped her into a taxi.

When he got back, Susie was telling me about one of the other composers. "I'd read about this guy. He's into really heavy electronics, and has stuff we haven't even heard of in Boston. He recognized me from the *Musical America* article. Isn't that great? We got talking and he invited me to visit his studio, so I called the airline and delayed my flight two days. They're charging me extra, but it's worth it. I'm staying with Colette."

I caught my breath. Frantic to know about her, I tried to sound casual. "Little Pierre's really sweet. You never told me you had a brother."

"What's to tell? I probably have siblings all over the planet." She slammed her suitcase shut and put on her coat. "But, he is very sweet and smart, and I love Colette. She's better than Dad deserves. A lot better. 'Bye all." She threw her arms around me. "You were so great today. At first I thought you were freaking out, but when you finally started to sing, you were fantastic."

"Thanks. You've always been fantastic." I held her tight.

Josh took Susie's suitcase, but she grabbed it back. "Thanks. It's not heavy."

He was too tired to argue. "Sue, you must know you were the best pianist in the competition. Have you really given up performing?"

"Yes. Yes. Yes." She looked happy as a kid at Christmas. "And, yup—I sure have. Whatever second thoughts I'd had, this week finished it. God, it was awful. I'll let Jenna tell you all the gory details."

My heart stopped. I would never tell Josh all the gory details, and she knew it.

Josh squeezed her hand. "I know this week was rough, but you were working with Eric on his own composition. It will be different with other conductors."

"Not that different. Conductors are all sadistic bastards." She cocked her head. "Unless they want to sleep with me. Then they can be lovely." Slipping the strap of her small case over her shoulder, looking calm and relaxed, she sighed happily, "Nope— no more performing. No more tendonitis. No more headaches. I killed myself getting a doctorate so I wouldn't have to put up with that kind of abuse anymore. 'Bye you guys. Come up to Boston and see my electronic studio. It's hot now. After this trip, it'll be steamy."

"We will, soon as we can." Josh gave her a hug.

"Be happy, you two!" Triumphantly lifting her suitcase, she strode out the door.

•

It was late when Josh and I got back to his hotel. We had spent a lot of nights together, but were both exhausted and strangely ill at ease. Josh stood under a hot shower, letting steaming water wash off twenty-four hours of near perpetual motion. Standing naked in front of the mirror, I saw that I was overly thin and promised myself to eat more regularly when I got home. I washed my face, brushed my teeth, and crawled into bed under the soft duvet.

The shower stopped. Josh toweled down and switched off the light. Bright street lamps shed enough light through the drapes to show him the way to the bed. Climbing in beside me, pulling the duvet over us both, he wound his arms and legs around me. "Hm, you feel good. I'm glad you're still awake."

"You must be exhausted, traveling all night, schmoozing all day." I snuggled against him. He felt smooth and warm, and smelled sweet.

"I am. The shower just gave me a second wind." He kissed my cheek, but I didn't respond. "Are you all right?"

"Sure." I held him tight.

Content and sleepy, he sighed. "I am so glad I came. That was an amazing competition. You three were brilliant. I couldn't believe it. You made that mathematical muck sound like music." He yawned,

"At least Eric didn't prepare the piano. I was sure he—"

"He did, but it didn't work. I couldn't hear my pitches. Susie got a bad cramp and they had a terrible fight. The third day, he took out the fiberglass strips and did some rewrites. After that, it was easy."

"Everything's easy for Eric." Giddy with fatigue, he laughed quietly. "That bastard's so damn lucky. Everything he touches turns to gold."

"Not everything." I gritted my teeth.

"Yes, everything. He screws almost every woman he knows and still has a woman like Colette to come home to."

We stayed quiet for a few moments. A lump formed in my throat. "Did you really come here, just to be with me?"

"Hm?" He stirred awake. "Sorry. What'd you say?"

"Never mind. I'm sorry. Go back to sleep."

"No. Tell me."

I needed to know the truth. "It's just … Did you really come here just to be with me?"

"Of course. Don't you believe me?"

"It's just hard to believe anyone's that nice." I needed to ask a tougher question, and swallowed, hard. "Josh?"

"Hm?"

"Did you mean what you said about loving me more than my voice?"

"Sure."

"Even after today, after I sang so well?"

"You did sing well." He rolled onto his back. "I sat in the last row of that hall, listening and trying to recognize the girl I'd fallen in love with. You were a diva. You glowed with sexual energy. You've always been sweet and beautiful, but so cautious. You're a great musician. Your voice is like crystal. But frankly, I'd envisioned you in a quiet career, soloing with prissy chamber groups and oratorio societies. That woman on stage could sing anything. Your personality radiated. Better than beautiful, you were forceful, charismatic, and your sound was big enough to be heard over a full orchestra. You were wonderful. You were a star and, my lovely, you're going to make bucks. Mega-bucks. As soon as you've had some rest, I want you to start coaching heavier repertoire."

"Really?" All this praise was nice, but I'd asked if he loved me, and not just my voice.

"Yeah. Until today, I never knew you had that much sound. Do you know the Liu arias?"

"I learned them in school. You think I could sing Puccini? Over a big orchestra?"

"I think you should try. There's a lot more money and glamour singing that stuff than Monteverdi."

"I love Monteverdi." That sounded like an attack.

"I love Monteverdi, too." He looked confused and concerned. When I stayed quiet, he rolled over, to face me. "Hey, what's going on?"

Close to tears, I was afraid to look at him. "Well, Eric only cares about my voice. He pretended to care about me, to get me to sing well."

"Flattered you along, did he? It certainly worked."

"Well, yeah ... When he wasn't yelling at me. It was horrible. Susie screaming at him. Him yelling back. Amy walked out. When we weren't rehearsing, we didn't even talk to each other."

"At least he wasn't able to get you alone."

Not having a ready answer, I hedged, "Right. It was like you said. We were all together, all the time like rats in a cage."

He took me in his arms, gently and sweetly. "Jen, you're a great talent. You want a career and I'll work my tail off to see you get the career you deserve, but I love you more than I love your voice. I want you beside me, just like this, for the rest of my life. Anytime at all. Tomorrow, next year, ten years from now, you can say, 'Josh, I want to stop singing,' and you can stop. Just like that."

Slowly, the tension eased out of my body. I felt myself smile.

He held me even closer. "I love you. I want to marry you." I stiffened and he hurried to soothe me. "I know we've only known each other a few months, and I don't want to pressure you into anything, but I'd like to get you pregnant tonight."

Startled and amused, I laughed uneasily. "Well then, I'm glad I took my pill."

Embarrassed, he laughed at himself. "I'm sleep deprived. I should shut up before I say something really asinine, but I really love you. I'm almost thirty-two and I want to start a family, with you. It doesn't have to be tonight."

"It won't be."

"How about tomorrow night?"

This time, I laughed full out. He joined me and we fell into sleepy, silly hysterics. Kissing me long and hard, he reached between my legs, felt for my clitoris and rubbed gently. As always, I responded instantly, warm and moist. He loved that about me. Reaching my hand between his legs, I stroked his erection, then spread my legs. He rolled on top of me and slipped carefully inside. Almost too gentle, his movements were nurturing and loving. He always made sure I was satisfied, always made sure I felt safe.

Sex with Eric had not been safe. It had been scary and exciting. Eric was scary and exciting, but he was somewhere else. Josh was *here*. He would always be here. I relaxed into the rhythm of his easy lovemaking, and smiled to myself. Eric was wrong. Some people were dependable.

9.
New York City: December 1978
Moderato Tranquillo

After the Paris competition, some things changed. First off, Josh was quick to get my competition reviews and send press kits all over the world. Requests for auditions trickled in, and I started booking concerts and operas as far as three years ahead. My financial future looked promising but the present was still very tough. I kept my church job and sang every wedding and funeral I could get. True to his word, Josh sent me to an outstanding vocal coach so I could work on heavier repertoire. He knew I couldn't afford the lessons and would never accept charity, so he had the coach bill Atlas Artists. The fees would be deducted from my future earnings, which I thought was more than fair.

The one time I mentioned it to Sheila, Josh's astute, geriatric secretary, she looked up from her filing and raised a thin gray eyebrow over her bifocals. "A smart girl like you should know better than to think a rich agency like this spends money coaching clients. Josh is doing this for you. It's good and he should, but don't go believing it has anything to do with Atlas. Just take the lessons, learn, sing, and make us all lots of money." She winked. "I never said that, right?"

My cheeks burned. "Right! Thanks for telling me."

"I told you nothing." She winked again and went back to work.

I couldn't afford to move and I still lived in my shabby apartment hotel. The bedroom ceiling was stained from water damage, and the mismatched floorboards creaked under my feet. Mirror-glass on the back of the bathroom door was discolored and white paint continually chipped off the frame. The soundproof walls still allowed me to practice anytime, day or night, and that was a huge plus.

For years, my living room wall had been a shrine to the glory of Eric Ries. Right after the Paris competition I wanted to forget I had ever heard his name. I still believed he was a brilliant musical talent, but knew that Susie's first description had been correct. He really was "a world-class bastard." Now there were only three photos on the wall: a picture of me with Josh's family at their recent Hanukkah party, a posed photo of Eric, Susie, Amy and me wearing our medals on their red ribbons, and Eric's seventeen-year-old, black-and-white autographed picture.

Again and again, I tried putting that picture away. It never worked. I would take it off the wall, leave it in a drawer, hear myself talking to it, and put it back up. Twice I stashed it on a high shelf in the closet, still found myself talking to it, brought it down, and stuck it back on the wall. Nine years ago, when I entered Newell Conservatory, Mom called that picture my "transitional object," my "blankie." Would I ever transition out of needing it? My habit of writing to Eric was also ingrained. Every three or four months, I sent him a note via Atlas Artists. Unlike the passionate letters of my youth, these brief notes kept him up to date on my singing engagements. I told myself that I wanted to keep up the professional contact. Deep inside, I knew I wanted more.

•

December twenty-third, I sang the *Messiah* in Pittsburgh, caught a late flight back to New York, and arrived at my apartment in the early hours of December twenty-fourth. I went to bed at dawn and slept most of the day. By 6:00 that evening, I was showered and dressed for Mom's annual Christmas Eve party. I stood in front of the full-length mirror, brushing my silky ash-blond hair. It had grown almost to my waist. I noticed some split-ends, made a mental note to get them trimmed while parting it down the middle, and smoothing it behind my shoulders.

Dangly green earrings hung alongside two-dozen other pairs, on thin chains tacked to the wall. I slipped the wires off the chain, slid them through my lobes, and shook my head to send the glass beads sparkling. The playful image made me smile. I pinned a fake holly sprig to the turtleneck on my red velour dress, straightened the calf-length skirt over my dark red boots, and sighed. This year, Mom would not be able to complain that I didn't look Christmassy enough. She knew I had to leave the party at 10:00 to sing a Christmas Eve candlelight service.

The WNCN radio disc jockey announced selections from Handel's *Messiah* and I cringed. After singing the oratorio with five different orchestras, I was sick to death of it. A key turned in my front door lock, so I switched off the radio, double-checked my makeup, and went to greet Josh.

"Hi, hon." He let himself in, and put two shopping bags full of presents on the daybed.

"Oh, no. What's that?"

He laughed. "Sorry. I couldn't resist. This bag's for you. That one's for your Mom." We had to leave immediately, so he kept his coat on, took my face in his hands, and kissed me sweetly. I carefully emptied my bag under the Christmas stockings tacked to my fake fireplace. He took the other and started for the door. "We'd better go. Allison wanted us there at six."

I raised an eyebrow. "The way you spoil her, she can wait half an hour for her free entertainment."

"She won't make us perform. Not unless we want to."

"Tell me one time you've turned her down." I went for my coat and gloves.

He laughed. "I like your mom. She has chutzpah."

"She loves you." I hurried into my soft, purple down coat, and zipped up the front. "I think she loves you more than she loves me. I love your mom. She's an angel." I wound a warm scarf around my head. "You're whole family's great—even the babies. I'm so jealous."

"Just say the word and they'll be your family, too." His smile was very inviting, but I shrugged it off.

"I'm not Jewish."

"They don't care. Just look at that picture." He pointed to the Hanukkah photo on the wall. "You're already part of the family."

I shook my head. "They've been wonderful to me, but you know as well as I do, when push comes to shove, if their brilliant, successful, number-one son actually decided to marry a *shiksa*, they'd—"

"I have ... and they've said it's okay. They love you. Why can't you believe that?"

"It's hard to believe even you love me that much. Let's go." I grabbed my purse and we hurried out of the apartment.

I really loved Josh. He was the smartest, sweetest man on the planet, and he worshipped me. I would never understand why, but I loved him for it. I couldn't imagine life without him, but I was terrified of actually marrying him. The very idea of blowing up with a child inside me was repulsive. I could deal with that later, but I couldn't put off marriage much longer. I didn't want to lose him, but I had to get my head straight. I had to talk to Mom.

•

Mom's annual Christmas Eve party had become a tradition happily anticipated by the New York Philharmonic Society set. I enjoyed this once a year reunion with people I had known my whole life, but braced myself for well-meaning, embarrassing probes into my career and personal life. This year, for the first time, I had really good answers: actual singing engagements with dates I could quote, and a steady boyfriend with a steady job. I expected the questions to graduate to the next step: "You're twenty-seven, dear. Isn't it time you were getting married?" and braced myself for that assault.

Even from the elevator, we heard people laughing over recorded Christmas music. Since the front door was open, we walked in. Josh stacked his presents with the others under Mom's tall Christmas tree. The fresh pine scent, along with fairy-lights and delicate handmade ornaments, brought back memories of childhood. Luscious aromas of fresh-baked biscuits and roasted meats lured us toward the dining-room buffet table, but Mom cut us off at the pass.

"Here you are, darlings." Dressed in a sleek green satin pantsuit adorned with gold and pearl cherubs, honey hair perfectly coiffed, and false eyelashes flawlessly glued, Mom glowed like the perfect Yuletide hostess. She hugged us both. "Everyone's been asking for you. Do be angels. Play and sing something." Josh and I exchanged smiles, and let Mom lead us into the living room, right up to the Steinway piano decked with a red tablecloth and pine garlands.

A pile of Christmas song books sat waiting. I skimmed through the contents, selected my favorite, and switched off the taped music. Josh sat at the keyboard, played a comically flamboyant version of the *Dreidel Song*, wove it into *Jingle Bells*, and finally the introduction to my song. I laughed at his musical clowning and sang, "Have yourself a merry little Christmas. Make the Yuletide gay. From now on our troubles will be far away ..."

A crowd immediately gathered. I looked and sounded great, and Mom beamed with pride. She loved me. She loved Josh, and she loved the way he loved me. She also loved the easy, confident way we made music together. By the end of the song, she had tears in her eyes. Party-goers crowded around the piano, applauding and begging for more. Mom hurried over. "Oh, darlings, that was wonderful! Do another."

"After we eat. I'm famished." I slithered around her, into the empty dining room. Too good-natured to refuse, Josh stayed where he was, graciously playing another carol so the raucous crowd could sing along.

Safely away from the piano, my hungry eyes were huge as I grabbed a turkey drumstick and gnawed it like a ravenous dog. Mom looked amused. "There's my ladylike little daughter. So, darling, what's the news?"

"Mm." I nodded, talking with my mouth full. "Last night was great." I swallowed. "The best conductor yet." I found a plate for the drumstick, and helped myself to a mug of mulled wine.

Mom gave a long-suffering sigh. "I don't mean your career, dear. I mean your life."

"My career is my life." I dove back into the drumstick, then helped myself to stuffing and cranberry sauce.

Mom followed, close enough to whisper. "A husband and children should be your life."

"Since I don't have either ..."

"You could. Just say the word. Josh will marry you tomorrow."

"I know." Suddenly, I wasn't hungry. Loud, happy, out-of-tune singing poured from the living room. I looked around. Sure no one could hear, I moved closer. "Mom, tell me the truth. If we do get married, will he stay married to me?"

"Yes, he will." Her words were strong and sure. She sighed sadly, "Oh, darling, Josh is nothing like your father."

"Listen, Mom, I know this isn't the time, but ... Why did you and Dad divorce?

Her jaw dropped. "Oh, great. For twenty years I've been trying to get you to talk to me, and you finally do it when I've got forty guests in the house."

I grimaced. "Sorry."

The carol ended boisterously and some of the revelers wandered back to the buffet.

Mom whispered, "To hell with them," put my plate on a sideboard and pulled me down the hallway.

I was frantic to know everything. "Did Dad hate us? Did he hate me? Was he just a selfish bastard? Did you drive him away? What?"

"Your father adored you."

"He couldn't stand the sight of me. That's why he said he didn't have any kids."

"No, that's not the reason. He thought you were beautiful and bright. He just wouldn't believe you were ..." Her hand went over her mouth. She forced back tears.

"Wouldn't believe I was what?" Alarmed, I dragged her farther down the hall into her bedroom, and pushed the door so it almost closed.

She pulled tissues from a box by her bed and carefully dabbed her eyes. "He wouldn't believe you were his."

I gasped. "Wasn't I his?"

"Of course you were. My God, just look at his pictures."

"I always thought we looked alike." Suddenly faint, I sat on the bed.

"You look exactly alike. And you have his blood type." Anticipating my obvious, painful next question, she dove ahead. "And yes, I slept with someone else, before you were born."

I thought I was going to be sick.

She sat next to me. "You must know that your father had affairs. Even at our wedding reception, he had one of my bridesmaids."

"So why did you stay married to him as long as you did?"

"Divorce was still a terrible scandal in those days, and despite it all, I thought he loved me. He was handsome and charming, and making more money than God." She paused, remembering. "I had charge accounts all over town and he never questioned what I spent." She shook her head. "A year after we were married, I learned he'd been engaged to another girl since high school. The poor thing was plain and mousy, and when he started climbing the corporate ladder, he saw he needed a wife with social connections. He jilted her and went shopping for me. He took my virginity on our wedding night, then said he wasn't ready to have children and barely touched me for the next two years. He'd leave early in the morning and get home late at night, smelling of … whatever. He traveled a lot. All the while, I made him a beautiful home, entertained his guests, got busy doing charity work, and helped him along with his career."

I braced myself. "That's all fascinating. What about—"

"Okay, okay. We were on vacation in Palm Beach with another couple, Doris and Fred Miller. I knew about Lester's affairs and pretended I didn't. One night, he disappeared with Doris, and Fred came to me. I was lonely. Fred was sweet …" She blew her nose. "But it didn't result in a pregnancy. Lester was furious when he heard about me and Fred. I thought he'd set it up. Anyway, he suddenly noticed that I was alive. For the next two months, we made love twice a day and I conceived you. I thought a baby would fix everything. I still don't know what went wrong, but it had nothing to do with you. I suppose if I'd have worked harder maybe I could have made him stay. I don't know."

My jaw tightened. "You probably didn't have time for him. You were too busy working for charity, for people you didn't even know."

"Is that how you remember it?" Her eyes refilled with tears.

"I remember you never had time for me."

"But …" Her fingers wiggled, grasping at air. "You never seemed to need me. I'm sorry. I didn't know."

"It's okay. You did the best you could at the time, but what do I do now? I don't want to have to make Josh stay with me."

"You won't have to. He loves you."

"Dad loved you and he didn't stay."

"He didn't love me."

"Never? Not even, at first?"

"I told myself he did, but I don't think so. I was just an ornament he could show off to his associates."

A cheer rose as the next carol ended. Seconds later, Josh found us in Mom's bedroom. He peeked around the door. "Is this a private meeting? Can I come in?"

I sprung up. "My shift at the piano." I hurried past him, out of the room and down the hall. He went inside and I was dying to know what Mom would tell him. I crept back, listening at the open door.

Mom had tears in her voice. "She loves you so much. Please don't give up on her."

"I won't, but I'm running out of ideas."

"I don't suppose you could get her pregnant."

"I've tried. I pounce on her in the middle of the night and she flies out of bed for her diaphragm."

Mom laughed sadly. "At least she's off the pill."

"Don't despair, Allison. I haven't given up."

Relieved that he wasn't giving up on me, I raced to the piano and played a rousing rendition of *Good King Wenceslas.*

A few hours later, Joshua Kendal, a Jewish boy from New Jersey, was in Greenwich Village, at the First Presbyterian Church, experiencing his first Christmas Eve service. I knew it would seem strange to him, but I also knew he would love the pageantry. The magnificently vaulted, hundred-and-fifty-year-old stone edifice was aglow with dozens of white candles, red poinsettias, and green holly wreaths. All the music had been wonderful, and he liked my plaintive solo, *The Holy Boy,* by John Ireland. Since he knew the *Messiah* by heart, he was familiar with many of the New Testament readings that had gone between the carols.

Minutes before midnight, the service came to a close. As a final ritual, the choir silently processed, two by two, from behind the altar. Swathed in floor-length blue robes, holding unlit candles and looking like rows of walking bells, we slowly moved down the center aisle, each one stopping at the end of a pew. The congregation had been issued small candles, and they held them up, ready to light. From the back of the church, smiling ushers made their way toward the altar, lighting the choristers' candles, pew by pew. On the minister's cue, we turned, offering our lights to the congregation. Soon the entire sanctuary was bright with tiny flames. Josh caught my eye as the organ began playing *Silent Night.* Sweetly and softly, choir and congregation sang together, "Silent Night, holy night. All is calm, all is bright ..."

The last verse ended, but the organ continued playing softly under the minister's benediction. After his final "Amen," all the candles were blown out. Quiet organ music continued as everyone wished each other a Merry Christmas and left the sanctuary.

I followed the line of choristers heading for the choir room. Lovely as the evening had been, I was tired, eager to hang up my robe, and get out into the fresh air. Josh took my hand, pulled me out of line, and led me into a side chapel. I whispered, "What's wrong?"

"Not a thing." He lowered himself onto one knee.

Embarrassed, but amused and pleased, I looked around to make sure we weren't being watched. With the organ still playing and the pew candles still burning, he looked like the most romantic of Victorian suitors. He opened a small leather box, and offered me a diamond ring. I thought my heart would leap out of my chest. Tears filled my eyes. I blinked them back, and looked at the medium-sized stone set in a delicate white-gold setting. He knew I would never wear ostentatious jewelry. This was perfect.

Gently taking my left hand, he slipped the ring on my finger. I turned it into the candle lights, and watched the diamond sparkle. He sighed with relief, stood up and gave his sore knee a comical shake. We both laughed at his clowning as bright electric lights came on, ending the romantic ambiance.

He pretended to wipe sweat off his brow. "Boy, I just made it."

Afraid of a fire, maintenance men moved up and down each aisle, extinguishing any lit candles and checking for hidden ones. In the bright light of reality, I looked at my ring. "This is beautiful, Josh." I bit my lip. "But I still need some time."

"That's fine. Take all the time you want. I was afraid you wouldn't even take the ring." He took me in his arms and kissed me.

10.
June 1979
Pesante Agitato

$\mathcal{B}$y summer, something else changed. I was sick to death of being poor. When I graduated from college, I rebelled against my affluent roots, moved into the shabby apartment hotel, surrounded myself with other starving artists, survived on green noodles and yogurt, virtually lived *La Bohéme*, and loved it. My high school wardrobe of classical, conservative clothes had kept me looking good year after year, but those skirts and blazers were now patched and mended beyond repair. I wanted a better apartment, better food, and new clothes. I was ready for a change.

Two to three times a week, I auditioned for opera and symphony conductors. I usually competed with the same sopranos, got to know them by their names, their arias, and their audition dresses.

Caro Nome wore black, and *Grossmächtige Prinzessin* wore green. I was *Chanson d'Olympia* in blue, but the blue seams were almost worn out and there was nothing left to mend. Desperate for a new dress, I swallowed my pride and let Mom take me shopping. She loved it, and I became *Chanson d'Olympia* in luscious rose.

Atlas Artists clients—sopranos, mezzo-sopranos, tenors, and basses—often auditioned at the same call. They knew I was Josh Kendal's girlfriend and thought I was dating him for his connections. They would never believe that he had pursued me.

He kept proposing. I kept resisting and wondered why. He was the sweetest, most nurturing being on the planet. Looks-wise he was pretty average, but that was where the averageness ended. He had the patience of a saint, a great sense of humor, a computer brain, and a consummate understanding of musicians, classical music, and the music business. This average-looking guy engineered the careers of two-dozen world famous musicians and two-dozen up-and-coming musical stars, like me. His roster was filled with pianists, singers, string, wood-wind, and brass players, trios, quartets, conductors, composers ... Twenty-four / seven he was on call to hysterical, angry, frightened, disappointed, or elated musicians in all time zones, on every continent.

We spent half of our nights together, either at his apartment or mine. I got used to his beeper going off in the middle of the night, his lunging out of bed, calling oversees to some hysterical client, and staying on the phone, making half a dozen calls, until the problem was solved. It was exhausting, but he loved it. Every time a new artist made a successful debut, or an established artist received a stellar review, Josh beamed like a proud father.

•

One steamy June evening I stood squeezed between smelly, sweaty bodies on a crowded subway car rattling toward my stop at Broadway and 86th Street. Afraid to move and drop everything, I clutched my garment bag, oversized purse, and faded music-case, and tried to ignore the stench of greasy fast food. The subway slowed. I excused myself, struggled to hold everything together, and squeezed through the other passengers. The train pulled to a stop and I braced myself for battle. Sure enough, the wide double-doors opened and, before anyone could get out, other passengers pushed themselves in. I yelled, "Getting off, please!" tackled more tight bodies and practically fell out the door onto the sweltering platform. I dragged myself up the crowded, gritty subway steps, watching energetic passengers rush down the stairs onto the platform. This was Saturday night. Most people were ready to party. I wanted a cold drink, a cool shower, and a soft bed.

I stopped at the corner kiosk to buy a *Sunday New York Times.* José, the elderly kiosk owner smiled through broken, coffee-stained teeth. For years I had been his steady customer. The few times I was stone-broke, he let me buy *Musical America* and *Back Stage* on credit. I lifted the huge newspaper, gave up, and set it back on the pile. He laughed, unfolded the paper, pulled out the Television section, *Arts and Leisure*, and *Week in Review*, rolled them into a manageable bundle and stuck that under my arm.

I smiled wearily. "Thanks, José. Good night."

"Goo' nigh', Jenna." He smiled and nodded as I walked toward my apartment hotel.

Crash, bang! Abrasive, electronic crashes nearly startled me into dropping everything.

"Damn it, Charlie!"

My stoned neighbor was in his usual place on the sidewalk, next to the apartment stairs. He pounded his synthesizer keyboard, stomped on the flat panels of his drum machine, and shouted a sophomoric lyric into the mike of his Maxi Mouse amp. I thought Charlie was my age, then learned from another neighbor that he was pushing forty. It seemed like a horribly wasted life. I clenched my jaw against his racket, and started up the front steps.

Suddenly, there was silence. "Jenna!"

I stopped and glared down at him. "What, Charlie?"

"Your boyfriend's a manager. I need one." His drugged-out eyes tried to focus.

I sighed dramatically. "Only classical musicians, Charlie."

"Wait a minute!" He reached into his pocket and took out a business card. "This guy wants me to write a jingle for some fruit punch. I don't want to get screwed, with the money."

I sighed again, laid my bundles on the banister, and let Charlie put the card on top. To my surprise, it looked like a reputable ad agency. "Well, like I said, Josh doesn't handle pop musicians, but he might be able to pass this on to someone who does."

"Cool!" Charlie smiled like a kid with a new toy.

Careful not to lose the card, I held it and everything else tight against my chest. At the top of the stairs, I looked through the glass door, hoping the guy behind the reception desk would see me and buzz me in. He was talking to someone and not looking toward the door, so I had to push the buzzer. Unfortunately, my hands were full.

"Hi, Jen. I'll get the door." My neighbor, Nan, was behind me. She had a shoulder bag and her violin, which left a hand free to push the button and open the buzzing door.

"Oh, thank you!" I smiled gratefully as we walked to the elevator.

Nan pushed the call button then stared at my hand. "Did you guys get married?"

I laughed. "No, my ring's just turned around. I don't show diamonds on the subway."

She nodded. "Yeah, that's an easy way to lose a finger. So, are you ever getting married?"

I shrugged. "I'm in no hurry. Things are good as they are."

The elevator door opened and we stepped inside. Nan pushed the buttons for both floors and the door closed. She shook her head. "Boy, if I was engaged to Atlas Artists, I'd marry him tonight before someone else got him."

Tired as I was, my blood boiled. "I am not marrying Atlas Artists. If I get married at all, it'll be to a sweet guy named Josh, who happens to work for a talent agency."

"That's a good line, Jen. Keep it up." She smirked as the door opened.

Too tired to argue, I shuffled out, and dropped everything in front of my door. I found the key and pushed the door open. Hot, stale air made me gag. I left everything outside and hurried to open the windows. A fresh breeze blew through my dusty curtains as I gathered everything together, made two trips, and dumped messy piles onto the daybed. The ad agency card was on the floor. I propped it on the mantel, hoping it really was legit. Crazy Charlie deserved a break.

The garment bag looked crushed, but the gown inside wasn't too wrinkled. I shook it out and hung it in the bedroom closet. My dress shoes stayed in their individual travel bags and slid into place, between other shoes on the closet floor. Almost too tired to move, I opened more windows, closed the drapes, and stripped off my sweaty traveling clothes.

The message light on my answering machine made single flashes. I pushed the play button.

"Hi, dear. It's Mom. Marilyn's visiting from Chicago. You remember, she's the one who always brags about her orchestra society. Anyway, she's coming over tomorrow, and I was hoping you and Josh could do that pretty song you did for my birthday. I left this message on his machine. Bye now."

The machine clicked off.

"No, Mom!" I pushed the erase button, shuffled back to the living room, and switched on WNCN. Satie's *Gymnopedie No. 1* played. The sweet, melancholy music washed over me as I went to the refrigerator and downed a large glass of cold orange juice.

Ready for a restful hour's read, I took the *Sunday Times*, stretched out on the daybed, unfolded the *Arts and Leisure,* and caught my breath. Upper right, on the front page, was a gorgeous picture of Eric Ries. He was forty-six-years-old and getting handsomer. How was it possible?

The phone rang and I hoped it wasn't Mom asking me to sing for her friend. I left the paper and picked up the receiver. "Hello."

"Hi, babe. You're finally back." Josh sounded tired.

"Yeah, the wedding was fine. They paid me in cash. The bride and groom both looked sixteen. Where are you?" I expected the call to be a long one, and relaxed onto the piano bench.

"At the office, waiting for a call from Tokyo. It's okay, I've got paperwork to do anyway. If this deal goes through, the Barkley Quintet will be employed for a whole year."

"I thought you were dropping them."

"If they don't book this, I might. They argue among themselves too much. Your mother left a message on my machine."

"Ignore it."

"Okay." He chuckled wearily. "I know you've got the church job tomorrow. I forget, is it the *B Minor Mass*? I'd like to—"

"The Bach is next week." I stifled a yawn. "Tomorrow's just the Vaughan Williams, nothing strenuous."

"Your second favorite composer."

"Third." I glanced at Eric's old framed photo. "Purcell's my second."

"Did you see the *Arts and Leisure*?"

"Just this minute. How'd you get him on the front page?"

"I didn't. I wish I had that kind of clout."

"If you didn't do it, he must have slept with someone."

He laughed. "Yeah, listen, something's come up—something important." He sounded anxious.

"I'm listening."

He hesitated, then took a deep breath. "Tom Epstein's leaving the London office. He misses his grandkids and wants to move back here. They've offered me the post."

My stomach cramped. "You love London."

"You will, too, and the Brits love your kind of voice."

"Could I get working papers?" I tried to sound calm.

"Only if you were married to a legal alien, like I will be. It wouldn't affect your American engagements. You'd just be traveling more."

I swallowed, hard. "So ... I have to marry you."

There was an uneasy pause. "I'm afraid you do. They want me there the middle of August. I know that's soon. You could join me later."

"No, I'd ..."

He waited.

"I'd want to go with you. I want to go with you."

"Oh, that's great." He sounded relieved and happy.

A nervous giggle bubbled from my throat. "I better call Mom."

"Yeah. Wait, Jen! Before you go, I had an idea. Once I hit London, it'll be nonstop work. If we left a few days early, we could have a honeymoon."

"Oo, that sounds nice. Where do you want to go?"

"Well, you never got to enjoy Paris."

"No, I didn't. That's great."

"Yeah. It'll be great." He sighed happily. "Call your Mom, get some rest, and I'll see you tomorrow."

I smiled into the phone. "Okay. Good night. I love you."

"Love you, too." He hung up.

I hung up, sat very still, and tried to decide if I was happy or scared. The decision had been taken out of my hands. Fate can be kind. I smiled at the old photo. "I'm getting married, Eric. Funny isn't it? I never thought I could love any man but you. And, I'll finally get to enjoy Paris."

Still watching his dark, sensual eyes, I picked up the receiver and punched a number. "Hi, Mom. Guess what?"

11.
August 1979
Adagio: Poco a Poco Accelerando

The gigantic jumbo jet was like a toppled skyscraper. It was a huge moving cage, come to take me away. I stared through the thick glass of a Kennedy Airport window and my throat tightened. I shivered, rubbed my sweaty palms together, and tried to get a grip on my runaway emotions. I was twenty-seven-years-old. I had just gotten married. I had everything: health, beauty, talent, and a loving, financially successful husband. We were on our way to Paris and a romantic honeymoon. We were moving to London and a small Victorian house I had never seen. That was okay. I could deal with that. Why did I feel like I was about to be tortured?

I shifted nervously from foot to foot, tried to shake off my imaginary traumas, and felt an attack of freezing air-conditioning. My ears were assaulted by humming fluorescent lights, squawking loudspeakers, screaming kids, frantic mothers, and uniformed airline staffers waiting patiently or treading loudly across the hard-tiled floors. I shivered, stamped my feet, and hugged myself for warmth. No one else seemed to notice the cold or noise. Since I alone looked like an idiot, I considered dancing and holding out a hat. At least I'd get warm and make a buck or two.

A few feet away, Josh looked unbelievably comfortable talking with Mom and her sister, my adorable Aunt Connie. Maybe marriage to Josh would teach me to take things in stride. Since I panicked every time the wind changed, I doubted it. I couldn't hear what Josh said but it must have been funny because the women laughed. Mom answered back, and they laughed again.

I rubbed my clammy fingers and felt the white gold ring, nestled next to the diamond ring Josh gave me last Christmas Eve. That night, I told him I wasn't ready to get married. I still wasn't ready, but, shit! I was married. I was Jennifer Adams Kendal. There was no turning back and the damned airport was freezing. I took deep breaths, and waited for the extra oxygen to relax my muscles and send blood through my chest. I read that was supposed to happen and wondered how long it was supposed to take.

At least I was wearing comfortable clothes. Josh and I changed out of our wedding outfits into soft slacks and blazers. I loved dressing up to go on stage and perform, but this had been a private wedding service with no audience. All the fuss had been for nothing —not true. It had been for Mom. She and Aunt Connie were still dressed up in their matching mother-of-the-bride and matron-of-honor silk-brocade suits. They looked lovely, but uncomfortable. At fifty-two, Mom was still stunning. Slim and statuesque, she would always be the perfect, untouchable Ice Princess. Aunt Connie had always been pleasantly plump and delectably huggable. I hadn't seen her in almost three years and her middle-age spread was spreading way too fast. She was two years younger than Mom, but looked like the older sister.

Josh and I didn't want a big wedding, but Mom had always planned on giving me a big white one. She didn't get the chance and I felt kind of sorry for her. I thought Josh's parents would insist we get married under a canopy, but they were so relieved we were finally getting married at all, they didn't care what kind of a ceremony it was. Trouble at the London office pushed Josh's transfer through so fast Mom had to settle for hostessing a quiet chapel service at the First Presbyterian Church and a lavish lunch at Café Des Artistes. At least she had an excuse to buy herself a new outfit and makeover her dowdy sister. She bought me an expensive white cocktail dress I didn't want. I hated shopping, but the dress was gorgeous. She paid for it, and I would use it later as a concert gown.

I was yanked into their conversation when Mom pointed a pink gloved finger at me. "Would you believe it? She actually wanted to keep her shabby little apartment. As if she'll ever have to live like that again." Her condescending laugh felt like an attack.

"Mom, I loved that apartment. The walls were thick enough so I could practice anytime I wanted to. The location was great. The rent—"

"I know it was cheap, dear, but the ceiling leaked, and your neighbors were derelicts."

"They were musicians." Some of them were also certifiable crazies, but I would never admit that to her.

Aunt Connie smiled maternally and squeezed Josh's arm. "Who knows where you two will be living in a few years. You may be in Vienna, or Rome, or anywhere."

Josh nodded. "You're right, Connie. We have no idea."

A sudden cold draught hit me and I glared at the offending ceiling vents. This damn air conditioning would ruin my throat. I never forgot flying to Paris with Eric. I was so jet-lagged and dehydrated, I couldn't sing for two days. Suddenly craving a cup of hot tea with honey, or at least a throat lozenge, I looked for one of the shops we passed on our way through the airport. There were none in sight. At least there was the silk scarf I always carried.

I reached inside my jacket pocket, pulled out a partially used Kleenex, three neatly folded dollar bills, a dime, two nickels, four pennies, but no scarf. I tried the other pocket: a comb, Chapstick, remnants of an old grocery list, but still no scarf. I couldn't have forgotten to bring one. Not today. I frantically searched my purse and went through my pockets again. Then I remembered. "The bag. Where's the green bag?"

"Right here, Hon." Josh looked startled as he slid the green tote bag off his shoulder. "Are you okay?"

"Sure." I clutched the bag and reached inside, past a thin package wrapped in brown paper. "Thank God!" I pulled out a long violet scarf, wound the warm silk around my throat, and exhaled. "I'm terrific. How could I not be?"

He smiled indulgently, put his arms around me, and squeezed. "Well, you're acting kind o' crazy."

"I know." I laughed at myself, slid my arms inside his jacket, hugged his chest, and relaxed against his warm body. He felt so good. "I'm just cold and tired." My heart pounded and I shivered again.

He kissed my forehead. "I know you are. You've had a tough few weeks and I've been too busy at the office to help with the moving. I'm so sorry. You did a great job shipping all that stuff, getting my landlord to break the lease. It's over now, so relax and let me take care of you." His fingers gently probed my over-thin ribs. He didn't say anything, but I guessed he was worried.

I whispered, "It's okay. I'll pig out once we get to Paris."

He whispered back, "Promise?"

"Yeah." I kissed him. His mouth was so sweet.

Mom leaned into Aunt Connie. "I can't believe my little girl is finally married. They're so in love."

"They certainly are." Aunt Connie sent her sister a knowing smile.

A voice from overhead speakers announced that the flight was ready to board. I pulled away from Josh to give Mom a last, frantic hug. "Oh, Mom! Thanks for everything!"

She held me tight, and blinked tears off her false eyelashes. "Just be happy, darling."

"I am happy. Very happy." She let me go so I could hug Aunt Connie. "I've missed you so much, Aunt Connie. I'm so glad you could make the wedding."

She held me tight. "Oh, you beautiful girl. Nothing could have kept me away. Now take care of your gorgeous new husband."

"I will. He deserves it. More than you know." I gave her a final squeeze, and turned back to Mom. "I'll call you tomorrow."

"Please do." Mom smiled and dabbed her eyes with a monogrammed handkerchief.

Passengers lined up, handed attendants boarding passes and started down the walkway onto the plane. A few minutes ago, it looked like a scary cage. Now it looked like a big, comfy escape pod. I reached into the green bag, pulled out the thin parcel wrapped in brown paper, and slid it into Mom's shoulder bag.

Before she could ask what it was, Josh stepped in to hug his new mother-in-law. "Thanks, Allison. Don't worry about Jenna. I'll take care of her."

His words made me feel all warm and cuddly. He really would take care of me. I trusted him completely. Mom held him close, then gave his cheek a maternal pat. "This is the first time in twenty years I'm not worried about her. You're a saint, Josh, putting up with her all this time."

Readily agreeing, he rolled his eyes and laughed. I laughed, too. Putting up with my vacillations had been a challenge. He turned to Aunt Connie. "It was so good to meet you. Thanks for coming to the wedding."

"I'm so happy to finally meet you." She gave him a hug. "Good luck to you both."

Josh picked up our carry-on bag, handed the attendant our boarding passes, and stepped back so I could walk in front of him through the gate. We waved, joined hands and started down the walkway.

"Jenna, Jenna." Mom shouted. "Where's the …" She hesitated, then moved her hands in a square shape, like some weird charade.

"Where's what?" I had no idea what she was doing. She gestured some more, but it still made no sense. "What is it, Mom?"

"Oh … Never mind, darling. We'll talk tomorrow." She waved us on.

Josh and I shared a questioning look and hurried onto the plane.

Two hours later, we were fed and tucked into our reclining seats. Josh read a magazine. I was almost asleep when it hit me. The picture! Mom's crazy charade was about the old black-and-white photo of Eric Ries. I started laughing and Josh gave me a sideways look. I shook my head. "I just remembered something Mom said. It was really silly." I snuggled back into my seat and I closed my eyes.

I would have given anything to watch Mom get home and find Eric's picture inside her bag. I hoped she would be elated. I was. I had finally transitioned from needing my "blankie." I finally grew up.

12.
Paris, France
Allegretto Giocoso

*W*arm and cozy under a foot-thick duvet on a huge bed in Paris's Hotel DeCrillon, I felt like I was floating on clouds. My sleepy eyes focused on a modern alarm clock, incongruously perched on a marble-topped, inlaid-wood bedside table. I shifted to read the numbers: 13:05. After a moment's calculation, I realized it was five minutes after one in the afternoon.

Last night, after the wedding and the long plane ride, we finally arrived at the hotel. Tired as I was, I admired the Louis XV decor, complete with crystal chandeliers, ornately carved antique furniture, bright-purple drapes and upholstery. Everything was sumptuous, elegant, and luxurious. We both flopped into bed and passed out. This morning, or actually this afternoon, sun shone brightly through cracks between the heavy brocade drapes. I closed my eyes against the invasive light, and buried my head under the covers.

Josh wasn't beside me. I heard water running and knew that he was shaving. For two years we had spent weekends together. It was his habit to get out of bed early, shave, then come back to make love. He was sweet and considerate in a hundred ways. I stretched voluptuously, waiting for my brand new husband to come and service me. I was actually on my honeymoon. Good grief!

Startled by a knock on the door, I sat up and pulled the duvet around me. Josh hurried out of the bathroom, wrapped in a fluffy, oversized white terry-cloth robe with the hotel insignia on the breast pocket. He grinned at me, and opened the door to a waiter pushing a table laden with goodies and covered with a pristine white cloth. Theatrically flipping off the cloth, the waiter revealed a plate of scrumptious pastries, croissants, and an array of covered silver dishes. Wonderful aromas of coffee, chocolate, and ham filled the room. Josh tipped the waiter and closed the door after him. "*Bonjour, Madame Kendal.*"

I laughed fondly. "*Bonjour, Monsieur Kendal. Comment ça va?*"

He nodded emphatically. "*O! Oui Madame. Ça va!*" He tore off the duvet and pounced on top of me.

"It's cold!" I kissed him hard, struggled to slip my fingers inside his robe and tickle his ribs.

"No fair!" Still laughing, he pushed me off, hurried back to the bathroom and brought me an identical white robe.

Naked and shivering, I leapt at the table, took an éclair, and bit into the sweet flaky pastry. "Hm! This is so gorgeous." I set down the gooey morsel, long enough to slip on the robe and tie the sash.

Josh shook his head. "I couldn't eat anything that sweet for breakfast, but I knew you could."

I finished the éclair, laughing, "It's afternoon. This isn't breakfast." I lifted the silver lids and catalogued the dishes: "The world's fluffiest scrambled eggs, beautiful sliced fruit, gorgeous, paper-thin prosciutto." There were two coffee pots. I opened one lid, sniffed and smiled. "Um! Great coffee." I opened the other and gasped. "Will you look at this hot chocolate?" I took a long-handled spoon from the table, and stirred the creamy brown liquid. "Look." Chocolate shavings floated up from the bottom of the pot. "This is made from real slabs of chocolate. Not Nestlé Quik." Contented silence accompanied our wedding breakfast. We savored every delectable bite.

The past few weeks had been stressful. I was very thin, and Josh looked pleased to see me feasting on cream-filled pastries, croissants, eggs, and prosciutto, and washing them all down with highly caloric cocoa. He enjoyed the strong coffee, spread creamy butter over his croissant, but left the sugary sweets to me. When we finished, only crumbs were left on the plates. I sat back holding my over-full, extended stomach and feeling slightly embarrassed.

Josh laughed fondly and knelt beside me. "I'm looking forward to your belly being a lot bigger than that." He lovingly ran his hand over my swollen flesh and I flinched. I was in no hurry to get pregnant. He was just being sweet, but I gently pushed his hand away and started for the bathroom.

"Jen." He held my arm. "Don't put in your diaphragm. Please." He took a deep breath and geared up his courage. "We're married now. We can try to have kids."

I kept silent and stared at the floor. Every sinew in my body tensed.

He forced a smile. "That's why people get married."

"That's why *some* people get married." I got married because my boyfriend was moving across the ocean and I was afraid of losing him. I ripped apart my entire life, gave away my favorite useless knickknacks, and spent weeks packing boxes for the London house. I even allowed my mother to drag me through the tedium of a church wedding. I needed a vacation and I wanted this honeymoon to be fun. I didn't want to even think about sacrificing the next eighteen years to a screaming child. My career was finally taking off. I had been married for one day. Couldn't he love me for me alone? Did I have to become an instant baby machine?

He smiled sweetly. "You love kids. Last weekend at my sister's you had a kid on your lap the entire day. They loved you, and you loved them."

Hurt, angry, and ready to snap back with something nasty, I made myself slow down and breathe. "Yeah. They're great kids, and yes, I loved being with them. I also loved giving them back to their parents at the end of the day."

"You weren't so eager to give back little Emily."

I smiled, remembering the impish four-year-old. "Yeah, okay. Emily's a trip, a really terrific little girl, but Josh we've only been married for thirty hours. We don't need to have a kid right now."

"We won't have one right now. It'll take at least nine months."

I cringed at his poor joke.

He put both arms around me. "Sweetheart, you're almost twenty-eight. I'm thirty-four. We can't wait too much—"

"I have engagements in nine months. It won't be a good time."

"A year and nine months from now won't be any better. Besides, it might take us a year to conceive—or never. I might be shooting blanks or something."

"With my luck, you'll knock me up in five minutes."

He flinched as if I'd slapped his face. We stared at each other. I had hurt his feelings, but couldn't take it back. He turned around, walked to the window and stared outside.

I raced to the bathroom, shut the door, and leaned over the sink. Why had I said that? It was horrible. He had been proposing for a year and a half. Every proposal came with a plea for children. I knew how much he wanted them. I did, too, I guess, but not now. I knew I could have kids and a career at the same time. Other singers did. Beverly Sills had two. Maureen Forrester had five, for God's sake. They never missed performances. Of course they both had huge boobs, and wore tent dresses, so no one could even tell when they were pregnant. If I ate an extra pea, it showed.

I dug into my toiletry bag, pulled out a tube of contraceptive gel, and the plastic box holding my diaphragm. At least Josh could wait till we were settled in London. Another few weeks wouldn't make any difference. I held the box over the sink, opened the lid, and let the small rubber cap bounce onto the porcelain. It looked like a moronic toy. In an angry flurry, I tossed the cap, tube, and box into the trash, washed my face, brushed my hair, and practiced apologizing into the mirror. Finally, I braced myself, and opened the bathroom door.

Josh was straightening the bedclothes. He looked adorable, standing barefooted in his loose bathrobe with shaggy hair falling over his eyes. He smiled sweetly. "You look like an angel."

How could he be so nice when I had been so awful? "Oh, Josh, I am so sorry."

"No, Jen! That was my fault." He hurried across the room and hugged me tight.

"You didn't do anything wrong. I'm just—"

"I did. I was an asshole. Kids or no kids, your happiness is the most important thing in my life. Ever since this move was offered, you've worked your tail off, for me. Your mom made us both crazy, and you've been a pussycat, saying yes to her and me, even when I knew you weren't happy. You've been wonderful. I acted like a jerk, but I'll make it up to you. I promise."

Before I could say anything else, he pulled off our robes, carried me naked to the bed, rolled the duvet over us both, and kissed me passionately. After the briefest foreplay, he pushed inside me, and stopped. "You're not wearing your diaphragm."

"I threw it away."

He sat up, staring. "Are you sure you want to do this?"

"Yes, I want your baby." Startled to hear the words come out of my mouth, I lay still, clutched him harder, and pulled him deeper inside. The sensation was thrilling. I was desperate for this to work. Sex was fun, but this was making love. This was working together to conceive a child. It felt totally different. "Oh my God, Josh! I really do want your baby!"

·

After a lazy afternoon of sightseeing, shopping, and more lovemaking, we took our time soaking together in the hotel's oversized bathtub. Relaxed and happy, we dressed up in our wedding clothes, my white cocktail dress and Josh's new suit, and went downstairs for a fashionably late dinner.

The maître d' led us through the main dining room filled with elegantly set tables, upholstered chairs and gold chandeliers. The walls were lined with gilt-framed oil paintings and huge mirrors. Ultra-chic patrons sipped expensive wines and feasted on beautiful plates of meats, vegetables, fish and fowl. It was too warm for a fire, so the wide fireplace was filled with a brilliantly colored flower arrangement.

We followed the maître d' into a smaller, adjoining dining room with a romantic corner booth, slightly off by itself. I guessed that Josh had prearranged the booth, and was sure of it when waiters magically appeared with champagne and an assortment of delicious hors d'oeurvres. The crystal glasses and silverware gleamed. Everything was so perfectly polished, I was afraid of leaving fingerprints. We sipped the tart bubbly, savored the exotic tastes, chatted, laughed, and thoroughly enjoyed each other. Now the honeymoon was perfect. I felt like we were alone on the planet.

I played the sophisticated Parisian, gingerly lifting my thin three-pronged fork, scooping a snail from its shell, and easing it into my mouth. I closed my eyes. The buttery garlic taste and rubbery texture were absolutely delectable. I swallowed as slowly as humanly possible, and elegantly popped another snail from its shell. This time, my charade failed miserably. The snail flew into the air, splattered melted butter and landed in my lap. I quickly retrieved the precious morsel from my oversized napkin, popped it into my mouth, then lifted my napkin and checked for stains on my white lace cocktail dress. I planned to use it as a concert dress, and was relieved to see that there wasn't a mark.

Josh and I laughed as I wiped my gooey fingers. By the time

I devoured all six prized snails, my hand was impossibly sticky. I gave Josh a quick kiss, and went to find the Dames.

"Jenna!" It was a man's voice.

Startled, I stopped and looked around. An elderly-looking man hurried toward me. He looked like an older version of Eric Ries. When he got up close, I realized that it was Eric Ries. He looked awful. His eyes were red. His skin was pale and drawn. He looked ill, but I didn't want to ask outright. "Eric? What are you doing here? Josh said you were in Rome recording your *French Horn Concerto*."

"I will be, day after tomorrow. I came here to see you." He moved closer. "My God, you look radiant."

I curtsied, acknowledging at the compliment. "My wedding dress." I held out my sticky fingers. "I look pretty messy right now. I just—"

"I saw that. It was a cute trick with the snail."

"You saw?"

"I admit it." He held up his hands in surrender. "I was spying from the bar, watching your reflection in the mirror."

"Why didn't you just come over and say hello like normal people?"

"Josh doesn't need to know I'm here. I came to see you." He moved closer, looking into my eyes. "I had to see you."

"That's a lousy line." A flash of long-buried anger flared inside me. "How'd you even know where I was? We made sure no one at Atlas knew which—"

"Your mother told me."

"My mother?" Now I was really angry.

"You're right, no one at Atlas knew your hotel, or if they did they weren't talking. I called your mother. Her number's in the white pages. I told her a lie about some missing contracts. It's not her fault. She was being nice. Don't be mad at her."

"I'm not mad at her. But, how dare you—"

"Please, don't be mad at me either. I know my timing's lousy, but there's nothing I could do. Listen, Jenna, sweetheart, if I hadn't been involved with Colette all this time ..." He shrugged sadly, then smiled and opened his arms. "We finally broke up. For good. I'm free now. She just married her conductor."

An elevator door opened behind me and half a dozen half-drunk party-goers practically fell out. Using the diversion, I waved my sticky hands. "Well, I just married my agent and I've got to wash my hands. Bye!" I glared and hurried away.

He was right behind me. "Meet me tomorrow."

I whispered, "Are you crazy? I'm on my honeymoon." I kept walking.

He followed. "You told me once that I'd saved your life. Now, I need you to save mine." I stopped, shocked, sure he was lying, but concerned he might really be ill.

He continued softly, "The elevator man heard you and Josh talking about going to the Louvre tomorrow, hearing some Wunderkind play a midday concert. Let him go alone. Say you're going to the museum shop. You want to surprise him with a gift. Men always fall for that. I'll meet you in the shop."

Two women pushed past me toward the Dames. "Why should I meet you?"

"Because I need you to."

"You don't need me!" I knew I should run away, but I couldn't move.

"I do need you ... I really do." He looked like he was about to cry.

I stared in disbelief. More stylish strangers hurried by, laughing and calling greetings.

He looked genuinely miserable. "Please, meet me. I'm depending on you." He hurried away.

Angry, but curious and concerned, I watched him go, then finally went to wash my hands.

•

At 11:45 the next morning, Josh and I stood at the back of a small gilded salon in the Louvre Museum. One end of the gracious room held a grand piano with its lid open. A dozen rows of delicate, gold-leafed chairs stood in a semicircle around the keyboard. The museum held free noonday concerts of new and established artists as a courtesy for their patrons. The artists were never paid, but could use these performances as showcases for invited press, managements, conductors, and contractors who might engage them to play for a fee in the future.

Josh studied a program and printed material on the nine-year-old pianist. He nodded with approval. "Good-looking kid. I hope he plays as well as they say. I also hope he's not a brat. A real prodigy would be great on my roster. It's a good program. Mozart and Ravel, intelligent choices for small hands." He turned the page, read the second half of the program, and chuckled. "Did you see this?"

"Hm?" I pretended to read the front of the program, while thinking about the gift shop and Eric waiting for me. I didn't have to go. I could pretend I never saw him. I turned the program over. The second half included *A Rainbow For My Daughter*. Shit!

"*Monsieur Kendal.*" We looked up as a smiling, very chic middle-aged woman clicked sharp high heels over the parquet floor.

Josh waved cordially, then whispered, "This is the kid's teacher. She's a real pusher."

I grabbed the opportunity. "Josh, I don't need to hear this boy, and you need to schmooze. I'm going to the museum shop to buy you something special — a surprise. I'll be back before he's finished." I hurried away, turned back, and saw Josh smile to himself. He really thought I was going shopping. I couldn't come back empty handed.

I hurried around confusing corridors, up and down a couple of wrong staircases, and finally found the gift shop. Just inside the entrance, a bored cashier sat on a high stool beside a glass display case, reading a book. Near him, two women studied jewelry locked in another case. The rest of the shop looked empty. Like a drug addict, frantic to ingest the very substance that could destroy me, I searched the aisles.

Eric stood in front of a book shelf studying a collection of renaissance reproductions. Last night he looked like he was on death's door. Today he looked rested, healthy, handsome, and I was annoyed. His eyes were bright. His thick dark hair and slightly grayer beard were freshly trimmed and glistening. The soft gray of a beautifully cut leather jacket emphasized his still perfect body. I clenched my jaw, pretended to study the books, and moved close enough to speak softly. "So, what's the matter?"

He manufactured a sad little smile. "You're the only friend I've got in the world."

"Bullshit!" I wanted to slap him.

"It's true. As long as I had Colette, I had an anchor. Whatever was happening, wherever I was, I knew one person loved me unconditionally."

"She finally gave you conditions?"

"I wish she had. One day I came home and she'd packed her bags. She was leaving to get married. It was Pierre's sixth birthday. I arrived, birthday present in hand—"

"You actually remembered his birthday?"

"I was a day late, but kids don't mind."

"Susie always minded." My blood boiled. I needed to leave.

"It wouldn't have mattered if I had been on time. Colette was already three months pregnant by the other guy. She'd been talking about wanting another child for a couple of years, but I hadn't taken her seriously. She works such long hours, training dancers at the ballet. She loves it."

"Does Pierre like his new stepfather?"

"He's ecstatic. They live in a country estate with horses, and older children who spoil him rotten. But, I was out in the cold. I expected a family celebration, and I was all alone in our four-room flat. I opened a bottle of Scotch and drank myself into a stupor."

"I didn't think you drank hard liquor."

"It's rare. But I needed it that night."

"Last night you looked awful."

"Yeah, I was jet-lagged. I'd flown to New York to see you, found out you'd just married Josh, and caught the next flight back here. For the first time ever, I wasn't able to sleep on a plane."

"You flew from Paris to New York and back again?" When he shrugged, I rolled my eyes. "There's this great new invention called the telephone. Wouldn't it have been easier to call me from Paris?"

"I almost did. I should have. That night, after Colette and Pierre left, I opened the monthly mailbag from Atlas Artists. It was full of the usual nonsense. You know—fan letters, questions from would-be composers, requests for out-of-print manuscripts. Then, there was the notice about Josh's transfer to London, and your letter. You wrote about coaching new repertoire, your singing engagements, but nothing about Josh or any other guy. You'd always told me everything, so I figured you were between boyfriends."

I laughed at his gigantic ego. "Did you even notice that I stopped writing after the competition? It was at least six months before I even sent you a hello note. When I finally did write, it was just to keep you up-to-date on my career." I stopped to breathe. "Let me get this straight. I didn't tell you about my love life, so you assumed I didn't have one? That's really funny."

"I guess it is." He nervously shoved his hands into his pockets. "Well, the timing seemed perfect. Josh would be gone. You'd be alone in New York. We could finally get together and stay together. All the mistakes I'd made with Colette, I was going to avoid with you. You really are the only friend I have in the world."

"Oh, please. Give me a break."

"I mean it. I've got colleagues and lovers, Jen, but I don't have friends. You're it. Even when you hated me, you never stopped writing."

"You never answered."

"I will now."

"It's too late. I'm married."

"I still can't believe you actually married Josh." Momentarily losing his cool, he sighed and shook his head. "I mean—now don't get me wrong, I love the guy. He's brilliant, but he's controlled and cautious. He certainly can't keep up with you sexually." He stared adoringly. "Oh, sweetheart, every time I think of that night in the cabin … You were so luscious. I wish with all my heart—"

"Stop it!" I hissed through clenched teeth. Memories of that night flooded back, excruciating and delicious. It was the one-time sexual highlight of my entire life, never to be repeated. I almost wished it had never happened. Now, I was married. I owed my allegiance to my husband.

I turned away and started for the exit, but he grabbed me from behind, dragged my back against his chest, and whispered into my ear. "Tell me the truth. Has it ever been that good with Josh? Ever?"

My stunned silence was a resounding *no*!

He held me tight enough to hurt, gently kissed my ear, and whispered, "I keep a flat in London. We could meet sometimes. You'll be flying out of the country a lot, so will I."

Horrified, but excited by his proposition, I pulled away and raced out of the shop. I was almost back at the salon before I remembered I hadn't bought Josh a gift. The opening bars of *A Rainbow For My Daughter* echoed down the hall. I cursed myself, raced back, and went shopping.

13.
London, England: September 1979
Adagietto Sostenuto

*J*osh and I arrived in London rested and happy from our Paris honeymoon. Josh had sailed across the English Channel several times, but this was my first crossing, and I loved it. The ferry was huge, the sea was choppy, but slate-gray skies, biting-cold mists, and swaying floorboards did not keep me from standing on deck, clutching the rail, and aiming my face into the stinging wind. The English shoreline came into view and we both sang, "There'll be bluebirds over the White Cliffs of Dover ..." I had seen English movies, but they never did justice to the real power and beauty of that chalky coast.

The sun came out a little, and we enjoyed a picturesque train ride from Dover up to London. A wonderfully roomy English taxicab easily held all our bags, and Josh gave the driver our address in Bloomsbury. We drove through narrow streets lined with picturesque shops, pubs, and churches. As we passed Russell Square, Josh pointed out the offices of Atlas Artists Management. Six short blocks farther, the taxi stopped in front of two identical four-story Victorian houses. There were high windows in the first, second, and third stories, and tiny ones in the fourth. I remembered *Upstairs Downstairs*, and knew that the top floors had been built for the live-in servants we would never have.

The buzzer on one door read *Macgregor*, and the other *Kendal*. I gave Josh a nudge. "Looks like home."

He laughed, "I guess so."

The last tenant had been Josh's predecessor, elderly widower Tom Epstein. I was concerned about the housekeeping of an older, single gentleman until Josh told me that Atlas Artists provided a cleaning service.

The landlord, Mr. Angus Macgregor, knew when to expect us. We rang his bell and Mrs. Katherine Macgregor answered. "Ah, it's Mrs. and Mr. Kendal, is it? Well do come in, and welcome. My husband Angus is at his printing business, but I'm happy to show you around."

Her hair was lustrous white and very beautiful. When I complimented her, she smiled proudly and said that it had been bright-red when she was a girl. She had lightly freckled, smooth, white skin, and must have looked like a perfect English rose. Now a slender, still pretty, very sprightly lady-of-some-age, she easily loped up the four outside steps and unlocked the outside door. It was made from thick, dark wood, and had a cut-glass window in the top half. I noticed that most English entrance doors had glass windows. Back in New York, glass windows were invitations to thieves. She led us through a narrow vestibule, another unlocked wood-and-glass door, and we found ourselves in a dark but roomy parlor.

I was relieved to see it was filled with our boxes, shipped from New York. Everything seemed to have arrived, but I couldn't be sure. Mrs. Macgregor enjoyed telling us how some boxes had arrived one day and some another. I loved listening to her lilting, musical accent. She used curtain-pulls to open the drapes on the front windows. A little dim light crept through. At a quick glance, the furniture and carpets looked worn out. Josh was given a generous moving allowance and I mentally listed items we would replace. The floorboards were polished and the walls were freshly painted. Everything smelled faintly of bleach.

The kitchen was behind the parlor. Mrs. Macgregor apologized because it was so small and I laughed. By New York standards, it was huge. The appliances looked modern, but strange. Learning to use them would be an adventure. A back door opened onto a small, shared garden of tangled vines and overgrown walkways. I didn't care that it was a mess. We actually had something green just outside the door. The weather wasn't very cold, but it was damp, and I shivered. I knew about English heating, but was still surprised to feel the same temperature indoors as out.

Mrs. Macgregor took us upstairs to the first floor bedroom and bathroom. There were two stand-alone wardrobes, but no closets.

To me, this should have been the second floor, but I soon got used to the Englishism. The bare mattress looked like it would serve, at least for now. Blessing Mom, I thought of her wedding presents packed in huge boxes downstairs. There were sheets, blankets, pillows, pillowcases, a mattress-cover, and a quilted bedspread.

The third story, or second floor, was office space, and the top floor was originally servants' quarters. Mrs. Macgregor explained that, these days, people used that space for children's playrooms or storage. Josh smiled at the idea of playrooms.

While graciously showing us all the light switches, electrical outlets, wardrobes, chests of drawers, explaining the plumbing, the stove, and the washing machine, Mrs. Macgregor babbled on, "There's plenty of hot water. No worry about that. You can even run your washing machine and do your washing up at the same time."

"Washing up?"

"Your tea things: dishes, pots, and such."

"Oh, I see." I smiled at Josh. "Lots of hot water. That's great."

She smiled and nodded. "Now if there's anything you'll be needing, day or night, my telephone number's by the phone, or just ring the bell. Daytimes, Angus is usually at his business. The printing shop's just three roads over. Some mornings, I'm at the shops. Most days I'm home."

I hesitated. "There is one thing, Mrs. Macgregor."

"Please, call me Kath."

"Thanks, Kath." I smiled nervously. "There's no piano."

She smiled, shaking her head. "Oh, no. Not for years. The chap before Tom had a piano. That was more than thirteen years ago. Tom got rid of it. Said he had enough music at work. Didn't need to bring it home."

Josh saw me stiffen, and squeezed my arm. "There wouldn't be a problem, would there, if we got a small piano? Jenna's a concert singer. She needs to practice. We don't need a—"

"Well now, I don't know. We used to hear the piano right through the walls. Angus likes his quiet in the evenings."

"I'll never practice in the evenings. I promise." I heard the panic in my voice and so did they.

She looked like she wanted to say, "No," then saw that I was about to cry, and smiled uneasily. "Well, I'll have to ask Angus. It's his house after all, but y' know, I wouldn't mind a bit a' music, in the afternoons." She winked, smiled, and left us alone.

I sighed loudly and collapsed into Tom's horrid stuffed chair.

Josh shrugged. "Don't worry. We'll get a piano. In the meantime, there are two at the office. You can practice there, anytime, day or night." I stared out the window, sulking. Josh chuckled quietly, knelt beside me, and spoke as if I were a cranky child. "It'll be fine. You'll see. Once we're settled in, we'll love it. I'm sure of it." He put his chin on my leg, looked up with big puppy dog eyes, and whimpered.

Always a sucker for his clowning, I laughed begrudgingly, and scratched him behind the ear. He pulled me out of the chair, hugged me, and went to work checking the boxes. We found Mom's, and pulled them into the center of the room.

The mantle clock struck four. "Look Josh, it's still early and we need groceries. The boxes can wait. Let's explore the neighborhood."

He sadly shook his head. "Not today. I've got to check in at the office." Ever the workaholic, he put on a tie and walked the six blocks to Atlas Artists. I unpacked a warm coat and went out to "the shops."

•

As Josh predicted, he hit town and disappeared under mounds of managerial paperwork. He spent long, aggravating hours at the office and seldom saw the light of day. Each evening we stole a few delightful minutes together, exploring the neighborhood, trying the food at various pubs and assorted meat pies from the local butchers.

A cleaner came to the house once a week, but I was left to figure out the backward plumbing, upside-down electrical system, do the laundry and the washing-up, shop, cook, unpack, and convince our charming but lazy landlord, Angus Macgregor, that one working electrical socket was not sufficient when two, or even four were already in the walls. The stove worked, after a fashion. The pint-sized washing machine and dryer were fine, but it took three cycles to do the one large load I used to do at the corner Laundromat on 85th Street and Broadway.

Angus begrudgingly agreed to let us have a piano, but we wanted a decent one. Taking time to shop was not a priority. With no performances scheduled for months, I hummed quietly, but didn't seriously vocalize. I was a housewife and oddly enough, enjoying it. In Paris, two weeks before, I had thrown away my diaphragm. I waited for my period, and sure enough ... Josh was disappointed. He joked that this month we had to try harder. I imagined a child growing inside of me. It felt scary, but exciting.

•

It was six-thirty in the evening, the end of our second week in London, when I finally unpacked the last of our boxes shipped from New York. I was on the floor with the carton between my legs. I cut the tape, wrenched the top open, pulled out yards of packing material, and stared at an oversized toaster. Josh's large front door key rattled in the lock. I waited as he walked into the house, looking exhausted. His suit was rumpled, his tie hung loose, and dark shadows circled his eyes. Before he even closed the door, I yelled, "I can't believe you brought this all the way to London."

He stared with dismay. "But that's the best toaster I ever had. It's the only one wide enough to toast bagels."

I rolled my eyes. "In the first place, the electrical current's incompatible, and in the second place, London doesn't have a decent bagel."

"I'll find one. I'm determined."

He looked like a little boy chasing a Crackerjack prize and I started laughing. "You looked wrecked." I put the toaster aside and went to give him a hug.

"I am, but I've got to go back." He hugged me hard, hung on me like a rag doll and sighed wearily. "I just wanted a couple of hours with you." We kissed sweetly, pushed boxes off the sofa, and collapsed. He rubbed his eyes. "Tom must have been losing it. Clients are calling, asking for confirmations on bookings, complaining about payments. They sound relieved I've taken over the roster. Some of the files are mixed up. Just catching up on bills will—"

The phone rang.

He sighed and picked up the receiver. "Atlas Ar—I mean ... Oh, hi, Allison. Yeah, everything's great. Here's Jenna." He handed me the phone and staggered into the bedroom to change his clothes.

I curled up on the lumpy sofa. "Hi, Mom. Yeah, I finally figured out the plumbing. It's all backward, but it does work. Yeah, okay.

Just give us a few weeks to get settled, then come and visit."

Mom tried to sound casual, but I heard an edge in her voice. "You're sweet dear, wanting me to visit, but I don't want to rush you. Um, you know it's fundraising time again for the Philharmonic Society. We're getting ready for the Christmas bazaar, and they're looking for celebrity memorabilia to sell. I was wondering if I could give them that old picture of Eric Ries. You don't want it anymore, and ..."

"No!" I clutched the phone. "Don't do anything with it. Not yet." My heart pounded and I didn't know why. "I ... I don't know what I'll do with it. Maybe nothing, just ..."

Barefooted, tie-less, and curious, Josh stood in the doorway, unbuttoning his shirt. He raised his hands, in a "what's going on" gesture.

Pleased by his concern, I smiled, shook my head, and continued talking into the phone. "I know, Mom. Just hold off for now, okay? Sure. I'll write soon. Love you, too. Bye." I hung up.

Josh leaned against the door frame. "What was all that about?"

"Just mother-daughter stuff. I'll get dinner. It's game pie again. Sorry." I went into the kitchen.

"No problem. I love it."

"Is there anything I can help you with at the office?"

He shrugged. "Only if you want to plow through reams of paper."

"Sure, anything. At least we'd be doing something together."

"Thanks." He smiled gratefully.

At six, the office had closed and the staff had gone home. At eight, fed, slightly rested, and dressed in casual clothes, Josh and I, solitary workers, were back at the offices of Atlas Artists Management. Sleeves rolled up, a mug of now lukewarm tea at his side, Josh sat at his large desk studying a ledger book, checking numbers with an electric calculator and cursing softly every time he found a mistake.

I was outside in the hall, sorting client materials into folders, and laying the folders on the floor in alphabetical order. "Josh, I don't see a folder for—" I checked the name on the paper. "Rosemary Bingham."

"There's a contract for her?"

"Yeah. Where's the date ...?" I checked the typing. "She was signed last month."

"Let me see that." I brought it to him. He looked at the signatures, started to tear it up, then slapped it on the desk. "I specifically told Tom not to sign her. She's a great technical pianist with absolutely no personality off the piano bench. She's plain, gawky, not Atlas Artists material, so he signed her anyway."

He was really upset and I was surprised. "Well, maybe he felt sorry for her."

"I feel more sorry for her now." He leaned back in his swivel chair and ran his fingers through his hair. "Telling an artist the truth can be unpleasant, but lying is cruel. We can't promote her, and I'm going to have to tell her." The phone rang and he glared at it. "Shit! Don't they know we're closed?"

I picked up the receiver. "Atlas Artists."

"Jenna?"

I froze. The voice was unmistakable. "Eric?" Not trusting myself to talk sense, I mumbled, "Here's Josh," and started to pass him the phone.

"Wait! Don't say anything."

I moved the receiver back to my ear.

"Jenna, are you there?"

"Yeah."

"Good. Just listen. My flat's four blocks west over the antique shop with pocket watches in the window. I'll be there tomorrow, after one. I'll wait for you. Now give the phone to Josh." I felt like a robot, as I handed Josh the receiver and hurried back to the safety of my filing.

Josh took the phone and leaned his elbows on the desk. "Eric, Hi. What's up?" He listened, then shook his head. "Even worse. Tom's a sweet guy, but ..." He listened some more, then smiled at me. "Yeah, she's helping me file papers." He stretched, shaking tension from his shoulders. "Sure. I can use all the help I can get. Okay, thanks." He hung up. "Eric's coming over." He yawned. "You never know who your friends are till you're in a crunch. His flat's somewhere near here." He rubbed his tired eyes and went back to his ledger book.

Fifteen minutes later, the front door buzzer sounded. "I'll get it." I set down my filing and hurried out to the reception area. Eric was on the other side of the glass doors, holding a bottle of wine. I braced myself, unlocked the door and let him in. One step inside, he pulled me close and tried to kiss me. I turned my head away, so he kissed my neck. The scent of his musky cologne, the feel of his arms around me, and the sweetness of his lips pressed hard against my skin were a huge turn-on. I was furious with myself and forced him away. "Josh. It's Eric." I broke loose and sped down the hall back to the office.

Josh saw Eric behind me and smiled with relief. "Thanks for coming, man. I hope you can help me sort through this shit."

Eric passed me the wine, then shook Josh's hand. The men laughed like old comrades, and shared a rough hug. Josh took a paper from his desk. "Look at this. I've got a contract for ... What's his name?" He turned over the paper. "Isaac Zimmerman. Last summer with the Berlin Phil, no confirmation, no receipt of payment, no—"

Eric raised an eyebrow. "Zimmerman died more than a year ago."

Josh balled up the contract, tossed it into the wastebasket, and shook his head. "Thank you, Eric." He gritted his teeth. "No thank you, Tom, for not bothering to tell me when clients die. You wouldn't know if there are anymore corpses in my roster."

Eric pretended to be Dracula, twisting his mouth into a ghoulish smile and comically rubbing his hands together. "Ahh! Yes. Let me see." We laughed, as Eric pulled another folder from the filing cabinet. "Ah ha! Margaret Müller." He laughed at himself and shook his head. "She's not dead, just retired to Graz."

Josh took the file and studied the paperwork. "You're sure?"

"Yeah, I had lunch with her last month."

"This contract's still good. Does she need a termination letter?"

"I wouldn't worry about it. She didn't mention being owed any money, and she would have." He looked through some more files.

Josh sat back and sighed loudly. "Thanks for coming, man. You're the best." Eric nodded, humorously acknowledging the compliment. "I mean it. Even when I first started, you were one of the few Atlas people who treated me like a person."

I felt stupid standing there holding the wine. "Thanks for this, Eric. It was sweet of you. Josh, is there a corkscrew?"

"Should be. In the pantry."

I left the wine, and went down the dark hall, feeling my way like a blind woman. I found a light switch, chose a corkscrew I knew how to operate, got three wine glasses, switched off the light, and started up the dark hall. I stopped halfway back, watching the men through the opened office door.

Eric stood next to an open file cabinet, reading the names on the labels. "You were a promising composer. Whatever happened to that?"

Josh shook his head and smiled. "I had technique, that's all. You made me realize that one night when I was working at the piano in the conference room. You walked in and said, 'Sharp the last A.'"

Eric smiled at the memory. "Yeah, I remember that. I played your piece."

"And you sharped the last A. It was brilliant. That instant, I knew I had to spend the rest of my life promoting you, and talent like you."

"Like Jenna?"

"Yeah." Josh smiled, then sadly shook his head. He looked toward the door, didn't see me hiding, and thought that I was out of earshot. He leaned toward Eric and spoke softly. "Ya know, I feel bad. We knew this move would be hard, but this is crazy. I'm here fourteen hours a day, and she deals with domestic hassles. I promised her singing engagements and she's not even vocalizing. Sometimes I think if we hadn't made the move, she wouldn't have married me."

"Really? You're kidding."

"No." He sat back, looking drained. "I'm not as dashing as you are." He drummed his fingers on the desk, thought for a moment, and glanced up before speaking. "A couple of years ago, when you had the girls locked away, rehearsing in the cabin, I was a nervous wreck." He took time, twirling a pencil. "Did anything happen up there, besides music?"

Eric didn't lose a beat. "Oh, come on. Besides, my lips are sealed." He sent Josh a good-old-boy wink.

Josh pretended it was funny. He laughed nervously, then settled back. "My God, Eric, I love that woman so much. She is so loving, so sweet. When I get home from here, wiped out and useless, I make love to her and nothing else matters. Nothing in the world. You're so lucky you have kids. I don't think she's ready for that, but I sure am."

Eric moved to another cabinet, saw me listening in the shadow, and winked. I smiled back, then felt guilty for smiling at him.

Josh glared at the papers on his desk. "Maybe I should just set fire to all this and start over."

I tinkled the glasses and walked into the office. "Don't worry, darling. We'll sort them."

He smiled gratefully as I put down the glasses and opened the wine.

FINALE: *Presto Appassionato*

The next morning started like any other. Josh shaved and showered while I cooked us an abbreviated English breakfast of eggs and bacon, tea and toast. He kissed me goodbye and left for work. I did the washing up, showered, washed and dried my hair, and saw myself taking extra pains with my light, daytime makeup. I also took extra pains picking out my best fitting jeans, a pretty blouse, sweater, belt, and earrings. I tried not to stare at every clock I passed, but the witching hour of 1:00 was still hours away.

I knew the antique shop Eric mentioned. It had a wonderful pocket watch collection in the window. I had passed it several times, but never dreamed he lived upstairs. I told myself I wouldn't go, and dove into my self-appointed chore-of-the-day: sorting the mismatched clothes hanging in our wardrobes and piled in the chests-of-drawers. It was a tedious but mindless job.

Around noon I finished, felt peckish, ate an apple, and stared at the clock. 12:15—12:17—12:20, this was crazy. If I didn't go, I would be tormented thinking about Eric. If I went, I could clear the air, get him out of my system, and maybe me out of his. I knew him too well to believe his sweet talk. Once he was sure I wasn't available, he would stop bothering me and find another woman, or more likely, women.

At 1:15, nervous and breathless, I stood on the busy sidewalk in front of a plain door with a glass panel in the top half. Next door was the ornate entrance to the antique shop. I read down a short list of names corresponding to apartment buzzers and found "Ries." My trembling finger pushed the button. I waited. There was no answer. Half of me was relieved and the other half disappointed. Suddenly the door opened. Eric stood holding that door and an inside door, at the same time.

I scurried past, whispering, "I'm not here to fuck. Where's your flat?"

He chortled at my unaccustomed language, slid past me, up a flight of stairs, and through the opened door to his flat. I followed, into the living room. He closed the door behind us.

Most of the room was filled with a grand piano and a small table layered with used manuscript paper. The back wall was painted dark-rose and covered with shelves of trophies, awards, and framed photographs. The living room set was upholstered with soft-brown leather. Fluffy sheepskin rugs covered parts of the gleaming hardwood floor, and I recognized an upscale version of his cabin. Everything was warm and inviting.

His bedroom door was open, but I averted my eyes and blurted out, "We both know Josh deserves better than a wife who cheats with his best friend. I love you and I love Josh, in very different ways. Whenever I'm with you, I'm neurotic and crazy and I hate it."

I expected him to argue, and was annoyed when he smiled kindly. "I know and I'm sorry. But that was in the past, when you couldn't depend on me. Everything's different now. I'm—"

"Nothing's different. I know there are no guarantees in marriage, but I've got to try to make this work. You heard Josh last night. For the first time in my life, I'm sure someone loves me. I'm not going to throw that away."

He smiled casually. "So why exactly are you here?"

I searched for an answer, stammering, "I ... I just needed to say that."

"You would have said it better by not showing up." He allowed himself a slight smirk.

"You told me to come." I sounded like a moronic infant. My cheeks burned.

He stifled a laugh, then put a fatherly arm around my shoulder. "Come here. I want to show you something." He led me to the piano and closed his nearly finished manuscript.

I read the cover page. "*The Happy Prince.* For High Voice and Orchestra. Music by Eric Ries. Words by Oscar Wilde. Commissioned for Recording by the English Chamber Orchestra."

Fascinated, I read through the first pages of music. "This is lovely."

He smiled. "They want me to score this for tenor, but I think I can persuade them to use a soprano. I want you to sing it. I was going to wait to tell you when I was sure, but well ..."

Tears filled my eyes. I blinked them away, turned another page, studied the melody line, and harmonic construction. "When I was eleven, you said you might write me a song. I've dreamed about it ever since. This is so beautiful." Suddenly my insides froze. My jaw clenched. "What do I have to do to earn it, just screw you, or leave my husband?"

He rolled his eyes. "Who's talking about anyone leaving anyone? I need Josh as much as you do. He's a great agent, besides being my friend." He scowled and stomped across the room. Afraid I had just lost myself a recording contract, I became even more alarmed when he picked up the telephone, punched a number, and said, "Josh Kendal, please. Eric Ries calling."

Terrified, I lurched after him, then froze when he pushed a button, transferring the function to speakerphone.

We heard Josh's voice. "Eric. Hi. What's up?"

Horrified and trembling, I put a hand over my mouth.

Eric smiled mischievously, then spoke into the speakerphone. "Hi, buddy. I know you're crazed. I just wanted to give you an update on the English Chamber Orchestra commission. They want Ian Partridge, but I want Jenna to sing it. I think I can convince them. You'll back me up?"

Josh's voice crackled through the speaker. "You bet I will."

Eric chuckled. "Thought you would. We'll probably record in March and premier live in May, so don't get her pregnant before then."

Josh laughed. "No promises, pal."

My stomach lurched. My legs wobbled, but I didn't dare move and make a sound.

Eric enjoyed his power, and milked my torment. "Oh, Josh, since you were wondering. When we were rehearsing in the cabin, things did get pretty tense ..."

I was ready to faint.

"But—" He smiled, and took an overlong breath. "Nothing happened."

I doubled over, silently gasping for air.

Josh sounded very relieved. "Thanks for telling me. I really appreciate it. Keep me posted on the other."

"You bet. Say, Josh, rather than meet at Selby's office this afternoon, why don't I come to Atlas? We can grab a cab together."

"Good idea. See ya around two-thirty?"

"Righty-o. See ya." He pushed a button and the phone went dead.

I collapsed onto the sofa, clutching my chest, gulping air. Eric took me in his arms, kissed me passionately and ran his hands over my very willing body. Like a kidnap victim loving my abductor, I clung to him, hungry for his mouth and grateful to be alive. He toyed with a button on my blouse, then changed his mind, and covered my face with gentle kisses.

I whimpered, "This is crazy. What am I going to do?"

"For now—" He kissed the end of my nose. "You're going to enjoy being loved by two men."

I swallowed a sob. "I don't think I can."

"Sure you can. Just relax. You'll get used to it. It's easier than you think."

He tried to push me down, but I pushed back and stood up.

"Yeah. You'd know all about having a harem. I've got to go."

Without another word, he stood up and politely opened the door. "Come back soon."

Totally confused, I grabbed my bag, hurried out, and made a beeline for Josh's office. I walked quickly, dodged other pedestrians on the crowded sidewalk, and only stopped when a streetlight turned red. It wasn't my habit to go to the office in the afternoon, but I wanted to make sure Josh didn't suspect I had been with Eric.

Why the hell had I been with Eric? Last night, on the phone, he said, "Come!" so I came. Why had I blindly obeyed him? What was I, his dog? His dependant child? He kissed me and I kissed him back. Why? As a thank-you for not telling my husband where I was? This was crazy. Eventually Eric would invite Josh and me to his flat. Now that I had seen it, I would have to pretend that I hadn't seen it, make a fuss, look surprised, and one lie would lead to another. Suddenly, life was just too complicated.

When I got upstairs, Josh and two assistants were deep into piles of papers. He rushed over. "Thank God you're here. I've been phoning the house. You've got an audition for the Royal Philharmonic, tomorrow at four."

I swallowed. "Tomorrow. But, I haven't sung a note in—"

"I know. Go practice. Your music's in the conference room."

"What's it for?" I was flushed and nervous, but hoped he'd think it was just performance anxiety.

"Mozart: *C Minor Mass*."

I gasped. "That's the hardest piece there is."

He nodded, calm and smiling. "I know. So, go practice."

"Can I get back in shape that fast?"

He put his hands on my shoulders, steadying me. "You are a great talent. You can do anything you set your mind to. Oh, Eric called. It's not for sure, but he wants you to record a commission he's doing for the English Chamber Orchestra."

"Really?"

"Really."

He nuzzled my ear. "Between the two of us, we'll make you a star."

I forced myself to breathe. "Yeah. Between the two of you."

"Okay. Go practice." He turned me around, gave me an affectionate swat on the behind, and sent me down the hall toward the conference room piano. A dozen thoughts crowded my head. *Between the two of them. Oh, dear God. I have an audition tomorrow. Shit!* I banished thoughts about anything but Mozart.

•

The conference room was not as large and inviting as the one in New York. The ceiling was high, white, and bordered with a floral plaster molding. The bare floor was dark wood that hadn't been polished in eons. Stark white walls made it seem like a Victorian hospital. A row of tall windows at the far end opened onto the narrow street below. A modern chandelier with dusty flame-shaped bulbs shed lots of ugly, utilitarian light. An old grand piano and a large wooden table with six chairs filled the entire space.

Josh had already put my copy of Mozart's *C Minor Mass* on the piano's music stand. This was one of the most technically difficult concert works ever written, and my blood pressure soared just looking at the cover. It was a very beautiful work, lushly scored for full chorus, orchestra, and soloists. I had been practicing the solos for years, but never performed them. They would be a joy to sing, if

I could sing them well. If I wasn't in outstanding voice, it would be a disaster. The big soprano aria, *Et Incarnatus Est*, was five pages of sustained high notes, huge register skips and slow coloratura runs. The duet with the mezzo, *Domine*, was vocal gymnastics, ending with us exchanging high and low B flats two octaves apart.

I opened the keyboard cover, played a C major triad, took a deep breath, and began a series of slow scales. After a few minutes, I became self-conscious and wondered if Josh and his secretaries could hear me. When I didn't hear the incessantly ringing phones, I knew that they probably couldn't hear me, and sang my next scales and arpeggios full-out.

Like any careful athlete who has not worked out in a while, I resisted the dangerous urge to dive right into the gymnastic aria. I carefully warmed up my voice, singing one exercise, resting for a few minutes, and singing another. It took a full half-hour, but finally the gears clicked into place. My nasal passages opened, my diaphragm muscles moved into automatic pilot, my throat relaxed, and the high notes soared. I was singing really well, but vocalizing should have taken ten minutes, not thirty. I would never again let two weeks go by without vocalizing.

I sang through my part of the duet, took another break, left the conference room, and went to the kitchen for a glass of water. Now that I felt confident, I looked forward to the audition, and mentally arranged my wardrobe. I sipped tepid water, meandered back into the hall and practically ran into Eric. I forgot he was picking Josh up for a meeting.

Before we could speak, we heard Josh yelling, "I've got the contract. Let's go, Eric."

"Oh, good!" Eric called back and winked at me. "Nice to see ya, Jenna." He turned on his heel and marched after Josh.

Josh saw me and waved. "Bye, hon. Back in a couple of hours. You sound great."

So they could hear me. Oh, well. I smiled and held up my water. "Bye, guys."

They left as I went back to the conference room, and made a mental note to iron my rose-colored audition dress when I got home. I shuffled to a window, pushed it open, and looked out onto the narrow street. Down below, I saw Eric and Josh leave the building. Eric hailed a cab. The two men got in and closed the door.

I went back to the piano, took another sip of water. *Crash!* I raced back to the window.

The cab's front end was on the sidewalk. A battered van was sideways in the middle of the street. A dozen people crowded around the cab, blocking my view.

"Josh!" I screamed, raced out of the office, and flew down four flights of stairs. I prayed Josh wasn't hurt, while flashing mental pictures of mangled bodies.

Outside, a small crowd had gathered. I pushed through them, screaming, "My husband's in there! Let me through!" The people moved aside and I was startled to see Josh and Eric standing calmly next to the cab. Its front corner was slightly crunched and the already battered van didn't appear to have any new damage. A thin trickle of blood ran down the cab driver's face, but he was only concerned with getting the van driver's information.

"Josh!" I grabbed his arm. "Are you okay?"

He turned and looked surprised. "Yeah, I banged my shoulder, but we're—"

I sobbed with relief, and hugged him hard.

"Jen—" He rocked me back and forth. "Sweetheart, I'm fine. Really." He kissed the top of my head. I turned my face and kissed his mouth, hard.

"Okay, lovebirds." Eric sounded annoyed. "We've got an important meeting. Come on, Josh." He hailed another cab and got in.

Josh gently pushed me away and smiled sweetly. I wiped my eyes, smiled back and felt kind of silly. "I'll be back soon." Josh got into the cab, and the two men drove away.

I watched the drivers finish writing each other's information, get into their vehicles, and drive off. My heart still raced. It felt strangely close to breaking.

Slowly, I made my way back into the building and thought about Josh. He could have been killed. I could have lost him that fast. Up until now I had taken him for granted. He had been like a solid rock I could always rely on. This was really scary. I would never take him for granted again.

Back in the conference room, I sat on the piano bench looking at the Mozart *C Minor Mass*. Now it was just a book of printed paper bound with cardboard. I wasn't afraid of it, or excited by it. I almost lost Josh. Mozart didn't matter. Right now, Josh was in another cab. He could be in another accident. The second cab could have a collision. He might be—

My imagination ran wild. I told myself that Josh was fine, that he and Eric were on their way to a meeting, and I suddenly realized that I had totally forgotten about Eric. He was in as much danger as Josh and I hadn't even noticed. Wow! I started chuckling, then laughing, and hoped the secretaries couldn't hear me. They'd think I was nuts.

Most of my life, Eric Ries had been my whole world. As a kid, I really needed him, or at least my fabrication of him. The perfect nurturing and musically brilliant father. I was thrilled when he had asked me to sing in his Paris competition. Rehearsing his music and finally sleeping with him had been the most exciting, scary, fulfilling, and joyful few days of my life. His brutal rejection immediately afterward had been the most humiliating few minutes of my life.

He screwed me so I would sing well and it worked. That screwing was such an emotional high, I sang better than anyone thought possible, including Josh. It served all three careers, but it also screwed up my head. Eric was the most sexually electric, musically brilliant man on the planet. I had been desperate to possess him, but no one could do that. A few hours ago, I came close to sleeping with him again. I had asked if he wanted me to leave Josh and he said, "Who's talking about anyone leaving anyone? I need Josh as much as you do. He's a great agent." Shit! Was there no end to Eric's pimping? Was there no one he didn't use? Didn't screw? Didn't throw away? After all these years, I still let the jerk steal so much of my energy. As a kid I didn't know any better, but now?

Okay, Eric was a brilliant composer. Okay, he was sexy as hell, but I already slept with him. Okay, I wanted to sing more of his music, but he needed me to be his singer. He loved my voice. I made him sound good. He needed my talent just as much as I needed his.

I came back to the present, looked for my water glass, and found glass shards scattered across wet, battered floorboards. I got a broom and dustpan from the kitchen, swept up the mess, and dumped the shattered pieces into a wastebasket. It felt really satisfying. The broken glass was sharp and dangerous and I threw it away. My obsession with Eric was sharp and dangerous and I threw it away. Eric would always be a part of my musical life, but he would never again be my whole life.

Next to Josh, Eric was an empty shell: resonantly vibrant, gorgeously colored, exciting as hell, but empty inside and hollow through-and-through. Josh wasn't flashy, but he was smart, sincere, warm, solid and totally dependable. I loved him so much I wanted to cry. I felt so lucky he stuck with me and waited for me to marry him.

I went back to the piano, opened the *C Minor Mass* and found the aria, *Et Incarnatus Est: And He Was Made Man.* Now the pages were just black ink. The musical notes were beautiful and demanding, but I could sing them. I pictured Josh and Eric together, getting into that second cab. Between the two of them, they might make me a star. That would be great. I would love it.

Eric was my muse and I was his singer.

Josh was my husband and I was his wife.

◆ *FINE* ◆

New York City: December 1980
POSTLUDE: Allegretto Spiritoso

Dear Jenna,

I can't believe it's almost Christmas, and you won't be with me. I'm finally feeling the empty-nest syndrome for real, and I don't like it a bit. Your Aunt Connie flew in for the Philharmonic Society Fundraising Bazaar. She stayed a week, and we had such a good time. She's gone now, and I'm all at loose ends.

The bazaar was better than ever, bustling with shoppers and volunteers working the booths and tables. Three darling college girls came up carrying musical instruments. They reminded me of you and your friends at that age. They chatted and sorted through the merchandise. One of the girls found your old photo of Eric Ries, shouted and waved her arms, "Is that who I think it is? Jane! You've got to see this."

The other two girls joined her, and the one named Jane shouted, "Oh, my God! It's Eric Ries! Look how young he was." The third girl said that he was even more handsome now. Jane said she had to have the picture and that it was even inscribed "To Jane." I started telling her that it was really "To Jenna," but the ink was smudged and she looked so happy, I didn't have the heart. It cost ten dollars, and the three had to scramble to find the money between them. I thought it was all very sweet until Jane said, "The next time he comes to New York, I'm going to meet him even if I have to camp out in front of Carnegie Hall." That frightened me. The poor girl was in love with him, and she'd never even met him.

Well, must run now. You're so good at writing, please keep it up. I'll call you Christmas day. Stay well.

All my love to you both!

Mom

Christina Britton Conroy

A native New Yorker and daughter of actress Barbara Britton, Christina Britton Conroy has sung on four continents, appeared on stage, film and TV. She studied music at Juilliard Pre-College, Interlochen Arts Academy and Camp, earned a Music Bachelors from the U of Toronto, and an MA from NYU.

A certified music therapist and founder of MusicGivesLife.com, she works with people of all ages in medical and social model facilities, helping them to deal with physical and emotional loss, disabilities and illness.

She lives in Greenwich Village with her husband, actor/media coach, Larry Conroy.

You might also enjoy these literary love stories:

Locked in a desk for decades, a lost poem destined to bring together the unlikeliest of partners.

ISBN: 978-0-9793252-9-8

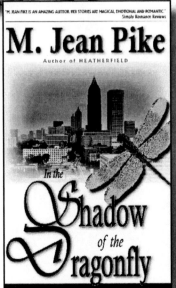

When Gray and Hope meet, theirs is a story of heartbreak, redemption and fate at its most devastating.

ISBN: 978-1-934912-07-2

Printed in the United States
144160LV00001B/2/P

9 781934 912102